CHAMPION'S CALL
The Hero's Code
Book 2

A.R. KNIGHT

The Cave

The skittering woke him. Forced Thane's eyes open to see the cave, silver in the Pacific ocean moonlight. Thane held his breath, that act alone almost too much effort, and waited for the sound to come again. The scratching on the cave stones had an animal's telltale signs, a creature's spastic motions; searching. The scratch's lightness, too, said the animal wouldn't be a threat, would, quite possibly, be food. And Thane could use food.

He'd done it again.

Thane knew why he lay on the cavern's floor, why his throat burned from thirst and his flimsy muscles ached from disuse. The reason why, back when the Paragons had left him in a cold north prison for decades, the staff kept him on a rigid routine. Kept him stimulated, if only so much. Kept Thane plied with pacifying drugs that fogged his mind and prevented him from going too deep down inside himself.

That's where Thane was now, rerunning the choices that had brought him to this moment and pursuing their infinite branching paths for a better present than the one currently killing him.

The scratches came again. A shadow shifted, then shot across the cave's floor towards . . . yes. Thane moved his eyes, scraped his limp cheek along the rocks to see the source of the noise heading right at its predecessor's bones, piled where Thane had left them. Slight meaty bits clung to the little white sticks, morsels Thane's tongue hadn't been able to scrape away.

What might be too small for him could, though, serve as bait for something larger.

The shadow approached the pile and caught the moon's full light, revealing a squat little rat nibbling its way through the remnants. The creature served as a lifeline, a focus that Thane could grab, could use to pull himself out from the dark pits where his mind had gone. Something here, now, to focus on.

Real. Physical.

The rat's possibility did Thane some good. He breathed again, easily this time. Feeling came back to his fingers and toes with the sparkling sensation of limbs left fallow for too long. An ordinary person, a normal, might have lost them entirely. As it was, Thane had to clench his own throat to keep him from groaning at the pleasure-pain as his body came back to actual life. It had been decades since he'd gone this far, and his body ached with the challenge.

Creaks and cracks rattled his bones, sent tremors along refreshed nerves, and all along Thane held his focus. On the rat, and everything the rat had that Thane did not.

The vermin had freedom, for one. It could go where it liked, at least within the limitations of its abilities. No need to worry about drones, or laws, only predators. The rat, too, could eat what it liked. No cooking here, no standards to cling to in order to be civilized. Its fur could could be dirty, its little teeth coated in plaque, and still the rat would be a rat and accepted as such. Thane, though, had been cast out of his society for . . . reasons that didn't matter here.

Stay on the rat. Use it.

Twist it.

How happy it looked, tugging on gristle that might have come from its own brother. How foul a creature. The rat perverted life. It deserved to die, more than Thane ever would. But who could deliver this just punishment on the rat? Who was here, in this cave, and capable of doing such a thing?

He could. And he would.

Thane burst up. Scrabbled towards the rat, arms and legs strong and kicking him forward. Thane reached out as the rat tried to scamper away, the tiny thing no match for anomaly-powered speed, reflex, muscle. It didn't manage a single squeak before its end, before Thane devoured it in a single, massive bite, spitting out the bones as he worked through the snack.

Thane wheeled around the cave, hunting, sniffing. The rat had been alone, yes, but there were other scents on the air. Close.

Bending his three meter frame, Thane shot towards the cave's hillside entrance, away from the ocean cliffs. His shoulders brushed and broke rock, the sharp edges leaving the tiniest scratches on vein-bristled skin.

Thane's feet crushed loose stones, ground leaves and other debris to dust. Through it all, Thane kept loosing rat bones like tiny rockets, spit flying everywhere. The rat had done little for his hunger, and for the first time in days, Thane demanded food.

Outside the cave's entrance, a ridged black-rock portal

revealed its origin as a long-cooled lava burst, the ground sloped away under a thick fern forest. Their gray-scale fronds drifted in the nighttime breeze to a cadence beyond Thane's comprehension or caring as he tore out into the moonlight, following his nose, his eyes, and every other sense sending him towards a back-pedaling human.

A small, younger man, the human held a sharpened stick with skeletal hands on a gaunt frame, a scraggly beard leading to eyes that, despite his whole wild, ragged look, held some intelligence.

Not that Thane cared. Food was food, and he would eat this one just as he had the rat. The man shoved a pointed stick towards Thane, who grabbed the weapon, tore it away and snapped it. He discarded the pieces and gave the man a spit-filled roar for good measure.

The food, his face in terror's frozen mask, stuck a hand towards Thane, and the monster's head jerked to the side, pushed by a strong, sudden wind. The man punched at nothing again and Thane's ankles slid, the arm reaching for his target blew out wide as gusts swept from nowhere to throw the monster aside.

But the monster was nothing if not adaptable. Snarling all the while, Thane turned back to his prey, dug in his large feet, and when the man's furious pumping shot wind into Thane's body, the beast didn't move.

Yelping, the man tried to run, flailing gusts behind him as Thane gave chase and, with a lunge through the leaves, snatched the man's trailing leg. Thane pulled his catch back, lifted him up and dangled the man upside down.

Where to bite first?

"I can help you!" the man yelled, eyes wide and rolling. "Don't kill me!"

Help? Thane leaned in, sniffed the man. Fear's sharp scent filled Thane's nose, frosted with unwashed stench and dirt. The man looked foul and starved. Like prey, nothing more.

"I saw when she dropped you," the man continued, voice finding a level footing at a pitch near a squeak. "That you're still alive means you're strong! Strong enough to get away, maybe!"

Away? Away was the ocean, and the murderous drones. The food was right here. Thane held the man closer. Opened his mouth wide.

"You're not the only one that wants Mynx dead!"

That name. Thane stopped, teeth pressing into the man's arm. Mynx. That name he knew, and knew well. She was his real prey, not this one. Because Mynx had been the first to betray him, the first to call Thane a monster rather than a Paragon. She had built his prison. She had caused him so much pain . . .

Thane dropped the man without realizing it, his arms too weak to hold him up anymore. Shrinking back to sanity, to the strength of a normal man. Aches returned with the reversion, and Thane traced those pains and understood them, grasped where he was, and turned to the groveling, crying body at his feet.

"Get up," Thane said, forming words instead of spitting them. "I'm not going to kill you."

The man froze, cutting off another panicked sob. On his knees, hands gripping the thin soil above the black rock, the man looked up at a much shorter, thinner Thane.

"The beast is back in his closet," Thane continued. "He'll stay there until I need him."

The man waited for an offered hand that never came. Without his anger's haze, Thane parsed the anomaly with an analytical eye.

Gaunt, yes, and ridden with dirt and, no doubt, disease, but Thane could see wiry strength there too.

Someone who'd been at the bottom for a long time and learned to live with it, survive on what he could scrounge. Who traded dignity like any other resource, and knew when hugging the ground counted for more than standing on it.

"Sook," the man said, finally rising on his own. He stood a little taller than Thane now, but that did nothing to erase the lingering fear in those eyes. "That's my name."

"I gathered."

"What's yours?"

"You don't know?"

Thane's record had been widely established. The sort of legend that makes it everywhere, in every language. The unstoppable beast that, when not on a rampage, turned into the Paragon's fountain of knowledge. Then again, he'd been in that prison for a long time. Perhaps the world did not care to learn about him anymore.

"Case you haven't noticed," Sook said. "We're kind of isolated out here. Don't read the news."

"We?"

"Yeah. All the other anomalies on the island. Most of 'em are a bunch of jerks, which is why I'm out here, looking for you. But there's plenty of us."

Thane had seen smoke, but tracing a little plume into the sky to an anomaly horde was a leap he hadn't thought to make. He'd assumed this island would be home to a scant few anomalies like him, but the Paragons may have gone soft since he'd been imprisoned. What would have once earned a summary execution from Aegis's fist might now mean a lifetime sentence here instead.

Gathering anomalies in one place would be dangerous, though. You never knew how their abilities would work together.

Maybe Mynx thought the anomalies would handle her executions themselves.

"Are you all right?" Sook said. "You're, uh, shrinking."

Not shrinking, exactly. Shriveling would be the better word. Stop. He was doing it again, chasing ideas and playing them to conclusions.

Thane faltered, his right leg suddenly unwilling to keep him upright on the slope. Sook reached out, grabbed Thane's arm and steadied him.

"It's a problem," Thane said, and tried to focus again. If he found the reason he'd been dumped here, a betrayal by the Paragons, their unwillingness to see him for who he was, he could bring back enough strength. "I will fix it."

The thought worked, pressing energy into his legs, his body, and Thane grew again, but he kept it in check this time. Leveled the hatred to a simmering bubble while keeping his mind clear.

"What are you?" Sook asked.

"Thane is who I am," the anomaly replied. "As for what I am," Thane looked around, at the cloudless, star- and moon-lit sky, the waving plants and endless black ocean on the horizon. "I suppose I am this island's new master."

Sook laughed. "New master? Buddy, there's already too many masters of this island. You're a little late to get a spot."

Thane reached out, put his hand on Sook's throat. The man stopped his laugh, froze.

"I spent too many years under the rule of lesser leaders," Thane said slow, even. "No more. You say there are others on this island? Then you will lead me to them. They will join us, and together we will find our way out of this prison, and give the Paragons the end they deserve."

Sook gulped.

"Do you agree?" Thane said, loosening his grip ever so slightly.

Sook nodded.

"Good. Then we start when the sun rises. We will not keep the new world waiting."

Knock Knock

She ran the tests without opening her eyes. Flexed her legs, her arms, turned her neck back and forth, and felt nothing. For the first time in the week since she'd fought Calvin in the scrapyard, Kat wasn't sore, wasn't bruised, and wasn't sick from the thick cold she'd caught while duking it out in a frigid night. Couple a healthy body with a bed she'd spent far too much reps on, and Kat felt like she could lie there all day. She'd feel a little lazy, because Kat had done pretty much nothing all week long, but why not? Hadn't she earned it?

Nearly dying deserved some time off.

A thick, slobbering tongue smacked Kat's face, left a dripping line along her cheek. Hot breathe lathered her, and paws pressed her shoulders into the mattress as Seeker, Kat's husky, attacked. She'd made a mistake, given a sign she was awake. A critical error.

"Seeker, stop it," Kat said with no enthusiasm and less force. "I'm trying to sleep."

She earned another lick for her troubles. Kat squirmed, tried to put forth a minimum effort to get Seeker off without opening her eyes and giving in to the day, but the dog didn't move.

"Tap, tell Seeker to leave me alone," Kat said.

"Seeker, bad dog. Not cool." Tap, her apartment's A.I. said. "Let her sleep. Not chill to wake someone up on the weekend, dog."

The surfer bro theme. The laconic attitude reminded her of golden beaches and sweltering sun, everything Chicago did not have on a February weekend. Seeker, though, obeyed Tap as well as he did Kat, and continued slobbering away. At a certain point the dog crossed the licking threshold and, sensing her time in bed had reached its end, Kat rolled herself away from Seeker, sitting up and pushing her chestnut hair out of her eyes.

Another gray day in the midwestern winter, going by the window to her left. What a shocker.

"Tap, the usual," Kat said, holding a finger up towards Seeker, now down on the floor but looking like he might resume his assault at any moment. "If you jump up here, Seeker, I'm not getting you anything."

The 'usual', a spread from a nearby third-shift diner, came with fried eggs, rye toast, and random fruits the place had available. A delivery drone dropped it in the package slot outside Kat's window not long after Tap placed the order. Just enough time for Kat to pull on some clothes, splash some water on her face, and start the coffee brewing. With a kitchen not much larger than her closet and a stove-top that preferred shorting out to heating up, Kat took the easy way out and boarded the take-out train.

It helped that the diner always threw in spare bacon for Seeker, who munched on the charred pork with gleeful, teeth-snapping happiness. Kat envied the dog's endless joy, as she picked at her own food over the coffee table from her couch. A leathery thing long since banished to doggy doom, the couch cushions remained comforting, and gave prime viewing to the massive monitor serving as Kat's work and entertainment. Right now, as the creeping clock went past mid-morning, she had Tap scrolling through her messages, reading the interesting ones and deleting the rest.

Not that there were many these days. The Paragons were still a giant mess. Ever since that video came out, the one that seemed to show Aegis dying—a horror Kat refused to really believe—the Paragons in Chicago seemed leaderless. Nobody posted new anomaly contracts in the region, and the Paragons themselves answered her calls with pre-programmed messages stating things were being dealt with, not to worry. While Kat could afford to wait, given all the anomalies she'd traced already who kept churning out reps for her, other trackers weren't so fortunate. They responded by littering message boards with increasingly panicked calls for work. It'd only been a week, but apparently people in her profession didn't keep much saved away.

Then again, given the likelihood you'd die in this business, maybe it made more sense to spend for the moment than save for the future.

"Hey Kat," Tap said after concluding another boring message extolling the tracker to update her beneficiaries in case of an untimely demise. Like she had any. "Just gonna say, you might wanna pay attention to this next one. It's from someone you might care about."

Tap's sun-drenched tone hid the under-the-hood calculations pretty well—Kat had no doubt the 'someone you might care about' line came from knowing everyone Kat bothered to contact through her computer—but she perked up from her breakfast's dwindling remnants and watched the screen as Tap pulled up the words.

"Hey Kat," Tap read, his surf voice ill-suited to Gordon Holyoak's midwestern lingo. "I know you might not care, but I'm getting out of the hospital today. Guess they think I won't die anymore, which is nice. But, uh, I don't know anyone else in town that would bother to show up and help get me to where I'm staying till I'm ready to get back to it. Do you think you could? I'll even buy you dinner. Not that it'd be enough to cover what I owe you, but, if you're around at four, think you could? And thanks, Kat. Thanks for everything."

Gordon. Able to pack so much sincerity into a paragraph, and so much callous ignorance into every other part of his life. Kat stared at the words, then told Tap to send a reply.

"Hey Gordon. Glad to hear you're not a corpse. Yeah, I'll get there at four. If you're up for dinner, you better believe we're going to the most expensive place that'll take a man in a hospital gown. See you soon, Kat."

Tap zapped the message away.

Too harsh? Nah. Kat finished her breakfast, drumming up excuses for her curt reply and why it was so very justified. Gordon had shown up in Chicago a little more than a week ago, roping trackers into chasing after a dangerous anomaly without telling them anything about Calvin. That the anomaly could take anything he touched and transmute it through his body into something else. A concrete wall could be shifted into flying stone spears. Air could be shoved into glass, blowing it into shards. Alcohol could be sucked—Kat's stomach churned at the memory—from a beer and sent right into someone's blood, instantly toxic.

Nobody died, but Gordon found himself perforated by ice inside his own body, damage Kat didn't even notice—the medic that'd picked Gordon up told her after she'd reached out, trying to find out if Gordon was still alive. As for Calvin, he'd been traced, picked up by a Paragon drone and taken to wherever the dangerous anomalies go before they're released as loyal servants or, failing that, imprisoned somewhere. Those were details Kat didn't want to know about.

Why blunt enthusiasm for a career that already suffered from more problems than solutions?

Anyway, now Kat had a plan for the day. Review her rep accounts. Take Seeker for a long walk. Find something for lunch after. Get downtown by four. Either Gordon would be up for dinner, or she'd drop him off at whatever place he'd be using to recover, and from there who knew. Odds looked good for a night in, with something warm to drink and something happy on the screen while Kat waited for another anomaly that needed capturing to pop up on the board.

Given the chaos enveloping Atlantis in the wake of Aegis's death, Kat felt a little strange to have a schedule so clear. As if she ought to be out in the streets fighting for . . . something. But, aside from the drones swarming the skies in huge numbers, the city around her hadn't changed. In the last week, the streets had the same crowds, the restaurants served the same food, and if she picked up a few nervous whispers, noticed the regulars at *Carver's* drinking more than before, that wasn't too scary.

The Paragons had the strongest, smartest anomalies on the planet. They'd figure out how to keep on going.

"How about that walk?" Kat said to Seeker, dropping the breakfast trash down her chute to the building's waste-to-energy incinerator. In a way, by eating disposable containers, Kat powered the building. How noble. "I need to stretch my legs, and you need to burn off your crazy."

Seeker agreed, grabbing his leash from the hanger near the door. Kat slipped on her boots, clipped the leash to the dog, and was in the middle of her did-I-forget-anything look around when someone pounded on the door. The heavy, fist-banging sound had Kat lunging for her desk and the secondary stun gun she kept holstered to the desk's bottom side in a concession to paranoia.

"Tap? Who's there?" Kat asked, keeping the gun leveled at the door.

"Haven't seen this dude before," Tap replied. "I can scan your records and find a match? Have to say though, he looks like he's having a rough time."

"Any weapons?"

"Nope."

"Seeker, stay," Kat said, then opened the door.

Standing there, blood dripping from a big, oval stain around his stomach, was the very same anomaly that'd put Gordon in the hospital a week ago, that'd nearly killed Kat at the same time. Sweat shone on his midnight skin, and while Calvin had upgraded his clothes from his old rags, the new ones already bore rips, stains and scars. If the past seven days had been a whole lotta nothin' for Kat, Calvin had been catching much worse.

"Please," Calvin said. "They're going to kill me."

Kat took a step back. Seeker growled.

"Who?"

"The Elementals."

Oh. Shit.

Restart

The loudest clock ticked in his mind.

Zhan-Yo heard every second as he lifted a finger and parted a sliver in the construction plastic coating the glassless window in the unfinished tower. The plastic fogged the late morning's light, and if Zhan-Yo had to spend any more of his day in the dark, he might very well lose his mind. Camping out among exposed wires and steel beams was far from the glorious revolution that Zhan-Yo expected, and the new world's presumed leader spent his hours watching his breath steam as he typed encrypted messages on his Tama.

The wrist-worn computer chirped with the thought, sending Zhan-Yo's eyes to a new note's blinking contents. Another status update from Wexley, no doubt as disappointing as the last several dozen. Promises had been made, had been catalyzed when Zhan-Yo drove his sword into Aegis and ended the Paragon's invincible leader. Yet, grateful companies and citizens failed to appear.

In the immediate hours after releasing the assassination's video, Chicago's streets remained calm, pods ferrying shoppers and diners and daters to their various ends. Perhaps with more tension, perhaps with a little fear and confusion, but a revolution? The end of days?

Promises had been made, and they had not been kept. Ziran, Zhan-Yo's company and the world's largest communications provider, found itself besieged without allies. When other companies failed to declare their allegiance, when citizen groups who'd called into Zhan-Yo's meetings and accepted his terms, stayed silent, Zhan-Yo had to change course. In what now felt like a psychotic episode, Zhan-Yo dealt away his responsibilities, fortune, and power to those around him with plausible deniability.

A Ziran standing alone would be destroyed, and if Ziran died, then any hope would die with it. Thus, Ziran had to be preserved.

So now, in hiding and at the utter mercy of the people he used to command, Zhan-Yo subsisted on a paltry diet of news and whatever Rhimes, his new bodyguard and handler, happened to bring up the sole working elevator. His bed had gone from goose down, fluffed comfort to a hard sleeping bag spread across the smooth concrete floor. A beautiful apartment where Zhan-Yo could watch the sun rise had been replaced by a new tower growing in Chicago's downtown, with scaffolding and plaster his companions. Zhan-Yo had often said, had often thought that he could survive without the luxuries his life had given him, and yet, this was damned difficult.

A chime came from the elevator, too cheery for this place, letting Zhan-Yo know that Rhimes had come back. With food, hopefully. Zhan-Yo settled back in his chair, the plastic legs scraping against the cement floor, as Rhimes emerged with a big bag smelling like grease and garlic. Rhimes himself had a small frame, packed over with a heavy winter jacket, faux fur poofing from the sleeves and neck. Brown gloves to match the jacket, dark jeans, and beneath it all, Zhan-Yo knew, shoulder holsters with lethal weapons so far from legal that Rhimes would spend his life rotting away in a Paragon prison if they ever caught him.

"Did you find anything good?" Zhan-Yo said.

"Same old garbage." Rhimes grinned, set the bag down and began pulling out the sandwiches, long subs laden with still-steaming toppings.

His earned decades meant Zhan-Yo probably shouldn't have been eating stuff like this, packed with fats and other junk, day after day, but being wanted had a way of putting problems into proper contexts. Zhan-Yo had ditched the cigarettes, though, on Rhime's recommendation. If the Paragons searched Zhan-Yo's apartment, they would find the ash trays, the burns on the walls, and tell the drones to look for the smell. Smokers were rare enough in the city that an idle puff might pull in the wrong attention. Greasy sandwiches, though, wouldn't give Zhan-Yo away, so he tore into the meal with gnashing gusto.

"How is it out there?" Zhan-Yo said, a question that could be about the weather, but Rhimes knew better.

"Getting better," Rhimes said. "Nobody's that nervous anymore. Too many drones for anything to go wrong, even if the Paragons are still confused." Rhimes caught Zhan-Yo's sigh and shrugged. "Sorry, man. Your revolution isn't going to come from the streets."

No doubt. Aegis was supposed to be the spark, but apparently his death hadn't been enough. The old Zhan-Yo would have waited, decided popular sentiment meant curling back up in his office tower and running Ziran like any other business, biding time until something else appeared. The new one, though, the one leaning over a space heater in a chilly construct, didn't have that time.

Sylvie, an old friend and the dagger that had pushed

this revolution to the brink, would have kept going. Fanned the flames, so to speak. She would be looking for what they could do right now, tonight or over the next few days, to capitalize on the chaos and force a reluctant populace to rise up. She would want Zhan-Yo to make a plan, and act on it.

And Zhan-Yo had found one.

The Tama on his wrist, a micro-computer about the size of a gauntlet, connected to the Internet and could give Zhan-Yo all the information he ever wanted. However, opening up that connection beyond the secure messages he gave and received with a few trusted allies put Zhan-Yo at risk too. Every Tama had a signature—a Paragon requirement, for their endless security state—and it's possible the Paragons could trace anything he did. Yet, to risk nothing would mean no reward.

"Rhimes, do we have the next place ready?" Zhan-Yo said.

"Always operating one step ahead," Rhimes replied. "Wexley had that spelled out in the contract. Why? You want to move?"

"We're wasting time. I'm wasting our chance." Zhan-Yo stood, went back towards the plastic-covered window where reception would be better. "Thanks for the sandwich."

"What're you doing?"

"Starting something."

"Wait, let me do it." Rhimes stood up, swishing sandwich crumbs from his hands. "You're compromised."

"That's the point. The world's going to know this came from me."

Zhan-Yo pulled up his Tama, bathed his face in the screen's blue light. For Ziran to push the revolution, the company needed allies. Those hiding in the shadows had to come forward. To do that, the risk of doing nothing had to be less than the risk of acting. Everything had to be on the line for these institutions to mobilize their resources against the Paragons.

So Zhan-Yo put them on the line. He sent a short message out to the world, tagged from his personal Tama, and called out every leader Zhan-Yo had met with in the shadows. Those basement conversations where lips spoke service to freedom, to rights, to a life lived without the Paragon's oppression. Now they were public, and now each of them would have to make a choice, push back and call Zhan-Yo a liar and themselves, inside, cowards. Or make public views private and bring strength to Zhan-Yo's position. With the world's oldest, strongest companies working together, even the Paragons would have to notice. Would have to concede the normals had a point, that they deserved their rights.

Rhimes's Tama beeped behind him, and the bodyguard spat out a curse. Good. Revolutions should grab emotions.

"We've got to go," Rhimes said, grabbing Zhan-Yo's arm and pulling him away from the window. "Should have warned me that you were going to lose it."

"I'm sorry, Rhimes," Zhan-Yo said, taking his momentum and snatching up the backpack already holding his essentials. He picked up the half-meter swords, his tachi, slipped on the shoulder sheaths that let them rest against his back, over his coat. One new after Aegis broke its predecessor. Made it hard to hide, but Zhan-Yo wouldn't leave them. "This had to happen."

"Did it?" Rhimes said, snagging his own pack. "Leave the rest. It's replaceable."

"Of course."

Rhimes took the lead, heading towards the elevator.

Zhan-Yo stepped over their sandwich wrappers, the space heater and sleeping bag that had served as home for the last three nights. He didn't look back.

As the elevator shot down, Zhan-Yo realized his heart had sped up, his nerves tingled and, despite a day spent pacing the empty floor, he felt wide awake. Thrill, excitement, things he hadn't felt in far too long, crackled. Before, Rhimes had shifted their locations in the deep night, with pre-planned routes and minimal civilian traffic. Now, Chicago approached noon. No hiding things here.

Did he want to get caught?

Maybe, Zhan-Yo conceded, he did. Sylvie had given her life for the cause and, thus far, Zhan-Yo's major play had reduced him to skulking in the shadows. Getting out in front of cameras, getting a chance to stand and probably die for his message would be a fitting end. Or, perhaps, seeing him playing the martyr would inspire all the nervous normals to finally take action themselves and push against the Paragons.

"Stay behind me," Rhimes said as the elevator opened. "Don't meet anyone's eyes. Don't say a word."

Zhan-Yo followed Rhimes into the barren ground floor, left waiting for better weather to complete its transformation into another glittering office. People here would run on reps instead of the dollar, dependent on an economy controlled not by market forces but by god-like beings. One mood swing and the lives that would be made here could be ruined through no fault of their own.

Why couldn't all the normals see this?

Rhimes didn't bother with the main entrance, instead going through a side door coated with maintenance and no admittance signs. The subsequent alley played home to snow-covered dumpsters and smoking vents from the neighboring building, an older, white concrete structure.

No souls save the two of them made prints on the ground as Rhimes led the way towards the street.

Out here, the sun gave enough gray light to make a cold winter's day, making it easy to see the drone pair swooping in on the alley's back and front. The black ovals swerved into view, hovering in place and shining their bright rays towards Zhan-Yo and Rhimes, who, with rapid back-and-forth turns, confirmed the trap. As the drones barked a robotic warning to surrender, Rhimes took Zhan-Yo and pushed him forward.

"Don't stop moving till I say so," Rhimes said over the drone warnings.

Zhan-Yo complied, managing to keep his feet going without slipping on the asphalt alley ground. The drones escalated their tones, the consequences, as Zhan-Yo and Rhimes refused to comply. Before killing Aegis, hearing these drone demands would have spiked fear throughout Zhan-Yo, no doubt filled his mind with all the criminal consequences. Now it all felt, if not fine, then acceptable. His chosen life's cost.

"Here," Rhimes said, pulling Zhan-Yo to a stop beside a thick door into the concrete building. Given the adjacent dumpster, Zhan-Yo figured they'd found the trash entrance. "Watch it."

With Zhan-Yo moving aside, Rhimes pulled back and delivered a sharp kick to the door's handle. A metal bar linked to what looked like a metal door, painted a dull red, Zhan-Yo wouldn't have thought a single kick could break it apart, but apparently Rhimes had some strength, because the barrier popped and swung open, the bolt's shattered pieces sprinkling the inside floor.

The drones didn't take the move without action, and even as Zhan-Yo darted forward, a two stunning bolts lanced out and scarred the ground where Zhan-Yo had been. Rhimes grunted behind him, and Zhan-Yo thought he'd been hit, but Rhimes kept on moving, joining him in a surreal dash through a crowded kitchen. Various chefs abandoned their cutlery as Zhan-Yo and Rhimes barged through. A dishwashing drone dropped a pile of plates as Zhan-Yo shoved it aside, clearing a path. The waiters by the exit, stalling in the brief moments before their tables' entrees appeared, at least recognized the threat and opened the doors for the pair.

"Keep going" Rhimes breathed behind Zhan-Yo. "I sent the safehouse to your Tama. Follow the directions."

They stood in the building's lobby, with people watching but just as many continuing to sift in and out for late lunches, early afternoon meetings, and more. Weird-looking people on the run weren't worth noticing, disrupting a tight calendar.

Rhimes, though, seemed like his day had been plenty disrupted. He leaned against the wall outside the kitchen, his hands on his knees and eyes on the ground. Zhan-Yo had always thought Rhimes a thick man, broad muscle on a body built to hold it, earning the man's heaping meals. Bending over and breathing hard, though, Rhimes looked less like an intimidating guard and more like someone in need of a hospital.

"What's wrong?" Zhan-Yo asked.

"They hit me," Rhimes said. "Can't run. Get going. I'll be fine."

Running a company as large as Ziran meant Zhan-Yo had to rely on employees, had to trust them and act on their words without doubt. So when Rhimes told him to run, Zhan-Yo ran. The main entrance and its foot traffic hordes made for good melding, and Zhan-Yo slowed to a normal walk as he went back outside, slipping his hood over his face. The tachi pair didn't make for an easy disguise, but Zhan-Yo didn't claim height as a personal success, so even with the sword hilts, he didn't stand out too much among city traffic filled with spastic fashions and mammoth winter gear. Even swords weren't all that out of place in a Paragon world, where anomalies and normals had redefined what could be possible.

Drones clogged the air above, dark and ominous. Facial recognition would catch Zhan-Yo before long, but the crowds bought him enough time to get half a block away from the building, and its adjacent alley. Zhan-Yo slipped into another big skyscraper, this one with a hefty restaurant on its bottom floor. Zhan-Yo went right for the bathrooms, made it inside and into a stall without attracting much more than a few stares. He shut himself in, brushed back his sleeve and looked at his Tama while his heart kept up its rapid race.

No doubt the drones were plotting his likely routes and Paragons would come crashing in here soon, looking for him. He'd be caught, he'd fulfill his destiny. A martyr for his cause.

That was a bold move. Could have warned me.

The message beeped onto his Tama, from Wexley, Ziran's new leader trying to keep the company afloat with its former head the most wanted man in the world. Wexley wanted the revolution as much as Zhan-Yo, but Zhan-Yo had kept the man away from the fateful night with Aegis for precisely this reason: Zhan-Yo still needed someone with real power.

Sudden inspiration. Need help. Rhimes down. Distraction?

Zhan-Yo heard someone else come into the bathroom, closed his eyes as they used the toilets for their intended purpose.

Where?

South loop.

Done.

Zhan-Yo wasn't in the south loop, but there was just enough chance that he could have run there to fool the drones. Ziran still ran Chicago's, the world's, communication networks, and with a bit of seeding, a few false pings from people's Tamas claiming Zhan-Yo sightings, Zhan-Yo could appear anywhere. Not a tool to call on too often, lest the Paragons catch on and strip Ziran's control away, but this counted as an emergency.

After ten more minutes in the bathroom, Zhan-Yo emerged and, finding the streets drone-less, meshed back into the crowds, following the map to the next hideout. Above and around, on scattered giant screens playing out the day's news, he saw his own headlines. His message, its many recipients among the world's most powerful companies, blasted out to a walking populace already beginning to talk, to look around with frowning faces and wide eyes at a world changing in front of them.

At a revolution's true beginning.

4

Call Me A Champion

She looked at her friend's faces and sighed. Mynx swiped away the Champion portraits hovering over the marble table, one not on her deck overlooking the Pacific ocean but instead a monolith inside a bulky, menacing downtown Los Angeles tower representing the Paragons and their complete control. Control they didn't have anymore.

Reeves, her AI and, Mynx wouldn't hesitate to say, her best friend, had minimal presence here. No drones swooped in to help her stand, none brought her hot tea. Instead, Mynx had to ask the secretary, who continued to be stunned that Pacifica's leader and one of the eight—now, seven—Champions, really existed. The shock was annoying: Mynx might have spent most of her time working in her Factory's digital mines, building the bigger drones that now surfed the skies looking for Aegis's killer, but she wasn't a myth.

Confronting her Paragon leadership went about the same. Regional runners so used to autonomy hadn't taken Mynx's return over the last seven days with the deference and happiness Mynx expected. The mood hadn't hit open rebellion yet, but if Mynx thought Pacifica her realm, then Pacifica didn't agree.

"Reeves," Mynx spoke to her Tama, on her wrist and tied through satellites and signal towers to her AI Outside, the noon sun drifted over a clear winter sky, not that you could really tell around here. "Why isn't it like the old days?"

"That is a nebulous question."

"We used to trust each other," Mynx said, fully aware she complained to a computer program, albeit a very savvy one. "The Champions all worked together. We saved the world so many times. Now it feels like everyone works for themselves. Did you listen to them on the call? All about their own regions, their own goals. Not a word about our collective future."

"Perhaps they expect you to take care of that."

Mynx looked out the window, itching in the Paragon-blue uniform she'd worn. Reeves suggested it, supported by studies showing people, both normals and anomalies, respected the uniform more than standard business fare. In other words, if she looked like a Champion, she would be treated like one.

But looking like a Champion might not be enough anymore.

"How many Champions responded?" Mynx asked.

"All made public declarations of support and mourning for Aegis," Reeves replied. "None acknowledged your call for a summit."

Mynx nodded. Not surprising. She probably would have done the same had one of the others called for a meeting. The Champions hadn't exactly parted on the best terms. Or any terms at all, once they'd carved up the world so nicely that they'd never need to talk to one another.

If, though, there was one thing she could do that the other Pacifica Paragons, scattered among North America's western half in population-mapped districts, couldn't, it would be bringing the world to bear on the crisis nobody wanted to talk about: the Champions would likely die or, like Mynx wanted, disappear into their true passions within a decade or two. Others would need to step up, or everything would fall apart.

The world had barely survived a fight between the Paragons and the normal nations that refused to give in. The world would not survive anomalies fighting over Aegis's scraps.

"Aegis always used to be the one to do these things." Mynx tapped a finger on the glass, her nail's click rattling around the room. A steady sound, ongoing. She would have to be the same. "Reeves, if I have to do what I hate, I may as well get it over with."

"What do you mean?"

"Let's start with Naija. We were always kind to one another, and it shouldn't be too late there."

"You want me to call a Champion?"

"Do it."

"And you're aware you have no scheduled time with her?"

"Reeves."

"Calling."

Mynx didn't hear a ring. She watched her Tama's reflection in the glass, but otherwise kept her focus on the cityscape. Millions went about their days here, and above them drones flitted about by the dozens. She tended to forget just how many humans, normals and anomalies, existed under her watch. Easier to act, really, when she didn't feel a Champion's weight pressing on every moment. Mynx couldn't get back to the Factory soon enough.

Naija answered with a click, her face haloed in the Tama, lit by what looked like firelight. Ever the stately warrior, Naija's glinted stare held level in the Tama's view. Gold—paint or real, Mynx didn't know—rimmed her eyes, while the rest looked unvarnished. Possibly covered by a mask now removed. A dress's barest hint climbed Naija with a straight silver line at her throat. If Mynx both felt her age and, if she was being honest, looked like it, Naija had captured time and bent it to her will.

"Ten years," Mynx said first to those emerald eyes. "Too long."

"Too long for you to call without a warning," Naija said. "There is a reason for those years. I sent my condolences, Mynx. What more do you want?"

Hostility, suspicion. Traits the Champions all acquired as their war on the normal's world swung their way and the inevitable aftermath became apparent. How do you divide a planet, a populace with a million differences between eight people? With catastrophic compromises. Endless bickering, deals and diversions corroding bonds that had lasted throughout the Paragons' founding, throughout society's transformation. None had left truly happy, but they hadn't killed each other either.

"You, Naija. You and the others," Mynx replied, summoning up her own steel will. "I asked for a summit, and you didn't answer."

"Did anyone else?"

Mynx didn't reply. Naija would know from the look, and Africa's Champion gave a single, sharp nod.

"We split the world, Mynx. We broke it because we couldn't stand to be together anymore. And even after, we kept trying. For years we gathered, and every time we splintered into our little factions. Played our little games in the name of Paragon unity, and we always left someone behind. You, me, Aegis, Apinya. One of the others made to sacrifice for Aegis's almighty Paragons."

"It worked, though. Earth's still spinning."

"Then let it keep working. Atlantis will figure itself out." Naija tilted her head. "Or you can take it for yourself. I don't think anyone will care."

"I don't want it." Mynx hadn't wanted Pacifica either, but she'd agreed to the region to keep things roughly equal between the Champions. Played a game she wanted to be left out of, one she now ran. "What I do want is to find who killed Aegis and stop them before they do it again."

"You think they're going to try to kill all of us?" Naija said. "Bold."

"Maybe. Did you see the message they released today? It's causing havoc here. We're taking over companies, pushing more drones to the streets to discourage anything open."

"A weak hand needs strong tools."

Mynx frowned, looked away from the screen. Always blunt, like herself. She couldn't take Naija's cut personally. Not now, not when there were more important things than pride.

"Then you're my strongest tools," Mynx said. "You and the other Champions. We need a summit. Need to put out a clear plan for everyone that explains what's going to happen when we're done. Who's going to take over, how things will keep on going. It's time, and we have to do this together."

Naija softened, shook her head. "Mynx, you tell me that someone is planning to kill us all, then you ask us to all come together? Why not just arrange this over the Tamas?"

Mynx would have loved nothing more.

"The Paragons need to see us united again. In person," Mynx replied. "A press release won't pack the same power as all of us together. We bring the Champions in for a summit, and nobody will talk about anything else. We'll have time to find a future for Atlantis, and when we make our play for how the world will work, everyone will be listening because we'll stand together and say it. Aegis taught me that much."

Naija shook her head slow, closed her eyes and rested a hand around her throat. When she opened her emeralds, Naija softened with them.

"Aegis had too much bravado in him," Naija said. "I agree, though, that he may be right about this." She looked away from the camera for a second, and Mynx wondered if the hard-hearted Champion had found herself a family over there. "Fine. Mynx. If you can get your summit together, then I will show."

"I will," Mynx replied. "And Naija? It was nice talking to you."

A slender smile. "It was, wasn't it? Take care of yourself, Mynx. There's only seven of us now."

The screen blinked off and Mynx let her wrist fall to her side. One down, six to go. She would drag all the Champions here, to Los Angeles. In her home, Mynx would have the slightest advantage in the negotiations, and when you pulled the Champions together, you needed every advantage you could have.

"Mynx, I want to tell you," Reeves said. "We still haven't found Celice. Atlantis is struggling to keep itself organized, and Pixie is asking for your help."

"Help how?"

"You're a Champion. They have none. Pixie wants you

to choose an interim leader. She thinks the rest will respect your choice."

"So I'm going to New York?"

"That's what Atlantis wants."

"Then that's what Atlantis will get," Mynx replied. "You keep calling me a Champion, Reeves, and I might just act like one."

5

Island Tour

Thirty years had passed since Thane last woke up in the same space as another human being. Trusting Sook not to kill him during the night's remainder was an easy leap— Sook would die a horrible death if he botched the murder, and everything the wiry anomaly said indicated a desperate desire to change his dismal life. While Thane couldn't promise much from his cave on the island's edge, he *could* promise change.

By coming to Thane's cave, Sook pried open a door already cracked, and now that the sun had risen and the paths were clear, Thane would not wait any longer.

They found breakfast in the fruits and berries dangling from nearly bushes and trees; Sook climbed the frilled wooden palms with alacrity, batting coconuts to the ground with a branch or blasting them with his wind gusts. Thane first bashed the fruits on the cave's walls, using frustration at their seeming invincibility to grow strong enough until he could split them with his hands alone. Sook kept his distance during that rage, watching from behind dew-coated ferns. Thane could smell the anomaly's fear and, as he slobbered down each coconut's contents, fought the desire to tear Sook apart. Still, he relished the natural taste. Real food, rather than vitamin intakes and caloric injections.

Back in the Paragon prison, the feedings came at regular intervals. Precise times, precise doses meant to keep Thane alive but weak. Laced with sedatives that would only be relaxed if the Champions needed to ask a question from the world's greatest, most unstable mind. Left to pace in an isolated chamber, fed books and print-outs of scientific journals and newspapers, Thane had been blessed by knowledge and time, and cursed by the inability to do anything with what he learned. Like an ox raised to plow a field, Thane would be called upon when needed, and, when not, left in his cage to rot.

"That might be the scariest thing I've ever seen," Sook said when Thane calmed himself to an older man's size and stature.

The two sat down to scrape white, meaty coconut insides with rocks.

"Then you have lived a charmed life."

Sook laughed. "Charmed? Me?"

"You are alive. You have no immediate demands. You are on a beautiful island with plenty of food." Thane munched. "Matched with all of human history, your circumstances are quite wonderful."

Sook stopped. Looked at the coconut in his hands. "I don't know about all that, but you stay on this island for a while and see how you like it."

"Compared to where I was," Thane said, "this is a paradise. When you found me, I was so relaxed that I nearly died."

"So relaxed? You almost killed me!"

"Before that."

"Uh, sure." Sook tossed away the shells into the ferns. "So, you know I came up here to look for you, right?"

"You mentioned this island has masters. I assume one sent you?"

"Let's go with that." Sook looked up and away, towards a seagull pair winging through the sky. "Thing is, they're not really masters. Just anomalies who grabbed a bunch of friends and decided part of the island was their's. Now they fight each other all the time."

"Of course they do. Because they lack a true leader."

"And that's you, right?"

"It is." Thane could never understand how so many people so awful at leading others found their way into powerful positions. Greed and strength could get you to the top, perhaps, but they could not keep you there for long. Wisdom, patience, ruthlessness had to play a part in order for a reign to stand. "We will wrap these others into our fold, Sook, and together break away from this prison."

"Didn't you say a minute ago that this prison was better than most of human history?"

"Sook, a good servant knows when to hold his tongue."

"Right."

Sook lead as they left, taking a slow walk through the brush. A gusting breeze gave cool breaks from the sun's tropical heat, though it provided little relief from the island's native flies and other flitting insects. Sweat proved tastier than the white and purple flowers dotting frond ends, and soon Thane and Sook found themselves besieged by pests. They sought protection by snapping off leafy ferns and using them like giant fans as they marched down the hill, through jungle that grew progressively denser as they moved. The ferns thickened, the trees grew deeper trunks, and they found numerous streams trickling beside them on their march towards the coastline.

Black smoke curled up from several fires, markers pointing their way.

"You mentioned several masters," Thane said. "Which one are we heading towards now?"

"She calls herself the Void," Sook replied, stepping around a mossy log. "Think that title's a little grand, but nobody's going to call her on it. Least if they do, they tend to die."

"So she rules by fear."

"They all do," Sook replied. "What else are they going to use? Money?"

A promise of safety. Communal society. Thane could find many reasons for people to work together, but perhaps an island of Paragon rejects and criminals wasn't the ideal place to expect such things.

"Are you afraid of her, Sook?"

The anomaly looked back at Thane, tripping over a stick as he did so and stumbling forward, catching himself against a palm. Sook set his thin face in that false confident pose so favored among the weak-willed. Mock bravery to let you live with the rest of your cowardly decisions. If Thane didn't know how so many incompetents found themselves leading others, he knew well how the sniveling found themselves stuck following in their ruts.

"I'm not afraid," Sook said, keeping his back to the palm trunk. "But I can't beat'em by myself. That's why I went to find you. Way I see it, everyone on this island needs to team up or they're going to die."

"Aren't we going to die here anyway?" Thane pointed out towards the drone wall. "Mynx will never let us leave."

"Yeah, I'd prefer dying my way rather than by a stab to the back, or getting my insides blown out."

"Does that happen here?"

"I've seen anomalies die in more ways than I thought

possible." Sook shuddered. "You need friends to survive here. Otherwise, someone you don't know's gonna walk right up to you and blow you to pieces with his eyes or something."

An interesting image, and, here, very possible.

So many weapons being turned against each other right now. If Thane could point them in the right direction, unite them under a specific goal—say, getting off this island—then they might very well get through the drone wall. Get back to the world. Then, with all the firepower at their disposal, Thane could aim them at the Paragons and let loose. Propose a different way to rule the world, one backed with strength. Not the artificial autocracy brought about by the Paragons, but a free-flowing, enterprise-driven society with Thane and his anomalies serving as the boundaries.

People could go as far as their abilities could take them. Wasn't that the ideal Thane had grown up under, back in the old days? A return, but this time with anomaly-powered guard rails.

"You all right?" Sook asked as they ducked beneath and through a waterfall pouring off an overhang. Thane didn't mind the cool soaking, reducing his already-filthy, stretched clothes to rags. "Being quiet back there."

"Pondering," Thane replied, but he tried to shut off the mental exercise. Already his bones felt weaker, his muscles thinner, and he was breathing harder than before while taking smaller steps. "When we reach this Void, what will she do?"

"Depends on her mood, I imagine," Sook said. "If she's happy, maybe she'll add us in to her crew now that I've brought you. If she's not, then we're dead."

"You, maybe."

"Don't think you could take her either," Sook shot

back. "Get as big as you want, that won't stop her from putting a hole through your head."

That threat would suffice. Thane could nurse the angry spark to keep himself strong, keep him going as the day spun through and they came closer and closer to sea level. Already he could hear waves lapping the beach, and the flitting birds further up the island had been replaced by ones more apt to scurry across the ground. Scattered streams had formed into more formidable creeks, rustling towards their salty mother. A beautiful place to begin the end of the world.

6

Come Together

A bullet. That's what caused Calvin's wound, an ugly blast that'd managed to miss perforating any organs as it clipped the anomaly's side. Kat maxed out her first-aid kit, spreading ointments over the bloody gash and pondering whether she could stitch it together before remembering they were going to a hospital. She'd promised Gordon she'd be there to pick him up, and while Calvin's immediate needs seemed to trump being a good friend to an otherwise capable tracker, why not deal with two problems at once?

"I'm not going to a hospital," Calvin said, doing an admirable job keeping the pain out of his voice.

"Don't be dumb," Kat said. "You're traced. You're on Paragon rolls now. They'll pay for it."

Calvin sat silent at that, while Kat slipped some gauze over the wound and taped the stuff in place. Not exactly the preferred medical treatment, but the fix ought to keep the seeping blood in check until they could get downtown. She'd already had Tap call a pod using her emergency tracker designation, a handy tool when she needed to get somewhere fast. Abuse it and lose it, but thus far, Kat had managed to keep on Mynx's good side. So many rules and regulations trackers had to follow, but Kat had been at this long enough that most felt like habit.

Calvin, meanwhile, didn't speak. Just sat on the bed staring at nothing. Lost in thought maybe?

"You all right?" Kat asked, standing up away from him, starting to put her coats back on.

"Yeah, I'm fine," Calvin said, snapping his eyes back to her. "It's just . . . you're right. I can see a doctor. I, uh, never really have before."

Kat quirked her mouth. "Far as I can tell, you've still got your teeth, and you don't look like you're dying of some disease?"

"Foster families got me through at first. Wasn't too hard to keep myself clean."

"You definitely weren't clean," Kat said, then buckled as Seeker buffed his head against her knees. The dog wanted to go out for another spin around the block, a walk that wasn't going to happen now. "C'mon, let's go. Gordon hates you enough already, and it's not going to be better if we're late."

"Gordon? That the other tracker you were with?"

"The one you nearly killed? Yeah. He's going to be so thrilled to see you again."

GORDON DID NOT, in fact, look thrilled to see Calvin again. Kat and the wounded anomaly—Seeker, disappointed, had been left behind—took a pod to the sprawling medical complex that had grown up around the University of Chicago Medical Center. Driven by Paragon rep infusions and anomalies with various regenerative powers, new buildings emerged like weeds, each one promising patients a full cure to specific ills, all guaranteed by Paragon funds. Anomaly abilities to erase cancers with a touch or restructure skin and bone like molding clay, made healthcare's difficulties fall away. Now the hype focused on life expectancy, and whether true immortality was just one anomaly away.

None of that meant you couldn't get yourself destroyed if you picked the wrong battle.

Gordon didn't look quite so devastated as Kat remembered him, but the tracker had lost weight over his wounded week, and had traded a subtle tan for the pallor of those whose bodies had priorities other than skin care. Gordon had shaped his hair, though, and had managed to put on a Paragon-branded shirt and jeans, giving him a passable appearance as someone who belonged in society instead of a bedchamber.

Gordon sat in a chair in the main lobby, beneath a soaring sculpture depicting Hippocrates—not the ancient Greek, but an anomaly by the same name who could, like Jesus turning water to wine, convert one blood type to another with a touch—the statue had his arms spread, smile wide, all benevolent.

Kat never had to capture these anomalies, the ones with kind and gentle abilities. All her missions sent her out after the killers, the rogues and the vagrants who declined participation in a system that could produce places like this. Still, given Kat's likely, eventual, alcohol-induced liver failure, she couldn't begrudge medical miracles all too much. Hard to complain when you could get half frozen from the inside out and still live.

"Isn't that right?" Kat said, walking up behind Gordon, engrossed in something on his Tama.

"What?" Gordon said, turning to look at her, breaking

into that flashpoint smile that used to give her heart the ol'
jolt.

"You owe me," Kat said.

"That's the hello I get?"

"Stand up and maybe you'll get a hug." Kat crossed
her arms, her jacket sleeves crinkling against each other.

Gordon managed to move without too much creaking,
though he used the chair for support. He stepped towards
Kat, spreading his arms, and Kat backed up accordingly.

"I said maybe." Kat waggled a finger, then laughed at
Gordon's hurt face and darted in to wrap the guy up.

"Thanks Kat," Gordon said, his chin brushing against
her temple. "Mean that."

They broke apart, Gordon's arms drifting down as if he
didn't know what to do with them anymore. Kat re-crossed
hers, tilted her head to the side, and prepped to call in a favor.

Without letting Gordon get a word in, Kat spilled
Calvin's story—the anomaly had skipped into the emergency room to get himself properly stitched up, ditching
away from this reunion—and finished with a loaded question, "So Calvin thinks the Elementals are after him. Do
you have any contacts here, in town, that could help?"

Gordon stared at her, then chuckled and shook his
head. "Man, Kat, I thought you'd be coming here because
you were nice. You think I'm going to help Calvin? The
guy who put me in here?"

"To be fair, we were chasing after him."

"Because he broke the law!"

"Because we'd get reps if we caught him," Kat said.
"Don't get all noble on me, Gordon. We're not saints."

"Not devils like that one either."

Kat turned up a glare, but Gordon shrugged it off.
Reached for his pack, another Paragon-issued hospital gift

full of, Kat guessed, the tracker gear Gordon had been wearing during his Calvin confrontation. He slipped the pack across his shoulders, gave Kat an icy look, and started a slow walk towards the exit. Without a coat, without anything close to what the weather required.

"Gordon, stop it," Kat said to his back. "You're being stupid."

"At least I'm not stabbing you in the back."

"And now you're being dramatic."

Gordon didn't turn around, kept going until he hit the giant revolving door meant to feed patients in and out at alarming rates. The security guard, pulling double duty as patient protector and guide, gave Gordon an are-you-insane look, but didn't manage to intercept the tracker until Gordon had stepped into the door's unstoppable swirl. While the door adjusted to Gordon's glacial walking pace, Gordon did not adjust to February's sudden slap, which sent him back into the door and around until he exited inside, right into Kat's smirk.

"Have fun?" Kat said.

"No." Gordon tried to go past Kat to who knows where. Kat moved in front of him once, twice, earning a scowl. "What are you doing?"

"Would you grow up?" Kat pointed back towards Gordon's chair. "There's more going on here than your pity fest."

Those words drew a sigh from Gordon, who appeared to accept his poor state and give in to Kat's demand. Together, with Kat providing a shoulder to lean on, the pair took over two chairs.

"Everything's gone to hell this week," Gordon said. "Have you been keeping up?"

Only one thing Gordon could mean by that comment.

"Aegis?" Kat said. "Yeah."

Not much else she could add. What did you say when a legend died? Aegis had never felt all that real to Kat, someone who seemed to exist but that she would never meet. Who showed up in pictures and news, but was so far beyond her daily life as to avoid much thought at all. And yet, without him, without the Paragons in strong working order, it did feel like a protective blanket had vanished.

"I thought I had life pretty well figured out," Gordon said as the two of them watched patients and providers and medical drones mill back and forth in front of them. "I like my job, even if it almost kills me every now and then. I like the people, like you."

"Thanks."

"But I never thought it could all go away." Gordon flicked his eyes to his Tama, revealing the—in Kat's opinion—somewhat hysterical editorial Gordon had been reading, declaring that everyone ought to horde what food and water they could to survive the end times. "I wonder if anyone sees changes like this coming."

"Probably the guy who killed Aegis. He probably saw that coming."

Gordon gave Kat a weird look, "You're able to joke about this?"

"You're not?" Kat shrugged. "It's not that I'm not nervous, Gordon, but if I can't throw up a sarcastic wall, I'm gonna fall apart. Besides, there's nothing I can do about Aegis. There is something I can do about Calvin."

"Right. Help the deadly anomaly, ignore the world falling apart."

"Yep."

Gordon huffed. Would he launch into another rant about how Kat didn't care enough about the world at large? That'd been a classic staple from their dating days, Gordon's towering news onslaughts, declaiming this and that detailed diatribe to Kat with withering condescension. Kat had often weathered these by, well, recapping her latest hunts in her head, plotting out her mistakes and how she'd do better, or by singing, silently, the newest pop star anthem. Not that Kat didn't care about the world at large, she just didn't revolve her life around it.

This time, though, whether due to his lingering weakness or the realization that Kat wouldn't change, Gordon held himself back. Stayed quiet, and then asked, "So what do you want?"

"The Elementals. I want to know how to find them," Kat said, then launched into her meetings with Beth, the Elemental who'd asked her to capture Calvin and turn him over to them. "But she's the one that found me. I can't, like, whistle and have her appear out of thin air."

Kat hadn't tried that, actually, but it seemed unlikely.

"You've been in Chicago more than I have lately," Gordon replied, but his voice had that slippery side to it, someone trying to get away without revealing it all. "Don't you know anyone?"

"If I did, I wouldn't be asking you," Kat said. "I don't like big anomaly fights, so the Elementals are way out of my comfort zone."

"Yet you're going to find them. For this guy."

"Hey, Calvin's my trace. He's supposed to earn me reps. I'm protecting my investment."

"That's all this is?"

"Stop changing the subject. If you know someone, tell me. If not, then I guess I'll have to dig something up."

Gordon rubbed his forehead, made his way to his mouth and down off his chin, a full on hand-face wipe, something Kat figured was a bad idea given all the germs running around a hospital, but hey, it wasn't her body.

"There's a meat market. A guy there used to run

messages back when the Paragons and the Elementals were talking," Gordon said. "I'll send you the info. This was a while ago, though. Back when Mynx agreed not to dump all the Elementals into the database for us to hunt. I was pretty new then."

With the dam broken, the objective achieved, Kat and Gordon settled into more casual conversation, whiling away the next hour until, looking uncomfortable and out of place, Calvin walked up with a freshly bandaged side. Apparently his wound wasn't serious enough to get the anomaly spot treatment.

"Calvin," Kat said, standing and putting herself, partly, between Gordon and the anomaly. "This is Gordon. I know you've met before, but how about we shake hands? Try not to kill each other?"

Neither one extended an arm. Neither one offered a smile.

Great. This was gonna be great.

7

Reflections

Twilight's last gasp put Zhan-Yo in front of a glossy apartment building. A green neon bear, rearing up on its hind legs, provided the aggressive logo for the tower's name, a fitting choice. While the building itself shared the subtle curves and glass-coated, solar-meshed design that'd overtaken all newer construction in the city, a furrowed copper edge created a bear's fur feel. Zhan-Yo hadn't been to this building before, which made it a good choice for hiding—while Zhan-Yo had long ago disabled his Tama's location tracking, he couldn't control other cameras seeing and cataloging his every move, and the Paragons might have his frequented locales on a drone-snooping list.

Wexley had approved every hiding place, though, and this one seemed a unique fit for Zhan-Yo's lieutenant. Climbing the steps, Zhan-Yo saw no doorman, and the doors themselves splashed a greeting across their dark glass surfaces. As little human interference as possible. The matching green letters sprawled cliched statements about home and hearth as they ran across the glass, as if the phrases themselves were running away from the building's bear. A light outline appeared in the center, layered over the line separating the two entry doors. According to some observing algorithm, the square positioned itself at the perfect height for Zhan-Yo's eyes, and the revolution's leader, champion of the free peoples, waited for a fancy lock to give him access.

"I'm sorry," the door said from a speaker embedded in its base as the green circle faded red. "You're not a resident, or on the guest list. If there has been an error, please contact your host or the building's manager."

Had he gone to the wrong place? Zhan-Yo glanced at his Tama, checked the address Wexley had sent to the glowing green numerals set in the wall on the door's right. Those checked out. This ought to be the next hideout . . . unless the Paragons beat him here.

Zhan-Yo whirled, keeping his feet level on the step and reached his hands back, gripping his tachi hilts. The swords might do nothing against a drone force, but Zhan-Yo would prefer to go out fighting than helpless. Revolutions could use martyrs, and while he didn't exactly endorse that route, Zhan-Yo would accept it.

Nothing waited on the side street save a couple across the way who turned, saw Zhan-Yo's reach for the weapons, and put an extra spring in their step. His paranoia added spice to a date night, and little else. Zhan-Yo stood, watched his breath mist, and calmed himself down. No drones, no Paragons. They hadn't found him yet.

"Did someone follow you?" Wexley said as the soft sucking sound announced the locked doors sliding open. "Are you all right?"

Zhan-Yo glanced back to see Wexley's hand beneath the man's great black overcoat, no doubt reaching for a very illegal gun. Wexley's eyes scanned the street as Zhan-

Yo acknowledged that, no, he wasn't being pursued. Just overly tense.

"With what happened to Rhimes, you should be," Wexley said. "Come on, get inside."

Wexley stayed in the door's path long enough for Zhan-Yo to get by, the security system defeated by the overriding need not to crush someone between the doors. Beyond, the building's lobby opened into a faux-rustic elegance, again milking the bear theme for all they could. Warm yellow lights flickered, mimicking candles, against blood-red carpets lined with gold patterns. Dark wood chairs, over-laid with burgundy cushions, sat in formations around similar coffee tables, each one sporting a pine sprig or two wrapped around a potpourri bowl pouring out north woods scents. The elevator banks at the lobby's rear ruined the image, though, burning through the effect with their digital panels and gray metal doors.

"This is quite the place," Zhan-Yo said as Wexley led him through. "Not what I expected."

"That's the point," Wexley replied. "It's ridiculous. Everyone that rents here is as insane as we are."

"You might be right," Zhan-Yo had never been to a hunter's cabin, never experienced the truth behind a setting like this. This lobby did not make him regret it. "The door didn't let me in."

"Intentional," Wexley said. "One fewer system with your information embedded in its database."

Right. Growing up, living during a time in which every action he took was cataloged and leveraged for his supposed benefit, Zhan-Yo had bad habits to kill. Owning Ziran, a company with a large revenue pile coming from data mining, didn't make it any easier. Now every bit of that data could be used against him.

Ironic? Perhaps.

Inconvenient? Definitely.

Wexley's apartment proved a defiant act against the building's stated theme. Blazing silver and chromed pieces scattered everywhere, as if purchased with the sole regard being how much a given chair, appliance, or picture frame could grab white light and reflect it around the room. Zhan-Yo shaded his eyes as he stepped in behind Wexley, who slipped on sunglasses without comment. Manufactured lilac filled the air, and soft house music bounced in the background from speakers Zhan-Yo couldn't locate. A red wine bottle, with two glasses for company, held center stage on a featureless glass-metal table.

"This place fits you," Zhan-Yo managed.

"It has a purpose," Wexley replied. "All the reflections and light make it difficult for outside eyes to see in. You want to hide from drones, you come here."

"Couldn't they assume a place designed to block them ought to be the clear target?"

Wexley didn't say anything, then moved to the wine bottle, unscrewing the cap and sloshing liquid in. Zhan-Yo found a chair and took it, dropping his small pack and his swords into the corner next to the door. He'd move them into the bedroom later, keep them at arm's reach, but the day's dashing had him exhausted and getting the weight off his back seemed a higher priority.

"Your message didn't make very many people happy," Wexley said as he took a seat next to Zhan-Yo's, the wine between them. "You're being aggressive."

"They're being slow."

"Big ships take a long time to turn, especially this far."

"They had ample warning." Zhan-Yo swirled the red, watched it sink from the glass's sides back to the base. "If we don't give them a shove, they'll never move. My father never did."

Instead, Zhan-Yo's father had spent the Paragon's rise at first denying the implications and then complaining about them even as he guided Ziran to take advantage in the new world. Years and years spent in toothless rage, and now that Zhan-Yo had acted, it seemed the remaining normals with any power didn't want to risk losing it. Faithless cowards.

"You won't earn their loyalty by costing them everything." Wexley had kept his coat and gloves on, as clear an indicator that Zhan-Yo would be left here as any. "I was working on them, Z. They would have come around eventually."

"Yes, easy to say when you haven't lost anything. The drones are hunting me all the time, Wexley, and they'll keep finding me."

"Rhimes had done well, until today."

"I'm sorry for that, but I didn't do this to sit silent," Zhan-Yo said. "Sylvie didn't die for me to hide out in abandoned buildings and wait for humanity to find its courage."

"She didn't have to die at all. It was her own fault."

Throwing the wine in Wexley's face would have been so, so satisfying, but Zhan-Yo relied on the self-restraint that had brought him this far. Wexley was about all he had left, and if Zhan-Yo drove his lieutenant away, then the revolution would die before it ever really started. So instead he swallowed the anger and turned the conversation to the idea that replaced it.

"Sylvie lived apart from it all," Zhan-Yo said. "Somehow, she did what needed doing and never feared the drones, or the Paragons. How?"

Wexley downed his glass, stood. "I don't know, Z. She had training, didn't she?" A look at his Tama. "But I've got your mess to clean up. You should be safe here for a while. Just let me know before you decide to lose it again, okay?"

"You're going to get Rhimes back?"

"Among other things." Wexley went to the door, didn't open it quite yet. "I'm going to see if we can't get anything from your outburst. If we can force someone to make a move, that should draw some heat away from you. From Ziran. When we're not running and hiding, we can put a real plan together."

"Right." More than half the wine bottle left, and all night for Zhan-Yo to drink it. "Thanks, Wexley. Let me know what I can do."

"Stay quiet, for starters," Wexley replied. "Good night, Z."

After his first glass, Zhan-Yo turned down the lights. Turned on the news. The talking heads blathered on about this and that while Zhan-Yo sipped more and more, until he'd emptied the bottle and his mind spun faster than the room.

Sylvie had done so well. She'd pulled on strings Zhan-Yo couldn't see, and then left him before he could learn. Some might say Zhan-Yo, nearing sixty, was too old to become a deadly agent, but he was fit, knew how to kill a man. What Zhan-Yo needed now were the resources Sylvie had, the tools that let her get around without being seen, the contacts in the shadows to complete the deadly jobs that needed doing.

If Wexley had taken Zhan-Yo's place at the top of the corporate tower, then Zhan-Yo had to find a new role. Sylvie's spot was open. He would fill it.

She would've liked that.

A Locked World

New York City's skyline changed more than any other Mynx knew. The city continually reinvented itself, so often the center for a cultural earthquake, then rebuilt anew. The new lights combing the skies now, though, didn't belong to buildings: drones patrolled at all hours. Scoured for insurrection, revolution.

Decades ago those same drones would've been enemy number one. A clear weight on the liberties and ideals the Champions adopted in their first forays together, once the world's governments decided an anomaly team ready to annihilate any threat made sense. The Champions had been plastered with so many inspirational platitudes—each of them had to stand, especially, for a chosen right; Mynx's had been knowledge—that, like an addictive drug, the constant posturing had changed their perception. Almost as one, the eight Champions realized the very basis for their power was, at the same time, violating the liberties the Champions sought to preserve.

"Do you remember when we tore them down?" Mynx asked Reeves, as her single-person jet homed in on the

Paragon's great tower, near Central Park. Bastion shone a deep blue tonight, as it had every night since Aegis's apparent death—Mynx had told no one she had the Champion's former leader frozen deep in her Factory—and while Bastion was not the tallest building in that row of sparkling metal teeth, she couldn't miss Bastion's curved, iconic facade.

"Perfectly. My memories don't degrade," Reeves said. "Would you like me to play them for you?"

That would mean crossing the threshold, and Reeves knew it. The Paragons hadn't taken power with peaceful well-wishes. The armies hadn't rolled over, neither had the free leaders. With only eight Champions, conquering billions would have been impossible. Apinya, that mind reader, had come up with a better strategy than open war: the people. Apinya had argued during one of their later discussions, when all eight wore increasing frustration on their faces, that the public's loyalty was a fleeting thing. They didn't care who ran things so long as the people and their families, had what they needed and a little of what they wanted.

Give the people stability, and they'll choose you.

"No, I should focus on the landing."

"You haven't gone back to those recordings in a long time."

"I don't like them."

"You used to say they kept you centered."

"Reeves, you're a computer, not my therapist."

Drones came in all flavors, but the ones coasting above New York City were among the most complex. Stopping crime, helping those in need, both required complex reasoning, numerous tools, and the flexibility to use them. Mynx hadn't perfected her modern drones, but they did well enough to keep casualties low enough for civilians to accept their constant protection, even with the occasional cost.

It had been far easier to build a targeted fleet with a single, murderous purpose. Tiny things, able to insert a few oxygen bubbles into the blood. No deep logic there. They did require timing, though. And something to handle it should any lose their way on their trek across the world.

"I like to think I'm far more than a computer." Reeves had the capability to sound offended, and Mynx often had to remind herself that Reeves really was just a collection of code. "I am, after all, your friend."

"A bold statement." Mynx smiled as the jet's engines rotated vertical, allowing the plane to lower itself onto Bastion's rooftop landing pad. "But I think you're right."

Mynx had disabled the little murder bots after the mission, after Reeves' first job had been a resounding success. The world had been thrown into chaos in a single night. Mynx and her drones handled the leaders, Aegis and his anomalies handled the weapons, and the Champions, along with the Paragon's newly formed ranks, promised peace. There'd been struggles, but for a total takeover, there'd been very little blood lost. Aegis had proclaimed it evidence that they were destined for this all along.

Now he'd left them to figure out what came next.

Mynx had entered Bastion several dozen times through the rooftop doorway, a curling entry that kept winding up past the door to the big antennae capping the building with its slow blinking blue light. The door itself didn't have a knob, a handle or other mechanism to force it open. Instead, the steel slate gave no quarter, no hint as to its secrets. To someone unfamiliar with its workings, it would look as though this was nothing more than a particularly shiny wall. Twin yellow lights flickered on as

Mynx approached, and she gave the door a clean, straight stare.

Tiny cameras would be sending Mynx's image to Aegis's apartment, which must belong to Celice now. Mynx would be showing on one of the monitors by the glassy overlook, or perhaps on Celice's Tama if she wasn't in the main room. Aegis's daughter would see Mynx had arrived, and while she hadn't replied to Mynx's earlier hail, Celice wouldn't leave her friend on the cold rooftop. Mynx wore one of her special Paragon uniforms, designed for flexible action, kinetic fabric set to burn its energy keeping Mynx warm. Kinetic energy, though, required momentum to charge, and standing still in front of that door provided none at all.

"Celice," Mynx said—the cameras could pick up audio too. "Open up."

Mynx counted off ten seconds, every numeral puffing white breath into the air. No response.

"Polly?" Mynx tried Bastion's AI. "Is Celice home?"

No answer, not even for Mynx.

"Your suit's running low," Reeves spoke from the Tama. "Want to head back to the jet? We can reroute to La Guardia and you can go in the normal way."

"This is *my* normal way," Mynx said. "Bring me back if I get too cold."

Pacifica's Champion strode to the door, reached out, touched its icy surface, and sank in.

Bristling black thorns rose around her, excepting only the soft, moss-covered patch on which Mynx found herself. The glistening thorn tips looked menacing, but Mynx looked for the little bright red lines curling back from those sharp ends, each one tracing its way through a Paragon's name, past or present. A beautiful routine, drawing from Bastion's own active database. Art for an audience of one, because as far as she knew, Mynx was the only human, anomaly or otherwise, that could enter these places.

The chill vanished, and her smoky breath, unneeded here, didn't puff from her lips. Mynx couldn't feel her heart beat, and no longer tasted the lingering cinnamon in the protein bar she'd had on the flight over. If she'd had a mirror, Mynx could have seen herself forty years younger, with skin, hair, and health more perfect than she'd ever actually achieved. In this digital Elysium, such things were attainable.

Mynx went straight ahead, long strides carrying her towards the thorns, which pulled away and parted like gardens for a fairytale princess. Silver light from an omnipresent full moon slid through the thorny canopy and contrasted with purple-pink mushroom caps that sprang up at her every footstep, guiding her way. Mynx had little time for beauty in the real world, where cosmetic concessions often created costs and construction challenges. Here her imagination could spin up its wildest ideas and let them flourish.

Beyond, the thorns pulled back into a wide, mossy oval, which contained the star of this particular demesnes: a pool surrounded by an ever-cascading rose petal flurry. Mynx almost laughed at the sight, so absurd, and a product of her younger self. Back when Bastion had been new, had marked Paragon power achieving its absolute height, and soaring with its peak came Mynx's pride. She could make beautiful things, yes, but the rose petals took an ugly turn now, a gaudy indulgence. All this lock needed was a simple switch for Mynx to flip, not this grand exercise in useless fluff.

She went beneath the petals—without smells in this place, the flowers were even less pleasant—and looked into the pool. Here was that mirror, turquoise warning Mynx's face, making her look, again, like one of those fairy-tale princesses. They could wish away their problems, or wait for some prince, or a turn in the script to save them. Mynx didn't have that luxury, so she stuck both her arms into the pool and felt for that switch. She found it, not far beneath the surface, but rather than the slender lever to pull, Mynx instead found a seal. A casing keeping her hands from the lever.

Someone had adjusted the door's security. Had strengthened it, changed it, had—

Mynx, your temp is getting low.

Reeve's voice crashed around the space, breaking through the sensory barrier. Ironic that the words wouldn't be heard outside as Reeves had to speak them at a frequency too low for human hearing. They could, though, be parsed as data, and they meant Mynx was running out of time. She could leave, try going through the front door, though if Mynx encountered resistance here, the main entrance probably wouldn't be any easier. And whomever had changed this lock would know she'd arrived.

No.

Aegis could out punch anyone. Apinya could break down a mind and put it back together however he saw fit. Mynx ruled the one-and-zero realm.

Mynx pulled her arms out of the pool. Tilted her head and focused. Forms and functions began to overlay across the water, detailing the lock's inner workings and the very precise set who could trigger its release. Mynx brushed these outer barriers away, erasing routines meant to verify voice, image, touch, emptying the water until only the single true and false, a boolean barrier, remained. This should have been the lever, but now the box covered it instead.

Your extremities are numb. You may not be able to stand much longer.

The box itself was simply another set of secure functions, designed to bar anyone that did not possess a single element from entry. Mynx leaned over, read through the fussy, lime green lines. Thick code, and sloppy. No wonder they'd only managed a crude box. As for the code key, that wasn't hard to find, though reading it wasn't easy.

Aegis's real name. The one he'd been born with, and had sought to bury under a legend's guise. Which meant only one person could have put all this in place.

Mynx fed the name to the function and the box faded away as the water had, leaving the lever. Mynx reached for it, flipped the switch. There wasn't any noise, no other sign. Mynx would have to trust Celice hadn't actually disabled the door and left the box as a tantalizing trap. Reeves called again, saying something about losing her fingers. Time to go.

She pulled back from the well, shut her eyes—a motion more for her own comfort than any necessity—and left her enchanted world.

And found pain, searing cold pain and an ache on her left side, now lying on the ground outside the open door. Mynx couldn't feel her legs, her arms, and every breath brought with it unstoppable tremors. Her suit had run dry, and she was freezing. Bastion's steel entrance lay open in front of her, the wall peeled aside and a simple, handled door waiting for her to pull it open and walk inside. She could, she had to, she must.

She reached—

9

Making An Entrance

The burnt orange twilight played overhead as Thane and Sook approached the Void's apparent . . . outpost? Lair? Thane didn't quite know what to call the place, but stronger terms like fortress or headquarters didn't fit the broad dune rising several hundred meters back from the beach. The golden sand wall, stitched with debris and darker dirt, revealed its unnatural origins as the harsh wind this close to the ocean failed to nudge even a single grain away. Cooking seafood wafted back towards Thane, whose stomach grumbled for protein after a day spent devouring coconuts and berries. Music played too, light drums and a makeshift guitar's tinny twangs. Someone laughed, and, behind it all, the waves continued their eternal crashing.

An advanced existence for a desert island in the ocean's middle. Thane had been trained by movies to expect a haggard gaggle crouching over a few driftwood sticks, attempting to roast a fish carcass that'd washed ashore. Once again, anomalies were proving their superiority. Stick them anywhere, and their powers would give them a better life than any normal could expect.

"The dunes came later," Sook was talking. He was always talking, and Thane had developed a knack for blocking out the man's needy voice. "From what I heard, it didn't start out with everybody trying to kill each other. That only happened when Arthur tried to take control."

"That's usually when the fighting starts," Thane said. "People are often too stupid to accept their rightful leaders."

Ahead, the battered trail, which had been joined by other connecting paths leading deeper into the island, finished its journey at a split in the dune wall. The sand simply cut off, as if it were stone, with flat sides creating a gap filled by a palm-frond-wearing pair. Each, a man and a woman, carried a sharpened stick not unlike the one Sook had brought with him to Thane's cave. They didn't react as Thane and Sook approached, at least until Sook came close enough for the man to inhale and spit towards Thane's hapless guide. The splatter fell far short, but Sook recoiled anyway.

As opening seconds went, that was less than promising.

"Who're you?" the woman asked Thane, ignoring Sook, who stood several paces behind.

"Thane. I'm here for the Void."

He would not banter with trifles.

"Then you shouldn't have come with Sook," the man said. "He's not going to help you get anywhere."

"He brought me here. I'm not an enemy. I want to speak with your leader."

The guards glanced at each other, the woman laughed, "Are you outta a movie or something? March up here, ask to get in? You could be working for anyone, and even if you're not, maybe you're just going to try and kill her."

"Sook said she was more than capable of defending herself."

"Maybe so, but she doesn't pay us to let unknowns inside," the man said.

"What does she pay you with?" Thane asked, honestly curious. "Sea shells?"

"Food," the man replied. "The only thing worth a damn on this island. Work a shift at the gates, you're guaranteed part of the day's catch." The man lowered his sticked, sharpened end pointing towards Thane. "You want to see the Void, convince us."

Sook, still behind Thane, coughed and started to speak, "You don't know who he is—"

"Stop." Thane held up a hand, didn't take his eyes from the guards. "I am a new arrival. I crashed near the cave up that way. Sook found me there, and told me about the Void, about how she would be the person to work with to find a way off this island."

The guards laughed again, but a weaker chuckle this time, sadder and derisive. Thane knew that laugh well, for he'd done it himself plenty of times. Back when he'd fought against the Champions, he'd dismissed his own chances at survival in the same way. Even so, Thane still tried. No matter how small the chance, Thane still tried.

"You're trying to convince us to let you in," the woman said. "And you say something like that? What'd Arthur say he'd do for you? Or did the Duchess give you something? Nobody's getting off this island. Never have, never will."

Trifles. This was over.

"Move aside, or I will make you," Thane said.

"He will," Sook added.

"Good," the man replied. "I was getting bored anyway."

As soon as the guard finished his sentence, Thane felt the air around his ankles thicken. He looked down to see a soupy fog forming around his knees, with small, micro flashes sparking inside as raindrops began to pour over his feet. Those flashes started hitting his skin, each one burning him like a tiny match. A strange power, but then, most were. Thane used the sparks, the pain, to fuel his anger and drive what would come next.

"Watch out!" Sook cried, and Thane looked up to see the woman throw her sharpened stick at him, and when Thane tried to move, he slipped on the muddy ground made by those miniature storms. The thrown spear struck Thane in the shoulder, embedding in his skin and sticking up like a flagpole as Thane hit the ground on his back.

More pain tearing through, starting fires Thane needed.

The woman, heedless, ran over to Thane and plucked the spear out. In her hands, the wood extended, becoming clay-like until, with its ends drooping down to form a crude arch, the wood hardened again. She jammed the altered spear down, pressing it across Thane's chest and into the dirt. Deep enough to pin an ordinary man to the ground. As she completed the motion, more mini storm clouds formed over Thane's face, his chest, again sending lightning sparks into his skin, forcing him to close his eyes.

Sook continued to yell, now arguing with the male guard.

Not that it mattered. Things had been pushed far enough.

Like someone sliding down an icy slope, Thane both gave into the inevitable fall and tried to keep what slight control he could. As his body grew, his perception of himself shrank until instinct overran coherent thought.

The monster ruled the man.

Thane lunged upwards, pulling the flimsy stick from the ground with his shoulders alone and letting it fall away. The two guards turned from Sook and Thane smelled their sudden fear as the weak, older man they had been threatening now stood near double their height, eyes ablaze and toothy maw wide.

The little lightning bursts grew and swarmed across his body, and Thane saw those same flashes reflected in the man's eyes. Miniature clouds burst in front of Thane's face, attempting to obscure his view, but Thane had more senses than sight, and used them. A quick leap forward pierced the barrier and pushed his target into the dirt.

A crack came with a dull push on Thane's left, and he stepped on the man, crushing him into the ground, as he turned to see the other guard, holding another broken spear across both of her hands. She glared up at him as both of the fragments stretched and sharpened into dual wood daggers.

Worthless weapons.

Thane needed only his hands to grab the guard, lift her as she broke her new toys against his arms, and throw her into the dune wall. The hardened sand didn't provide much cushion, and she bounced off to the ground, unmoving.

"Thane?" a sniveling voice said behind him, and Thane whirled.

The little man who'd led him here cowered, hands up by his face, as if by hiding his eyes Thane might disappear. A nightmare banished. Thane, though, was no dream.

But this wasn't the enemy. Couldn't be a threat. That question, that tiny uncertainty, provided the hook that Thane needed to start his climb away from the hazy rage. Up and out, back to sanity. His muscles shrank, his heart slowed its thunderous chorus, and Thane once more enjoyed real thought coursing through his mind. The rage could be, was, an intoxicating freedom from consequence. A delving into violent id so enticing . . . if Thane had nearly starved himself bathing in cold knowledge, up there in the cave, falling so totally into the anger would result in what?

"Are you normal again?" Sook asked, chasing away the thought. "Because you're going to have to say something."

Sook pointed towards a growing crowd clustering in the dune breach. Torchlight replaced sunlight's last remnants, though it took Thane a moment to notice nobody held actual torches. Small, burning globes appeared in the air around him and the newcomers, as though a swarm of giant fireflies had found them. The light revealed a filthy, wretched cast. Anomalies of all types, yes, but universal in their thin frames and sun-scorched skin. The men wore disheveled beards, the women had hair frizzing below their waists, or braided into haphazard bunches. None seemed especially hostile, even though Thane stood over the unconscious bodies of their chosen guards.

Sook had said the island held three rulers, and the two guards had mentioned the others before engaging in the worst fight of their lives. Perhaps the Void was the least of these. Perhaps Thane had chosen the wrong course.

"Aren't you a little old to be picking fights?" said a voice from within the crowd, one that at once seemed to come from the heart of the cluster and yet also from the dunes, from the ferns behind Thane, and even from Sook.

Anomalies were amazing, and, Thane was beginning to find, exhausting.

"Not too old to be winning them," Thane replied. Having nowhere else to look, he addressed his remark to the people. "But I did not come here to threaten, or hurt, you. Your sentries refused any other path."

"Then why did you come here?" said that same voice, feminine steel. None of the people he saw, and Thane counted now over two dozen, moved their mouths, yet the words came anyway. "To join us?"

"To make you an offer."

"Then make it."

A crossroads. Either Thane gave into the Void—he assumed that's who he was speaking with, who else could it be? Or he made a demand of his own, that she reveal herself and they speak as equals. Pride dictated the latter, but pride made many fools. Thane had given up what remained of his pride when he let the Paragons use him, when he refused to die for all those years in that makeshift dungeon. He had no use for the follies of younger men.

"I want to get off this island," Thane said, projecting, drawing on enough of that always-burning anger to give his words depth. Add some bulk to his arms, shoulders. "I believe it is possible, but not for one alone. Together, though, we can be free."

No sound. Thane had expected something. Maybe laughter. Instead, only the waves.

"Do you know what makes you different from us?" the voice finally replied. "You were sent here by the Paragons, just as we were. You want to escape, just as we do. You might have family, as some of us do, or you might have nothing but hatred pulling you away from here, as many of us do. But the difference? You have not tried to leave. You don't know how impossible it is."

"I've seen many anomalies do the impossible, myself included."

All at once all the burning globes winked out, giving the moon full command of the night sky. Thane stayed still. This looked like a show, best let it play.

When the globes re-appeared, this time higher, like a halo around the dune breach, they revealed not a crowd between the dunes but one ringing Thane, Sook, and the downed guards. No longer haggard, but clothed in various makeshift tunics, dresses, and cloaks, the washed and somewhat civilized eyes of the Void's army stood far stronger than the rabble he'd seen a moment ago. It also meant the Void had an anomaly capable of an illusion, or at least twisting Thane's vision.

Anomalies really were exhausting.

Standing alone in the breach, wearing a thick dress made from molten lava rock—orange threads ran through the craggy, yet somehow flowing, outfit—and standing short, was the person Thane presumed to be the Void. Her face set in a grimace, her arms folded, the Void didn't seem thrilled.

"You have bravado," the Void said, her words now coming from her actual mouth. "I'll give you that much."

"And you put on quite a show," Thane replied. "Are the games over?"

"This isn't a game. This is life on this island, and now it's the only life you have. Tread carefully, Thane, or you won't live to see another sunrise."

She turned away from him, towards her town.

"Wait," Thane said. "You know my name. How?"

"We're not all Sook. We know who you are, and we are not afraid."

The Void led the way through the dunes, the rest of her force forming up around Thane and marching him inside. From what he saw, the Void spoke the truth: fear had no hold here, but in its place hovered the doomed's dead-eyed stare. These anomalies might have power, might have formed a community, but they had no hope.

Thane had worked with Aegis, had seen the Champion inspire billions. He could manage this much.

He had to.

10

Fresh Meat

Kat had the pod drop her and Calvin at a greasy spoon tucked into the corner a block away from Gordon's contact. Kat had a few rules before going into a dangerous situation—any contact with the Elementals qualified as dangerous—and a good breakfast splashed with coffee entered the top five on that list. Just behind bringing the suit and ahead of bringing Seeker, who she'd left back at the apartment. Despite missing his slobbering joy, the huge husky made an easy target in a close quarters quarrel, and Kat preferred her doggo happy instead of hurt.

Another rule barred bringing extra people, though Gordon hadn't pushed to come along. They'd all spent the evening downtown, grabbing dinner, with Kat performing a conversational dance to smooth the rough edges between Calvin and Gordon. Every time one or the other threw a glare, Kat hard-switched the topic, ordered another round, or pointed to one of those slow-moving statues orbiting the park. Not exactly her preferred role, but they'd left the restaurant alive. Dropped Gordon at his hotel, and then

Calvin had crashed on her couch, Tap the surfer AI watching everywhere for an Elemental ambush.

Now Kat had a latte steaming in a saucer between her gloved hands. Her shock-white suit, already bearing dirty-snow splatters here and there, seemed overkill in the diner's omelet-flavored confines, but Kat couldn't take it off like a coat. More like armor than clothing, the suit came custom from a trackers-only marketplace that Mynx kept stocked with useful tools meant to put normals on par with the anomalies they chased.

Across from her sat one such anomaly, staring at his black coffee as though he'd left the diner far behind on some mental journey. They'd had Tap order Calvin some new clothes last night and they'd appeared, dropped by drone, with the dawn. A slim royal blue arctic jacket, faux-fur hood, and gloves designed to dig out avalanches. A little absurd for city living, but Calvin insisted the cold wasn't his friend, and as he paid for it all with his own Paragon reps, Kat didn't care.

"You all right?" Kat said as the waiter, a real human one who looked like she might've been working there since before the Paragons were a thing, dropped off a motley eggs and toast batch.

"Yeah," Calvin replied, blinking himself out of his stupor and taking a slow sip. "Just thinking that I never used to like coffee till I started running away."

Kat spread some strawberry jam on the toast, gave Calvin a chance to keep going.

"Then I learned a cup of black cost less than just about anything else."

Kat glanced up. "That's it?"

"Yeah." Calvin started in on his own toast. "What, you think I had some profound insight comin' from a cup of coffee?"

.   .   .

DELANO'S LOCAL MEATS. The signage looked like it'd last been updated a century ago, with big, white block letters on a black span lined with red and coated with dirt. Kat figured the place had to have straddled the transition from actual meat coming from actual creatures to the modern, grown stuff. An old-fashioned hanging sign said "Open" in the glass door's center, the two big windows on either side giving view to freezer cases showing steaks, chops, and more. All of'em in that advertisement-red, marbled to perfection.

A quick view through the glass, though, gave little further insight. The place seemed as empty as the sidewalk they stood on. A weekday morning, but late enough now that anyone going to work was already there, and cold enough that anyone who wasn't would be curled up inside. Kat caught all this on a single walk by, turning once she'd cleared the window's sight lines to wave Calvin across. The anomaly tried to follow Kat's method, but the man's stare held too long. Wasn't casual enough.

"Next time," Kat said when Calvin reached her, "try not to look like you give a crap about the place."

"What?"

"You pay attention to them, they pay attention to you."

"There wasn't anybody there."

"Hi, I'm the world we live in," Kat said. "There's cameras everywhere, and most of them have algorithms that tag interest. You look that intense at this place, they'll catalog you, let the owner know so they can send you ads."

"So?"

"Calvin, if the Elementals are trying to kill you, everyone working for'em probably knows your face." This was why Kat far preferred hunts on her own, where amateurs couldn't get her killed. "If the cameras tell him you're outside, now he's going to be ready for you."

"Then why are we waiting out here?"

Kat shut her eyes for a second, took a breath. "Okay, you stay. I'll call you when it's clear."

Calvin tried to protest, but Kat pushed by him. In the same motion, she reached up and tapped a light latch on her suit's collar. Unlocked, the suit's mask shot up from beneath her chin to wrap her face and connect with her hood. A dark screen covered her eyes, then faded as it adjusted to her vision, giving Kat a better view. Releasing the mask set the suit's other parts in motion too: the ends of her gloves sealed with the bracers on her arms, which rotated to her default gadgets, her waistband holsters popped open to allow easy access to the stun gun pair on either side, and the suit swapped its target temp from resting to active.

Kat had wanted to go in soft, play it nice, but these people had tried to shoot Calvin, tried to kill him. They'd failed, but they wouldn't even get the chance with Kat.

She pushed open the door, sounding that oh-so-old bell jangle from a faux-gold set hanging above her head. Kat's mask filtered out the details, highlighting in red the two back doors, one a double-set for wheeling out meat stock and the second, on the right side, a single one probably leading to an office. More meat cases filled the space, containing a ludicrous variety that included elk, moose, and kangaroo. How those qualified as 'local meats' in Chicago, who knew.

Kat caught the whole room in a single swinging look. Didn't seem likely anyone had crouched behind the meat cases. The ceiling sat low, fluorescent lights hitting the pale, flickering white that said they hadn't been upgraded in decades. Nothing hiding up there either. The two doors, then.

As if anticipating her next move, the small door swung open, revealing exactly the man Kat would have pegged to be running a place like this: an older, flagging body hiding better days beneath a long life opening early and closing late. A half-hearted gray beard made incursions up the man's long face to his speckled hair. An apron covered a worn t-shirt and jeans combo pack. And a wholly illegal shotgun sat in his hands.

The mask identified the threat before Kat did, sending a vibration on Kat's side that she used to guide her dive. The calculated trajectory took her out of the blast's potential range by putting the place's main meat case between her and the gun, at least for the moment.

"What're you runnin' for?" the man said. "I'm not gonna kill you!"

Yeah. Sure.

Instead, Kat drew one stun gun in her right hand, while sticking her left wrist out and clenching that fist. The trigger shot a strong wire with a steel grappling hook on the end out and up, where it wrapped around one of those fluorescent lights. The man's face appeared over the case, looking at her and aiming that shotgun.

Kat triggered the hook and she shot up off the floor as the man fired, the pellets blasting a hole where Kat had been a moment before. The hook brought her up a couple meters before the light, groaning, broke. Not that it mattered: the height took her over the meat case, giving her a clear shot with the stun gun. The dart hit the man right in the neck and he stumbled back, hitting the wall, then plunging forward and banging his face on the back of his own meat case.

The light snapped off its hinges and swung down, Kat

taking the landing and ducking out of the way as the meter-length light smashed into the meat case's front and sent broken glass everywhere. Ignoring the destruction, Kat quick-stepped around the case's side, slipping another stun dart into the gun's chamber while her grapple retracted back into her wrist slot.

With Calvin, it'd taken more than one dart to bring him down. She wasn't going to take any chances.

"WHAT WOULD YOU DO, person comes into your home looking like you?" Delano said an hour later, after Kat had taken away the shotgun, bound the man to a chair in his office, and turned the sign out front to 'closed'. "I see you on the cameras, and what'em I supposed to think? You're here to get a filet?"

Delano's office doubled as his living space, breaking back into a small kitchen and a bedroom. Two TVs split between daytime programming and the camera feed from out front sat on a huge green-metal desk overlaid with photographs and a small, old-fashioned laptop still showing what looked like a sales spreadsheet on its tiny screen. Shelves filled the rest of the space, which apparently assisted the kitchen by functioning as a pantry and held myriad dry goods. Without her mask and its air purifier working, raw meat's heavy iron smell permeated everything.

Calvin stayed on the periphery, leaning near the exit door and looking towards the ground more than anywhere else. Not used to playing the interrogator. Which, fine. Kat could, had, and would continue to ask all the damn questions, and she had enough vinegar for the job this time: Delano had tried to shoot her. With an actual gun.

"So because you think I look weird, you decide to shoot

first, ask questions later?" Kat replied. With Delano sitting, Kat stood taller than the man, a position she so rarely occupied that, hey, she was going to enjoy. "What if I'd been a Paragon? You'd already be locked in some cell, or dead."

Delano shrugged. "Look around this place. Think I've got a lot to lose?"

"Stop it. Seems like every time I catch someone all they talk about is how their life's so terrible that it can't get any worse. Then why are you still here? That's a lot of meat waiting to be sold, and it looks fresh, which means you're doing well." Kat surprised herself a bit. Seemed like a lot to say to a man she'd never met before, and didn't get them anywhere close to what they wanted to know. Guess it felt good, sometimes, to go off on someone. "Anyway, that doesn't matter. You have your own problems. We're here so you can help us with ours."

"Dunno if I can do that, lady," Delano replied, barking out a short laugh at the end. "With a suit like yours, don't think I'm part of your world."

"I'd be thrilled if you weren't," Kat said. "But my friend here's in some danger, and I'm trying to get him out of it. Answer the questions, and we'll forget you ever existed."

"Then ask'em," Delano said. "You've already wrecked my shop and ruined my day. I'd like to forget you too."

In the movies, they'd cut to a different frame. The official interrogation music would start playing and Kat would lean forward, plant her palms on the table and give Delano a withering glare as she laid into him with incisive questions. Here, she just spoke and wished she had a glass of water to compensate for all the talking.

"We're looking for the Elementals," Kat said. "I heard you know where we can find them?"

To Delano's credit, he didn't change his expression one bit. The cocky grin stayed plastered on, his wrinkled eyes stayed bright, "Whaddya mean, the Elementals? Are they a band?"

"You're not that stupid."

"You don't know me that well."

Kat rubbed her forehead, stalling what could well be a coming headache.

"They shot me," Calvin said, without moving from his wall. "The Elementals did. Yesterday, outside the place the Paragons gave me."

Now Delano turned, his smile twisting a bit, "You're a Paragon?"

"He's a Paragon, I'm a tracker," Kat said. "You said you didn't like your life, we can ruin it for you, but I'd rather save his."

"For the first time," Calvin added. "I'm a part of society, and now someone's trying to kill me. I want to know why."

Delano shook his head, "That's not how they do it. The Elementals aren't assassins. I'm not saying they're heroes, but it's not about murder. That doesn't help them."

"You said you didn't know them," Kat said. "Maybe things have changed."

"A lotta things are changing right now," Delano agreed, falling into a shrug that withered away his remaining resistance. "Anyway, yeah, whomever your guy is, they've got it right. I did know some of the Elementals that worked this city. Knew some of the old Paragons too."

"How?"

"Meat, duh. You want the finest specimens in the city, you come here. Catered to both groups, then they see each other here one day and I'm expecting fire'n'hell to rain down, but they start talking and soon my shop is like the chosen meeting place for Chicago's powered-players."

A lot to unpack there. Paragons and Elementals working together? Laying out agreements? Kat wasn't far enough inside Paragon circles to know how that would happen, but, if you wanted to keep a city this big safe, you probably had to work with the ones you hated. Especially when they could nuke a city block whenever they wanted.

Like Kat had opened a valve, Delano poured out more, going on and on about the last couple decades as the Paragons and the Elementals negotiated one arrangement after another, before finally getting to what Kat and Calvin were really there for, the most recent Elemental enclave. Not all that far from here either.

When Delano ran out of stuff to say, the clock neared lunch and Kat needed to get out of the iron, sweaty smell. She freed Delano from her grapple's binding and reset the gear. Told Delano she'd buy some meat in a few days to help pay for the repairs to his shop. Then she and Calvin made for the exit, stepping over the glass on the main floor.

"Hey," Delano said as Calvin reached for the door. "I've been trying to place you, Kat. What'd your parents do?"

"Paragons. Why?"

"Yeah, I thought so. Got your dad's eyes, your mom's hair," Delano said, broom now in hand. "Sorry to hear what happened."

"You knew them?"

"Where d'ya think your meals came from?" Delano replied. "They were two of the good ones. Always came in here with happy faces, ready to talk about their girls. They said you were a fighter." Delano pointed the broom at the wreckage. "Guess they were right."

11

Apartment Hunting

Leaving a half-filled wine bottle within easy reach in a place Zhan-Yo described as his personal hell had consequences, and they were throbbing. He'd used the Cabernet, after Wexley's departure, to sink through the day's adrenaline and then resorted to staring at his Tama, watching for any sign his plea to the world had any effect. Denials spread everywhere, as executives and boards that had endorsed Zhan-Yo's plan a week ago now disavowed it in grandstanding public proclamations. There were no clashes in the streets, no overthrows, no invitations for Zhan-Yo to come forth and lead the proud normals of the world to their rightful place in it.

Thoroughly soaked, Zhan-Yo reconciled to the clock and proceeded to spend his last conscious hour in a futile quest to turn off the lights in the apartment. He realized, after combing every wall several times, establishing a handhold network to support his veering steps, that, in a concession to the most modern of modern conveniences, Wexley's place had no switches at all. Zhan-Yo confirmed this discovery when the apartment's AI finally spoke out, insisting that it was worried about Zhan-Yo's health. In a rambling slur, Zhan-Yo gave a list of demands, most of which were far beyond the AI's capacity.

Zhan-Yo settled for darkness and some water.

LATE MORNING PROVED A THUNDEROUS AWAKENING, one only silenced by rote processes, worked slowly, designed to blunt a hangover's power. Zhan-Yo nibbled on crackers, worked out as hard as he dared in the building's basement-level gym, and took a long shower. Headache-destroying pills practiced their magic, and by the time Zhan-Yo had himself bundled back up, he could call himself alive again.

He also had a plan.

Wexley's building presented a safe haven, but, even after and perhaps especially because of yesterday, Zhan-Yo wanted no part in that. The adrenaline, the feeling like he was doing something proved a drug no amount of common sense logic could defeat. After all, Zhan-Yo hadn't started his revolution by sitting around in Ziran's offices. He'd gone out there, risked himself and everything else for the sake of his cause! Stopping now would render all of that worthless.

Sylvie had operated from the shadows. Zhan-Yo lived there now, in the margins. He needed to learn what she had known, to understand how to make change without being seen or sensed. Sylvie had resources, connections and methods that Zhan-Yo had never asked for, but Sylvie would have kept them somewhere. Certainly not on a public server, where Ziran could have found it: after her death, Zhan-Yo had searched. Wexley had searched. They had found no trace. But unless Sylvie kept everything in her head, and Zhan-Yo couldn't discount that possibility, she would have stored it somewhere. And of all the places that somewhere might be, Zhan-Yo had settled on her apartment.

Registered under a false name and in a neighborhood of so little distinction, Zhan-Yo might not have found the apartment at all save for careful digging through Sylvie's pod records. Even the master spy herself couldn't foil every digital tracker in the modern world, and, with Wexley's paranoia powering his choice, Zhan-Yo had dedicated a tiny slice of Ziran's network to tracking her movements. Delivered to his Tama in daily bursts, the records confirmed Sylvie's loyalty, and once confirmed, Zhan-Yo had forgotten about the program until Sylvie died. Then her movements, colored lines over Chicago's grid detailing where her Tama's constant connection put her, became a bittersweet guessing game. Why had Sylvie gone here or there on this day, was this her favorite coffee shop or where she liked to shop for her clothes? An apparent love for the Field Museum? Her life's hidden pieces revealed.

Now he stood in front of her complex, his tachi tucked beneath his ground-to-neck warm trench coat. Wexley had left the garment in the closet with a note suggesting it would be better to keep the swords unseen. Zhan-Yo smiled amid a slight shiver—another chill day, despite the winter sun—Wexley wouldn't want him out at all, but the man knew his boss well.

If Wexley's apartment lived in Chicago's beating tech-noheart, then Sylvie's laid its stakes in the city's bones. People flurried along the streets here, ducking into and out of pods, hustling to the shops or inside their homes. From what Zhan-Yo could see, incomes ran across a wide scale, but he didn't feel a society hustling under stress. Smiles showed more than frowns, though Zhan-Yo attributed the nervous edge on many to his recent proclamation, his invitation to shatter a status quo that, evidently, served this community well.

But he meant to save the entire world. One couldn't look at the good pockets and assume things were fine everywhere.

Contrary to Wexley's building, Sylvie's had few security features. A sole Tama-matching lock held vigil on the front door, and Zhan-Yo simply waited, smoking a cigarette—Wexley, ever considerate, had left him a pack—and watching the walkers until someone left. He caught the door, stubbed out the tobacco, and drifted inside. Five floors up in a drab elevator, a minute-long hike through a pocked cream hallway and a carpet that screamed store-closing-sale, and Zhan-Yo arrived at a door he'd never managed to see when it really mattered.

He'd blamed the whole planning-an-assassination-and-other-dark-deeds for their relationship never progressing past occasional dinners. A hopeful view, and potentially a delusional one: Sylvie may not have seen Zhan-Yo in the same light that he saw her, but all the same, he wished Sylvie had opened this door for him.

Just once.

Without her, though, Zhan-Yo needed to figure out a different way in. Random passersby wouldn't be opening Sylvie's door, and if Zhan-Yo loitered outside the apartment long enough he'd attract the wrong sort of attention. A Tama lock, no doubt tied right to Sylvie's signature, glistened on the right side like a black slate. Zhan-Yo found it ugly against the door's own navy coat, but this whole placed looked like it'd been around long before Tamas became a thing. Modernity forcing itself on the past.

Zhan-Yo looked up and down the corridor. The building shaped like a square, and the hallway matched the outer frame, with Sylvie naturally choosing the unit farthest away from the elevators. Her apartment sat against a corner and, for the moment, the hallways on either side were empty. Zhan-Yo opened his coat, used his right hand to draw one of the tachi. Shifting the coat to hide the blade, Zhan-Yo wedged the sword between the door and the frame, then slid the edge down. A converted building like this, like Zhan-Yo's old apartment, would substitute the keyholes for the Tamas, but he bet they wouldn't change the bolts themselves. Solid metal, yes, but Zhan-Yo's tachi were made to cut through harder things. With a couple of hard presses, their sharp pings muted by Zhan-Yo's coat, the bolt split and Sylvie's door hung free.

Sheathing the sword, Zhan-Yo pushed the door open and went into a place he'd imagined going many times. Those imagined versions, it turned out, were wrong. From the moment he stepped inside the entry, gliding the door shut behind him, one word dominated everything he saw:

Plants.

Chicago had its gardens, but its location didn't lend itself to tropical lushness or the pine forests found further north. Zhan-Yo considered plants a garnish rather than a place's highlight, but here something changed. Nestled between aloes and orchids, Zhan-Yo picked out normal life's sparse, scattered evidence: a table, a single chair. The windows let in enough natural light, though hued through flowers that had attached themselves to the biggest sun source they could find. Vines ran across the floor, crawling over each other and most everything else.

Chaos, but in a natural way. As if Sylvie had wanted her apartment to showcase what might happen to the world if humans disappeared.

Pollen and plant perfumes thickened the air, which was far too warm for this time of year. His Tama put the temp at eighty degrees, a ridiculous energy waste, but a necessary one to keep a greenhouse like this alive.

Zhan-Yo went further into the kitchen, seeing beyond it, through a doorway overhung with a bright yellow climbing rose, what looked like the main living room. Between the leaves, Zhan-Yo tried to find some evidence that the woman he'd admired, even loved, had lived here, but there were no pictures. No letters left on the counter. Every product he could see, from the toaster to the knife set latched onto the wall near some cutting boards, looked brand basic.

Mystifying. Zhan-Yo had always assumed Sylvie lived a vast life beyond their interactions, but now he wondered if this was her refuge. If, after completing yet another blackmail job or assassination, Sylvie would come here to this green-filled place and simply be. This many plants would have required so much care, so much time, but they wouldn't judge her actions either. Wouldn't ask her to consider the implications of overthrowing the world's government.

He laughed as he passed beneath the climbing rose. What had he expected, really? Pictures of Sylvie at her weekly bowling league? Vast bookshelves detailing ancient philosophers? A knitting yarn collection?

Sylvie always defied his expectations. Why would that stop now?

The living room furthered Sylvie's commitment to a green thumb, with twin dwarf lime trees flanking a gigantic screen. Had he found her true passion? Movies? But no. A glance at the coffee table showed a dedicated Tama-tablet, and he understood. Video-linked windows on the screen would display operations in progress. By the end, Sylvie didn't need to get her own hands dirty. She could command from afar, watch every dagger find its throat without ever leaving her couch.

"You're not supposed to be here," the heavy words came from behind Zhan-Yo, and he whirled, tripping over an ivy tendril and back-stepping against that big screen.

Watching him, standing in front of what Zhan-Yo suspected was the bedroom, was a large man. Heavyset, but level, comfortable; Zhan-Yo bet the man knew how to use his weight. Jeans meshed up into a sweater. No coat, even though it neared zero outside. Hollow eyes, deep bags beneath them, followed Zhan-Yo's haphazard retreat. Gloved hands, but no weapons. Still, Zhan-Yo drew his tachi and kept them both ready.

"Who are you?" Zhan-Yo asked.

"Her brother," the man said. "And you're the man who got her killed."

A brother? Zhan-Yo wished he could be surprised Sylvie had never mentioned that, but her family held firm on the list of things she'd never brought up with Zhan-Yo. A conversational collection deflected with ease whenever Zhan-Yo had tried to breach Sylvie's defenses.

"But I didn't kill her," Zhan-Yo replied. Sylvie's brother hadn't moved, and keeping the couch between them seemed like a good plan. "Aegis did, and I did the same to him."

"She talked to me about you. How you had big dreams. She never said whether they were worth dying for."

"I would have died for them. We shared that."

"But you're still here."

Zhan-Yo had always prided himself on his patience. He'd kept Ziran growing through innumerable twists and turns not through intractable anger or split-second decisions, but with careful analysis and deliberate moves. He'd watched rivals crumble chasing trends or ignoring their bottom lines for risky, ill-fated investments. To Zhan-Yo, Ziran wasn't personal. It had been a puzzle to solve, and little more.

Sylvie had been a puzzle, and so much more.

Zhan-Yo crossed the room before he realized what he'd done, both tachi pointed right for the brother's heart. He stopped with the points pressing against the brother's sweater, creating small indents in the black cloth.

"Question my feelings for Sylvie again," Zhan-Yo said. "It will be the last thing you say."

The brother walked his eyes from the sword points up to Zhan-Yo's face, "If you're telling the truth, then why are you here?"

"I never saw this place while she breathed," Zhan-Yo said, not moving the swords. "I wanted to know how she lived, and I need to know her secrets."

The tension broke there. The brother stepped back from the tachi, nodding at Zhan-Yo's reasons and echoing them himself. He too had come here to try and find what his sister had done, how she might have died. There weren't any answers here that he could find, save possibly in a small digital storage unit in the closet that the brother hadn't been able to unlock, and no longer cared to. Sylvie had decided to keep her life a mystery even after she'd died, and her brother could accept that.

"So what are you going to do now?" Zhan-Yo said as the brother made his way to the apartment's exit.

"You run your family's business," the brother replied. "Sylvie ran ours. Now it's on my shoulders."

"Then, good luck," Zhan-Yo said, giving the brother a slight bow.

"My sister liked you, wanted your work to succeed,"

the brother said, pulling on his shoes. "After I get the pieces picked up, I'll be in touch."

As the door shut behind the brother, Zhan-Yo realized the man had never said his name. A life in the shadows, just like Sylvie.

Hero's Daughter

Hot chocolate. The warm, luscious scent traveled through Mynx's slow consciousness, thawing out her mind with happier memories until she came back to the present, one where she should have been frozen on Bastion's roof. A stiff prize that wouldn't be found till the spring thaw brought hungry birds, as Mynx didn't think anyone else used the tower's top-tier entrance.

Instead, pushing through sun-burn-like irritation, Mynx opened her eyes to a room she knew very well. Aegis's control center, living room, kitchen, all of it combined into a huge half-circle chamber with floor-to-ceiling windows on one side, looking over Manhattan's southern half like a god surveying her works. Going by the room's soft light—no direct sun here—the time had slipped into afternoon already. Mynx hadn't come to New York to spend the day lying on the floor—though her back felt all right, suggesting someone had stuck a blanket beneath her —but coming back from certain death had a way of putting a day's tasks in perspective.

Mynx turned her head and followed the hot chocolate's

steam to the hefty blue mug beside her, emblazoned with the Paragon's slanted P logo. Though her muscles protested at the motion, giving clear evidence that this thaw would take a few days to heal, Mynx managed to roll to her side and reach for the cup.

"It's hot," said the only possible voice from somewhere behind Mynx.

"I could use something hot right now." But Mynx didn't drink quite yet, instead holding the fluffy brown mix up to her nose and inhaling, sucking away some warmth and reveling in the flavor. Pacifica rarely chilled enough to warrant hot chocolate, but here? In the Northeast? She could indulge. "Thank you."

"For the hot chocolate?"

"For saving my frozen self. I assume it was you?"

Celice, Aegis's daughter and a Paragon, despite lacking anomaly abilities, didn't stride into view and Mynx had to complete the rollover onto her chest to see Celice standing at the kitchen's modern-metal counter. In the week after her father's apparent death—Mynx kept Aegis's frozen status secret, both because she didn't know how, or if, she'd be able to bring Aegis back, and because Zhan-Yo might try to finish the job—Mynx hadn't heard anything from Celice. Mynx had imagined that meant Celice had been doing some soul-searching, possibly some vengeance-seeking, but imagining and witnessing were two different things.

Practicality had been Celice's defining dress code for as long as Mynx could remember. As a young girl, Celice had defied dresses for pockets, an attitude that had grown into a full-on obsession with keeping multiple Tamas handy and making her the Paragon's premier coordinator in the western hemisphere. What Mynx saw now wasn't a turn against that ethos, but Celice redirecting its intent. The pockets still existed on the blue-black getup Celice wore, but they were long and narrow, cinched around her thighs and along her waist. A setup for the field, rather than the office.

"You didn't tell me you were coming," Celice said, twirling a spoon through what Mynx assumed was her own hot chocolate mug.

"I didn't think you'd want to see me."

"I don't."

"But you pulled me inside anyway."

"What was I supposed to do? Leave you out there to die?" Celice dropped her hands away from the mug, gripped the counter's edge and stared at it as if lasers were going to shoot from her eyes. "I couldn't lift you all the way to the bedrooms."

"I'm alive, Celice. It's fine." Mynx tried to stand, but her legs, still in shock, didn't want to cooperate. While it felt a little absurd, she'd have to carry on the conversation from the ground. "I came here for you, because you haven't been answering my calls."

"I've been busy."

"Apparently."

Mynx dangled the word, inviting Celice to take the bait.

As Mynx cooled off from the thrill at still being alive, relief at seeing Celice alive suffused her. Nightmares had plagued her over the week, hinting that Celice had gone on a suicidal quest to kill someone too dangerous for a normal with little field training, no matter how much sparring Aegis might have done with his daughter in this tower. The former Champion had made it clear Celice wasn't being groomed for wet work, that her destiny lay outside the violence the Paragons had used to carve up the world.

"You know who killed him," Celice said. "But you don't have Zhan-Yo, do you?"

"We're looking."

"How is it taking you this long? You have all those drones. His picture is on every screen on the planet. Every time he takes a breath, you should know." The words suggested Celice should be erupting in a rage, but instead they came out limp, flattened.

"He's smart, but he can't hide forever."

"He doesn't have to," Celice said. "Zhan-Yo's trying to turn everyone against us. The normals. If he can keep sending these messages, he might turn more people before too long."

"You're assuming too much," Mynx replied. She took a sip from the chocolate, cool enough now to enjoy, and its liquid sugar was, indeed, amazing. "Normals and anomalies are doing too well to risk anything. The world is a good place, Celice. He might find a few, but hardly a revolution."

"I think you're wrong," Celice replied. "I think he can do more damage than you believe."

"You sound like you have a plan."

"Zhan-Yo has friends. He had a whole company. They'll know where he is." Celice stood away from the counter. "I'm sorry I sealed the door up top, Mynx. I didn't want you getting in unannounced, because I didn't want you to stop me."

"Guess you succeeded."

Celice accepted that, then came over and stood over Mynx, and in Celice's eyes, Mynx could see the condemning thoughts: old, crippled, useless. A swallowed sigh confirmed the diagnosis.

"I'm leaving, and you won't find me here again," Celice said. "This was father's place, not mine. If you catch

Zhan-Yo before me, maybe I'll come back. If I catch him before you . . ."

"Do what you have to do. I'm not going to stop you. But if you get into trouble, you know how to reach me."

Celice grew a small smile at that, reached down with her left hand and squeezed Mynx's shoulder. "Get better."

Before Mynx finished another slug of the hot chocolate, Aegis's daughter disappeared down the elevator.

Mynx sat up, started massaging her legs. To say that the visit to New York had been unsuccessful would be giving it too much praise. She'd nearly died, and now the visit's sole objective, to bring Celice back into the fold, had vanished without a whimper. Mynx hadn't even protested as Celice slipped away.

And she knew why. Because, in her position, Mynx would've wanted to be left alone. When her own parents had died, not through any cataclysmic means but through life's ordinary pace, Mynx hadn't sought out comfort in the arms of others. She'd started on the journey that had led her to Denise Jones and the potential for life everlasting.

Of course, that had been a miserable failure, but maybe Celice would find what she was looking for. At least she seemed stable. Coherent.

"Reeves," Mynx said, continuing to rub feeling back into her body. "Celice is on her way out of the building. Tap and tag her, please."

"Of course," Reeves replied. "I already have several drones in the area. Must say, it's good to hear your voice."

"You knew I was alive."

"A human's vital signs tell only a small part of the story. I didn't know how much of you would be left in the thaw."

Mynx twinged at that. "How long was I up there, Reeves?"

"More than an hour. Bastion's own defenses blocked a

drone rescue, and by the time I convinced them it was really you up there . . . "

Not even the remaining hot chocolate melted that fear away. Mynx wasn't one for dying. She could play the hero, but there was a reason she preferred the drones, liked to mesh herself in thick, resilient metal before entering combat. Underneath all her talents was a simple, frail human body that could be broken like any other.

"Next time, break me out any way you need to," Mynx said. "I'm authorizing it. No more chances."

"You'll remember that?"

"No, but you'll remind me, and then I'll be grateful."

Reeves didn't sound so sure of that, but the AI accepted the revised parameters. Mynx continued chatting while she warmed up, stood up, and limped her way to the bathroom. A hot shower restored her missing humanity, and after ordering a meal up from the Paragon cafeteria thirty floors below, Mynx felt rather good.

Until her Tama buzzed with an incoming call.

Eight Champions worked together to found the Paragons, and after the world's nations refused to accept the obvious benefit to letting the most powerful anomalies keep things safe and secure, those eight Champions created a movement that flattened any foolish force that tried to stand in their way.

Mynx would have preferred to end the story there, but life kept going even after the final countries signed away their independence. The sun rose again on the next day, and soon enough Lukas declared that he would be returning home, and that his home would belong to him. Of the thousand small splinters breaking the Champions apart, Lukas had decided to become the wedge, and had relentlessly poured acid on their differences until Aegis had split the world to mend them.

Now the man's face appeared on her Tama, looking puffy despite Lukas's height. Colored splotches marred part of his skin, and his hair had thinned to a wispy set, but those damn eyes still looked the same. A colored barcode, that's what Aegis had called them and what Mynx had seen ever since.

Still, he was a Champion, and Mynx needed him to show.

"Lukas. Thanks for calling." Mynx tried to stand straighter, adjusted the Tama's angle to show Bastion's window rather than the dull kitchen. "I take it you received my message?"

"Of course, of course I did!" Lukas said, and he blinked. When he did, the color lines across his iris shifted, slotting red into the center. "What a fine idea, to have a summit. It has been so long, and I imagine all of you have changed so very much."

"Some of us more than others," Mynx replied. Lukas blinked again, and the colors moved. Mynx tried to remember what each one meant, then gave up. She had nothing to hide from Lukas. "Things are moving. We're getting older, and we need a plan."

"And such plans can only be made in Los Angeles? Not in London, or Amsterdam?"

"I called the summit, I choose."

Lukas looked like he might contest the point for a hot minute, and Mynx countered with a deep, stern breath. The two of them had gone at it plenty during their Champion days, and both had their strategies. The difference here, it seemed, was a small beep on Lukas's end. He looked, still at the camera but obviously away from Mynx's face, and grimaced.

"Another day, another time," Lukas said when he looked back up. "In the spirit of our companionship, my dear friend, I will make the trip. Send along the dates and the details, and I will be there."

"I appreciate that."

"And Mynx, you may want to visit your physician," Lukas said, putting his hand to his large box of a chin. "Looks like you may have some worries going on inside that big brain of yours. I'd hate to see a Champion felled by a stroke."

"Goodbye, Lukas." Mynx swiped away the call, collapsed on one of Aegis's hard metal chairs.

The media had called him Spectrum. Lukas liked it because the word was the same in Dutch and English, and it matched. Those eyes let him see what any light frequency could show him, and plenty beyond that. Mynx wasn't sure how it worked, but every time Lukas performed one of his ad hoc readings, she felt violated.

The Champions had too many mind readers, emotional manipulators. Apinya, Lukas, and Burov turned normals against themselves. By the time their victims realized they'd been twisted against their wills, Mynx and Aegis had already claimed vital infrastructure, decimated any confused resistance.

Except, when the fighting stopped, those same mind-bending powers angled at Mynx, at Aegis. The only way to keep any secrets, to be sure her motivations were truly her own, had been to split the world apart and send the dangerous Champions to their homes.

Now, Mynx was bringing them back.

"See Reeves?" Mynx said, finishing the last of her reheated hot chocolate. "This is what it means to be a Champion."

And why, when the summit had finished, Mynx would give up that mantle.

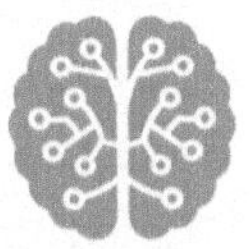

13

Beach Diplomacy

Thane woke to the ever-soothing waves, this time as they rustled up the beach towards the sand patch he'd declared his own. Sook snored nearby, a noise alternating between loud rumbles and high-pitched nasal squeaks, as if playing a haphazard accompaniment to the ocean's song. Behind him, as dawn grew, the village picked itself up. Fires ignited, and several anomalies already stood at the water's edge, with a younger woman swinging her hands back and forth in wide circles, each one pulling a flapping fish from the water and into her comrade's dashing, catching hands. Others looted water from giant rain barrels dotting the village, filling thin rock pails made, Thane discovered, by that same guard who stretched the wood spears the night before: molding stone, apparently, listed among her talents.

In all the world Thane knew, there wasn't a single society functioning on anomaly power. By the time anomalies had appeared, humanity had developed ways to meet all its needs without 'magical' means, though the Paragons seemed intent on fitting anomalies in where they could increase efficiency. Here, though, anomalies required their abilities to survive. An interesting dynamic, and Thane, after last night's long gathering where he met the twenty-odd people living here, saw both the benefits and costs.

Using one's ability to survive brought you closer to it. The girl drawing fish with her hands—Thane wondered at the crime that had dashed her here—showed more control, more ease with her power than most anomalies he knew. Like another limb, she leveraged every phantom pull as if she did it with her literal fingers.

In last night's casual conversation, Thane had heard the anomalies boast, time and time again, about how their abilities let them roast dinner with ease, or sculpt ferns into useful clothing, or add flavor to otherwise bland rainwater. All useful, all dull. While everyone here had done something terrible, they seemed to have forgotten that potential and instead settled into a primitive existence.

Thane would shatter that calm. He had to, or they'd never leave this prisoner's paradise.

After shaking the sand out of his new palm dress, a loose-fitting frond shirt and what amounted to a grass-weave skirt, Thane stomped past the sleeping Sook and headed up towards the town's main structure, a thatched hut serving as the Void's home and the only private meeting place in the camp. As he crested the dunes, Thane counted three cooking fires burning, closer to the ocean than to the main gates, each tasked with a different meal. As the sun hadn't hit full illumination yet, those dancing fire globes proliferated again, bouncing their flickering brilliance over anomalies carving up vegetables and bird's eggs to add to the fresh catch.

The Void's hut sat in the camp's center, and to its left, most people slept under a large overhang protected by layered palm fronds. To the right, smaller huts provided private spaces. One anomaly, last night, had explained the need to cater to anyone sick, or those who required privacy to complete their work or to sort out themselves. A benevolent move, until Thane remembered that all of these people had done something heinous in the past. Providing space to decompress might be less a kindness than a survival mechanism.

Woven boxes sat all around the camp, storing dried goods. Enough makeshift spears to arm a phalanx lined the dunes inside the main entrance, while three bow-and-arrow sets sat on a rack near the village's center. It would be easy to question this stone age weaponry on an island with so much power, but a well-placed shot would do the same to an anomaly as it would to a normal. Not many could take mortal wounds like Thane and Aegis.

The Void sat inside her hut, sipping something steaming from an earthen mug. The rock dress from the night before lay to the side, and she wore a woven getup similar to Thane's own. She didn't look up as Thane entered, though the light assent she'd given after Thane asked to come in proved she knew he was there. Instead, the Void kept her focus on a meter-wide sandbox in the hut's center. Thane came closer and looked down on what appeared to be the island, immaculately carved into the dirt. The instruments, sticks stretched into fine brush tips, lay set on the right.

Little circles and lines denoted sections, and Thane figured they marked the territories and positions of the other islanders. From this view, it seemed like the Duchess had taken the island's majority, a hold around the central peak, with her lines almost reaching the coast between the Void's village and Arthur's encampment on the island's far side.

"Eyre draws this every morning," the Void said, a softer voice in private. "She throws her gaze as far as she can see and looks down on our home. Ridiculous luck that she wound up with me."

"What is her story?" Thane asked, sitting across the sandbox from the Void.

"Does it matter?" the Void replied. "She's here, same as you. I think she spied on the wrong people, and rather than kill her outright, Mynx dropped her on this island."

"Maybe the Paragons think they can use her."

The Void looked up from the map, crinkled her mouth at Thane. "The Paragons? I'm using her now, and she's using me, albeit for different things."

"Of course," Thane said. He needed to feel his way around this power dynamic. For all his life, Thane had either been the strongest leader in the room, or a prisoner forced to do the Paragon's bidding. "You want to know where your enemies are."

The Void shook her head. "Not enemies. Rivals. Arthur and the Duchess aren't dumb to fight each other for this rock, and I'm not dumb enough to fight them either. We have a balance, and that works for everyone."

"But you post guards every day and night?"

"Because I'm not stupid. Because the balance only works when we believe the costs are too high to act."

"Ah. Deterrence."

"We're waiting for a chance." The Void pointed at the Duchess's line creeping towards the sea. "Once she gets ocean access, then she won't have any reason to trade with us anymore."

"Then why don't you stop her?"

"Because she has double my anomalies, at least. She gets the most Mynx drops. And she's good at persuading them to stick around."

"You're saying there's a reason she's called the Duchess?"

"I'm saying that we're outnumbered," the Void replied, and while Thane wouldn't call himself a mind-reader, she seemed annoyed. "Nobody's loyal enough here to die fighting a pointless war.'"

"You need a leader."

"I *am* a leader."

Thane hesitated. Another knife's edge that could tumble him off into oblivion. If what Sook said was true, then the Void might actually be able to kill him. Even if she couldn't, Thane didn't want to fight off all of her anomaly supporters either. But he hadn't come to this place to wallow days away catching fish on the beach and counting coconuts with fellow criminals.

"What's your name?" Thane asked. "Your real one."

The Void stood up, brushed the sand from her knees. "Come with me."

Not an answer, but at least she didn't seem so defensive.

Thane followed the Void outside the hut, and she led him past the fires, where they each grabbed a leaf-wrapped fish portion along with some roasted roots. The Void greeted everyone they passed with their first names, though rarely with a smile. A commander reviewing their troops, checking morale.

Sook made the island seem like a chaotic battle between anomalies, where the strongest held sway, but the Void's little village felt more like a controlled operation. Everyone knew their part, and played it, just to live one more day.

The Void led him down to the beach and away from the village, walking along a crystalline shore in the morning sun. Shells littered the sand, and a look to the sea showed dark forms scurrying around beneath the surface. Crabs raced away as they walked, and, above, the day's early birds took their first flights, chirping all the while. As idyllic scenes went, and Thane didn't consider himself a romantic, this took a top spot.

"You're the oldest anomaly on the island," the Void said once they'd cleared the sole sentry watching the beach approach, a woman with a curt nod for her leader. "So you might see this differently, but the rest of us came here facing a long life imprisoned."

Thane laughed, "I spent decades in a cell."

"Then look at all this and ask whether you would risk it to go back? What do you think Mynx and the Paragons would do if we escaped? Let us go? Give us a prize?"

Looking at her, Thane guessed the Void to be somewhere north of forty. She'd had a lot of sun on the island, but the grays hadn't made an incursion on her hair, the wrinkles hadn't marked wisdom's valleys on her cheeks, but neither did she move or speak with Sook's more youthful fire. She knew what it was to play, and lose.

"This island is a prison," Thane replied. "By staying, you let them win. They rule without consequence, without a check. With all the anomalies on this island, we could resist. Force them to change."

"All the anomalies on this island?" Now it was her turn to laugh. "A hundred of us, maybe, against the millions of Paragons? Thane, I don't know how strong you are, but we would not survive that fight."

"We wouldn't be alone. The Paragons aren't beloved everywhere. We would find allies."

They reached a narrow sandbar that extended out into the ocean like a spear and the Void chose to walk along it, the cool water kissing their feet. Behind them, a giant palm grove stretched, wearing ferns across its base. Behind that, the island's central peak rose high and gray into the cloudless sky.

"Have you forgotten why we're here?" the Void said,

leading their walk. "Every one of us turned on their friends, families, society. What makes you think we could stick together at all? We're not soldiers."

"Everyone wants their lives to mean something," Thane said. "Right now, every one of us on this island is nothing to the world. You grow old and die here, that's all you'll remain. Nothing."

The Void stopped at the end of the sandbar. Out beyond, dotting the horizon at regular intervals, were the drones. Malevolent black spots. The Void reached out with her left hand, and Thane felt sudden heat. Almost searing, radiating from her. And out in that ocean, incoming waves burst apart, holes appearing between their roiling crests, causing them to fall into one another. They smashed together again and again until a foamy chaos surrounded their little sandy walk.

The Void practically glowed with the heat, and Thane took a step away, until she stopped and the breeze stole the warmth from her.

"I come out here because the waves don't care what I do to them," the Void said. "And nobody can see how angry I am."

"We're all angry. We've been wronged."

"This is a lot to lose."

"This is nothing to what you've already lost."

The two of them kept looking straight ahead, out at those drones. That implacable wall.

"You want to change our fates, you'll have to convince the Duchess," the Void said. "She has the most of us. Get her to follow your dream and maybe I won't think you're that crazy."

"But you won't? Now?"

The Void shook her head. "Before all this, I was a teacher. If you can believe it. A teacher that had a few bad breaks, took it out on the wrong people. Paragons found out I never admitted to being an anomaly, threw me this way. But you don't get to be a teacher without understanding what it means to care for the little ones, and all those back there are mine."

"They're not little. They need you to lead, not baby them."

"Maybe." The Void brushed a stray hair from her eyes. "Thane, prove that you can back up your talk. Then, if you're still you, I'll agree to what you're asking. Get the Duchess on your side."

Another anomaly to persuade. If it kept moving things forward, fine. Thane said as much, and they turned to walk back to the village.

"And Thane?" the Void said as they returned to the beach proper. "My name's Cassidy."

14

The Hunter and the Hunted

For once, the enemy had a hideout in the city. Kat loved Chicago's outer wilds, where industrial wastelands separated the bars so crucial to their employee's existence, but every now and then going into the city's techno-embrace made for a nice change. Leaving the L station, with the mag-lev train's whooshing whistle behind them, Calvin and Kat marched through urban miasma as the afternoon grew into full swing. Most people saw Kat's suit and gave her and Calvin a wide berth, squeezing over towards buildings or slipping inside cafes or stores and watching till the tracker passed. Above, a drone interrupted the sky, its soundless black bulk drifting along. Restaurants gearing up for dinner filled the air with tantalizing tastes that Kat ignored—who knew if any would even seat her, armed as she was?

Delano's intel put the Elemental's current base not far down this street, across from a square-block park. Snow and ice rendered the park's playground equipment into abstract art, while people hugged the benches, bent over their Tamas and snacking on sandwiches. Pods crunched along the road, and while Kat watched what she could, her mask saw the rest.

No potential threats appeared while they closed on the cafe. That seemed a little odd—the Elementals had to know they hadn't killed Calvin, and that attacking a Paragon would come with retribution—but maybe they were all out to lunch?

"Your parents were anomalies?" Calvin asked as they walked.

The man had been silent almost the entire way from Delano's to here, and now he chose to start in on that conversation?

"Yep."

Kat would murder this topic a thousand times.

"But you're not?"

"Nope."

"Strange."

"Yep."

Her Tama beeped and Kat looked at it. The Elemental's cafe should be close now, just ahead. As if reality conformed to the Tama's data and not the other way around, when Kat looked back up, she noticed a soft blue overhang with coffee cups stenciled in white all over it. Tiny icicles hung off the overhang's edges, making the awning look like a comb.

"That's the target," Kat said, choosing to nod instead of point, keep their already-conspicuous appearance from going completely wrong. "You should hang back."

"Kat, look, I'm not helpless."

"Really? You're not armed, and that coat's not going to protect you. I don't want to watch your back."

Calvin sputtered something about watching hers. Kat put a finger to his chest, a firm one.

"Listen, I know these people. Or some of them,

anyway," Kat said. "I can talk to them, and we can figure out why they tried to kill you. Like I said, assassination isn't really their thing, so they have to have another reason. Unless you can think of one? Right now?"

"No idea. I'd have told you. The shot came out of nowhere."

"Then stay behind. I'll signal when you can come in." Kat stepped back from the anomaly. "If you want to help, keep out of sight. Watch for anything weird."

Calvin didn't argue. So much more refreshing than Gordon, who seemed to like butting heads with her on everything. Kat hadn't ever wanted a sidekick, or a partner, but if she had, Calvin and his total obedience might be the only type she'd accept.

The cafe didn't expand much beyond the awning, its long and narrow profile going back from the street. Tinted windows gave a dim view inside, though tan tables pressed up to the glass made it clear the space did, at some point, serve something. Not now, though. A red-lit Tama panel near the door declared the place closed, despite an hours display showing the cafe should very much be open.

Seemed suspicious.

Kat kept moving, following her own advice about the cameras and turning down the next trash alley, another building away. She tapped out a quick message to Calvin from her Tama, and circled around to the block's dividing line. A narrow space with high buildings on either side, with metal fire escapes climbing up and down and dumpsters occupying every square inch along the walls, the alley hardly looked inviting. Kat, though, wasn't expecting a welcome.

The Elementals were an anomaly collective that'd made their name on various demands for freedom, rights, and other things that amounted to rebuking the Paragon's system without offering anything better. As if the normals, and the Paragons, were supposed to accept a rogue anomaly band could freely run around without any monitoring, any control. As Aegis had proclaimed in countless addresses, the last thing the world needed was another war, much less one between multiple super-powered forces. As such, with the Paragons swooping in to cut their numbers down any time the Elementals made any serious moves, Kat wasn't surprised to find the alley, and the cafe, empty.

Strike out, then huddle up and hide.

Yet Kat kept her left hand on her stun-gun's hilt anyway, the weapon resting in its thigh holster. Anomalies could be anywhere, could be invisible or, like Vedder not all that long ago, could project a visual image that made things look far safer than they actually were. Nothing, though, sent fiery bolts from the sky or melted the concrete beneath her feet. Kat's insides didn't combust, her mind didn't fall into madness. Despite the interrogation, Kat wondered whether Delano had told them the truth.

The cafe's back door, labeled with a thick sticker on the beige-painted surface, had its own Tama plate with the same closed message. Locked too. Which meant, if Kat was going to go inside, she'd have to break in. That would be violating Paragon law, tracker or no. Before she'd cross that line, Kat figured they could do some observation. Find a bench in the park, get some lunch and see if the cafe found its way to opening up. Or the Elementals might see Calvin and decide to make a move, bringing their people into the open.

Kat tapped away the idea on her Tama, turned back towards the alley's exit, and her mask screamed red.

She dove forward as a concrete divot exploded behind her, the crack coming later and rattling along the alleyway. Kat rolled right when she hit the ground, putting a dumpster between her and the alley entrance, the direction where the shot had come from. She pressed her body up against the rusted green metal, read the translucent blue feedback pouring across her mask.

Her vitals, the suit, all of that was fine. She hadn't been hit, but the sound and the divot where the bullet struck suggested an illegal rifle. The mask didn't point out that almost all rifles and guns that shot lethal bullets were illegal now.

A real gun. Kat had dealt with flame-launching anomalies, ones that could shapeshift or, like Calvin, turn anything into a deadly tool, but she'd never been shot at by real bullets. The suit wasn't designed to be bullet-proof, because anyone using those weapons put such a huge target on their own backs as to be, well, stupid. Or too powerful to care. Already her mask told her the drone they'd seen drifting overhead was turning around at the noise.

The mask beeped again, the suit's visual sensors picking up someone lining a shot. The mask's right side lit up, telling Kat where the shot would be coming from. She jumped again, but this time no shot came, only the constant beeping as the mask screamed she was in someone's sights. Kat needed cover, needed to get inside somewhere. Fear balled up in her throat as Kat scampered back into the alley's center, then lunged behind another dumpster on the opposite side, cutting off the mask's panic for a second.

Kat hated being hunted. Hunched behind a trash pile, heart beating a thousand beats a minute, hands shaking and breath whooshing in and out, Kat had to calm herself down, had to stop thinking like prey.

Be the predator instead.

"Hey! Kat, you all right?" Calvin called, his voice coming from the alley's entrance.

Damn. Guess she couldn't play coward today.

"Calvin!" Kat cried, lunging around the corner. "The shooter's on the roof!"

Her mask didn't light up, and even as Kat ran towards Calvin, gesturing with her arms for him to run, she looked up, to the only possible place a shooter could be and still track her between the dumpsters. She spied him, and the mask outlined the crouching figure in light green. Hard to hide on top of sparse rooftops when you're hauling a long gun like his around; the weapon's thin barrel extended over the roof's edge, angling towards Calvin.

The anomaly did not obey Kat's instructions, but he stood close to the alley's entrance, hand on the nearest building's corner. As Kat came around, she saw the air in front of Calvin shimmer, harden and turn into the thick red clay making up most of those bricks Calvin touched. The clay shield moved up with Calvin's hand as it grew, and when the shot rang out, the bullet puffed into the barrier. Calvin didn't flinch, so his makeshift defense must have worked.

Kat didn't want to give the shooter any more time. With the sniper's attention on Calvin, she aimed her wrist towards the sniper's rooftop and fired her grapple. The hook spun up and over, and as Kat sprinted towards the wall, she twitched her wrist to retract the grapple, letting it bite into the stone roof's edge. The sound caused the sniper to turn as Kat hit the wall with a running jump, the grapple's retraction pulling her up at the same time.

Wall running. Of all the things a younger Kat would've called super-heroic that Kat did on an almost-daily basis, this still gave her the thrill that came with defying the normal order. Physics be damned, Kat ran straight up the building's side, led by her left arm.

The sniper, still visible, made a lunge towards her grapple, but when a single tug couldn't dislodge it, the man—with his black tactical gear and the way he moved, Kat pegged the killer as a male—grabbed his rifle and ran.

Kat cleared the roof's lip a few seconds later, puffing hard after sprinting up four stories, but ready to go. The sniper had retreated another building over, and looked to be making for a maintenance entrance. Black drones were coming close, zooming in from several directions, and the sniper wouldn't have a chance getting away from them if he didn't bust it now.

Kat wasn't going to let that happen.

She broke towards the sniper, even as the grapple snapped back into her wrist. Kat drew a stun gun with her right, aimed, and fired a running shot as the sniper yanked open the maintenance door, curling himself behind it. The dart bounced off the makeshift shield, but the move put the sniper on the wrong side of his chosen stairs. The mask beeped, a yellow line appearing at the bottom of her vision, and Kat caught the warning in time to plant her foot on the edge and press, leaping over the narrow gap and onto the next tiled roof.

The sniper pushed the door away, and Kat's mask screamed again. In the second he'd been hiding from her vision, the sniper had dropped his rifle and drawn a smaller handgun. Kat tried to dodge, leaping forward—always forward, because shooters didn't expect it. She pulled out of the somersault, aimed her stun gun at the masked man, and he fired.

It felt like being punched, a breath-killing blow to her chest that knocked Kat to the ground. She tried to pull the trigger on her own weapon, but her nerves were otherwise occupied, focusing on the sudden pain, shock, and blood streaming from places that weren't meant to lose it. Her head fell back, hitting the cold rooftop. The mask screamed at her, those perfect vitals marred and quickly getting worse.

But the sniper. Kat couldn't lose him. Not now, not yet.

She tried to sit up, tried to get her eyes on the target, but all she saw was the flash as the door slammed behind him, leaving her up here, alone, cold, and dying.

Of all the ways to go. Trackers died all the time, but not like this. Not shot in the streets at random, not left to bleed. This wasn't how it was supposed to work. Even as the cold spread from her chest, Kat tried to focus, tried to think of what she could do, who she could call. If these were her last moments, then she should call someone. Just not to be alone.

"Call him," Kat said to her suit, her mouth at once cold and hot at the same time. "Call Gordon."

Her Tama connected, rang, as the clouded sky darkened with hovering drones.

She didn't hear if he picked up.

15

Crack the Inbox

Zhan-Yo had been looking at the computer for hours now. The storage device, a disconnected, hardy machine built to last decades with minimal power and maximum instability, sat in Sylvie's closet, tucked into the corner and hidden by hanging ivy tendrils. Without her brother's hint, Zhan-Yo might not have found it at all, as the device wasn't much larger than his own Tama, made no noise, had no lights.

The screen, gray and dull, without a backlight, presented Zhan-Yo with a blinking cursor and nothing else. A tiny keyboard on the device's bottom edge offered the chance for inputs, and Zhan-Yo stared at it for a long time without touching a button. Who knew how many attempts he might get before the thing locked him out? Every try would have to be precise, planned.

At first the infinite possibilities were despairing—Sylvie knew a strong password's value, and she wouldn't play games. She would have set letters and symbols in a random series with no connection to anything, a couple dozen characters meant to befuddle any attempt at getting in. If that was the case, short of taking it to the Paragons, who might have an anomaly able to crack the thing, Sylvie's secrets would stay just that forever. And Zhan-Yo, obviously, wasn't taking this thing anywhere near the Paragons.

He sat in that plant-ridden apartment, taking breaks from wracking his brain by browsing the day's dead news on his Tama: the most interesting story, a live rooftop shooting not all that far from here, had concluded quickly and without an obvious body count. The drones had missed their man too, just like with Zhan-Yo and Rhimes. Perhaps the machines were getting old.

The cerebral stewing started his mind running down different paths, lighting on the tantalizing idea that Sylvie had to have known death could come at any moment. Zhan-Yo, looking at his own life, could see how much it had changed in the short time since he'd joined the shadowed side: When every action presented a mortal risk, you assessed those actions differently.

So how would Sylvie have acted?

She would have prepared. Like Zhan-Yo, she'd committed to a post-Paragon future. Everything they'd done together had been moving towards that, and Sylvie had kept pushing even as the risks became greater. Aegis had been her plan. What would she assume Zhan-Yo would do if she died, and he lived?

"Anything else gets me nowhere," Zhan-Yo said to himself, then took a long look around the room, as if Sylvie's ghost might appear to confirm the fact.

If Zhan-Yo didn't believe that Sylvie assumed he would come looking for what he knew, then he was back at square one. Infinite possibilities. But if he chose to believe that Sylvie would want him to find this, would expect him to try and crack its secrets open, then Zhan-Yo had a chance. The plan limited the potential passcodes to what Zhan-Yo might guess. But, also, what Zhan-Yo *alone* might guess.

Common terms weren't plausible, neither were easily guessable words they had shared, like 'Ziran' and 'Revolution'. Both could be found by anyone with cursory knowledge. Zhan-Yo kept looking at the device, not really seeing its grayscale display, but instead a thousand threads branching out behind it, each one leading to a possible choice. Time to start cutting those down. First, the password would be personal. Something between only the two of them.

Some of the threads disappeared, plenty more remained.

Sylvie played a hard game, constantly pushing Zhan-Yo and everyone around her to greater things. She wasn't sentimental. She let ambition swallow softer feelings. Little things, like the meals they'd shared or the name of their favorite restaurant wouldn't fit her style.

More threads floated away.

They contacted each other through encrypted messages. A notification would show up in his Tama, inviting him to click out to an anonymous portal and enter a one-time code to view what she'd sent along, then reply in the same manner. Every message deleted shortly after it had been read. Would Sylvie have gone in that direction? A passcode relating to their passcode-driven life? Zhan-Yo wondered, his hands drifted over the keyboard, ready to type the name of the mutual service they'd employed for so many years.

No. The service itself was well-enough known. Not emotional, but not personal enough either.

He cut those threads.

Few remained, and of those few, only one seemed strong enough for this. They preferred to meet along Lake Michigan, at night, and along a particularly deserted stretch between Soldier Field and Navy Pier, where, except for nighttime joggers, they didn't have to share space with anyone. Pods navigated by address, and this particular spot didn't have one.

The first time they'd really met, it'd been on that stretch, on Sylvie's suggestion they both start from opposite ends and meet in the middle as a way of keeping things random. From there, when they were done, they would call a pod to their particular spot, generating a specific location code. Clever on the part of the pods—the code would let you return precisely to where you were picked up, in case of a lost item or memory, with your own personal identifier tied to it so you could share the spot with anyone else.

To Zhan-Yo's knowledge, Sylvie's code for that spot on Lake Shore Drive had only been sent to him. At that spot, they'd made their plans, they'd shared their dreams, and they'd done the work to pull those dreams closer to reality. The perfect password, the only password.

He pulled up the code on his Tama, then entered the twelve digits. The grayscale screen blinked once, then presented him with options. He was in.

In that plant-filled, dark apartment, Zhan-Yo allowed himself a small smile.

Now what?

First, Zhan-Yo read. While browsing the device felt like reading through a massive tome with no table of contents, Zhan-Yo fumbled his way through documents detailing Sylvie's thoughts on everything from himself to Ziran to the world at large. At first, the possibilities felt fascinating: a window into Sylvie's private musings on him? On his cause? But rather than heartfelt missives, Sylvie proved to be a straightforward analyst. Zhan-Yo's own file, beyond a rudimentary physical description— capable but hesitant? Zhan-Yo took issue with that—had little more than several lines declaring him a strong leader but too idealistic to be counted on to make the hardest decisions.

More valuable were the rosters and contact methods for the copious mercenary clusters still hiding out in the Paragon's underbelly. All those soldiers had to go somewhere when the army disbanded, and if, on the surface, they took up peaceful professions, plenty exercised their skills in deep cover work the Paragons largely ignored unless the body count grew too high. With these lists, and enough reps, Zhan-Yo could have himself a dangerous army in little time, though it would be scattered across the world. Still, if he could tip public sentiment, these names would give him the kindling to turn a spark into a full-blown fire.

And yet, sitting amongst those plants, disappointment loomed. Zhan-Yo thought he'd come for exactly what he'd found, the tangible items that would push his cause forward. Instead of happiness, a gnawing sadness settled into the gloom as night fell across the city. Sylvie either didn't use or didn't have automatic lights, and Zhan-Yo didn't feel like leaving the couch. So, with his Tama shining, he kept reading through one file after another, hoping something would fill the void.

Zhan-Yo wasn't dumb. He knew, now, that what he'd wanted was something deeper. Some note or video—even though this device didn't seem to show images—just for him, telling him goodbye, revealing what Sylvie had secretly felt but never said. His heart talking when his head knew better.

Sylvie had planned for the worst, but she'd done it the same way she'd done everything else: with an eye towards results, not emotions.

And perhaps that was the best way to look at it. Sylvie trusted Zhan-Yo to take the reins, to carry on without her and bring their dream to fruition. She didn't get distracted by romantic foolishness, and neither should he. Revolutions like their's required hard hearts, determined wills. Sylvie hadn't put a note in here because she didn't need to. Zhan-Yo already knew what she would say.

Get going. The world's waiting for you.

Zhan-Yo stood, cramming the device, awkwardly, into one of his larger coat pockets. It sank to the bottom, making Zhan-Yo's left side bulge out like he'd grown a particularly fantastic tumor, but carrying the old-style computer in his arms would've been even more conspicuous. He took one last look at the various plants, started to tell himself that he'd get Wexley to buy the place, send someone over to care for them. Zhan-Yo would check in every now and then, make sure things looked like they were now.

No. That was sentiment. Sylvie wouldn't approve.

He'd send an anonymous message to the complex's ownership instead, let them know the owner of this particular apartment had died and let them figure it out. They'd probably turn the place over, and in a month there'd be no trace Sylvie had ever lived here.

Though, apparently, someone seemed to think she still did.

As Zhan-Yo approached the door to leave, he noticed a simple white envelope had been slipped through the door. He picked it up, flipped it over, and saw nothing written on the back. There was some chance it'd fallen out of her brother's pocket, but that man didn't seem like the type to lose something like this. And since Sylvie wouldn't be opening her own mail any more . . .

The message wasn't long. Barely two paragraphs, typed out and spaced wide, like a schoolboy's first paper. Its message, though, concerned things decidedly heavier than a book report.

Multiple sources confirmed: the Champions are setting up a summit. Most likely location is Los Angeles. Mynx said to be the originator. Pulled together fast. Starts in days. Send plan.

Letters and numbers followed in a twenty-character code. Something Sylvie might know how to parse, something Zhan-Yo would have to decipher. The message's point, though, wasn't hard to figure: a summit? Where all or most of the Champions would be in one place? Legends, every one of them, and vulnerable. If Aegis had been a failed start, the world wouldn't be able to deny a clean sweep of its premier heroes. Sylvie wouldn't let this opportunity slip past. Zhan-Yo wouldn't either.

He'd felt lost on the run, hiding from windows, from messages, from responsibilities. His revolution hadn't come to pass, but what had looked like the finale to a decade spent preparing now seemed like the opening act. The Paragons were giving Zhan-Yo a second chance to bring them down. He wouldn't fail.

Sylvie wouldn't let him.

16

Long Island Enemies

Sometimes, you had to turn getting frozen into opportunity. In the hours Mynx had spent recovering during the day, while her body thawed, while a drug cocktail went to work restoring her physical equilibrium, while a full cream assault waged a successful war against Mynx's dried and damaged skin, Pacifica's Champion had gone digging. With Polly, Aegis's AI, helping her, Mynx brought a monitor army up from slots around the viewing window looking across Manhattan and combed through to find any idea that might lead to the why.

Why had Zhan-Yo, with everything going his way, decided to act now?

The Paragons, as a worldwide force, seemed to be as strong as they'd ever been. Mynx's own drones covered the Americas and were expanding into Europe as the other Champions realized Paragons were better sent to handle actual problems than patrol the streets. Opinion polling proved the public loved their Paragons—stability counted, it seemed—and peace, generally, reigned throughout. Zhan-Yo also had a lot to lose, which made such a turn like this make even less sense. Logically, he would only make a move this drastic if he had some support from another powerful corner, one that might be able to nudge Zhan-Yo to becoming a real threat.

While they hadn't yet made a big move, Mynx could only think of one group foolish enough to challenge the Paragons in the open: the Elementals.

The damned terrorists had been around like a disease almost from the beginning, anomalies claiming they didn't want to work in the new order but, instead, defy it in solidarity with some imagined freedom. The Paragons weren't slave-drivers, they were protectors. The Elementals claimed new laws, like conforming to reps, like anomaly registration, like Paragon positions being restricted to those same anomalies, were dictatorial and punitive, but they missed the point: in a world where anyone could be a walking nuclear bomb, it just wasn't viable to leave things wide open. If a city block exploded, or a full stadium turned into ash, you either knew, with the Paragon's anomaly laws, who did it, or you lived in total fear.

Zhan-Yo apparently wanted a return to that fear, with groups of super-powered, but otherwise very human, people fighting in the streets while the normals looked on in useless horror. The Elementals would back that goal, as stupid as it was, and perhaps had guaranteed Zhan-Yo their firepower if he made this play.

Of all the things Apinya had done, and Mynx respected most of them, getting the Paragons to let the Elementals live on as a political group rather than annihilate them as the Paragons would any other terrorist, was the worst. Yes, there would have been damage all over the world if the Paragons had waged anomaly war against the Elementals. It would have been painful, even catastrophic in some places, but the Paragons would have won. They would have stamped out this problem.

Mynx would revisit the question at the coming summit, but if she wanted to turn the Champions against the Elementals, she'd need some evidence first. To that end, Polly helped Mynx rifle through Aegis's records, looking for and finding what she wanted: a strong Elemental enclave, not all that far away on Long Island. Mynx could go, ask some hard questions. Learn if these monsters had truly turned a corner and deserved elimination.

"Polly, activate reserve suit five," Mynx said, standing up from the counter. "And open up the roof. It's time to do something productive."

Going back out to the place that'd almost killed her didn't phase Mynx in the slightest. You had to learn to brush off near-death experiences in this life, or you'd never be able to do anything.

ONCE AGAIN IN her kinetic energy suit, the batteries charged through her steady pacing back and forth along the room, Mynx put in some last minutes cleaning up Aegis's old home. Cleared the counter, ran the combo dish washer-sterilizer, and had Polly return the monitor forest to its resting place. It felt a little like saying goodbye to her friend, doing what Aegis ought. With Celice leaving, who knew how long till someone else would come in here? The Paragon throne left vacant, perhaps rightly so.

Outside those winds continued whipping, and Winter's dipping sun didn't do much to keep her warm. However, by the time Mynx had taken three steps towards her jet, reserve suit five found her. The light Paragon-blue metal oval launched from its storing station in Bastion's roof, one of many secrets Mynx and Aegis had put into the building to handle an armada of just-in-case scenarios.

Using its plutonium battery, the suit had enough power to go for a long time, though any puncture of that battery's thick shielding would mean a swift end to the occupant. Risk, though, was ever-present, and Mynx had at least designed this one. If it failed, it'd be her fault and no one else's.

The oval approached, its tiny jets keeping it afloat, and, as it did, the various latticeworks making up the suit's outer shell split apart and swallowed Mynx like a jungle cat's maw. Mynx stepped forward into the embrace, sliding her hands and feet into cushioned slots while the oval's back reformed around her, tightening a strong brace along her back. Mynx entered her metal cocoon, and as soon as it closed completely, the walls disappeared.

All around her, Mynx could see as if she floated in a bubble. A glance down showed Bastion's rooftop walkway, and above showed the deep purple clouds. Straight ahead sat her jet, and alongside it, floating in translucent blues and blacks, were readouts detailing the suit's systems, the outside temperature, time and more. Mynx hadn't used this one in years, but it felt good to be back. Like plugging in an old gadget and finding it worked as you remembered.

"Reeves, you hearing me all right?" Mynx asked.

"Clear. Must say, it's nicer knowing you're in that thing rather than freezing out there."

"Nicer for both of us, I think." Mynx punched in the coordinates for the Elemental base. As she did so, in front of her, a satellite image floated and helped her narrow down the target. "Aegis thinks there's an Elemental center over here, and I think they're helping Zhan-Yo. I'd like to find out for certain. Let's get a few drones ready for back-up in case things get strange."

"Of course. Are you feeling up to this?"

"I'm less than twenty-four hours removed from near-death. It's just like the old days," Mynx replied as her suit began lifting off, the omni-directional jets coating the suit's exterior giving it a smooth, precise glide.

"I'm not sure you want to go back to the old days."

"Don't have a choice," Mynx said. "They came for me."

AS YEARS PASSED, the techno-makeover took different areas at different speeds. Those places with history tended to burnish and preserve it, keeping iconic facades alongside shimmering new ones. This trend continued apace as Mynx flew over the Burroughs towards the eastern ends, where quainter elements continued to wage their culture wars against New York's modern demands. Fishing boats blinked their night lights in starlit skyscraper shadows. Pods moved in endless lines along highways, while smaller delivery drones clogged prescribed flight paths beneath Mynx, creating a luminescent lattice.

Beautiful, in its way.

Her destination was less so: a watered down shopping center surviving on its corner stores and little else. The Elemental's chosen home made sense in its invisibility, if not in its amenities. A vast parking lot spoke to the area's lethargy—pods made such wastes of space exactly that—but gave Mynx room to touch down near a defunct light post. A few pods did meander around the area, picking up waiting people perusing a nearby liquor store and the twin restaurants sustaining the mall. The freezing air had limited numbers and Mynx didn't think anyone bothered to glance her way.

Funny, that. Easy to shake her head at the changes

that'd come in over the decades, how little notice people took when a flying object landed in their midst. Funnier still that Mynx would find it funny. As much as she resisted the idea that people become their parents, the young become old, and the cycle repeats itself, she had to concede its truth in this: what had been, and still were, miracles to her meant nothing to most of the world.

The Elementals had chosen a smaller lot, billing itself as an exceptional members-only spa. While the Paragons, with Apinya's agreement, wouldn't slaughter the terrorists wholesale, the Elementals had also pledged to keep their own operations out of the open. In other words, no running ads to recruit the disaffected anomalies too scared to live up to their birthright blessings. Instead, the Elementals hid in places like this and sent street-savvy salesmen running around, recruiting their members through gamesmanship and false promises.

Yes, anomaly, you can change the world. Just hide out in this squalid mall for a few decades until we want to do something other than annoy everyone else.

Now Mynx had to make a decision: either go in with the suit on, armored and ready for anything, or play the Champion and assume invincibility until proven otherwise. Through the suit, she displayed the nearest drones and their distances in the sky around her. The two she'd requested were close, and could get to her within a few seconds if necessary. That might be enough. Mynx didn't want to start a war, not yet, and barging in with this weaponized shell around her wouldn't pitch a peaceful premise.

Back in the cold, relying on her kinetic suit to keep running, Mynx approached the spa. While a sign blazed *Closed* in red neon on the front window, the spa's mint-green outside lights shone, and she could pick out people moving inside too. None, though, watched the door as the Champion approached.

"Reeves, keep the drones hot and ready," Mynx said. "If I give the word, I expect to be grabbed in under ten."

"Done. Should I alert the local Paragons as well?"

"No, they're busy enough."

Aegis didn't mind Mynx working in Atlantis when she'd had to, but not every Paragon appreciated Champions going vigilante outside their set regions. Pixie, the Boston woman who'd taken provisional charge, had always seemed friendly, but there were better ways to start a working relationship than a late night call revealing an aggressive mission on home soil. Of course, if this all went sideways, Mynx would have to explain the decisions.

She'd take that risk.

Mynx tried the single-pane glass door leading in, glancing at her own washed-out reflection in the process. She looked tired, and she refused to concede anything else about her appearance. Mynx did stand straight and put on a sharp glare for the Elemental that came to unlock the door, a younger man bearing a faltering smile.

"We're closed?" the man said it like a question.

"I'm not here for the spa," Mynx replied. "Who's in charge here?"

"Uh, what?"

Another anomaly appeared from the back, an older woman in a soft-looking sweater-and-sweats bundle that actually looked like it belonged in the spa, and she rescued the young man, telling him to head back and keep cleaning up. She then beckoned Mynx inside.

"Thank you," Mynx said, stepping through the door and running her eyes around the inside. Black nubs gave corner cameras away, but otherwise Mynx didn't catch any obvious ambushes in waiting. "I need to talk with whomever leads this branch."

"You're speaking with her. I'm Rosamund, and I handle the northeast for the Elementals," the woman replied. "But let's get ourselves somewhere more comfortable. I imagine a Champion is used to better than an entryway."

Mynx let Rosamund lead her back into the spa, back to a massage area and a room that looked like sales presentations were its primary purpose; posters and brochures littered the area, declaring numerous opportunities for stress relief, muscle relaxation, and more. Soft flutes played over jungle tones, and curling flower stencils lined the walls. Mynx would have pegged the space midway between dirt cheap and actual luxury, about right for a dying mall in what was otherwise a flourishing city.

Rosamund clasped her hands on the table and set a smile on her face, like she was about to stream pleasantries out in a windy road to the point. Mynx didn't care to wait for that, so she started first.

"Did you kill Aegis?" Mynx said.

That smile settled into a frown.

"We did not," Rosamund replied. "In fact, I was sad to see his passing. We had something of a relationship, worked well together."

"Did you."

"To a degree," Rosamund said. "Two sides that want different things won't always see eye-to-eye, but I believe we kept the bad blood to a minimum."

"So I'm supposed to believe you just because you say so?"

Mynx, though, did find herself believing Rosamund. The woman's serious-yet-sad face and sagging pose told a story of someone still gripping with a tragedy, not preparing to take advantage of one.

"You saw the video," Rosamund said. "The killer admitted his own act. Ziran's leader would have the resources to pull off the attack without our help. Besides, he wants a return to normals. That's not our agenda."

"So you'd help us find him?"

That smile came back, "When the mighty ask the weak for a favor, the weak must ask for something in return."

"And what would the weak like?"

"A seat at your summit."

Mynx hadn't expected the summit to stay a secret for all that long. She wanted to wait until every Champion had committed before announcing it, but enough people knew that Mynx couldn't be surprised the meeting's existence had made its way here.

"I thought you were sad about Aegis," Mynx said. "Now you're taking advantage."

"If we waited for the perfect time, we would never move."

"You're not moving here. The summit is for Paragons. Not happening."

Rosamund didn't nod, didn't shake her head or shout. She did sit there, listen to a few more flute measures glide by, before tapping the table with a single finger.

"Thane did not release himself," Rosamund said. "Other disasters could happen, if you don't respond to the risks."

"You're threatening someone who could level this building in a second."

"I am."

Mynx met Rosamund's stare, contemplated calling the bluff. She could tell Reeves to have the drones deliver a precision strike a meter in front of Mynx's current location and watch Rosamund turn to ash. Yet, of the things the Paragons couldn't afford right now, open war with the Elementals numbered pretty high up there.

Time to throw another ball in the air.

"I'm holding the summit so those who deserve it can decide what's next for our world," Mynx said. "Prove you do, and I'll get you a seat."

That the Elementals never would, never could deserve such a thing went entirely unsaid.

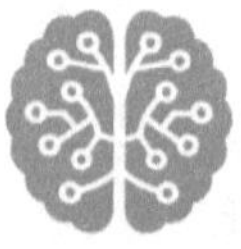

17

Traverse

Thane woke, again, at dawn's cusp. Without electricity, the nights started sooner and the days began at their earliest whisper. Thane took his time moving, listening to the waves and the birds beginning to stir. The first fires let their crackles play beneath the island's natural sounds. He embraced the ambiance, because he might never get it again.

Yesterday had been spent with Cassidy, a.k.a. the Void, and her anomalies. Thane had fished, had helped thatch together a new sleeping hut, and gone foraging for fruits and berries. In the evening, he sat with Cassidy and enjoyed their labor's fruits, plus a little bit of a strange, wine-like concoction one of the anomalies made with salt water, coconut milk, and their ability. It had been, Thane had no problem saying, the nicest day he'd had since the Paragons first slapped cuffs on him and jammed Thane inside their prison.

One nice day was enough.

Thane rolled up off the sand and assembled his grass

skirt, careful to nurture that tiny, ever-present angry flame. He wasn't all that large now, and wrinkled, tanning skin abounded, but so long as Thane could keep enough frustration boiling towards Mynx and the Paragons, he'd have the strength to push forward. And no matter how nice the island happened to be, the real goal lay out there, beyond that omnipresent drone line.

"Get up," Thane said to Sook, snoring close by. "We're moving."

The scrawny anomaly muttered something, swung his arm across his face, but Thane saw his eyes open. Sook would obey. He couldn't risk being left without Thane's protection.

Cassidy's tiny village once again hummed with motion as Thane made his way through it, towards the exit between the dune walls. A thatched backpack lay on the ground next to the gap in the barrier, stocked with smoked fish and roasted roots. A single cracked coconut sat on top. A leathery, older anomaly played guard to both gate and goods, one of those pointed sticks in his hands, though Thane knew this particular man could make his left hand as hard as diamonds, and as sharp.

"These are for us?" Thane asked, approaching.

"The Void ordered it," the man, Hiram, said. "I'm glad she did."

"Are you?"

"You see this island for what it is, rather than what we pretend." Hiram nodded past Thane, towards the open ocean and the death that lay beyond it. "I've lived here for almost fifteen years. The third anomaly, I believe, put on this cursed place. If you would get us away, then I will do whatever I can to help."

Thane reached out and shook Hiram's hand, the right

one, and then pointed back towards the village, "If you want to help, convince them to leave."

"We will, if you show us the way."

Hiram's words, so earnest and honest, knocked Thane's mind for a spin. He'd led mercenaries before, but those people came for the reps and stayed out of fear. He'd never been a Champion, never been tasked with guiding others towards some moral purpose. But then, how hard could it be? Thane wanted something, these people wanted the same thing, and trusted him to help get it. That, Thane could do.

Sook arrived not long after, as Thane struggled to find a fit for the backpack that didn't feel like its stiff straps were slicing his back open. He wound up handing the thing to Sook, and the anomaly accepted his role, shrugging on the backpack with a wince. Ready, the two began walking past Hiram and towards the jungle.

"Wait!" Cassidy's shout came clear, and Hiram put his hand on Thane's shoulder to turn him back around. Cassidy approached, wearing a pack of her own, with several other anomalies, each carrying spears and looking ready for a journey. "If you're going to see the Duchess, we're going to tag along."

"I didn't think you believed in me?" Thane asked.

"Nothing to do with you." Cassidy grinned, shrugged on her pack. "The Duchess likes smoked fish, and we could use some of the metal she's been mining from the volcano. It's just coincidence."

"Right," Thane drew out the word, letting Cassidy know exactly what he thought about this coincidence. Then he flipped his expression, his attitude. "Regardless, I'm glad to have you along. Sook seems to know his way around the island, but I'd rather not get lost."

"I wouldn't have gotten us lost," Sook muttered. "Best guide this island's ever seen."

Sook continued his complaining as the group set out, as they clomped through the ferns, and walked away from the sea towards higher and higher ground, where the lush tropical feel gave way, meter by meter, to long grasses and wildflowers. Bees hovered from one purple petal to another, while songbirds flitted overhead. The group continued to salve themselves with plant oils to keep away the worst sunburns, something Thane appreciated now as they left behind palm trees for the wide plain. Without shade, the sun bore down hot, and only a steady breeze kept things bearable.

"Why did the Duchess choose to live this way?" Thane asked as they walked. "The seaside seems to offer far more benefits."

"If you don't have a way to make fresh water," Cassidy replied, "you're going to get thirsty by the ocean. And it was crowded."

"Crowded?"

"Before we sorted things, Arthur, the Duchess, and I, everyone clustered together at the beach. A whole collection of murderers, cheats, and frauds with all kinds of power."

"A dangerous situation."

"I think that's what Mynx wanted." Cassidy spat to the side, her eyes flashing. "Get us to kill each other and she could justify putting us here. The Paragons could say they were right."

"But you didn't?"

"We did. Every day would bring more anomalies dead. I slept in a tree, used my power to carve handholds and then ruin them once I made it up. Not the safest, but better than getting my throat cut or my insides boiled. The ones who couldn't handle the stress, or who thought they could, tried to escape on their own. I saw one who could fly by summoning up these fantastic wind gusts, he launched himself towards the drones, thinking he could get over them."

"And?"

"He didn't make it a kilometer off shore before they swarmed. No stunning here. A few pinpoint flashes and he became fried fish food. Others tried going through the ground, or under the water. Never saw any of them again."

"Maybe they made it away?"

"You ever hear of someone escaping this place?" Cassidy asked.

"No."

"Exactly."

Having seen Mynx's drones in action, Thane couldn't argue with the story. Any solo breakout would result in similar consequences. Batch a bunch of anomalies together, with their complementing powers, however, and those results might be flipped, or at least delayed long enough for some to get through.

That, of course, was the real key. Working under some illusion that all of these anomalies would get off this island with some symphonic operation weaving their abilities together would mean slaving himself to a fantasy. The objective wasn't to save everyone, but to save those that could make the most impact.

Like Thane.

"So you were captured all this time?" Cassidy asked as they kept walking through the morning. "They used you?"

"I tried to fight them, and lost," Thane replied, the grass tickling his feet beneath his sandals. All the sensations here, just being beneath an open sky, felt wondrous. "They should have killed me, but Apinya recognized my value."

"Isn't he the nice one?"

"The others prefer physical punishments. They struck me with fists, machines, bullets, swords and spears," Thane said. In truth the battle blurred together. His angry self didn't care much for memories or detail. "Apinya takes a different approach. He'll turn your mind against itself, break you apart. He could have turned me into a madman or reduced me to a slurring pile of nothing. Instead, he broke my rage, and let the rest of them take hold."

Thane noticed the other anomalies listening in. They marched in something of a ball, with Sook out ahead a few meters keeping tabs on the trail. The eavesdroppers didn't hold Thane back, and he spoke louder because of it. Every one of these anomalies would be in the Duchesses's camp later, and every one could spread his legend.

"But now you're here?"

"I made it out." Thane leveled a look at Cassidy, to make sure she understood that this was no small feat. "It took decades, but I broke their chains and smashed my way to a small taste of freedom."

Cassidy laughed. "Must have been real small if you're here already."

Someone who hadn't been chained to a bed, force-fed, force-moved to prevent bed sores, and made to use a bedpan for all those years might have had pride to get hurt by Cassidy's words, her tone. Thane, though, had nothing left there. Only burning ambition, and that could take a hit without losing its fire.

So he laughed with her, "It was not, perhaps, the greatest breakout in Paragon history. I think, though, it's led me to where I need to be."

"Guiding us to a doomsday mission that'll leave us all dead?"

"You don't believe that," Thane said. "If you did, you wouldn't be here."

"We're delivering the smoked fish." Cassidy shifted her backpack, as if to remind Thane, though the constant, nigh-overpowering smell did that already.

"A trip that had to happen today, at just this time?"

Now it was Cassidy's turn to level a look at Thane, "No, it didn't need to be today. But it's been a long time since anyone offered hope in this place, and even if the only thing I'm going to see today is you getting thrown into a volcano, at least it'll be something different."

The Duchess, apparently, had an execution variety pack at the ready. She'd developed a reputation on the island for being ruthless to enemies and traitors, and inspiring die-hard loyalty among those who chose her tribe. Of those executions, her favorite, according to Sook and his random knowledge from traipsing the island, involved paralyzing an anomaly somehow—Sook wasn't sure if the Duchess herself did this, or some other anomaly in her employ—then carrying them up to the volcano ridge and dumping them in.

"She sounds like a cartoon villain," Thane said. "Nobody really does things like that. Too much time, too risky."

"We have nothing but time here," Cassidy replied. "And as for risk, what does she have to lose?"

Thane did not want to get thrown into a volcano, nor did he want to start a fight. Every anomaly lost meant one more he couldn't use to defeat, or distract, the drones. If the Duchess wanted supplicants, then she would get them. Until Thane convinced her to fall in line.

"When we arrive," Thane said. "I'll act like I'm one of

your new anomalies. I'll pretend I want to defect to the Duchess, and get a meeting with her. Then, I'll convince her to join our goal."

"So sure of yourself," Cassidy said. "When did you learn to be so cocky?"

"When I left Aegis beaten and broken in a frozen field."

Life Price

Kat didn't wake up so much as find her way through the thick cobwebs clogging her mind. She pushed and pulled, ripped and tore against the sticky silver threads, heading towards a blue glow. Flickering and distant, the light drew her through the strands, and Kat's steps grew faster as she went. Soon the webs parted and fell like dust as she came closer and closer to the light, though the glow's tiny size remained the same. She stood over the blue dot, almost blinded, and while Kat couldn't feel her hands, her legs, or see any part of herself, she reached for it anyway, that only thing left in this endless dark.

And saw a soft teal room that looked like it belonged to a schemer, daylight pouring through a sole slit window high up on one wall.

Were they harvesting her organs?

Kat tried to breathe, found a tube connecting to her mouth that ran along her chest and off to the side. Air pushed through it, keeping her lungs full. She couldn't move her hands—she could feel them, but they were tied down by something she couldn't see beneath the broad yellow blanket laid on her. Kat's other senses came online to tell her about the chilly air, the iron flavor in her mouth, and a vast emptiness in her chest.

She'd been shot. The instant came back to her in what was less a flash and more a hallucination, a slow motion replay with the black-masked man and her forward roll, the steady-aimed pistol and the single crack that sent her to the dark world she'd woken up inside. While Kat hadn't encountered guns like that in the wild, she'd seen the movies, read enough accounts running through their damage to know she shouldn't have survived.

Which made this either the world's most dingy, hostile hospital or some sort of surreal afterlife. Kat hadn't put much stock in any particular religion, but this didn't seem to fit the end-game definition for any of them. Unless she'd found her way to Hell, and this began her eternal torture.

A familiar weight tugged on her attention. On Kat's left wrist, the Tama. Its presence confirmed Kat's own life, while simultaneously putting doubt as to her impending demise. A Tama would respond to any true peril with a radio out to emergency services, and its combination GPS and cellular tracking would send drones and more to Kat's position. If she still had her Tama—then whomever held her must be keeping her alive and healthy, or they'd already be caught.

Which meant what, exactly?

One, she'd been saved. By who, she didn't know, but of the people who knew she'd been on the rooftop, who would have known she'd been shot, Calvin stood out as the only option, unless the black-masked man had decided to kidnap her and keep her alive after shooting her, which seemed like a reach. If drones had made it to her, Kat would be waking up in a hospital now, a real one, so that struck them out. So Calvin must have done something, taken her somewhere.

Two, even with drugs, Kat couldn't believe she didn't feel anything from the gunshot. No aches from her chest, no feeling of a giant hole, or even the weakness she'd assume would come from a near-mortal wound. Unless Kat had been out for weeks in stasis—she hoped someone had fed Seeker—she shouldn't be feeling like this, feeling good, if tired. Which meant she'd been party to some special healing.

Three, if someone not a part of emergency healthcare had decided to bring her back from the brink, they must have done so for a reason. Organ harvesting again flared its horrifying head, but Kat squashed that far-fetched plot. Her savior could be wanting anything. As a tracker, Kat had access to all kinds of information. They might want to see where a certain anomaly had gone, or who else did her work in Chicago or another city. Maybe they just wanted reps, though that too seemed unlikely.

Regardless, Kat felt alive and all right, which meant she needed to get off this bed, out of this room. Find her suit, get it fixed, and track that black-masked man. Get some payback first, then come back here and learn what was really going on. Who she owed a debt for saving her life.

Kat jerked her right side, trying to get the bed to tip, but someone had anchored it to the floor. Nothing there. Next she tried to wriggle her hands, her wrists out of the restraints, but whomever had tied the things knew what they were doing. Her legs were tied at the ankles, putting them out of commission too. The best Kat could do was shake her head until the tube dislodged and fell to the side, letting her at least gulp in some real air. It tasted sterile, plastic-like.

As her escape plan failed, another door opened.

The literal door.

A large, not particularly fit man wearing little more than a tank top and baggy shorts led the way, and Kat found her eyes crawling all over the tattoos everywhere on his body. Rather than some sort of grand artistic expression, the tattoos seemed to be random symbols and abstract lines, often layering on top of each other, like a child coloring the same page repeatedly. An ugly look, but mesmerizing in the sheer color the man had packed onto his skin. Kat expected malice, or a nasty grin, but instead the man cleared away the tube and set about untying Kat's restraints without a word. Kat, too, didn't talk.

Instead, she looked at who came through next, because Beth changed everything.

"The next thing you do better be cutting me out of this bed," Kat said to the blonde woman, who smiled around her creased face like a patient mother listening to a toddler whine. Annoying. "I'm guessing you saved my life somehow, but that doesn't mean I'm your prisoner."

"He saved your life, actually," Beth said, pointing to the tattooed man. "You see all of those shapes on his skin? One of those belongs to you."

"Belongs?"

The man glanced over at Beth, who nodded, and he started to undo the rest of her restraints.

"We found you nearly dead," Beth said. "We came out when we heard the gunshot, and who should we find, but Calvin, the anomaly we'd been searching for, who says the tracker that betrayed us needs our help."

"I didn't betray you," Kat said. Her left leg popped free, and she moved it around, letting the blood wake up the stiff muscles. "I never agreed to anything."

"Semantics," Beth replied. "Taro here saved you. Took

your wound and all its damage and turned it into that long line across his cheek, that bright red one right there. He made a choice too, the right one."

"Thanks," Kat said to Taro, who released her left and started making his way around to the right side. "I've got it."

Kat had the ties undone in a couple of seconds while Taro moved to stand near Beth. Kat slid herself off of the bed, stumbled when her legs weren't quite ready for her yet, and wound up leaning against the wall, glaring Beth's way.

"You've been on that bed for almost eighteen hours. Your body is going to need time to recover."

"I thought you said Taro took all that." Kat threw a forced smile Taro's way. "Again, thanks for saving my life. I mean that."

"I'm sure you do," Beth said, "and I'm sure you know that a severe injury like yours leaves effects that last beyond its healing. Unfortunately, you can't stay here to recover from them."

"Don't worry, wasn't planning on it," Kat said, then tried to look past Beth. "Where's Calvin? You're not coercing him, are you?"

"Calvin left not an hour ago," Beth replied. "He's been walking your dog."

Wow. Not too long ago, Calvin had almost killed Seeker with a creative, concrete use of his power, and now here he was taking the dog for walks. What a turn. It also proved Kat had made the right call in turning the man into the Paragons: a good heart would go farther there than with these manipulative anomalies.

Beth shifted and let Taro walk by her, leaving the two women alone in the room. Kat noticed, though, that Beth blocked the door. She wanted something, and Kat didn't have much choice but to ask what it was.

"You saw the shooter," Beth said. "You're not his first victim."

"I know, Calvin showed up with a bullet wound a couple days ago. That's how this whole thing started."

"Calvin wasn't the start." Beth's facade started to crack, that smooth smile slipping down a few notches. "I don't think the shooter has hit any Paragons, yet, but we've been suffering."

"Wait, you think he's targeting Elementals?" Kat tried to follow this revelation. "I thought he was one. That you wanted to hurt Calvin for going to the Paragons."

"We're not assassins. We wouldn't try to kill an anomaly just for being a Paragon. How would that serve our goals?"

"Hey, I don't know you. All I hear is the news telling me that you're all out to sow chaos, cause panic in the streets and all that."

"That's not all wrong." Beth slid the door shut. "But we're not doing this. Not shooting anomalies with a weapon like that." Beth looked a little green now, a little gut-punched, and she leaned forward onto the bed. "He's killed five of us in the last two months. We can't find him, and the Paragons are too scattered because of Aegis."

"Five?" That many murders was unheard of these days, when even looking aggressive would get a drone on your ass before you'd managed an angry word. "All out in the open, like me?"

"Everywhere. At night, during the day. Not all snipings either." Beth shook her head, Kat noticed her tight fists. "We need to find him, Kat, but we're not trained for this. We're not trackers."

Ah. Now it made sense why Beth saved her life, why

they'd kept Kat here instead of healing and dumping her off somewhere anonymous. A favor.

"Guess what?" Kat said. "Normally, I'd charge you for this. Charge you a lot. But when someone shoots me, I make it a point to get even."

That this was a new policy, enacted now after she'd been shot for the first time, went unsaid. Beth didn't question it, and began laying out the where and when of the prior assassinations. Midway through, Taro returned with Kat's suit, its fabric already repaired and, minus some red staining across the chest, ready to go.

As new color went, Kat didn't mind the bloody splotches. She was going to get her hands dirty. Might as well look the part.

19

Deal's Made

Waking up in Wexley's hyper-modern apartment, less overwhelming without a hangover's mental bomb, Zhan-Yo did what he'd been doing ever since he returned from Sylvie's old place: try to confirm the summit's existence, or learn who the contact might be.

No news organization had printed anything about the Champions converging anywhere, though with the Paragon's iron-fisted rule over said news, that wasn't surprising. Zhan-Yo, though, couldn't find any little notes on social media showing heightened security, rapid construction, or anything else. He did find Aegis tribute videos, everything from young children to grizzled elders posting stories of how the Champion had made their lives better.

Not one talked about the freedoms Aegis stole from them. Not one explored how normals had no part to play in today's government.

Then again, how could Zhan-Yo expect anything different? The Paragons swept fair representation from the planet. Nobody considered it anymore, nobody cared. If someone who, with a wave, could annihilate city blocks wanted to run things, might as well let them. Anything else would mean disaster.

So Zhan-Yo turned to the contact instead, trying to figure out who Sylvie might know with information like this. Sylvie didn't seem like the type to have an open tip line, leave her contact information around random places so random information could get dumped her way. She'd also never mentioned a bounty program for hot news, which meant Sylvie must have known this person somehow. And this person kept things anonymous, which meant they were in a position with some power.

Combining those two things restricted the possibilities to one solution: a Paragon. One of Aegis's soldiers turning traitor. The idea would seem ludicrous, except Zhan-Yo had already seen Sylvie do it with Innis, Chicago's Paragon leader who seemed to be benefitting more from Aegis's death than anyone else. Paragons, it seemed, were just as power-hungry as the rest of them, willing to take a shot to reach the top.

But if there was anyone who didn't know Paragons, who actively avoided them . . . Zhan-Yo stared at the hated chromed appliances, their gleaming surfaces some sort of metaphor for the life he'd led compared to the life he led now. Hunting for traitors. Using his—was crush still a term used these days? Not for him. Sylvie, that's who she was, and that's whose resources he used to root around for someone to corrupt.

Seemed a long way from that moral high ground he kept insisting he stood on.

"You're looking glum," Wexley said when he opened the door, refined as always in his slick hair, glasses, long black wool coat. Black leather gloves came off and slapped on the counter. "Heard you took a trip today."

"Heard?"

Was his own lieutenant spying on him now?

"Some people snapped shots with their Tamas," Wexley said. "Outside Sylvie's old building. Had to look that bit up, because it didn't make sense why you'd risk it all for a daytime walk."

Wexley slid out a chair, set himself down on its edge. Zhan-Yo couldn't see that part, but he could see Wexley's perfect posture, as if the chair's back were radioactive. The man crossed his legs, folded his arms and let his hands clasp beneath the table; Wexley, a psychologist coming to hear Zhan-Yo's troubles. Then, Wexley waited.

As Zhan-Yo used to wait for him.

Very well. Sometimes the balance shifted. Wexley had his name on Ziran now. Zhan-Yo still served as the revolution's scion, the face that the supporters, whomever they happened to be—if there happened to really be any—looked to for inspiration. In real terms, though, Wexley could evict Zhan-Yo to the streets and let the drones hunt him down. That should have been a sickening realization, but instead Zhan-Yo felt free. His only accessible assets sat in this room. He could do anything without contacting a secretary and clearing a calendar, without having a cadre follow him around and pester Zhan-Yo about this or that market, meeting, or motion.

"So what?" Zhan-Yo almost laughed as he spoke. He sounded like a teenager. "I can do what I want."

"Of course you can. The question is whether what you want is in your best interest. Our best interest."

"You'd rather me stay inside this place all day and wait? That's what I did before, only I had an entire company to distract me."

"That's actually why I came," Wexley replied. "I've put together another meeting this evening. Those people you reached out to, the ones who don't want to touch this publicly, they still want to talk in private. They haven't abandoned the dream, Zhan-Yo, they're just not ready to commit yet."

Zhan-Yo pushed back the chair, stood up and went to the window. Not as high as the one in his office, not quite so majestic a view, but he could still see the morning crowds wandering. People waiting for him.

"I committed," Zhan-Yo said. "I had the most to lose and I committed. What's holding them back?"

"Fear." Wexley didn't hesitate, didn't hold back his contempt either. "You risked everything on a chance. They'll only do it for a sure play."

"What about you?"

"I'm here, aren't I?" Wexley said, though he didn't follow Zhan-Yo to the window. "Wherever this road leads, I will walk it. The Paragons need to be destroyed."

Zhan-Yo nodded several times, pursing his lips and puzzling over the right way to put this before going with the blunt approach, "I went to Sylvie's to see if I could find anything. She always had more happening than she let on."

"That's why I never trusted her."

There were times to be annoyed, and times to ignore.

"She has someone inside the Paragons. Not Innis," Zhan-Yo said. "They sent her a message yesterday saying there's going to be a Paragon summit. All the Champions in one place."

"With more security than anywhere else on the planet."

"Maybe," Zhan-Yo said. "But I don't think we can pass on this. If Aegis couldn't kick-start our revolution, then this might. Think about the chaos if we took out all of them? The people would need someone to turn to."

It would happen fast. With the Champions dead, Paragon in-fighting would break out as anomalies tried to stake their places. They'd destroy each other while Zhan-Yo gathered everyone else, promising peace, order, and a representative government for the world. At first, yes, there would be pain, but after? As the need for stability overwhelmed all else? The people could take back the power. One region after another falling in line. Zhan-Yo would even offer the Paragons places in the new government to prevent bloodshed. A clean transition.

"The world would never turn itself over to someone who killed the Champions," Wexley said. "Never. I think you don't realize how much people hate what you did to Aegis."

"That was necessary."

"You destroyed the childhood hero for billions. I didn't like the idea at first, and now you're seeing why. Zhan-Yo, you can get this revolution started, but you'll never lead it."

"Words from someone who's never led anything. When the time comes, I'll explain and they'll understand."

Wexley didn't nod, didn't say anything. Zhan-Yo frowned. The man was spoiling the day, the find. The summit should be a good thing! A reason to celebrate and then get to planning. Instead, Wexley seemed more intent on crushing Zhan-Yo's spirit than anything else.

"That's all in the future anyway," Zhan-Yo said. "What matters now is the insider. We need to know who it is, how to correspond with them. Like you said, it will be difficult to penetrate a place with that many Paragons. But if we have someone on the inside, then we have an opportunity."

"Do you have any leads, or is this a wild grasp at straws?"

"All I have are wild grasps, Wexley. That's why I'm in your ridiculous apartment after what should have been my biggest triumph. Look at me, look at this." Zhan-Yo followed his own directions, saw his thin-skinned hands, a body showing signs it wasn't up to fighting the world. "I'm going to find that Paragon, we're going to go to this summit, and we're going to kick-start a better world."

Wexley didn't have an answer for him, and after the man extracted a promise that Zhan-Yo would hop up to the mall that night, and that Zhan-Yo would spend the day not getting himself seen by everyone on the planet, he left.

Zhan-Yo waited till Wexley had gone, changed into a nondescript sweater and jeans, tugged on a faux-fur hat, left the swords and ventured out into the late morning. He had a destination, not all that far from Wexley's gleaming building, an old-style restaurant tucked mid-block into a side street off Michigan Avenue, a space looking like time had forgotten its existence, with wood everywhere, spotted metal lanterns that may not have been cleaned for centuries, and a long bar home to a hunched over crowd sipping black coffee and staring vaguely at scattered televisions.

Zhan-Yo took his own table over zero objections from a hostess busier with her Tama than her job. An unlit candle adorned the tabletop, refinished so many times as to glisten like plastic. Besides the screens, around Zhan-Yo hung old items without any rhyme and certainly no reason, as if someone had perused estate sales and grabbed objects at random and nailed them to the walls. Here a bicycle wheel, there a movie poster from the last century, and yes, that was a real jukebox in the corner, its lights on but no records ready to play. Those would have been too expensive, and the bar had sports coming over its speakers anyway.

"I didn't expect a two a.m. message from you," Sylvie's

brother said as he pulled out the opposite chair and set his large bulk in it.

"I am always working," Zhan-Yo said, and would have gone on except the waitress blew by with a look that said order now or forever hold your peace. Eggs, bacon, and more coffee secured, Zhan-Yo turned back to Sylvie's brother. "Your sister received a message from someone, and I want to know who that someone is."

"Lot of someones in the world."

"They had knowledge that most wouldn't," Zhan-Yo replied. He took a glance around, nobody seemed to be paying attention to them. Microphones could be anywhere, but nobody would listen to all that recorded noise without a reason. "I think they're a Paragon."

Sylvie's brother didn't react to the statement, then rolled his eyes and looked at his Tama. "Sure, I'll get right to asking every Paragon if they knew my sister. That's what you want, right?"

"Look," Zhan-Yo said. "I don't know how these things work, but I need to get inside that summit, and I can't get inside that summit without a Paragon helping me."

"You assume that, because this one sent a message to you, that they'll be willing to go that next step?"

"I assume."

"Dangerous." The big man canceled the eye rolls, the shrugs. Gave it straight, now. "Everyone's willing to risk it all when the stakes aren't real. You ask this Paragon to chance their future, their whole organization on you, they might back out."

Zhan-Yo nodded, "I have to try. As soon as the Paragons get themselves back in order, they'll find me, and when they do this dream is dead."

"And this is what Sylvie died trying to do?"

"Yes."

"Then show me the message," Sylvie's brother said. "Digital fingerprints are easy to read."

"Thank you."

"Don't thank me, I haven't sent you the bill yet." The man offered a half-smile. "Name's Mathieu, by the way."

"Zhan-Yo."

Hands shook, breakfast came, and they plotted the new world over bacon and eggs.

20

A Champion's Advice

Amazing what a good night's sleep and a morning enjoying drone operation reports over tea could do for you. Mynx finished her update list and sent it to Reeves, who'd spend the day tweaking the software to account for some of yesterday's issues—particularly a new fashion style involving reflective bands that could play havoc with drone cameras. By tomorrow, the drones would account for the coloring and register the wearers as people rather than, say, construction cones or signs.

Aegis would've called it boring, not being in the field throwing a fist against some goon. That'd been, in part, why they worked so well together: Aegis and his constant daring drew the press to him, letting Mynx work magic behind the scenes to keep the world safe. Without him, Reeves had to block the press constantly, referring them to regional Paragon managers, inevitably not to the satisfaction of reporters and institutions.

"You could make the reporters illegal, you know," Reeves asked.

"No, I'm happy they exist," Mynx replied and swiped

away another interview request from her Tama. "Not so happy I'm the focus."

The Champions had taken a saw to society, at first. In those heady times after the last governments had given in, everyone clustered in Geneva's relatively safe confines, the Champions had gone on a wish fulfillment spree. They'd shot out directives, forced countries to redraw into regions, folded currencies into the singular rep, and then used that overhaul to re-align industries that'd suffered, in the Champions' opinion, under capitalism's yoke. Mynx had driven her vague support towards journalism—more because it made an easy opportunity than a noble drive: improving the drone program already had its claws in her time and energy. Publications of all types and quality proliferated with service-earned reps providing a healthy supply to write up and spin out just about anything.

Now Mynx received calls from prestigious outlets, ones that'd survived the Paragon takeover, and the tiniest and most niche places, each one hoping to be the first one to break her sealed lips. Since Aegis died, Mynx had issued one statement. For mourning and calm. She hadn't had time for anything else. She didn't know what she would say when they asked.

"They won't leave you alone until you give them something," Reeves said. "I performed an analysis on the call volumes you've received during previous crises, and they all dropped as soon as you spoke up."

"Reeves, I hope I didn't build a super-powered AI to tell me people will stop asking for quotes once I give them a quote."

"I'm confirming the obvious."

"Right."

Mynx had to keep the Tama clear anyway. She expected another call, this one from the nebulous region encompassing eastern Europe and central Asia. Burov ought to have his embattled mug, always at war with itself, showing up soon.

Of the Champions, Burov was most like Aegis. He'd built himself up as a legend in his own native Russia first, then grown beyond its national borders through one highlighting performance after another. Unlike Aegis, the man didn't use his fists.

Mynx shivered. Looked away from the Tama towards the city below. Paragons with physical abilities, even ones that mocked physical laws, Mynx could understand and appreciate. The others, like Apinya, like Burov, that could mold your mind like putty, made her sick. Burov, in particular, always felt wrong. Not the man's fault—he didn't choose his power—but not really her own either.

As if on cue, her Tama buzzed, drawing her eyes back. Burov's face, coated with the heavy make-up the man always wore to disguise the shifting shadows beneath his skin. He looked like a wax doll, refusing to wear a mask but also bowing to the inherent impossibility of talking with someone whose face looked like . . . well, like it had shadows crawling beneath the surface.

"Mynx!" Burov exclaimed when she tapped to answer the call. "How are you? It has been so long!"

"Sapped some enthusiasm today?" Mynx said.

They'd met, for the first time, in Japan. A joint earthquake rescue operation. While Aegis, Mynx, and others were there to handle the physical duties, Burov vacuumed up the panic, the fear, and replaced it with calm. Determination. Substituted confidence for despair, at least for a time.

"Of course!" Burov replied. "I visited a school this morning, young children looking to meet their Champion.

They were so excited I thought I'd quiet them a little. Not that I need the boost to talk with you!"

"Don't you, though?"

Burov's eyes darkened a shade, throwing off his sparse dark hair, "Mynx, you're asking me to come to your summit, but you are so cold?"

What did Burov do with all that sadness? All that fear he stole from the people clustering around the rubble, pulling at their families, waiting for news they suspected would be terrible? Burov stored it, kept it in those blotches stealing around his skin, and gave it back to his enemies.

If there'd been a secret to the Champion's world takeover, it'd been Apinya's mental manipulation coupled with Burov siphoning fear and sending it into the hearts of every world leader, every general, every politician sitting across from them. Mynx had watched opposing wills crumble in real time, had said nothing as coerced signatures handed the Champions their dreams.

"Sorry, Burov," Mynx said, pasting a tight-lipped smile onto her face. "It's been a long week. I don't have much happiness left."

"Ah, then I should visit. We can fix that."

"I'm sure," Mynx said.

"Oh, don't give me that look. I take a puppy's joy and it's back in a moment, but you get to keep it for a day. There's nothing wrong with a trade like that."

"Come to the summit, and we can work it out."

"Mynx, of course I am coming. What happened . . ." Here, for the first time, Burov's poise failed him. "What happened to Aegis was a monstrous act. He deserved better. I will come, and together we can find this Zhan-Yo. He will pay for what he did."

"He will." Having secured the commitment, Mynx wanted nothing more than to get off the call. She thought she could see a shape moving beneath Burov's left eye. Whose emotions were those? "Once I catch him."

Burov tilted his head, "I am surprised he is still free? If this had happened here, such a criminal would not last a day without getting captured."

"The drones will find him. Things have been chaotic."

The conversation dithered after that, despite every effort Mynx made to get Burov off the line. The Russian wanted to cover all the details for the summit, the coming changes to Atlantis—Burov insisted on meeting Pixie before giving approval—and then he asked about Mynx's personal life, which was so far over the line that Mynx finally told the Champion straight out that she had to leave.

"Still sensitive, even after all these years?" Burov said at the dismissal. "What does Apinya say?"

"He says nothing, because he understands boundaries."

"And look at where that has brought you." Burov did manage to look disappointed, a feat for his blocky head. For all the man's ability to steal emotions, his body language had a rock's finesse. "A cut only heals if you let it."

"Goodbye, Burov."

Mynx swiped away the call before the Champion could get another word in. Of all the times to tread that well-worn path, now was not one.

"Any sign of Celice?" Mynx asked Reeves via her Tama, watching drones drift over Manhattan.

"She hasn't popped up yet," Reeves replied. "An analysis of your last conversation would suggest she intends to go to Chicago."

"Both of us, then. Burov did have a point, Reeves. New York doesn't have what we want. Send the confirmation to

Pixie and tell her to relocate here after the summit. She's the provisional Champion now, and she needs to get Atlantis in order."

"Done. Shall I warm up the jet?"

"Yes." The cloudless blue sky looked nice, but she could see snow whipping around between the buildings, cold and sharp. "Make it very warm."

Zhan-Yo had escaped the drones for too long. Mynx needed to find the man before Celice did, because the world needed to see that the Paragons were more than capable of delivering their own justice.

Revolutions would not stand.

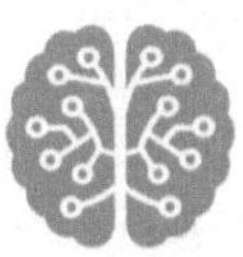

21

Meeting Royalty

From the coast, the island's volcano loomed black and pointed, a spire aiming into the bay-blue sky. Up close, and Thane felt the slope with every step in his unsparing sandals, the volcano exposed its true features: crags, hardy plants nestled in rocks, and steaming vents making clear this geological wonder lived.

Cassidy walked beside him at the small collective's head, Sook hidden back towards the rear where his presence, apparently a constant offense to every faction on this island, would hopefully go unnoticed. Sook himself had suggested the idea, stating they might get attacked on sight with him at the front.

And that, given the Duchess's town, would make for a quick ending. Rather than Cassidy's hut gathering on the beach, this seemed more like a fully functioning space where an actual ecosystem flourished. Smoke rose, but not only from cook fires: pounding hammers, shouts for supplies, and fizzling sparks from anomaly power inside the rock walls overwhelmed Cassidy's meager offerings.

"I never denied it," Cassidy said, her mouth set. "She

has the most land. Most people dumped on the island start here."

"How did she take it?"

"Her power," Cassidy almost spat these words. "You hear about anomalies messing with minds, but this is something else. I've never felt it. Never let her get close enough."

"Is that why Mynx brought her here?"

"No idea. But I think you'll get the chance to ask her."

The city's rock wall looked like it had been mashed together, ill-fitting rocks ground into one another with the fix clear in an emerald, moss-like substance lining their intersections. At the front entrance, where Thane and Cassidy's group approached, the mossy seal rose to coat the sides all the way up from ground to top, preserving space for a ten meter-wide gate.

Cassidy's village seemed half done, a temporary habitat meant to keep people alive until a better alternative came along. This one, though, felt permanent. People were creating lives here, even if 'here' was a prison they hadn't chosen.

What that meant for Thane's own objectives, he wasn't sure, but he doubted that it would help. People didn't mind leaving a makeshift shelter, but a home?

Three guards came forward to greet them, a mixed trio sporting grass weaves like Thane's own. No weapons visible, and with no belts to hold the hilts, it seemed unlikely there were any hidden options either.

Not that anomalies needed normal weapons.

"Cassidy," the lead guard, a stringy man whose letters glued together with syrup when he spoke, said. "We saw you coming. The usual is almost ready."

"You can call me the Void." Cassidy shrugged off the smoked fish pack, set it down in front of her. "First name's for friends only."

"We're not friends?"

"Mort, we're not friends. But Thane might be interested, if you're offering."

Mort's eyes shifted Thane's way, but nothing friendly showed on the man's face. Thane matched the glower. Despite what Cassidy said, this wasn't about making friends. He needed an army, and a loyal one. That's all.

"I need to see the Duchess," Thane said. "I have a plan to get us all off this island, and it's going to take her cooperation."

"Cassidy," Mort said. "Your friend—does *he* count as one?—has nerve. He thinks he can walk right in here and see her?"

"I do," Thane answered as Cassidy glared Mort's way. "And you'll take me. Now. The rest of you can finish your trades."

Mort shook his head, folded his arms. "Ah, no can do. You see, the Duchess is busy today. No audiences. No new entries. Cassidy—"

Thane didn't see her move, but he saw Cassidy's results: Mort's weave shucked off his skin, pulled towards what Thane guessed was a point just a couple centimeters in front of Mort's chest. The grass strands hit that point, swirled and ground first to dust and then to nothing.

Mort, naked and looking none too thrilled about it, yelped and back-stepped behind the other two guards.

"I said, call me the Void. Next time I'll take more than your clothes."

Behind his human shield, Mort's head stuck above their shoulders. He spat their way, a failure that hit the ground well short of its mark.

"Next time we'll take your heads," Mort said.

"I don't think your Duchess would like that very

much," Thane said. "Not if she wants fish like these. Now, I asked you nicely. Take me inside."

Being a leader required many traits, not least understanding when a man could be commanded. Mort's anger aside, Thane could see the man breaking, sputtering to keep his stature. The other two guards failed to suppress their grins as their naked boss tried to hold his authority. Cassidy's band laughed.

Mort, too, recognized he'd lost this one. He took a deep breath, with everyone waiting, then cleared his throat like some pompous advisor, which, now that Thane thought about it, fit the man exactly.

"Fine. I will lead you inside. The rest wait out here, complete your trades, and leave," Mort proclaimed. "I warn you, though, the Duchess won't want to waste her time."

"That's my problem. Let's go."

The day had already reached its noon-time zenith, and, now that his plan was marching forward, Thane felt every passing, useless hour. The world needed to be rescued, and spending time on this piddly island wasn't helping.

Cassidy and the others didn't protest Mort's final arrangement, and after a few minutes scrapping pieces of other weaves, Mort assembled a crude grass skirt and led Thane through the gates into the Duchess's town.

"Welcome to Avalon," Mort announced as they went through the gates, passing by several anomalies heading the other way, sacks filled with wood, polished stones, and what looked like smoked meat of a heartier variety.

"Avalon?" Thane almost laughed. "Isn't that presumptuous?"

"You haven't met her yet."

Truth. Thane hadn't met the Duchess, nor ever heard

of her before arriving on this island. While the Champions hadn't told Thane everything that happened during his years locked away, he felt he would have learned about some god-like anomaly coming forth, attempting to remake a mythical city.

That the Duchess played into her ego as a means to control desperate, trapped anomalies seemed far more likely. Why not make your island village a magical place? Who here would complain?

Avalon did not follow Cassidy's town template. As inland cities differ from coastal ones, Avalon stocked black-rock buildings, including a few too large for houses that, when questioned, Mort indicated were used for production. Forges for tools, weapons, a weaving space for warmer clothes.

Whereas Cassidy's village relied on the ocean for everything, including entertainment and exercise, Avalon had no such opportunity. Anomalies clustered around a large rectangle in the middle, kicking a rudimentary ball back and forth between makeshift goals. Others played a game with rock chips at a standing table, stacking them on one another.

"Not much compared with home," Thane said to Mort. "But, considering, I'm impressed."

"Nobody cares whether you're impressed."

"I do. The Duchess seems to care about you."

"Yes. We belong to her. Caring for us is like caring for herself." Again Mort's voice, his eyes, gained that faraway glint when he spoke of the Duchess. "We're going to her home now, where you will wait until she is ready to see you."

The Duchess's house proved to be modest in size—the forges and such were larger structures—but by far the most beautiful. Volcanic rock, smoothed and layered together, formed what seemed to be a black icicle in reverse, coming to a point some ten meters in the air. Smoke curled from the tip, sending its black finger to the sky.

In any other city on Earth, the structure would make for a strange statue. On this island, with no other competition, it suited a goddess.

Mort deposited Thane outside the building's entrance, which had no guard. Thane stood alone, and after watching the ball game for a few minutes and drawing curious looks, went inside.

Black stone floors greeted his feet, and Thane realized this was the first time he'd walked on true hard ground since he'd left the cave. After a lifetime spent on such surfaces, it'd been pleasant to give his feet a rest, feel the contours in the earth. Now, inside this cavernous space, Thane felt divorced from the planet. Small and insignificant.

Cascading runes carved into the building's walls emphasized that last. Giant letterings in different languages spun down from the point at the top, illuminated by a small, dazzling fire. At first Thane thought the runes were laws, or maxims, but as he read around, he realized they were much . . . dumber.

Duchess. That's all they said, but in different scripts. She'd left one in Roman lettering there, removing all the mystery. This wasn't some paen to wisdom, the runes were for herself.

Royalty, even self-proclaimed, needed her castle.

"Mort said I had a visitor?" said a lithe voice behind him, and Thane turned, already falling into a bow as he did. Dictators tended to like supplication, and Thane had no qualms about giving it, for now. "But he did not say who it was."

"Thane," he said, raising his eyes to see a hardened woman in front of him.

Like some costumed orphan, the Duchess wore robes that seemed stitched together from so many fabrics, many wearing through. They piled around her and her long silver hair, an outfit Thane would have considered ridiculous anywhere but here: power came in different ways, wearing actual clothes while everyone else sported grass weaves proved how far the Duchess stood above them. While Thane assumed she'd taken those very clothes from the anomalies when they'd landed here, technicalities like that wouldn't matter to her followers.

"I know who you are," the Duchess replied, coming into her home and walking left by Thane. "The long prisoner finally set free, only to find himself in different chains."

"Indeed," Thane said, following the Duchess's walk with his eyes. She gestured for him to sit in one of several rock stools—the Duchess had what looked like a crude, squared throne—and Thane did so, enjoying sitting anywhere other than the ground. "It was not the release I had hoped for."

"So now you're planning another?"

Thane cocked his head. How would she know?

"Thane," the Duchess continued. "There are only a few anomalies on this island that I would consider a threat, which, in this place, is the only consideration that matters." She leaned forward, those clothes clumping along her lap. "The Void and Arthur keep to their roles. The others work for me. What should I do with you?"

"Listen."

She did.

The Duchess, stirring the fire every now and then with a scorched stick seemingly for that purpose, heard Thane's story, sprinkling in questions from time to time as if to show interest.

Thane hit the highlights, from the breakout in New England to the drop on the island, Cassidy and the journey here. He concluded with his plan to escape, which, to this point, meant uniting the anomalies and seeing what they could do together.

At the end of this, the Duchess stood, paced a long circle around Thane. Inspecting him. Thane followed, turning in place.

"Old, but hale," the Duchess said. "A fair characterization?"

"Strong and wise, I think."

"So wise you would walk in here alone? With no friends, no reinforcements outside my walls?"

"As I said, I'm not here to fight."

The Duchess kept up her pacing, her grass-cushioned sandals leaving bits and traces on the rocks as she moved. Her hands were at her sides, though Thane noticed the Duchess seemed to be holding, kneading something with her fingers. Grains falling to the ground.

"No, and you won't," the Duchess replied. "You will believe."

"What?" Thane said, but as he finished speaking, he began to understand.

The Duchess glowed. A faint white aura like an angel in old movies, and more than that, she didn't drop grains from her hands, but tiny sparkling stars. Her silver hair, which had been matted and tangled, now flowed free in long strands down below her waist.

Those clothes were no longer patches, but a seamless, glittering golden robe. If Thane felt artistic, he would have called it dawn's own color.

The Duchess kept moving around Thane, always talking, telling Thane all the things he would be believing from now on. That he would be safe now, with his protector, his queen.

That after so long a journey, and such hardship, Thane could finally rest. Thane heard those words, and his heart, for so long brittle and angry, melted. Peace found him, and Thane could want for nothing else.

Dog Walk

Returning home after nearly dying didn't feel right. Kat went down the steps from the mag-lev train towards her street, the metal grates wobbling as she went, though nobody else seemed to notice. The snow didn't squish to the side from her boots like it used to. Street lights reflected from everywhere, harsh and bright. Things had an edge, a twist to them. Like a dream, but sharper.

She couldn't get away from Beth, the Elementals. What they'd said and asked for. Work for them? Catch a killer who'd almost killed her? Kat wasn't supposed to be a hero. She wasn't supposed to be chasing evil on the streets.

Trackers were meant to hunt anomalies who'd jumped their responsibilities, who were dangerous, yes, but weren't killers. Confused, or just afraid, most Kat caught accepted their role in society once the Paragons provided it and moved on. A few fell back, tried to run, and paid for it with their lives.

None had shot people in the street. None had shot her.

And all of them, when caught, had given Kat a healthy

rep reward. For this, if Kat could trust Beth, she'd get her life. Higher stakes, higher payoff.

"You think that's going to happen?" Calvin said, sitting on her couch with Seeker in his lap. "I've always heard the Elementals were the bad guys. That's why I never wanted to join 'em, even when they offered."

"What's my choice?" Kat shot back, leaning against her desk. "I don't find this guy, either he kills me or Beth makes good on her threat and I fall over when captain tattoo over there makes me disappear."

"We could turn them in to the Paragons," Calvin said, then blinked. "Hell, I'm a Paragon. I could get some drones over."

"Thought about that," Kat said. "Still don't know how the tattoos work. He could kill me before they came close."

"Wait, what about this? We bring you to the hospital, get you all rigged up, then call in the cavalry. Right? Tattoo guy makes you explode, everyone's ready to help."

"See, the problem with this idea is that I would get hurt. Again."

Calvin shrugged. Kat glared. Seeker barked, and that's when Kat declared they were going for a walk. After so long in the Elemental's cramped basement, doing a lap around the nearby park would be good.

Late afternoon meant people were out and about, coming back from work or just taking the chill air for a spin. Clouds were moving in, but not so many to ruin the sunset, still so early. Pods trundled along the streets, and the occasional sign and storefront promised distractions, none powerful enough to push away their continual conversation.

As Seeker sniffed at everything he could, Kat and Calvin continued to hash through the options, but there were no good ones. Everything led to danger, but only one led to revenge.

"So you really want to go get this guy?" Calvin said. "Like, really want to chase down a dude who shot you point blank? Again?"

Kat did not. As was often the case, what she wanted was a hot chocolate and a movie. Or dinner out somewhere nice, for a change. Such things, though, seemed to be a perennial dream rather than a reality.

"You've had it hard, right?" Kat said.

"Is that a real question?"

"What I mean is, I didn't have it easy either." Kat pulled Seeker away from a compelling trash bin, and the big dog took the cue and bounded forward, pulling them along. "So, you might say I'm not well-adjusted."

"What does that even mean?" Calvin replied.

"I mean all these people here. This city. This world. It's like everyone accepts where they're at, and they just want to get home at the end of the day and be happy."

"So you're, what, not one of those?"

"No, I am, but I don't know how to be."

"Did getting shot mess with your head?"

They reached the park, a big square with leafless trees providing a skeletal canopy. A small playground, snow pushed to make a sort-of pit out of the slide, monkey bars, and swing set, claimed the center. Benches, some with people, some without, bordered cleared walks. Serene enough to make Kat twitch.

"Think getting shot messes with most people," Kat said. "What I mean is, I don't know how to be that way. I can't do it."

"Okay?"

"So when you're saying to call the Paragons. When

you're saying take the way that leaves me out of it, I don't know how to be that person."

"Kat, I ran for a long time. It works. You get used to avoiding conflict, and you know what? I might not have been happy, but I was alive."

"You lived in a scrapyard."

"Never said it was perfect."

Kat laughed and that felt good. Calvin laughed, and you know what, that felt good too. Sharing a moment with a friend. Damn. She needed to do that more often. Needed more friends.

"So you're going after him, is what you're saying," Calvin said.

"Yeah."

"Going to let me help?"

"Like you did so much last time?"

Calvin reached down, scooped up some snow. Most of it crumbled away in his hand—too cold to make a real snowball—but he tossed the remnants Kat's way. She ducked, and Seeker, noticing, darted back and barked. Calvin threw more snow at the dog, who leapt and caught the sprinkles.

From there, things descended into madness. The two of them tossing makeshift snow shards at each other, Seeker jumping in the middle. Others in the park watching with, so far as Kat could tell, smiles on their faces.

Kat managed to get a pretty good chunk in her left hand and tossed it, right at Calvin's chest. The anomaly caught it in his left hand, and the jagged chunk shrank, as though melting on a hot day. In Calvin's right, a perfect snowball formed. He tossed it towards Kat, and Seeker snatched it, crunching the ball to dust.

An anomaly. Kat had almost forgotten in the moment. Calvin was a Paragon, not some friend tossing snowballs in the park. Like her parents, he'd be sent away on missions, be tasked with jobs and be a part of something she could never join. And if he had kids, then one might—

"Hey, you want to head back?" Calvin said. "Don't know 'bout you, but it's getting dark and I'm getting cold."

"Order some takeout, try to figure out who this guy might be?"

"Not my ideal night, but I'll take it. If you're buying."

"For saving my life?" Kat said. "Oh wait, that wasn't you."

"I, uh, kept your dog company?"

The two managed to get Seeker away from the park and went back, a plan somewhat in hand. They'd find the shooter together. Stop the killings, then get the Elementals to release Kat from their binding. Simple enough.

Dark had taken hold by the time they made it back to Kat's building, though prolific streetlights kept things cozy. They'd decided on something hot and spicy, with Calvin holding Seeker's leash while Kat reached to brush her Tama against the building's entry scanner.

Seeker's yip came first, a panicked sound that had Kat turning back as the bullet whipped by her head and blasted a hole in the wooden door behind her. Kat didn't think, just dove forward down the steps, trying to get behind the trees along the street.

Calvin yelled something, dropped Seekers leash, and touched the sidewalk. As Kat scrambled down, another shot rang out, crashing into Calvin's makeshift concrete barrier, which grew out and around the two, and the barking Seeker, whom Kat snagged by the collar.

"I'm calling the drones," Kat said, huddling close and tapping the alert into her Tama.

As much as she wanted to catch the guy herself, doing

it in the dark, without her suit or any weapons, seemed like a bad idea.

No third shot came, and in thirty seconds, as drones appeared overhead and cast their lights around the surrounding buildings, no arrests came either.

Calvin waited till the drones issued an all-clear before letting his dome drop. Kat looked at the buildings around them, looming in the dark, each one a potential sniping point. The shooter, apparently, knew who she was, knew where she lived.

"We can't stay here," Kat said.

"Don't ask about my place, because I don't have one," Calvin replied. "I crashed with the Paragons, but they're a mess right now."

"No, no." Kat closed her eyes for a second. "I know where we can go."

"Don't like how you're saying that."

Gordon wouldn't like it either, but he'd get over it. Gordon always did.

23

The Underground

Aegis's death didn't faze the mall.

Zhan-Yo left the pod and stopped on the curb, awestruck at the shoppers careening in and out. Drone deliveries alone ought to have rendered this place an empty husk, but as stores adapted to create experiences rather than sales, people returned. Supposedly, believing that the Paragons, society's structure, were about to collapse would keep people at home. Instead, it seemed like the people's plan to keep things afloat was to spend, spend, spend.

Some walked by holding bags, others went with drone carts hovering behind them, walking to every-size pods to take their victories home. Zhan-Yo saw all those faces, unconcerned, wrapped or rosy in the cold. As though he hadn't done a single thing. Music, some insipid, wordless beat, played.

This, this was his revolution at work.

For now.

Zhan-Yo followed the lights inside, through the vacuum pressure doorway designed to force out cold air and keep the warmth where it ought to be. The slight pressure pushed against his face, but on the other side, he slipped off the nondescript overcoat Wexley had lent him and embraced the warmth.

Tiles in some unsolvable pattern splayed out in front of him, and the mall's two floors stretched up to a far away ceiling, from which hung artwork and sales signs. Things Zhan-Yo wouldn't have noticed before, except he hadn't expected all this to be here.

Zhan-Yo's disappointment built towards hope as he continued to see normal life continue. He'd been spending so many evenings concerned with how much destroying the Paragons would alter the world. If, though, society could press through such a big event like Aegis's death with so little change, then perhaps his own efforts would leave a recognizable civilization still standing. Zhan-Yo could take charge of a damaged, but functioning humanity.

That thought put some enthusiasm into his step as Zhan-Yo wandered to a store bearing the Ziran name and logo. Selling techno gear, from Tamas themselves to accessories and every home device known to man, the store too looked unchanged. Despite Ziran's former CEO declaring an end to modern life, the employees inside looked just as bored as they had before. The red and black colors just as splashy.

They did, though, notice as Zhan-Yo walked through the store towards the back. A sign noting restrooms, and declaring they were for employees only, marked the doorway. Zhan-Yo didn't stop.

"Can I help you?" one of the employees, Zhan-Yo thought the scatter-haired boy looked fifteen, said, walking Zhan-Yo's way with the nervous gait of someone unused to confronting adults.

"You cannot," Zhan-Yo replied, and kept walking.

"That's, uh, for employees?" the boy tried again.

"I'm allowed," Zhan-Yo said, then stopped his march to the back, and what lay beyond. "How many have come already?"

"What?"

"Back here. How many?"

The boy's face changed, and he even took a step back. "Some, I think. Wexley told us to let them go. Sorry, I didn't know?"

"You're doing fine. Nothing to be afraid of."

The boy stared, so Zhan-Yo turned back, blew past the employee's only entrance and, with his Tama, scanned through a locked door. Soft yellow lights guided his steps down the stairs to a simple lobby, occupied by a couple cheap chairs and not much else.

A single thick wooden door led further in, and Zhan-Yo hesitated before opening it. On the other side would be, for lack of a better word, his destiny. What power he had left hung by the thinnest thread, and even if Mathieu found the traitorous Paragons they needed, Zhan-Yo couldn't make a move without these people's support.

Zhan-Yo would need their reps, their men, their resources, and he would get them.

He pushed through without knocking, causing conversations to cease, and the half-dozen or so men and women in the room to freeze, looking his way with panicked glances that gradually settled into the frowns and glares Zhan-Yo expected.

"You made it," Wexley said, stepping over from the room's left side where he'd been sharing whiskies with a leader in the world's transportation business. "Wasn't sure if the pods would pick you up."

"I used your account." Zhan-Yo glazed his eyes over the guests, logging each who'd come and showing, outwardly at least, that he expected no less. "This is a good turn out."

"They wanted to make sure you know they're not happy."

Zhan-Yo smelled the whiskey on Wexley's breath, and noticed his lieutenant wasn't wearing the business attire normally stuck to him like glue. Instead, Wexley sported more active-wear tonight, as though he'd gone running before heading here. At least it matched the whole group's penchant for black.

"Welcome," Zhan-Yo opened. "Please, sit down. We have a lot to discuss, and I imagine most of you would rather be anywhere but here."

"You're right," said a woman, accented and representing some natural goods firm across the sea, in what had been Africa. "We're here because you don't seem to understand what we've been telling you over video."

Zhan-Yo knew all their names, but refused to dredge them up now. They were all one and the same in this moment, creatures to be controlled by any means necessary.

"You're upset because I started something you all believed in," Zhan-Yo said.

"We weren't ready!" Another man, on Zhan-Yo's right, said. "It wasn't the right time!"

"And when would that be? When would be the right time?"

The man threw up his hands. The others in the room looked at each other, their Tamas. Because, of course, there would never be a right time. Speak big words, and forget them when you had to back them up.

"I believe the right time is when you have a chance," Zhan-Yo said. He leaned forward in his chair, arms out, palms up. Supplicating, for now. "Aegis gave us an opening, so I took it. Whether that means anything now is up to you."

By the faces around the table, Zhan-Yo's words didn't mean much. Most were impassive, and a couple even looked sick. Like they were uncomfortable sitting in the same space as a killer. Zhan-Yo might have been the same a few years ago, but he'd moved on from denial.

Change required sacrifice, and these people didn't understand that. Yet.

"Wexley," Zhan-Yo said. "Can you lock the door?"

"I . . . can?" Wexley said, but he stood up and followed Zhan-Yo's instruction anyway, swiping his Tama against the black scanner alongside the door, whose light blinked from pleasant green to warning red.

Zhan-Yo again ran his eyes across his opponents, settling them in a dead-straight stare, "Before anyone leaves this room, you're going to commit to this course. I have a new plan, and it will require funds, and resources. You will support it."

"You can't force us," a man to the left said, pushing back his own chair. "You've lost your vision, Zhan-Yo. We didn't sign up for a bloodbath."

"And I didn't want one," Zhan-Yo said, standing up to meet the man, who stood taller, but not fitter, then him. Zhan-Yo trailed a hand, index finger raised, to forestall Wexley from coming to any defense. "Plans need to change to meet the circumstances. The objective remains the same, the methods differ."

Sizing up the man, Zhan-Yo could tell he came from privilege, and not the flash-in-the-pan kind that splurged on luxury brands for the name alone. The man's suit had understated quality, his Tama new but showing, with colored tags, modifications made by those who knew what they were doing. He could probably override Wexley's door lock if he wanted to.

Puffy eyes showed sleep escaped the man, likely due to overwork, and while he had softened around the edges, enough remained to fill out his clothes with a fitter history. That Zhan-Yo's approach struck no discernible fear in the man suggested experience with adversity.

All in all, an imposing individual, and while Zhan-Yo's perception had helped him in innumerable business meetings, finding the right words and desires to get a contract signed, here it only showed that what Zhan-Yo was about to do could end poorly.

With all Zhan-Yo had risked for this, though, what was one thing more?

"Sit down," Zhan-Yo said.

"I came for a discussion, not orders. I'm leaving."

"No, you're not. Not without accepting the new arrangement."

The man, shaking his head, took a long step around Zhan-Yo, heading towards Wexley and the door. Zhan-Yo let him go by, then, with the man's back turned, delivered a sharp kick to the man's left ankle. A solid leg, but Zhan-Yo hit it right and swept the ankle forward, causing the man to tumble backward.

Gasps and shouts, both swallowed and not, filled the room.

Zhan-Yo caught the man's large head before it hit the floor, then let it down gently, delivering a somber look to the man's wide eyes.

"This is not what I wanted," Zhan-Yo said, glancing back at the crowd. "However, I hope you see how serious I am. We are doing this, and you will help. There is no backing out now."

As Zhan-Yo finished, he saw a twitch beneath him, and the man he'd downed threw a wild punch from his knees towards Zhan-Yo's stomach. Zhan-Yo blocked the blow down, back-stepping and letting the man get up to his feet, that fancy suit marred from its encounter with the concrete floor.

"The Paragons are holding a summit," Zhan-Yo said, dodging back from another lumbering swing. "All the Champions will come."

The man stalked him around the table, everyone watching the dance. Wexley, getting out of the way, returned to his seat.

"Before that time, we must marshal our weapons, both physical and digital," Zhan-Yo continued, ducking another swing.

The man's face grew ever-redder as they continued around the table, sweat making its mark on his long forehead. He held his fists like a boxer, but one who only threw haymakers.

"When they gather, we'll strike," Zhan-Yo said. "Shut down their summit and prove that we deserve to have our place in their world. Every camera will be there, everyone will hear our words."

They passed by the door leading out and the man stole a look at it, his Tama ready to make that freedom swipe. Then he turned back, nodded at Zhan-Yo's legs.

"Big talk, for a coward," the man said. "You kicked me, now you want me to fight with you?"

"I'm not asking."

The man growled, no doubt very used to getting what he wanted and frustrated that wasn't happening here. He started forward again. Lurched—perhaps Zhan-Yo had done more than clip that ankle—into another big swing.

This time, Zhan-Yo stepped into, around it. Went right up to the man's face and, sliding his right leg behind the man's, pushed his opponent forward. This time, he didn't catch the fall.

With the man groaning on the ground, Zhan-Yo turned back to the rest of them, these hesitant leaders, so un-willing to risk what they had to put normals on par with the Paragons.

Before, when he'd delivered rousing speeches about a better future, Zhan-Yo had seen hope in those faces. Had read courage in their shoulders, their nodding heads. Now, Zhan-Yo saw fear.

He would use that too.

24

Traitors

As buildings went, the Paragons tended to choose the tallest, most imposing structure they could find in their cities. Even so, for Chicago, occupying the Willis Tower's top quadrant seemed excessive. But then, Mynx lived in a mountainside outside of LA, so what did she know about lording over the populace?

Near enough to dinner meant few Paragons occupied the offices, and those that did were either the young and fresh or the old and dedicated, standing or sitting in spaces and reviewing ongoing cases or digital city maps overlaid with drone alerts. Some spoke to those drones or people in them, orders and advice peppering through otherwise sterile space.

Every Paragon office had its own character. Chicago's celebrated local culture, the city's roots, both in the distant past and its more recent, Paragon-driven era. Pictures, real, physical ones, lined the walls with faces from the local ranks, either in portrait style or in-action, saving someone or something.

Funny how few of them Mynx knew, or even recognized. So many Paragons now, so many anomalies running loose under their name. Long ago, the Champions had welcomed every new recruit personally, had reviewed their abilities and placed them in their respective divisions with the same care someone might take with color in a painting. Now algorithms handled everything, and the regional leaders stepped in when required.

The Champions? Theoretically, they considered the larger problems. In reality, they fiddled with their passion projects and let the world glide on.

Her target, a conference room in the Paragon block's center, had a single, thick white door with a lit red line bordering the outside. Mynx glanced at herself, now wearing a classic Paragon blue uniform. Defiantly far from business formal, ready for action at any moment, the uniforms matched old comic book clinginess and, also, matched those outfit's seeming invincibility.

Killing a Paragon took a lot of work even without this thing. With it, whomever attacked Mynx would be lucky to survive, even with surprise on their side.

Which is why she didn't feel anything more than curiosity as she looked at the door, then pushed on through. Her Tama beeped a single chirp as she did, announcing its signal loss as Mynx passed the threshold and the door shut behind her.

Unlike the picture-laden walls beyond the room, slate gray dominated every surface in here. A long table, enough for a dozen, sat centered. A single, burly, red-haired and bearded man held position at its head, nodding to Mynx as she came in.

"Welcome, Champion," Innis, supposedly the last Paragon to see Aegis alive, said. "I'm glad you finally made time to come."

"Innis." Mynx took her own seat opposite the man, at

the table's other end. The distance between them was absurd, but Mynx felt no desire to close it. Innis seemed too composed, his smile too false and his eyes too hard. Mynx hadn't ever liked the man, and the formal greeting did nothing to thaw her attitude. "As you know, it hasn't been easy."

"Nah, it hasn't," Innis replied. "We're keeping it together well enough, though. You saw, it's normal out there."

"As I'd expect. But I'm not here about how you run your office. I want to know why you haven't found him yet."

"Who?"

Mynx narrowed her eyes. "Don't be dumb. I don't have time for it, and neither do you."

"He's slippery," Innis allowed. "Zhan-Yo has a lot of reps, a lot of powerful friends. I've got people looking for him day and night."

"Yes, you do. I checked into that. Seems like it's your most junior teams doing the hunting, and they're also the first ones pulled if a call comes in. My drones are the only things doing the real work."

"Aren't they going to be better at it?"

"If Zhan-Yo wanders into the open, perhaps," Mynx said. "You have anomalies that can see through walls, that can go inside people's minds and tear out their secrets. Why don't you use them?"

Innis leaned back, cocked his head, "Didn't think we were the kind of heroes that did those sorta things."

"Found killers?"

"Tortured innocent people."

Mynx started to reject the idea—what the anomalies could do wasn't painful, most who could dig through thoughts would mine secrets without the target even knowing what happened—but instead she took a deep breath and used the moment to study Innis's look, the little smug grin that'd taken home between his burning bristles.

"Why are you fighting me on this?" Mynx asked instead. "Do you even want to catch him?"

Innis swept his palms across the table, as if brushing imaginary crumbs to the floor, then brought everything together beneath his chin, mouth twitching.

"See, Mynx, that's just it." Innis's face went manic, and Mynx's stomach lurched. "I don't. Not one bit."

Innis stood up from the chair, pressed a button on his Tama, and the heavy door behind Mynx, the only way out of the conference room, locked with a loud click.

"You don't know what it was like living under Aegis's boot," Innis said, beginning a walk around the table towards Mynx. "He said something, you had to jump. He changed the rules, you had to change with them. And he didn't like me. I wasn't ever going to be a Champion. Wasn't going to escape."

Mynx heard the words, and divorced her emotions. Just as she might reprogram a frustrating routine, or deal with a day's annoying and necessary requirements, Mynx pushed away the dead, cold anger and considered the situation.

Innis had threat all over him. As traitors went, Innis would occupy a pretty high spot in the Paragon structure to go turncoat, but a betrayal like his wouldn't be unheard-of. With all their power, some anomalies thought they'd make better rulers than the Champions. Some tried to act on those thoughts.

They all failed.

"So now you're going to sit right there, and we'll get the rest of the Champions on the line," Innis said, walking slow now to give his own words time to spill out, as if learning his plan as he spoke it. "Then you'll tell them you're giving me Atlantis. Not Pixie. Then we'll all be good."

Innis passed the table's halfway mark. Closing in. Without a Tama signal, Mynx couldn't call for help. Reeves couldn't hear her. And, with the door locked, she couldn't scramble outside.

Fine.

Mynx, still sitting, cocked her left leg and kicked the chair to her left, sending it scooting into Innis while shooting her away from him. He grunted, tossed the chair to the side as Mynx stood up.

"Not happening," Mynx said. "Never will."

"So stubborn. Just like Aegis."

Innis rushed her, pushing around the table and running towards her with intent to tackle. The man had enough muscles, and Mynx had thin enough bones, that such an assault would leave her a broken ruin. So she ran, shoving her chair into Innis's path and getting around the table.

Now she stood opposite the door, opposite Innis.

"Did you ask Aegis to retire?" Mynx said. "How'd he take it?"

"About as well as you." Innis jumped on the table, the thing creaking under his weight. "The man wanted to keep punching until he dropped dead."

Another lumbering charge. This time, Mynx slid beneath the table as Innis ran by above. Crawling along the carpet didn't feel all that heroic, but it kept the man's mitts off her. Right now, that's what mattered.

She started to roll right, then switched back left as Innis, his legs visible as he dropped from the table, gave clues to his direction. Mynx pushed herself up as soon as she cleared the table, and managed a single step before Innis grabbed her right arm.

"Gotcha!" Innis shouted, pulled Mynx back.

Mynx used the momentum, used the years spent with Aegis, sparring on his insistence that a Champion could never depend on gadgets alone. Heroes, Aegis would say, needed to be ready to use their hands. Now Mynx used her left to pop Innis in the nose, palm-heel making a crunching connection that had Innis stumbling back, clutching his face.

Innis cursed, and Mynx ran for the door. She reached for the handle, hit the lock, and fell into it.

A blank white landscape stretched to infinity beneath a grey sky. Shifting numbers formed floating pillars gliding by overhead and around her, melding with the white plain here and there as they bobbed to an unseen, unfelt wind.

Time might not have meaning here, but it passed just the same outside. Mynx had to find the lock, and fast, before Innis realized what she was doing and knocked her out. Every lock had its own character, but they all shared some traits: one of these pillars would be the key.

But there were thousands, maybe millions, floating across all she could see. Impossible.

So rather than find the key, Mynx changed the lock. She stuck her hands down into the white floor—it felt like nothing—and purple-black spread from her touch, corrupting and changing the lock's code.

In little more than two seconds, Mynx warped the lock's standard Paragon program—one she'd designed—to a new one tied to Mynx's Tama. At its signal, and her Tama's alone, the door would open and shut.

As the final variable slid into place, the last of those number pillars disintegrating into virtual dust, the entire space blurred, like static coming over an antennae.

Innis had her.

With a blink, a hard shift, like standing up fast from a nap, Mynx whirled away from the lock's virtual 'verse and woke back in the sealed room. Just in time for Innis to throw her away from the door and onto the table.

"You know," Innis said, breathing hard, twin blood trails marring his face in their journey south from his nose. "I wanted to make a deal. Now I'm thinking it might be better to just kill you too."

Kill her *too*?

Interesting.

"You missed your chance." Mynx tapped her Tama, sent the signal to the lock.

The door obeyed, chimed bright and swung open. Outside, already waiting, perhaps drawn by the sounds from inside the room, were a half-dozen Paragons. Uniformed, ready to come to their Champion's aid.

Then Innis laughed. Waved out the door to the gathered Paragons.

"Come on in!" Innis barked. "Mynx doesn't see things our way, so come help me persuade her."

Relief died before it had a chance to grow. Mynx barely processed Innis's words, their implications, and what the sudden constriction around her chest meant for her survival. A Paragon stepped forward, reached out with his hand and closed it into a fist, crushing her further.

The man lifted his fist, and Mynx floated off the table. He pulled his arm back and she moved towards him, Innis nodding the entire time to her right.

"See, Mynx?" Innis said, following Mynx outside the room. "Kevin's beat you already. He's clearly better, so why's he stuck here when he should be running a region?"

Mynx would have replied, except Kevin's fist made it hard to breathe, to talk. Thought, though, ran freely.

At least a dozen traitors here. From the looks on their faces, too, these gullible goons no doubt thought Innis would lead them to power, if not glory. That they would achieve some sort of stature denied to them by working here. As if preserving civilization wasn't enough.

How many times had the Champions cleansed rot from the Paragon ranks? Apinya and Burov would make their world tours, peering into hearts and minds and destroying any who harbored seditious thoughts. Cleansings had sufficed to convince the Paragon ranks and the world at large that dissidence would not be tolerated.

But those sweeps ended years ago, when the Paragons became too large to monitor with individual examinations. Mynx proposed the drones instead, autonomous incorruptible bodies watching over the tempted and twisted. Her machines missed this mark. Every system had flaws, and it seemed like this one might kill her.

Kevin—looking somber, yet pleased with himself—guided his invisible fist to put Mynx in the Paragon crowd, which parted with the Champion in the middle. Blue uniforms surrounded her, grim faces split here and there with the half smile of someone finally about to get what they wanted.

"What do you think happens?" Mynx managed as she drew in her breath. "You kill me, you betray the Paragons? How long do you survive?"

There were hundreds in the Chicago area alone. Unless Innis had turned them all, this little group would find themselves destroyed within hours. Without a plan, this was nothing more than suicide.

"We didn't kill you," Innis said, stepping into the ring. "You died trying to find Zhan-Yo. We found you. So tragic."

Mynx rolled her eyes, but stayed on the ground. She didn't want to die quite yet.

"You believe him?" Mynx said to the others. "You think he'll be able to protect you?" Dots kept connecting, tracing back through Innis's other words. "He's betrayed everyone else, why not you?"

"What do we have to lose?" Kevin said, crouching and looking Mynx in the eye. "A lifetime stuck with this, or a moment reaching for our true potential? I know which I'd choose."

Aegis would have felt like he'd failed these Paragons. He would have bemoaned their morale, that they could have chosen a path like this. What this unfulfilled ambition meant for the Paragons as a whole.

Mynx just laughed.

"Finish her, Kevin," Innis said to the sound. "We gotta get on the clean-up."

"Do it, Kevin," Mynx said. "Fulfill your potential, or whatever nonsense you're telling yourself."

That, at least, drew a frown from the young Paragon. He stood straight though, reached out with that fist of his, and Mynx again felt the air shift, press in close.

Not the way she thought she'd go, but how many get to choose?

The air closed around her, lifted her up above the Paragon traitors, then began to press her into a ball. As her arms folded inside, her legs came up, Mynx looked over their heads and out the windows, one last glimpse of Chicago's glittering lights.

Only she saw none. Slate black outside every panel, as though blinds had been drawn.

"End it," Innis said.

Innis spoke the command, and those black windows burst into bright light. Milliseconds later, even as the Paragons started to shout, the rattle-crack of shattered glass mixing with assault fire filled the floor. Bullets, designed to pierce Paragon armor, swept through the ranks beneath Mynx, razing the traitors.

Kevin's fist dissipated along with Kevin himself, and Mynx dropped to the floor as the fire stopped. She landed right where she'd been, this time surrounded by torn bodies. Innis among them. Lifeless.

"I was worried you didn't have enough time," Mynx said as she went from body to body, confirming their ends.

"The secure room opened five minutes ago," Reeves replied, his voice coming through the Tama. "I only needed three."

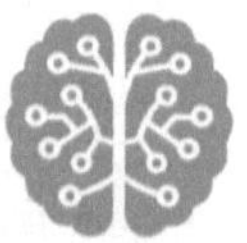

25

The Other Side of Desire

Thane lived in the space between dreams and waking. That reality sliver where he couldn't quite make himself move, where his cracked-open eyes saw black rocks blurring into memories. Incapacitated, yet understanding.

The vibrations, the ever-so-slightly cooler air, the changed breeze confirmed whomever carried him marched up a slope. Their step's clatter confirmed stone, the steadiness confirmed a well-worn path. Logic dictated where they were heading, and why.

The Duchess feared him.

As she should. From her position, leading a large anomaly group through her own ability, the Duchess ought to fear Thane, a creature that could, by purpose or accident, churn into a violent, thoughtless rage. Why keep a monster like that around? Why not kill him?

Ah, but killing Thane would not be so easy. Take a knife to him and Thane's skin would harden at its touch, his bones would turn to steel and then it would all be over.

So how, then, to remove this sudden, lethal inconvenience?

Thane jumped from that thought line. It didn't matter whether the Duchess had a way or not. The more interesting question was why she didn't want to get off the island, when, clearly, Thane represented the best possible way to do so. An invincible, rampaging monster like him could either destroy the drones or distract them long enough for the Duchess to make her escape.

The answer came over the same air as the breeze, but through sound. Thane counted two hand pairs carrying him, each connected to a mouth and each mouth whispering a prayer. Not to some old god or common religion, but to the Duchess.

Power's sweet nectar had her. Why abandon a devoted cult for the unpredictable other? The wide world had sent her here, and here she thrived, so here she wanted to stay.

Thane wanted what she did. The Duchess deserved everything, and by giving her everything, they would be happy. He would be happy. How funny that he could feel this way while knowing the Duchess would likely have him killed. But such is love, right? Holding someone above yourself, and Thane would hold the Duchess as high as he possibly could.

With his flimsy muscles and brittle bones, that might not be very far. All this placid worship had drained away Thane's strength to the point where his own heart pumped blood with feeble pulses, his lungs wheezed puffs in and out. If he stayed in this state too much longer, Thane would die even if the Duchess did nothing at all.

Which would not do.

The Duchess was having him carried up this rocky path for a reason, and if Thane expired before they reached the top, then she would be disappointed.

Thus, he needed to live. Thus, he needed to find some anger, some pain, some drive.

Thane tried to speak to the hands lifting his shoulders, the person holding Thane above their head. At first, a wheeze came out and vanished without much sound. Vocal cords shriveled and weak. He had to summon what energy he still had, dip the ladle into that shallow pool and scoop out what he could.

"Help me," Thane said, the words sounding like the wind.

"That him talking?" the voice beneath him spoke.

"I didn't hear anything," another voice, near Thane's legs, replied.

"Help me," Thane said again, this time scratching his throat with real tone.

Now the walking stopped. Thane felt a shuffle, felt the voices lower him to the ground, the front one telling the back that Thane was saying something. Definitely speaking to him now.

"You're telling me that wrinkled thing spoke to you?" the voice said. Thane's head rested on the rock, looking to the side. He didn't have the strength to turn his face to see who carried him. "Look's like he's dead."

"He said to help him. I swear."

The back voice laughed, "We're doin' that, aren't we? Who cares what he wants. We're almost there."

"I don't want him hurting me."

"How would that thing hurt you?"

Yes, Thane wondered, how could I hurt you? How could I hurt anybody?

"I don't know," said the front voice. "Duchess just said he was dangerous. I didn't think he'd wake up."

The Duchess said Thane was dangerous? The thought flooded him with sadness, the same as when Aegis had told Thane he no longer belonged among the Paragons, that someone as dangerous as Thane ought to be sealed away.

Kept where he couldn't hurt anyone. When Aegis had said that, Thane had wanted to destroy the little man, but now, if the Duchess said the same, perhaps Aegis had been right. Perhaps Thane ought to end.

"Do it," Thane wheezed. "Kill me."

The voices, still arguing, fell silent at Thane's words. Then Thane saw thick legs wander into his vision, tanned and ending in those same grass sandals worn by everyone on the island. The leg's owner squatted down, and Thane felt the man's breath on his face, hot and vile. Not much oral hygiene in a place like this.

"See?" the second voice, the one close by his face, said. "He wants it too." The second voice reached out, poked Thane in the shoulder. "He doesn't care what we do to him, he just wants it done. Like the Duchess said."

"I don't know."

The second voice moved away from Thane, went back towards Thane's legs. "You're so scared of this guy. He's just an old man. Watch."

Thane, feeble, brittle, felt the foot stomp down on his ankle, felt the bones snap. His atrophied nerves followed the sensation with the requisite pain, with shock, with paralyzing panic. The Duchess might want him dead, Thane could see that, but she would not want him, one of her devoted subjects, to suffer. No, that would not make sense. That would follow no plan.

She did not want pain.

They were traitors, these terrible voices. They had hurt him, for no reason. Just to be mean. Needlessly cruel.

The flame, once sparked, burned bright through Thane's fogged mind, at first clearing and then consuming him. As it did, those same muscles, with little more strength than a thread, grew like that same fire, expanding, healing, and boiling into furious energy.

"What the—" The words came from the first guard, and they ended in a cursing, increasingly high-pitched stream as Thane picked himself from the ground, growling like a trapped animal.

The Duchess had demanded obedience, worship, subservience. Such things meant nothing now. Such concepts lay beyond Thane's reach. The two guards did not. Thane pounded them to the beat of his heart on the mountainside, thick and red.

Crisp air invaded his nose, the breeze masking the aftermath of Thane's destruction. The island lay spread beneath his eyes, verdant palms and ferns mixing with grassy plains. Except for one place, not too far below, where fires burned and sent their smoky tendrils towards him, rich with cooking food.

Thane had not eaten for hours upon hours, and his stomach burned for the fish, the boar, whatever lay down there. He looked to the two bodies he'd just smashed, but they were too pulverized to eat. He would need fresher things.

Thicker things.

Running down the mountainside, bounding along the rock, roaring into the wind, Thane barreled towards the smells. Towards the food. As he neared, little people began to appear, to shout and run from him. Some manifested strange things, conjured lightning from the air or made the surface Thane ran on slick. Burning scratches racked his throat while sudden, blasting concussions hammered his ears. He roared through it all, kept pressing on to the flimsy walls and then through, into the town itself.

Which, seemingly, was no longer there. Instead, Thane stood in a great blue plain, with silver-clad, translucent spirits floating all around him. Mirrored copies of himself, they gestured as Thane turned, roared when he roared.

But they did not smell like he could smell. Could not taste the fear as Thane could. So when he caught the scent, whirled and dove, the blue grass and ghostly spirits disappeared, revealing the town and a smaller, shouting man in his grasp. An easy snack.

"Stop!" A command, not a cry for help.

Thane tossed the anomaly aside, bouncing him off a building and to the ground. He turned towards the person now repeating her order. She stood righteous and great, a glow wrapped around her, brilliance personified. Thane squinted as she ordered him to stop for a third time. He should listen to her, his mind whispered, and in that whisper began to sap the strength from his bones.

He should listen, and obey.

But Thane was so, so hungry.

She ordered him to sit down, and that Thane could not do. Would not do. She had come closer now. Three meters away. Far too close, and he was so hungry.

The monster didn't hear what else she had to say.

HIS RAGE LEFT Thane alone in Avalon's center, skin stained by his efforts. Not a soul remained, though the fires still burned. Rags clustered around him, torn like everything else. Ruined like everything else. The Duchess had taken him, and now he had destroyed her. Fragments played back as his fire dwindled: the carry up the mountain, the charge into the village.

If he hadn't given in to his anger, then Thane would be dead. Better her than him, right?

"Thane?" Cassidy called from the town's edge, flanked by those walls. "Are you . . . back?"

Thane stood, wiped the remnants off his hands, "I could use a wash."

The Duchess's surviving anomalies had decided switching loyalties to the Void made sense, so as they fled Thane's rampage, they found Cassidy beyond the walls and formed up with her. Most were still in a daze, owing to years spent under the Duchess's spell, and Thane saw tears coursing down many cheeks as they wandered back into their old home. They had lost their leader, their beacon. Thane himself even felt the loss, a sore wound in his heart, despite only being in her thrall for a day.

"How many do you think will come?" Thane asked Cassidy, eating some actual food after a long time spent rinsing himself off in a nearby stream.

"Come where? Are you still stuck on this stupid dream?"

"Stupid? I think it's the only dream. There are some powerful anomalies here. If we focus, we can—"

"Not without Arthur." Cassidy bit into the orange, licked its juice from her own chin. "I'm not going to throw these people out there into those drones unless we have everyone on this island working together."

"He'll see me coming now," Thane replied. "I won't be able to pull something like this again."

"Thane, that's a good thing. You're terrifying."

He wanted to laugh at that, but Cassidy was right. Thane was terrifying. But he also did what had to be done, and what was next required help. Required, dare he say it, friends.

"Why did you come back?" Thane said. "Here, after I finished? Why you?"

"Sook refused. Said you'd tried to eat him before." Cassidy shook her head. "I guess I didn't want to run knowing you might keep on going and tear up this whole island."

"So you had a plan."

"If you were still the crazy, snarling, monster you? Yes, I had a plan. I would have collapsed a hole in your heart, and in your head."

She took another bite from the orange, looked away towards the sky and the island birds flitting through the cloudless air.

26

Downtown

The glass fell like bullets, cutting into walkers beneath the Paragon tower as Kat, Calvin and Seeker rode by in their pod. At first she didn't understand why people were screaming, why shards exploded in a dire rain across the concrete, but as others pointed up, way up, Kat began to understand.

They stopped the pod and joined the crowd, staring at Chicago's law and order symbolized. Drones hovered around the tower's higher floors, more drones than Kat had ever seen in one spot before, illuminated by lights from below like alien starships. For a second, Kat wondered if the drones had betrayed the Paragons, if the same group that'd killed Aegis had somehow managed to turn society's protective machines against them.

Society wouldn't last long in that event.

"Don't know how to feel about that," Calvin said as the first emergency pods zoomed into the area, electronic orders pushing Kat and Calvin's original ride along. "I'm, like, a Paragon now, but I spent so long running from them . . ."

"Think you can feel bad for them." Kat pointed to the people on the ground. "And for us."

"For us?"

"The Paragons might not be the best all the time, but they keep most of the anomalies in check." Kat glanced at her Tama, no immediate messages. No emergency broadcasts. So either the Paragons had it under control, or they had no control. "Without them, this would happen all the time."

"So you think all us anomalies are crazy."

"Maybe." Kat nodded down the block, towards their target hotel. "C'mon, let's get going before anything else happens."

"I'm not going to forget what you said."

"Don't care, Calvin."

Their destination evoked past luxury left to dwindle over time, to the point where its gold lettering and overhang above the revolving door seemed a self-parody. A real, live doorman stood outside and waved them through. Kat had to pull Calvin in—he'd never gone through one of the doors before.

They marched through a lobby crowded with people browsing their Tamas, some stammering through what a Paragon attack might mean for their meetings, their vacation, or their dinner reservations.

Kat had been inside places like this before, old money bastions, but generally to chase down targets. Anomalies who dodged Paragon assignment came in all types and flavors. Not all were runaways like Calvin, hiding in junkyards and waiting for the end.

Still, the chandeliers, tile—some chipped—and the grand staircase to a literal mezzanine was not Kat's thing. Wasn't Gordon's either, so far as Kat knew, so why had he chosen to stay here?

Seeker drew looks as they went along, and Kat saw no other pets, but confidence ruled here. She knew what she was doing and everyone else seemed to agree. Just as likely, the hotel contracted with some anomalies to provide cleaning services. Dog hair, smells, didn't present much difficulty if someone could wave their hand and make it all disappear.

The elevators creaked their way up to the twentieth floor, and after winding through a faded green hallway with tarnished gold lights, Kat knocked on Gordon's door. Calvin stood off to the side, in sight but very much an accessory. Better, Kat had said, to keep the anomaly in the periphery.

"You look better than before," Kat said when Gordon opened the door, in a white shirt and pajama pants.

Gordon held deep circles beneath his eyes, and his skin had that waxy pale hue that comes from too much time indoors, in bed. Water dripped from his hair, proving Gordon had at least tried to clean himself up before Kat and Calvin arrived. Kat hadn't expected that, had expected a surly greeting and a mess beyond.

"Thanks," Gordon replied, standing aside and ushering them in, with a nod at Calvin. "I'd say I'm working on it, but I'm really just lying here."

"That's what you're supposed to do."

"They don't warn you how boring it is."

Gordon's room held the traditional hotel trappings; bland, comforting paintings scattered along off-white walls, a desk and a dresser with a widescreen on top. A queen bed nestled into the tiny room, with a dark wood nightstand filling the distance between mattress and wall. A closet-like bathroom sat on the right. A single cushioned chair occupied the corner next to the desk, looking like it hadn't been used in decades.

Seeker burst by them all to jump on the bed, prompting a laugh. Calvin slipped into the bathroom, shutting the door and leaving Kat and Gordon standing alone in the tight space. She took the chair, and Gordon sat next to Seeker on the bed, petting the husky, who gave him a couple big licks in exchange.

"Missed those," Gordon said. "I'm glad Calvin didn't hurt you like he did me."

"He tried," Kat said, then screwed up her face. Bad call. She needed Gordon to accept, if not like, the new anomaly. "Not really, though. Calvin pulled back."

"Mmhmm."

"Seeker still likes you."

"Seeing that. You haven't turned him against me?" Gordon cupped the dog's face with his hands. "Your mommy and I don't always get along, but I'll always love you."

Seeker delivered another slobbery slap.

"I was actually hoping you'd keep him for a while." Kat looked towards the window as she finished, into the office building across the street. Lights played checkers through the glass, people working late. Like her. "We're in the middle of something, and I don't want Seeker getting hurt."

Gordon looked towards the bathroom, "The middle of something? Did you go talk to Delano about the Elementals?"

Kat relayed the events, and by the end, Calvin had left the bathroom and joined them, leaning against the wall and looking at his Tama. Gordon's eyes flicked between them as Kat spoke, those circles getting darker as his brow furrowed deeper and deeper.

"So you're saying someone's trying to kill you, maybe

the Elementals too, and I'm supposed to watch your dog? That's what you want?"

"Gordon, you can barely walk. I'm not dragging you into a fight with this guy."

"A guy that almost killed you. Twice."

"We're getting better," Calvin interjected. "We know how he works. Rooftops, long guns. We can trap him."

Gordon laid back on the bed, completing the motion with an exaggerated groan, "If I know Kat, nothing I say will get her to change her mind, and while I don't know you, Calvin, you seem the same way. So if you know what you want to do, why are you here? Just for Seeker?"

"We need a safe space," Kat replied. "It's getting late, we're tired, and of the places I could go, I don't think the killer would know about you."

"What about the Paragon over there? Can't he get you inside their tower?"

"Tower's not real safe at the moment," Calvin muttered.

That led to a whole other review, replete with Gordon turning on the screen so they could get the news's full video version. The current spin had the event labeled as an anomaly accident, a test gone wrong. That didn't exactly square with a whole drone force deciding, as one, to light up a floor with lethal bullets, but nobody pushed the Paragons, so the reporter delivered the statement with a straight face.

"All right," Gordon said when the clip had finished. "So you want to crash here, then go out in the morning after this guy?"

"That's the idea," Kat said. "Would you mind?"

"Would I mind having the anomaly that made me like this, sleep in my room?"

"Self-defense," Calvin said.

"Quiet." Kat held up her hand to the anomaly. "You didn't seem all that angry when he showed up here with me."

"Changed my mind."

Gordon stood, a shaky move, but a successful one. Kat rose to meet him, and now they all filled the tight gap between bed, desk, and the hotel room's exit.

"Ah, look at this guy," Calvin said, stepping through Kat's cautionary hand to get right up to Gordon's face. "Getting all cocky after I smacked you down? Need me to do it again? Because I will."

"Tricks, that's all you had," Gordon replied, looking up at Calvin's face, fists clenched, mouth tight. "We go again, you won't win."

Calvin moved quick, reached out and gave Gordon a light shove. The tracker might have been able to catch himself if he'd been healthy, ready. Now, his legs hit the bed and Gordon fell back onto it. A hard thump on the firm mattress.

"Calvin, take a walk," Kat said, even as Gordon tried to stand. "You're both acting like morons."

"If he's going to call me out, he'd better back it up," Calvin said, but he did as Kat asked, and slipped out.

"Good," Gordon muttered, sitting up. "He's trouble, anyway."

"You're trouble, and stupid on top. Calvin's on our side. We need his help."

"Do we? Since when have we needed an anomaly? It's not like he knows how to hunt someone down."

"He saved my life, Gordon."

"He nearly took mine."

Kat opened and shut her mouth. Looked towards Seeker, who hadn't left the bed, who provided zero answers. Maybe she had been playing this fast. She'd beaten Calvin, so it wasn't much to her to give the anomaly another chance. Gordon, though, had been bruised in more ways than physical.

"I shouldn't have brought him here," Kat said. "I didn't realize how much he hurt you."

Gordon flipped a hand, "It's vanity, Kat, I know that much. I'm not as stupid as I look, but yeah, Calvin's not exactly my best friend."

And there was the Gordon conundrum. One minute he'd be a hot-headed jerk, pissing off everyone and demanding that he be treated like the coolest kid on some block, and the next he'd be staring at the carpet and Kat would feel sorry for him.

Would, if this whole mess didn't involve her getting shot.

"I'm going to need you to grow up, Gordon," Kat said. "Calvin too. Both of you. Right now, you can't back me up, so unless you want me wandering into gunsights alone, you'd better help get him back on my side."

Gordon nodded, still not looking at her, "Sure, yeah. I get it. But when I'm back, ready, he's gone."

"Whatever it takes to get me through tonight," Kat said, standing up. "Now be nice."

She went to the room's door, Gordon flopping back on the bed like a petulant kid finally giving in to the inevitable. Kat pressed down on the handle, opened the door into the hallway, starting to say that Calvin could come in.

Except the anomaly wasn't there.

Confront The Killer

Few things could lift Zhan-Yo's spirits like aggressive, successful negotiations. He had the physical adrenaline from slapping the idiotic man around the room, and the mental rush from everyone else giving in to his asks.

They'd agree to go full force if Zhan-Yo could pull off the summit stint.

More importantly, Zhan-Yo and Wexley had recorded all their answers. If this group pulled the cold-feet act again, the recording ought to act as some very compelling blackmail. One way or another, the world's major companies, all pre-Paragon relics, would come together to fight for their freedom.

The pod coasted along crowded, snowy streets, and for once Zhan-Yo delighted in looking out at the huddled crowds as they slipped into shops, restaurants, or other pods. With the holidays over, simply walking to revel in the nighttime cold didn't seem smart, but plenty in Chicago still braved a trip. Left their homes to join their community, their city.

These were Zhan-Yo's people. Citizens, living their

lives in hopes that each day would be a little bit better than the last. Zhan-Yo had brought them one big stride closer to that truth with Aegis, and now he would carry them across the finish line at the summit.

The pod beeped and Zhan-Yo glanced at the display hovering against the glass enclosure, right in front. Where before a faded blue line showed the pod's intended path, with an address appearing when Zhan-Yo looked, a city map appeared, showing a new destination.

One Zhan-Yo hadn't chosen.

Zhan-Yo reached for the pod's doors and tugged at the handle, which didn't respond. He touched the emergency release button, a red circle down by his shin, and that did nothing either. The inaction did, however, confirm that this wasn't a simple rerouting.

Only Paragons or their drones could restrict a pod like this.

The vehicle, though, didn't come to a halt so anomalies could pour from the alleyways around and arrest Zhan-Yo, neither did the pod pronounce some message warning him to stand down. Instead, it ground across the slush and merged with other traffic heading south, away from downtown.

Captive, Zhan-Yo took a look at the new destination, expecting an existing prison, a Paragon outpost, or maybe some forgotten dockyard where Zhan-Yo could be murdered and dumped into Lake Michigan. Instead, the pod planned to take Zhan-Yo to an old supermarket in an industrial neighborhood that'd be very quiet at this hour.

Why would the Paragons bring him there? Why not stage a flashy arrest?

Zhan-Yo couldn't read minds, but he could prepare for what might come. He pulled up his Tama and dashed a quick message to Wexley with the new coordinates.

Another oddity there: Zhan-Yo assumed any Paragon ambush would come with signal blocks, a freeze on his devices to prevent precisely this from happening.

Which meant Zhan-Yo wasn't dealing with Paragons, or even professionals.

Fascinating.

THE DESTINATION FULFILLED ITS PROMISE: a dark, fence-lined pit amid a quiet neighborhood undergoing much of the same change Zhan-Yo had seen spread outward from the city during the Paragon years. Whole economic sectors overturned as the Champions decided, based on their momentary whims, what would be legal and not, what would be tolerated and not. Beyond those top-down forces, anomalies alone wrecked the hierarchy; a single efficient anomaly could replace hundreds or thousands in factories and offices.

As a result, places like this lost their purpose. No need for supermarkets or stores on every block when you could get a drone to deliver anything for you. So unless you craved the exploration, or could get to the stores Zhan-Yo saw downtown, the ones conquering ennui with experience, why leave home?

And so these neighborhoods sat quiet in the cold, their families passing every day and night afloat on a thin rep cushion, provided for and depending on the Paragons.

Not for much longer. Zhan-Yo would bring purpose back into their lives. Soon.

The knock came from his right, and the pod reacted the way pods tended to when authority came calling: its doors opened up and the interior light, a bulge built into the pod ceiling's center, lit up a soft green. An appropriate color, as Zhan-Yo didn't have any visible weapons. He'd left his swords back in Wexley's apartment, where they wouldn't draw eyes. Or blood.

Two Paragons—so Zhan-Yo had guessed wrong—waited for him outside the pod, standing and, it seemed, shivering in the cold. Both had the stock blue uniforms on, and both looked like young men, arms folded and twitchy stares giving clues.

"You're Zhan-Yo, right?" the scrawnier one, with shock-white hair and a large black mole on his right cheek, said. "The guy that killed Aegis?"

"The guy that killed Aegis?" Zhan-Yo replied, slow. "I haven't heard that one yet, but I suppose it's true."

The other Paragon pointed at the ground, as if Zhan-Yo was a child, "Then get down. Hug the asphalt."

Zhan-Yo raised his eyebrows, looked at the black, slush-and-mud covered small parking lot where the pod had dropped him, "No, I don't think I will."

"Do what he says," Shock-white said. "Or else."

"Or else? You're a little young to be threatening someone like me. As you said, I killed your Champion."

"That's why we're here," said the other, and Zhan-Yo chose to mark him by the black stubble over his dark chin. "You killed Aegis. We want revenge."

"Then you'd better take it."

Playing with the executive had been one thing, a demonstration for the crowd. Zhan-Yo, though, hadn't had a real fight since tussling with Aegis in Chicago's undercity. He'd been running too much, talking too much.

Zhan-Yo exorcised those demons by rushing towards Stubble and, just as Stubble recoiled, pushing off his right foot and launching towards Shockwhite. The Paragon didn't see the move coming, because, like so many anomalies, they forgot about combat basics and relied on their powers. Shockwhite saw Zhan-Yo turn towards him, threw up his hands in a panic, and let a man three times his age sweep him up and slam him down into the asphalt.

Zhan-Yo didn't stay still, but pushed off the downed Paragon and kept running. Behind him, Stubble finally pulled himself together enough to unleash . . . something. Zhan-Yo saw lines, like green snowflakes, burst out around him before dissolving into smoke. He tried to dance around the tiny clouds, circling back towards Stubble, but couldn't dodge them all.

The clouds burned, caught his clothes and seared into them, leaving black, somewhat beautiful, outlines. Zhan-Yo felt an acid flake on his cheek, knew it would leave a red, or worse, mark. The cold air, though, tempered the burn and gave the pain an iced edge.

Stubble couldn't quite pull off Zhan-Yo's attack, and as the older man closed in, the acid flakes disappeared and Stubble turned to run. The kid took a step, forgot he stood on an ice patch, and bit it into the ground. Zhan-Yo caught him an instant later, planting his foot on the Paragon's back and putting a hand around the young man's throat, keeping Stubble pinned.

"Don't hurt him!" Shockwhite, more than a little pained, called from behind. "Or I'll kill you!"

"One twitch and I snap his neck," Zhan-Yo said, turning his head to look back at the standing Paragon. The words weren't really true—Zhan-Yo didn't have the grip here to deliver a mortal twist—but he bet Shockwhite wouldn't know that. "Why don't we start again, with you telling me how you found my pod, and why you're taking me out here, where nobody can help you?"

Shockwhite looked past Zhan-Yo to his friend, who must have done something, because all the bravado, all the confidence, or what was left of it, drained out of Shock-white and left him sitting on a slush pile next to the dormant pod. The Paragon ran his hands through his hair, marring it with mud, but he didn't seem to notice.

"You weren't supposed to fight back," Shockwhite said. "Everyone's seen the videos. It took like a dozen of you to get Aegis. He had you before you tricked him."

"Life doesn't always work out as you planned," Zhan-Yo replied. "Answer the questions, please."

"We're dumb. Does that work?"

"That's obvious, but not an answer."

"Tell him, man, so he'll get off me!" Stubble said from beneath Zhan-Yo, the words coming out scratched and tight from the ground squeezing the Paragon's chin.

"We worked for Innis!" Shockwhite said. "A lot of us here did. He kept saying we were going to get promoted soon. Have real stuff to do besides, like, patrols. When Aegis died, we were all sad, then Innis was like who's going to get the next big time gig? And who's gonna benefit?"

"You?"

"That's what we thought. Innis even had us feeding info to this woman. We'd send messages about Paragon plans, and he'd tell us this was the way forward," Shockwhite replied. "Then things started getting worse. Innis didn't get picked to be the next Champion." Shockwhite breathed, looked at the P on his uniform as if he expected it to peel off and fall to the ground. "Then this guy reaches out, says he knew what we used to do, tells us to get in touch with you. Now Mynx showed up, and we were out on patrol, but it's all over the news."

The fight at the Paragon tower. Zhan-Yo had caught word of it on his Tama. Some sort of drone attack and an explosion. News wrote it off as a test gone wrong, but this seemed far more interesting. Mathieu had found the Paragon insiders, though whether they would stay that way much longer seemed in doubt.

"Innis is dead," Shockwhite concluded.

That the whimpering Paragon traitor had died left Zhan-Yo feeling nothing, really. Innis had been Sylvie's mark, a man coated in mindless ambition's rotten smell. Zhan-Yo had let him leave the undercity after the fight hoping Innis would continue to infect the Paragons, and it seemed he had.

"So now you're caught out and alone," Zhan-Yo said, still holding Stubbles down. "Mynx might kill you if she ever finds out where you placed your allegiance, so you want to buy her goodwill with my body."

Shockwhite stared at the ground, gave a slight nod.

Tools came in many forms. Zhan-Yo's tachi, back in Wexley's apartment, served a physical purpose. People, though, could solve bigger problems, provided you fit the right person to the job. These two hapless anomalies might not be the best of the bunch, or even average, but plug them into the right problem, and they might work.

"Here's what you're going to do," Zhan-Yo said. "You're going to go back, tell nobody about your relationship with Innis, and work for me instead."

"What? Why?" Shockwhite said. Stubble tried to protest too, but Zhan-Yo pressed his face harder into the asphalt to stop it. "That's not going to get us on Mynx's side."

"Mynx won't be in charge that much longer. And she's going to be too busy to care about you two. Besides, I don't think you're in a position to disagree."

Shockwhite didn't fight those facts, and relented to reality. Zhan-Yo laid out the task, a simple one: find out where the summit would be, how it would be protected, and, if possible, get themselves there to help when the time came. Do that, Zhan-Yo said, and they would find themselves in high places when the revolution came.

"How will you know we're doing what you say?" Shockwhite asked when Zhan-Yo finished. "Maybe we'll just turn and kill you as soon as you let Marcus up?"

"Maybe you will, but I have friends, and my Tama's been recording this whole conversation. They'll get the message, and you won't live much past that." Zhan-Yo knew how to deliver a steel-eyed edict when he needed to. "You've dug yourselves in deep, little Paragons, and I'm the only one offering you a way out. Best take it."

Suitably threatened, Marcus a.k.a. Stubble and Xander a.k.a. Shockwhite confirmed their names, said they'd take the chance Zhan-Yo offered. They didn't sound thrilled, didn't look happy, but revolutions required prices to be paid by many, and these two uniformed anomalies could afford the cost. Would afford the cost.

Back in the pod, Zhan-Yo coasted the streets heading towards Wexley's apartment, reveling in the adrenaline, in the action. This was what Sylvie had been doing all these years, making deals in the dark, bending people to her will with threats and promises. Zhan-Yo understood, now, why she enjoyed it, why she kept at it despite the danger.

This was a powerful drug, and he wanted more.

28

Body Work

Carnage didn't happen these days. Wasn't supposed to, at least. The Paragons, the drones, all existed to ensure mass slaughter, for any reason, ended. The good guys were supposed to root out the problems and fix them before they could, like cancer, metastasize.

Mynx stood in the impossible, watching as Paragons from lower floors, ones still loyal to the Champions, to the cause, dragged their former friend's bodies to waiting drones. The bodies would be taken far away, cleaned up and returned at a slow pace for funerals, excuses developed for their deaths. Nobody would know what really happened here and these Paragons, in time, would realize it was healthier to forget.

You learned to do that in this life.

Disgust roiled with icy shock in her gut, refusing to dissipate even with danger's end. Because this wasn't about the danger, wasn't about Innis and his flunkies trying to do her in. So many people and worse things had tried to do that during her decades in the open. The traitors, though, stuck with her.

Innis going against the Paragons itself wouldn't be unheard of—anomalies often had great power, though Innis himself hadn't been all that strong—ambition always burned with anomalies at the top. Worse, and stranger, was the body count around her.

How had Innis, by no means the most silk-tongued person around, convinced this many Paragons to go along with his scheme? What had he been able to say to convince them that their efforts would be rewarded? After Mynx had chosen Pixie to be Atlantis's new Champion, Innis and his followers had to have known there would be no chance.

"Perhaps you should get cleaned up?" Reeves said, the message displaying silent on her Tama. "Cameras will be waiting, and a Champion covered in blood, according to data I've been analyzing, does not play well."

Mynx ignored the message, directed some of the loyal Paragons towards a newly arriving transport drone. Little moment-by-moment orders served to build back her sanity, restore some standards to her life. Perhaps getting the blood and worse off her uniform would be the next best thing.

"No cameras up here," Mynx announced to the floor. "If anyone asks, tell them I'll be on the ground level before too long to take questions about the accident."

She put weight on that last word, enough so that everyone understood. This was an accident, an unintended fallout from poor choices. That's how it would be explained, and that's what these bodies represented.

Terrible accidents.

As Mynx went towards the restrooms and a wash, she saw Innis himself, still splayed out near the door to his central conference room. It looked like the man had been making a break inside and had taken rounds to his back. A traitor and a coward.

But one with a Tama. There, on his left wrist. Splattered and battered, yes, but likely still functional.

"What are you doing?" Reeves asked as Mynx changed direction, as she knelt over Innis. "I don't think you want to take his clothes."

"Dima, watch me," Mynx said to a nearby, younger Paragon who looked stunned, but somewhat coherent. "It's going to look like I'm sleeping, but don't touch me, and keep everyone else away."

Dima came over, confused, "For how long?"

"As long as I need."

Mynx looked at Innis's Tama, reached towards it, and fell inside.

Barrels, barrels stacked as high as Mynx could see, including over her head and at impossible angles. Not the big, movie-style ones either, but refined casks meant to store whiskeys and wines. Her feet, too, stood on more barrels, balanced between two. Their stacks appeared to form walls, breaking and leading into different paths as Mynx took in the space.

Innis had a unique digital makeup, but then, so did everyone. Mynx wasn't quite sure how her ability formed the world—she could mold it herself into something completely different with time—but Mynx suspected the barrels had something to do with Innis's interests. In other words, looked like Innis was a bit of a drunk.

A closer look revealed the barrels were more than just decorations. Each one had a label, branded on in black-purple marks, declaring the barrel's contents. Here and there were messages between Innis and various people. The stack to her right contained all of his recent purchases, and the barrels Mynx stood on held Innis's various videos.

None seemed secure, and to test, Mynx reached down

towards one marked with a decade-old date, labeled 'Birthday'. She touched the barrel's face, not feeling the wood in this digital world, and no password came up, no encryption fought her inspection, and the face faded away.

The video began to play, forming a virtual square in the air, right at Mynx's eye level. Innis running around with several small children, acting like the big galumphing man Mynx had always thought he was. Behind him, cooking against a blue sky summer's day, were other adults. One kept yelling at the children to catch their uncle, and the collection finally did, Innis feigning a fall to the soft grass and succumbing to a tackling cascade.

Mynx wiped the video away. So Innis had a family. Aegis had one too, as did all these other Paragons who followed Innis into the abyss. Mynx would give their deaths the anonymity they didn't deserve. Buried as Paragons, their families would be cared for. Those children would never know their uncle's stain.

Though maybe they should. You had to get creative with people to keep their loyalty. A drone never required persuasion, didn't need career advancement as a carrot. If normal Paragon service wasn't enough to compel anomalies any more, maybe a little raw example would work better.

A dilemma for another time.

Mynx walked through the stacks, stalking across the barrels and reading their labels, looking for something useful. She didn't care about the correspondence, didn't care about the family heirlooms, or the large stack apparently devoted to Innis's heretofore unknown shoe obsession; the Paragon had hundreds of the things, in all shapes and sizes, photographed and laid out on forums for the admiration of virtual strangers.

Eventually, Mynx looked back up to the ceiling. She

focused and grew taller, or pulled the ceiling closer. Either concept worked in this world, and the end result let her read the labels that'd been too far away at first.

"Innis, perhaps I gave you too little credit," Mynx said, thought, whatever. No sound here to carry the words, but her digital mouth moved anyway. "Keep your secrets in plain sight, and maybe nobody sees them."

The barrels forming the ceiling lay well back in the nested files making up Innis's Tama. Deep down in the system's folders, but lacking any protective barriers, she'd overlooked their relevance. Clever, but only viable if you don't give an interloper time. And with Innis dead, Mynx had plenty.

These barrels held digital conversations too, but with more besides. Tracking signatures, address lists, names and Tama identifiers. All labeled with odd codes. Mynx opened a couple, and read their contents, but the actual values were nonsense.

Here was the real encryption. Make the files hard to notice, and then fill up a thousand of them with dummy data. If you didn't know exactly what you were looking for, you could sift through Innis's maze for days and never know if what you found was real.

Mynx, though, knew what she wanted. She placed her hand, palm spread against the ceiling. A light blue film spread out from her fingertips, running at increasing speed until it covered every hanging barrel. The blue flashed once to signal the search had captured every single object, and then Mynx put her function to work.

First, she isolated on obvious targets: Aegis, Ziran, Zhan-Yo, and keywords like Chicago's lower level. She also added herself, just for kicks. Each command zipped from her head down through her arms, to her fingertips and into the function.

The search began its work, and as the terms mined their way through the barrels, the targets began to disappear as Mynx filtered them away. The ceiling faded in whole sections as irrelevant barrels vanished. Others, which the blue film highlighted in a neon green, shuffled through their dissipating brethren, forming a neat box above Mynx.

Time didn't stop inside the digital world, but without references like the sun or a watch, Mynx couldn't track it, so she couldn't be sure how long her search took, how long she'd been inside Innis's barrel maze, but when the function finished, she had six targets above her.

With fast-acting swipes, Mynx scanned their contents. Found what she suspected: the initial plans concerning the ambush—Innis had worked with someone named Sylvie, who had, apparently, both fed Innis's ambition and threatened those very same family members Mynx had seen earlier to ensure his cooperation.

Another held thorough plotting with the other Paragons about their potential ascent to greatness, filled largely with fantasizing about future power.

The third held something better. Something she could use. A dossier Innis had been building about the one behind Aegis's assassination, a collection Innis himself had noted, in one terse description in the barrel, was for his own protection. If Zhan-Yo ever decided Innis wasn't worth it, Innis had been prepared to feed the man's information to Aegis, to the Champions.

And Innis had found the goods. The man was a back-stabbing monster, but he'd done better than Mynx would have expected. Here was what she needed, here was the key to the summit, to fixing the disaster that had started when Zhan-Yo plunged his sword into Aegis's back.

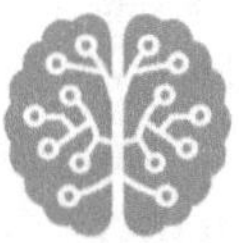

29

Hot Air

The narrow ledge proved enough room for the Duchess's former followers to watch as Thane tossed the collected rags the anomaly had once worn into the churning, orange glow far below. The clothes didn't even make it to the bottom, bursting into flame before they'd fallen a dozen meters. As a ceremony, quiet except for the burbles and cracks from the depths, the Duchess's funeral lacked just about everything, even the body.

"You made the right choice," Cassidy said after the early morning funeral had finished, as the assembled group headed back down the mountain. "They'll appreciate it."

"They were slaves. Why would they want to honor her?" Thane said. "I would never stand for someone who controlled me."

"You're strong," Cassidy replied. "Most of the anomalies here didn't work with Champions, didn't play with the Paragons. We were thieves, or people who had one bad idea that put us here."

"Ah, yes, you're not all evil. Sometimes I forget that."

"Sarcasm doesn't suit you."

"Things rarely do."

While Cassidy's prediction had turned true—the anomalies around here, leaderless, had looked to Thane and, as Cassidy called herself, the Void for guidance—Thane still had little idea what powers lived within the group hiking down with them, within the group still down at the village, pulling together what things they wanted to bring with them.

"You seem to think power suits you," Cassidy said, tugging him back to the conversation.

"Hasn't fit anyone that I've seen so far," Thane replied. "Might as well have a turn."

"It's not easy."

"Is that a warning?" Thane brushed away a rogue fly, trying to snack on the sweat coating him. Turned out volcanos make things hot, and the island breeze hadn't cooled him off yet. "Because I know what I'm getting into."

"Do you?"

"Are you going to keep peppering me with questions, or are you going to say something worthwhile?" Thane said, and saw Cassidy's face turn down at the remark. "Because what I struggle with is how I'm supposed to take you seriously when your grand accomplishment on this island is to catch some fish and build a hut on the beach."

Cassidy didn't talk again on the walk down, and Thane told himself he didn't care. The walk gave him time to think, to piece together a plan for Arthur and what would lay beyond.

KEEPING that little angry flame alive enough to prevent his muscles from shriveling away entirely, Thane focused on the drones, visible in their dark ring. Too many to destroy, too many to fight straight on, no matter the anomalies he had.

But the ring was shallow, and he couldn't see reinforcements. Get past the first line with speed and you might be able to keep going. Whether any anomaly on this place could produce that kind of acceleration, who knew?

"So, uh, have you decided who gets to be what?" a new voice, Sook, said. Cassidy had fallen back into the crowd, among the people she'd brought with her. Sook had replaced the Void at his side, and it seemed like he'd upgraded his clothes, shoes, and walking spear along the way. "I'd like to point out that I've been behind you this whole time. You'd probably still be in that cave if not for me."

Ah. Power drew leeches from every corner.

"Sook, I haven't forgotten. What would you like? What role would make you happiest?"

If Thane were a kinder man, seeing the sparkle that came into Sook's eyes at the question might have prompted some warmth, a fuzzy happiness at bringing someone so close to their dream. Instead, Thane frowned at Sook, pitied his small ambition.

Not that Sook noticed.

"I'd make an excellent guard," Sook said. "And, you know, running the guards. Your own guard. Like, bodyguards."

"Bodyguards."

"Everybody important has them. You're important."

"I'm invincible." Thane didn't know if that was technically true, but close enough. "Why do I need bodyguards?"

"Appearances, Thane!" Sook turned mid-step and gestured at the crowd. "They expect it. If you don't have armed anomalies standing watch at all times, you'll look weak!"

"And you, Sook, of all people, would make me look strong?"

Sook laughed, a gassed little thing. "Let me prove it to you. I'll pick some good ones from the mix, and we'll make you look like the leader you're meant to be, I swear."

Thane had led dozens before, but they were always military forces intent on completing objectives, never a society actively looking for leadership. Perhaps Sook was right, perhaps now Thane had to play by different rules.

"Then, Sook, I give you permission. Keep me safe, make me look strong. Choose four others to work with you. Succeed, and when we're off this island, you'll have your pick of positions in our new world."

Sook took the news exactly as a child would have, and the anomaly disappeared to go quiz everyone else on their abilities, martial and otherwise. Thane had to give Sook that much: the man had enthusiasm.

AFTER THE HIKE DOWN, Thane assembled the full allotment outside the village's remnants. He spoke slow, even, and clear about the goal, about getting Arthur on their side and breaking through the drones to a newer, better world.

The anomalies didn't respond to the speech with rousing cheers, but with grim or muted responses. A few nods, but otherwise, these looked like sheep content to follow the flock. Servants needing direction.

Well, Thane could give them that.

"Did you have a family?" Cassidy asked him afterwards, as preparations continued to leave, the Duchess's legacy getting packed into woven carriers. "Back home?"

"Not really. Long ago."

"Explains why you're such an asshole all the time."

Thane laughed, "All the time? And who here had a good family, a good home?"

"I did."

"So you chose to betray that family and wind up here instead?"

"I made mistakes. You did too." Cassidy said this like she knew Thane, like she had some idea of his plight.

Yet, Thane kept finding himself talking with her. As though magnets pulled them together after every event. It didn't take much analysis—Thane had enough brain power to spare for this one—to see that Cassidy simply had more interesting things to say than the other anomalies.

And the power to back it up.

"What I don't understand," Thane said, "is why you're still this kind. I'm barely suppressing my rage at all times. Not just at this situation, but at life in general. I didn't want this curse."

Not true. Not remotely true. Thane hadn't meant to lie there, but he relished his strength, his powers, and always had. Sometimes, though, it sounded better to deny it.

"Because I tried to push back and failed," Cassidy said. "That put me here and I'd give anything to go back, try it again. Change the narrative. But I can't, and after spending a lot of nights being angry about it, I decided not to anymore."

"You decided not to be angry." Thane reached down, plucked a little wildflower from the grass, watched it bend in the wind. "Woke up and said that was it."

"Not that easy, but yes," Cassidy said. "I was tired, and I kept finding more anomalies like me, that didn't know what to do on this damn island. We gave each other a purpose."

"Like a family. So you've said."

"You should join it. The island, our family."

"I don't want to say here. That's the point."

Cassidy looked up at the sky, always clear blue and getting brighter as the sun climbed higher. They'd need to get marching soon.

"They're not going to follow you to the end like this," Cassidy said. "I won't, either. You think everyone wants to get off of this island, but a lot of them have lives here. Lovers, even a family or two."

"That they'd want to raise here, on a small circle filled with criminals?"

"Where else? I think your problem is that you're too focused on leaving to see how staying might be better. You could, we could, make something here."

Thane held onto that 'we'. Cassidy wasn't much for inflection, or, that he'd seen, affection. He'd never played that game much himself, as those emotions came awful close to anger. After some disastrous results as a teenager—those years had put him on the wrong radars, before the Champions had even existed—Thane had avoided life's more physical pleasures for the infinite mental ones.

"What do you mean, we?" Thane asked, giving in to curiosity.

"You're an ideas person, I'm an empathetic one," Cassidy plucked the wildflower from his hand and stuck it in her hair, above her ear. "You bring them in with your vision, and I'll keep them here by listening to theirs."

"A partnership, then."

"A team."

Thane took that in, chewed it. If Cassidy could keep some of leadership's softer, messier bits off his back, then that might be worth it. Provided she would support his goal.

"I'm not staying on the island," Thane said. "So you'll have to accept that."

"I'll accept that you want to leave now. And that I might be able to change your mind."

Oh, how long it had been since Thane had held real conversations with, if not equals, then people close enough. Cassidy had fire, and he could use that fire. With time, he'd get her to see his way, to understand the island was a trap, a place to leave behind.

About Town

The clock on her Tama, blaze white when she glanced at it in the dark room, pushed midnight. Still no Calvin. Gordon had suggested she let the anomaly go off on his own for a while. Said the man was probably used to being by himself, that Calvin would come back when he was ready.

Now those words seemed like lunacy. A killer lurked out there, gunning down anomalies he didn't seem to like, and Kat had just let Calvin go off on a wander alone. Maybe Calvin was in an alley right now, bleeding out from a shot to the gut. Maybe he'd been kidnapped and the killer was enacting some torture to extract Kat's location.

Or maybe the hotel room and Gordon's soft snores were driving her insane.

Kat slipped out from the covers and stood on the carpet for a second, letting her body adjust to sudden motion. Seeker, passed out on the carpet at the bed's foot opened one eye, a motion Kat caught when the outside lights hit the eye's glint and reflected it back to her.

Kat stuck a finger to her lips, nodding towards Gordon.

Seeker opened both eyes now, and his tongue dripped out of his wide mouth. The husky could get excited about anything, but a late night journey?

Oh yes, definitely. Seeker wanted to go.

If there was an advantage to having little luggage, to just lying on the bed and floating in a semi-dreamless sleep for a couple hours, it sat in Kat's readiness to wander out. Still in street clothes, she didn't need to change. Would she have slept the whole night in jeans? Unclear, but the thought provoked some worry about her mental state.

When Kat forgot basic habits, like putting on pajamas, that seemed like a sign something needed to change. Like, perhaps, avoiding killers.

Kat did some gentle work on the door handle to let her and Seeker into the hall with minimal noise. From there, she walked the bland yellow-lit path to the elevator, and rode its humming descent to the lobby. If someone asked her what she thought about during those few minutes, Kat wouldn't have known. Beyond the desire to find Calvin, everything else had become a mental fog.

The lobby, because this was Chicago and things weren't that late, had people milling around. The fancy bar and restaurant off to one side seemed crowded with people doing their best to avoid the coming day, while the receptionists were handling latecomers from the airport or other destinations, arriving in their huddled masses. February temps equalized everyone beneath gigantic coats.

Kat, with Seeker padding along with her, stuck her head in the restaurant and scanned the bar seats. No Calvin, so when the hostess, who seemed exhausted by the hour, asked if she wanted a table, Kat just shook her head and went out to the street.

Flakes decided to make their nightly appearance, drifting between the big buildings in sparse numbers. Not enough to make things magical, but the flakes provided a texture to the glowing lights and scattered people tromping along the sidewalks. Pods didn't fill the streets, but they came by often, adding their rolling whoosh to the city's sounds.

All in all, compared with Kat's quieter apartment, the downtown mix felt pretty good. Like a harmless postcard.

"Any guesses?" Kat asked Seeker, busy chomping on a flake.

The dog looked at her, then focused on the smells attached to a nearby streetlight.

"Fair enough," Kat muttered.

Calvin wasn't in the most convenient option—the hotel bar —and Kat doubted he would have taken a pod back to the suburbs. Even with Gordon's hostility, Calvin was smart enough not to throw himself back into deadly territory without help. At least, Kat hoped he was.

At the same time, Calvin had only been drawing a Paragon salary for a week, which meant he might have skipped on the hotel's offerings on price alone. Might also mean he'd reject renting a pod. More than that, if Kat included pods as a potential option, she'd have too many possible destinations.

Instead, she raised her Tama, pulled up bars in the area, and found the cheapest, dirtiest one. A couple blocks away, in a place that functioned as a pod repair shop during the day and converted to a greasy spoon for overnighters once the sun dropped.

Oil and Vinegar had the look, and going by the menu someone had slapped on its outside wall, definitely had the prices. The signage had a flickering neon glow that screamed inattention, and the single door was so fogged over that Kat couldn't see inside. No doormen here, and its twin luxury shop neighbors—ones that probably hoped *Oil and Vinegar* would die in a fire—were closed, so the dive sat alone as the clock tripped towards one.

Inside, a narrow bar cut between equipment racks, with the mirrored shelves behind covered with bottles Kat could neither identify nor want to drink. Labels had been torn off, and the woman standing behind the counter looked like she'd been doing it for years. Despite smoking inside being illegal, she puffed on a cigarette and hit Kat with an icy look as the tracker, and her dog, came inside.

A half-dozen other patrons braved the bartender's smoke to chat along the bar or gaze at the sole TV in the joint, one that looked stuck on sports reruns from earlier in the evening. At the far end, nursing something dark, sat her quarry.

"No dogs," the bartender said, taking out the cigarette and jabbing it towards Seeker, who stayed behind Kat's legs.

"You're not supposed to have one of those either," Kat replied. "Seeker's not going to cause trouble, but I might."

"Then you can turn and walk yourself right outta here."

Instead, Kat went up to the bar, where the woman blew smoke into her face. Kat shut her eyes as the cloud ran over her, held her breath to keep from coughing. Then pointed at a brown bottle, something she prayed held whiskey.

"I'll have a double of that." Kat said. "Neat."

The bartender didn't move for a full second. Kat folded her arms on the bar. Seeker brushed her legs, started to jump up to see what was happening, but Kat moved her own calf in front of the puppy, keeping him down. This contest of wills only needed two players.

One thunk later, Kat had herself a smoky glass full of . . . something. The bartender moved on to other drinkers, and Kat moved herself to the back end, where Calvin sat eyeing the TV like he wished it would teleport him somewhere, anywhere else.

"What's on?" Kat asked, sitting down.

Calvin had a bottled beer in front of him, label still there. Smart man.

"Never did get attached to sports," Calvin said. "They tie you to a place, I think, and I never really had a home."

"I have a home, and I don't care about them."

"Why not?"

"Because I'm too busy trying to keep myself alive," Kat said. "You ever think about that? Because I'm starting to doubt it."

"No way that guy was going to be downtown after attacking us on the west side."

"How do you know?"

"A hunch."

Kat rolled her eyes, tasted her drink, and . . . wow. It wasn't great, but she definitely had whiskey in her hand. Not, for example, straight poison or, as the restaurant's name implied, oil.

"Were you going to come back to the room at all tonight?" Kat asked.

"Does it matter?"

"You know it does."

"Nah, Kat, I don't." Calvin lifted his left arm, looked at his Tama. "You know what this thing's been telling me since we got down here? That some accident, that thing we saw, took out a bunch of my new coworkers tonight."

"Took out?"

Calvin relayed what he knew in drip drop fashion, layering every detail with dashes about how he didn't know this guy or that girl, how he'd never even been to that floor. That he'd only met Innis the one time, with a half-dozen other newbies, and the man had seemed all right then, in the way that people you never think you'll have to see again can seem all right.

"Now they're all, like, gone," Calvin finished. "First time in my life I get something like a family and sure enough, they're dead."

"Hold on. A family? You didn't want to be a Paragon."

"Doesn't mean I can't see the good sides."

"So your solution, after reading all this, was to go to a bar and drink?"

Calvin's mouth opened and stayed that way, then he turned to his beer and took another swig.

"Dude," Kat continued. "You've got problems. And I say that as a girl who's got plenty of her own, but you're not going to deal with them in here, right now, with that beer."

"Like you're dealing with that whiskey?"

"This? This is commiseration." Kat reached down, gave Seeker a good pet. "Let's down one to the tragedy."

They clinked glass, had their swallows.

"Now," Kat said. "I'm going to ask you to do something for me."

Calvin leaned his head away, looked her way in mock terror.

"You're gonna have to be nice to Gordon," Kat said. "Because he's too stupid to be nice to you. Let him whine, complain, whatever, because we're going to need his help. Or at least a place to sleep. Because tomorrow we're finding this guy, and taking him out."

Calvin laughed, "Really? That's what you're delivering right now?"

"That's it." Kat said, and she started laughing too. Declaring a joint quest to catch a killer in this sweaty, metal place seemed ridiculous. "That's what I want." Then she stopped, just as quick as she started. "Because, Calvin, this guy almost took me out. Twice. I don't know if I can handle him alone."

"Don't know if I'll be much help." Calvin swirled his drink, then finished it. "But okay, Kat. Guess all those Paragons would want me to go along with you anyway. I'm supposed to be the do-gooder now, right?"

"That's right," Kat said. "Do what your Champion would want you to do."

"Know who that is now?" Calvin said. "This woman, Pixie, out east? You know who she is?"

Kat shook her head, "Nope, and I don't care." She finished her whiskey, stood back from the bar. "Want to know the real secret to surviving, now that you're in this world?"

"What?"

"Stay in your lane, Calvin. Stay in your lane."

31

Swordsman

If Zhan-Yo could hurt his father, he'd get to keep the tachi. A single touch, that's all the son needed to manage, there in the white-paneled, blonde wood room that had served as his father's sanctum for as long as Zhan-Yo could remember.

"But we've already practiced every day this week," Zhan-Yo said, feeling the aches in his arms and legs and wanting more than anything to get back to his phone, his connection to friends and things far more interesting than his dad's old swords.

"And we will keep practicing every day until you succeed," his father replied. "Perseverance has as much to do with winning as trying in the first place. You must continue."

Zhan-Yo had a hierarchy with his father establishing the levels that he was allowed to disagree. Smaller things, like whether and where Zhan-Yo could go out at night, represented easy wins. His father had too much work, his mother doted on community projects, and that split focus let him get away. These lessons, though, held firm towards the pyramid's top. No pleading, cajoling, or suggestions that they take the day off and get snacks took hold.

The wooden tachi—the live, edged ones sat on hooks against the room's walls—felt airy in Zhan-Yo's hand, a toy. He'd held the real ones, and those felt like they could do real damage. His father, though, maintained that the tachi were a privilege to be earned. Zhan-Yo, not yet fifteen, had not.

"Come on," his father said, holding his own wooden sword. "The faster you beat me, the faster you can return to your messages."

Inspiration provided, Zhan-Yo hefted the blunt tachi and broke into a sudden run, raising the weapon for an overhead slam. A telegraphed move that pushed his father to step aside, a telegraphed move that gave Zhan-Yo the opening he wanted. As his father evaded the expectation, Zhan-Yo changed his step, instead planting his left foot and sweeping the tachi wide.

The sudden panic on his father's face was worth everything. The older man jerked up his own tachi to ward off Zhan-Yo's attack with a thick clunk, and Zhan-Yo used the reversed momentum to back step, get something else ready.

"That was different," his father said, copying Zhan-Yo's move to build the distance. "I'm impressed."

Praise not given lightly. Zhan-Yo tracked his father's sword, how he held it ready in both hands. Not the relaxed stance from someone confident in their success, but rather someone ready to defend. A worthy opponent.

About time.

"Ready to see what else I can do?" Zhan-Yo said.

Because, for all his friends, for all the fun he'd have running through downtown with them later, Zhan-Yo had been practicing. Had been learning from a teacher better than his old man.

"SYLVIE WOULD HAVE RESPECTED a date like that," Wexley said, sitting across from Zhan-Yo as the hours crept towards dawn. "A pair of swords and a fight to see who could knock each other's teeth out?"

Wexley hadn't been happy, exactly, with Zhan-Yo's message from the pod on the way back, but he'd agreed to come over in a few hours, which had given Zhan-Yo time for a quick nap. Now, with fresh coffee at four in the morning, Zhan-Yo needed to convince his lieutenant that he wasn't crazy.

To do that, Zhan-Yo felt he had to connect, again, with Wexley, prove to him that Zhan-Yo still had his faculties. That he was still sane, and ready to lead a war against the world's greatest, and only, power.

"That's how they met," Zhan-Yo said. "My mother's parents ran a studio, where my mother taught when she was younger. My father came in for a lesson, I guess wanting something different from the office."

"That was it? Did he ask your mom on a date after she knocked him out?"

"Something like that," Zhan-Yo said. They'd never told him precisely how it happened, but his mother always maintained that his father had never bested her. "Then she started training me in secret. My father always wanted these duels, but my mother cared about technique. About actually getting better."

"Mine went to movies," Wexley said. "I played soccer."

They took long drags from their coffees, with Wexley's eyes gliding over to his Tama. To what was likely a devastating meeting and email list. The kind Zhan-Yo used to know, that he missed every now and then.

"So you have these Paragons in your pocket. You think you can trust them." Wexley said, his voice indicating just how little he cared for the plan. "They're going to deliver the summit details to you."

"They might," Zhan-Yo said. "Mathieu is leaning on them. They're kids. Ambitious ones. We might be able to use them to get into the summit itself."

"Then what?" Wexley said. "You want to bomb the place?"

"Exactly," Zhan-Yo replied. "It's not about how many I kill, or even wound. It's about the message. The world needs to see the Paragons, the Champions are too vulnerable to lead it. That will create our opening."

"So you're going to sneak a bomb into the most guarded place on the planet? There'll be anomalies there who can read your mind, who will be able to understand every motivation you have in an instant. You'll keep no secrets."

"They'll have to find me first." Zhan-Yo waved at the window. "The Paragons haven't found me here, yet, and I'm already the most wanted man in the world. What makes you think they'll be any better at the summit?"

"Because you're coming to them?"

"Trust me, Wexley. This is going to work. I just need you to keep the accounts topped up. Mathieu's doing the prep work for me, getting the people we'll need for this. They'll need to be paid."

"Can't say I expected to be funding a guerrilla war when I took the job at Ziran," Wexley said. "But a promise is a promise." The lieutenant stood up, tossed his empty coffee in the silver trash bin next to the counter. A perfect angle, a perfect basket. "You'll have your reps. Just be careful, Zhan-Yo. You die, and all this dies with you."

When he'd beaten his father, not too long after his sixteenth birthday, Zhan-Yo had expected pride in his father's eyes. Some happiness on his father's face. Instead, Zhan-Yo had seen painful acceptance. A reality long feared that had finally come to pass.

Perhaps Wexley felt the same. Perhaps the world did, too. All of them nervous about the inevitable.

Zhan-Yo had earned those tachi, and he carried them still.

32

Mila

Mila, the last Champion, picked up on the first ring. No video call this time, and Mynx, exhausted after the long night, didn't mind that Mila's own preference for mountain peaks left her with such poor connectivity that faces weren't an option.

"Mynx." Mila's caramel tones came through fine, though. "I'm so sad you came to me last. I thought we were friends."

"That's why I waited till the end," Mynx said, staring out over Lake Michigan from Innis's former office. "I needed something to look forward to."

"Then you should come down here, where there is always something beautiful on the horizon."

"Like what?"

"Oh, today? Today I am waking up on the sun-kissed slopes above Lima, with the ocean at my feet and the peaks at my head." Mila said. "The most beautiful sight."

"I'm sure. But I need you to leave it behind for a little while. The summit starts in a couple of days. I know you've seen the details."

"I have, and I will be there, of course, even if it pains me to leave my loves behind."

Mynx used to worry about Mila, after they'd first met. The woman described everything she liked as her 'loves', and appeared to view her world through a soapy, sappy lens. Everything drenched in emotion, either devastating or rapturous in equal measure.

Then Mynx saw Mila shift a killer's body, turning the strong, lean man into a weak, fractured one that couldn't even stand. As Mynx was to computer code, so Mila was to the physical form, she could get inside and rewrite a person into whatever she wanted.

Frightening, sure. Enough so that Aegis had wanted her destroyed before Mila decided to scramble the Champion's bodies. Instead, Mynx and the others had recruited her, proved to Aegis that Mila's abilities could be good. Could be incredible.

A promise only partially fulfilled.

"Thank you," Mynx said. "I know it's a risk gathering all of us together, but we have to show the world that the Champions remain united, and that we have a plan for the future."

"And do we? Have a plan?"

Others might have sounded accusatory, or even mocking asking that question, but Mila let a little laugh linger at the end, as if the idea that the Champions might not have such a plan was ludicrous.

"We'll refine it together, but the point lies in choosing who's going to replace you when you're gone." Mila should know this if she'd read the messages Reeves had been sending out with the Summit's various details. "Just like we chose the regional Paragons. Like we chose you."

Silence on the phone, then some rustling. Mila moving somewhere. Mynx took the opportunity to enjoy the coffee, the doughnut someone had brought up for her.

"I remember that day," Mila said. "How do you recall it? Most of you didn't trust me."

"Hard to, knowing what you could do."

"But you let me in anyway, and look what's happened."

"It's been something," Sentimentality wasn't Mynx's preferred playground. "But, Mila, I haven't slept well, and there's a lot going on here. Can we talk more at the summit?"

"Check me off your list and disappear, I suppose?"

"That's not fair."

"Oh, I'm only playing. Go, be queen."

"I'm not a queen."

"Whatever you say," Mila replied. "But if you do catch that one, hold on to him for me. Nothing calms a revolution down faster than its leader shriveling up into a little, silent raisin."

"Will do. Thanks, Mila."

The Champions clicked off as the sky transitioned from black to deep blue, orange's barest hints clinging to the horizon. Mila made a good point. Twist Zhan-Yo's mind, make him a whole-hearted Paragon supporter? Devious, but perfect.

Mynx stood and started pacing around the spare office. Innis had a big desk in there, two monitors. No personal pictures, no art on the walls. Either he rarely spent time here or just had no taste for decor. In a way, Mynx appreciated it—nothing to distract from the plan.

"Reeves, we have the targets," Mynx said.

"We do. The drones are ready to launch as soon as you say."

"Give it another two hours. I want the city to see it. I want the cameras ready to catch what happens."

"A visible capture risks energizing Zhan-Yo's base," Reeves replied. "They could see it as an inflection point and begin their revolt. Other revolutions were sparked with moments like this."

"No, we're not doing this quietly. We have to show everyone that this won't be tolerated. Allowed. Zhan-Yo put his move in the open, and we will too."

Reeves, as the AI ought, accepted the argument and began making plans. Mynx, exhaustion blurring the edges, left Innis's office and went back down to the broken floor.

Already, the bodies had been removed and several Paragons with constructive abilities were piecing together the glass with hand waves or simple stares. Another remolded spent bullets into spendable ones, ready to get restocked into the drones. By noon, the building would be its perfect self again.

Mynx watched them work, and wondered. How many were truly loyal, how deep had Innis's corruption gone? After the summit, she'd spend more time inside the man's Tama, dig through all of those barrels—or, more likely, have Reeves crack it—to find out who had tasted that traitorous apple.

Before, Mynx had thought she'd eradicate every one of them, and drop those too dangerous out on her island. But how many could she take? How many could she expect Apinya and Burov, with their mind-warping powers, to turn?

Drones didn't question their commands, or their commander. They did as they were told, and executed to their maximum abilities. The Paragons had human flaws, and they were increasingly difficult to tolerate.

So why tolerate them at all?

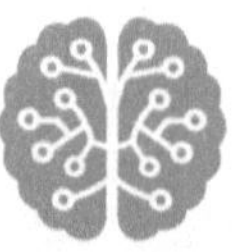

33

To Meet A Villain

The police found him alone, on a blood-soaked carpet, crying. His body shriveled and cold and stained red. Just past nine in the morning, and Thane should have been in school. Instead, he'd wanted to wear an old shirt. His mother had bought him a new one. For that, and that alone, Thane had killed them all.

For all his intelligence, for all the hours he'd spent curled up beneath the lights in the Champion's prison, Thane had never been able to figure why his abilities had chosen that morning to manifest themselves. Why a twelve year-old's protest had turned into devastation.

After he'd destroyed the hospital—where the police had taken his shrunken body for care—and demolished several buildings in a twisting rampage towards the slippery creek where Thane's father used to take him fishing, the first Paragons found him.

Soft and weak again, lying on the moss, and covered in debris.

"They wanted to save me," Thane said, brushing aside ferns blocking Cassidy as their band stalked from the island's center towards its east side. "They thought I could control it. A child."

"Would you have rather they put you in chains, like they did later?"

Thane had offered an apology for before, tried to salve any wounds. There wouldn't be time for drama once they reached Arthur, especially if the villain met Cassidy's estimation as the most dangerous on the island.

She walked beside him, and seemed happy to do so, if more cautious than before. One eye, Thane noticed, always stayed on him, measuring. A suspicion earned, he supposed.

"Looking back, yes," Thane said. "I had no understanding of myself, what I could do. I was a blind weapon brimming with hormones who'd slaughtered the only people he loved. I should have been locked away."

"They believed, back then," Cassidy replied. "I never got that chance."

"It wasn't belief." Thane felt his way on the ground. The thick undergrowth made it easy to slip up, sprain an ankle. "It was insecurity. They thought they could use me."

"I would have let them use me if I had known what was coming." Cassidy had taken up a branch and employed it as a walking stick, feeling out the path. "I thought, by defying their orders, I was making some sort of stand. Instead, I just spat in their all-powerful face."

The Paragons had taken Thane far away from the town, to an isolated spot in the north woods, near the U.S. and Canada border. To a camp where anomalies learned not to kill everyone around them. Was that place still around? Were powered children still sending novas into the night, protected by Paragons that could keep them alive?

How many times had they repaired bodies Thane broke?

"They mold you at those camps," Thane said. "They taught me to forget my family. I don't even remember their names, only the lesson."

Everyone required their own plan. Treatment, from day one through graduation, years or months or weeks down the line, when they thought you could handle society. Could handle real work.

"I heard they rip open the minds?" Cassidy asked.

"More than that. The idea is to make the perfect Paragon. Someone that can strategize, can lead and fight and serve, that will never have too many drinks and vaporize a crowd."

"That last doesn't sound like a bad goal."

"Do you think I hate what they did?" Thane shook his head, laughed. "No, I love them for it. The Paragons gave me a life to live. Without them, I would have been angry and unstoppable until someone found a way to kill me. Instead, the Paragons made me rational, made me forget how to be human."

"You're still plenty human, Thane. You definitely make enough mistakes to qualify."

"What I want to know, is why didn't they take you?"

"Too old."

"No. They would have taken someone with your power at any age."

Cassidy looked away, towards the horizon. The ever-present black drone line holding still beneath growing clouds.

"I told you. I didn't get a choice."

Cassidy didn't offer more and Thane didn't press. They were nearing the slope's end anyway, coming into a flat, forested stretch before the lagoon beach Arthur called home. They'd left the Duchess's territory, and stood on contested ground.

Unlike Cassidy's side, the island climate shifted here, with the volcano serving to stop and split clouds, such that rain coated the ferns, and the green seemed far deeper. Lush described everything. The ground became muddier, and Thane's woven sandals did little to prevent the sloppy ground from squeezing up through his toes. More insects buzzed around, taking the generous water and turning it into spawning beds. Flowering plants bene-fitted, their purple and red petals peaking out in shy brilliance.

Beautiful, and distracting.

The Duchess's former anomalies, during the march, had warned about this, had said Arthur kept a tight watch on what went on around the island. Rumor had it the man kept an anomaly that could see here and there, like a spot-light shining on a black building wall. The thought that they could get close, walk right up to the lagoon like Thane and Sook had approached Cassidy's town, was mocked.

So Thane marched at the column's head. While, with his mild anger always burning, Thane didn't appear as the most imposing monster, he could take a hit. If Arthur chose a surprise assault, Thane would likely live long enough to counter.

How often does the leader serve as the bait, the target?

For Thane, that seemed to be all the time.

That logic killed the shock when the first anomaly, wearing a sash across his chest, dyed purple-blue from crushed flower petals, stepped from the jungle. Unlike Cassidy's guards, this one didn't carry any weapons, though he looked fit enough. Tanned, muscled, and grim.

The call went up along the columns sides and Thane turned from the first newcomer to see the air shimmering along his force's length. More anomalies appeared, as if throwing off blankets, blue sashes across their bodies.

While a thinner line than Thane's group, within a few seconds the new arrivals had them surrounded.

The problem with anomalies: strategies became useless, because you never knew what you were up against.

"Well met," said another anomaly, ropey and small, with naturally brown skin. "Welcome to our adopted home. I am Arthur, and you are the intruder."

Given the name, Thane would not have expected what he saw: Arthur looked nothing like the European knight from legend. He'd expected someone physically imposing, willing to supplement his ability with brute force and a dire disposition. Instead, Arthur burst out with a wide smile. Arms spread, he walked forward and thrust a single hand towards Thane.

Who hesitated. Cassidy, too, sent glaring daggers Arthur's way, but the man's smile never faltered. The anomaly seemed determined to force his way through the situation with his dirty teeth on display.

"My name is Thane." He offered no hand. "Do you know why I'm here?"

"You're here to help us all get off this island," Arthur answered.

"Then you don't need to surround us. You're not the target."

Arthur laughed, a thin chuckle. "Of course I'm not. But I'm not letting you walk into my territory either. This is a takeover, and not one I will allow."

Options. Either they fight it out here, which, with Arthur's obvious advantages, would result in deaths nobody could afford. Or Thane could accept the circumstances and go along with Arthur, as he had with the Duchess, and time his strike later. Not all that difficult a choice to make.

"Do you remember Sienna?" Cassidy asked before

Thane could speak. "One of your teams found her, took her."

Arthur let half his smile die. Stuck a hand to his chin and sent his eyes skyward in an exaggerated look that had Thane putting a hand on Cassidy's left arm. She could be as mad at Arthur as she wanted, provided she didn't act on it.

"Sienna. Hmm," Arthur said, then snapped his left hand's fingers. "I remember! She's right there."

Arthur pointed back down the line, towards a younger woman—Thane guessed early twenties—who tried to duck back behind the others. Even from ten meters away, Thane could see the blush on her face.

Sometimes Thane forgot how long these anomalies had been on this island, how much history they had been able to rack up.

"So you lied to her too." Cassidy didn't bother turning around. Didn't crumple or shy away from Arthur's apparent triumph. "Gathering your pieces with sweet words about escape."

"Lied? Isn't that why you're here? To get off this island?"

"We're actually going to do it," Thane said, re-taking the conversation before Cassidy decided to act on impulse and open a hole inside Arthur's chest. "We heard you had a plan, so we're coming to help you make it work. This shouldn't be a fight."

"And you? Void? What do you say?" Arthur folded his arms. "Are you coming to work for me too?"

"Not for," Cassidy said. "With. Just this once."

This time, when Arthur extended his hand, Thane and Cassidy shook it in turn. Together, they would get off this island, or die trying.

34

Hunter Killer

Her suit did its level best to keep out the water, but Kat felt the slush making inroads between her boots and leggings. Cold, especially given the sun's unexpected, hot assault on winter's chill. The melting snow made her attempted disguise, lying prone in a rooftop pile near the Elemental's cafe, look dumber as the morning went on.

For the moment, Kat held a clear sight line across all the roofs for blocks around, and her suit's white blended enough to pass, so Calvin said, for a particularly stubborn snowdrift.

"Any sign?" Kat spoke into her Tama.

"Nothing on the ground," Calvin said. "I stopped counting the laps."

"Healthier that way. Stakeouts tend to go long."

"I'm also getting a lot of looks. Might have to bail for a bit."

"Take your coffee break if you need it." Kat didn't remark on her current situation, how her muscles were falling asleep, how she could use a restroom or some water. "I'll be here."

Mentally, she'd prepared for this. On the way back from the bar last night, Kat and Calvin had decided the best way to deal with an assassin would be to take the fight to him. They'd left Gordon's room in the early morning—after Kat extracted a promise from her tracker friend to look after Seeker—and ventured back to Kat's apartment.

She'd left Calvin to keep an eye out while Kat went through a side door, avoiding the entrance and the bullet that might come with it. Her apartment hadn't been ransacked, and a cautious door opening proved unnecessary. No ambushes. Apparently the killer limited his traps to the outside.

Which is what Kat and Calvin were doing. They'd gone back to the Elemental's cafe—Kat even sent them a heads-up, letting the rogue anomalies know to keep things going as per usual and not scare off the prey. Hopefully this guy would come and try to do his thing.

And Kat really, really hoped he would. She'd never thought of herself as a revenge person, always felt she was above that, but the last day had kept at her, whispering to Kat's subconscious about how close she'd come to biting it. And not only the near death, but that Kat had failed to get this guy twice now.

Deadly, and also insulting.

"Do you want, like, a latte or something?" Calvin popped in over the Tama. "This might sound weird, but I have reps to burn now that I'm a Paragon. Not used to treating people."

"What're you going to do, throw it to me?"

Calvin hesitated, "Maybe?"

"I'm already covered in slush. You get coffee on me, we won't need the assassin to get a body today."

"Sorry I asked," Calvin said. "Don't get too angry up there."

"Only gonna get worse."

Kat clipped the call. Shifted to get a better view across the eastern rooftops. Flatter that way for a bit, though the places over those next few blocks were mostly houses. Not like the assassin would be crawling from some attic window to snipe the streets.

And yet.

Over that way, looking like he didn't quite come from one of those houses but instead rose to the roofs by way of an older dry cleaning enterprise, a shape cut across Kat's view. Unlike the solid silver and snow-coated fixtures, the shape moved, looked like a human, and had the all-black outfit favored by their target.

Kat didn't even count the big ol' gun hanging from the shape's back, its barrel providing a straight contrast to the form's athletic shape as the assassin jumped from one roof to the next. He moved with a speed that suggested planning, or at least enough repetition to learn the ideal, least risky rout: every rooftop jump occurred at the closest possible point between irregular buildings, leveraging overhangs and built-up edges to give himself an advantage.

Kat would have applauded the display if she'd been watching it in a movie, or in some competition. Every landing came smooth and kept him moving, every jump timed with his push-off to give the assassin maximum air and space to land. Kat almost never found herself on the rooftops chasing anomalies, but even so, she wanted his talent.

Instead, Kat would take everything else.

"Incoming," Kat said to the Tama. "Looks like he's going to go across from the cafe to set up."

The assassin hit a snag in his journey just after Kat said the words. While he'd been progressing towards the main avenue and a skywalk across the boulevard connecting two offices—likely to scamper across the roof—drones interrupted his travel, passing over the area like the silent observers they were. No doubt the assassin's gun-slinging around here had the drones doing additional patrols.

So the assassin liked to play it dangerous. Sense dictated that he ought to make his killings random, space them around the city to keep anyone from honing in that they were being done by the same person. That he wasn't bothering suggested either insanity or that the assassin thought he was invincible.

Either way, Kat had her target. She shifted, twitched, on her chest to keep the assassin in front as he made his way towards the main avenue and the people clogging it. The warm day pushed everyone outside, a pleasure vice squeezing the populace into the open.

Standing over the busy street and trying to take a shot, though, would only get the assassin caught right away, so he settled a few buildings back, began unlimbering his gun.

"He's in the block's middle," Kat said. "Three back. Looks like an apartment building. He's setting up. What's your status?"

"Heading your way," Calvin said. "Hard to run with hot coffee."

"Then ditch it, you moron."

"This is, like, the fifth time I've bought coffee with my own money," Calvin replied. "I'm not throwing it away."

"Whatever. He's almost set. I'm going in."

Kat cut the chat and rolled off the snow drift as the assassin, four square rooftops away from her, hunched over the rifle to get its legs square. Kat left her roll and darted behind a ventilation stack, snuck a look to confirm the weapon still held the assassin's attention. The scope needed affixing, so the killer didn't look Kat's way.

Now the hard part. Jump between the buildings in a

rapid sprint. The roofs weren't exactly pillow cushions, but Kat would try to keep the landings as quiet as possible. Land on her feet, keep running, and all that.

She loved the precipice, the moment before the action began, when everything slowed. No turning back, once she took this next step. Kat became a tracker for many reasons, and these moments were definitely one of them.

So Kat seized the instant, turned around the vent stack and its belching white smoke, and ran. Her tight boots gripped the tiles, gave every leg pump all the momentum she needed. Breathing came easy. The suit moved with her, like a second skin.

The mask, highlighting the assassin in red, traced the optimal path to him. Roof ledges shone green, with yellow arrows pointing to the best arcs for running jumps—as if Kat could hit them perfectly. As Kat picked up speed, the first ledge flashed, then stayed bright: the mask thought she had momentum to clear the first gap.

Kat planted her right foot near the ledge and leapt, holding her breath as the alley passed by beneath her. Dumpsters, if they had eyes, would have seen her billowing white-silver body fly over them for a hot second and nothing else. She heard no shouts from below, her heroics unnoticed by living things.

The landing came up quick, that second hanging ending with a hard crash pushing Kat into a roll. Something on the rooftop squeaked as she went across it, hard and smooth. As she came out of the roll, sliding some on slush, Kat glanced down. Solar panels. Why weren't they raised, collecting sunlight instead of lying flat, coated in melting slush?

Because Kat had miserable luck, that's why.

Her mask beeped in her left ear as Kat gathered her remaining momentum and turned towards the killer. Who wasn't where she'd last seen him. The man's rifle still sat there, on stands and ready, but its owner . . .

Kat spun further left, making a straight line from her building, then another two roofs to the main street. The killer jumped the gap to the middle, landing smooth on the roof. No solar panels on that one.

With her sneak attack canceled, Kat raised her left wrist and squeezed her palm, triggering two silver balls to launch across her roof to where the assassin turned towards her. As the balls landed, Kat crouched and burst forward. Her left foot caught the roof's lip—because the assassin came towards her, Kat didn't have to run across the entire roof to jump—and she flew.

The assassin glanced at the silver balls, then raised that same pistol towards her. Kat, in flight, soared with zero cover. Her mask, as if deciding she didn't need to see her own death, blacked out her vision. Her stomach twisted, and Kat tried to hold onto her own space, where she was and where she'd be in a second.

Twin flashes, and Kat landed as her sight returned, a sudden clarity that showed the killer stumbling back from her, from those silver balls, his gun waving wide with his other hand grabbing at his face.

Never one to let an advantage waver, Kat pressed hers. She dove forward in a tackle, trying to close the range on that gun, make it pointless. The assassin's back-stepping kept Kat's attack from reaching glorious perfection, and instead Kat wound up grabbing the killer's ankles.

Use what you get.

Kat pulled the killer's feet towards her and the man dropped the gun to catch his fall, the pistol clattering on the tiles and bouncing away. Kat snapped her left wrist as she pulled herself up the man's many-pocketed pants, changing from the empty flash bangs to something more useful. With her right hand, she tried to pin the assassin's own wrist to the ground.

That didn't work. The killer leaned up, still shaking his head, and swung a clumsy punch with his left hand. The hit whacked Kat's face, with the mask blunting the impact, but stalling Kat's attack and letting the assassin find some grip with his feet and push himself out from under her.

Kat grabbed her stun gun, brought it up and fired point blank at the assassin. The dart buried itself into the man's black vest, then fell away. The killer didn't seem to care, and they both rose to their feet, staring dead on at each other in a frigid puddle.

"You should be dead," the assassin said. "How?"

"None of your damn business," Kat replied, then stepped into a kick, angling for the killer's ankles.

He danced back, letting the kick miss, but kept his own fists raised, "Anomalies?"

"The ones you haven't killed yet." Kat feinted for another punch, then angled her left wrist towards the assassin's right leg and fired.

The steel cable shot out and embedded itself into the killer's thigh, and the man shouted, high and loud. Not exactly a berserker's yell, but the panicked yelp of someone who hadn't felt much real pain. He would be feeling a lot more.

Kat jerked her left wrist and the cable pulled the killer down to his back again, hitting him hard on the roof.

"Kat, where are you?" Calvin's voice came from the Tama. "What roof?"

"Get up here and you'll see us," Kat said, walking towards the killer.

As Kat approached, the killer, his breathing hard, reached and pulled a buzz knife from his belt. Slid the blade towards his thigh and began working the edge against the cable, for all of a second until Kat kicked it away.

"Got me once," Kat said, looking down at the man. His mask hid his face, and while he had no coat like Kat, black gear covered everything, even the man's Tama. "Never again."

Kat aimed the stun gun right at the killer's neck, in what should be a soft spot in the armor.

"Stop! Lower the weapon!" The drone's stern-voiced order came blasting loud, the dark orb floating towards them from the main street, its tech out and pointed like a cactus towards Kat and the killer. "Freeze or you may be injured!"

The drones had been close by, but not so close as to get on top of them in seconds. There hadn't been any loud gunfire, and Kat wouldn't have expected someone from the street, even if they had seen a pair jumping between the rooftops, to call for help. But the drone was here, which meant Kat had to obey. She lowered the stun gun, glaring at the drone the whole way.

The killer didn't get the message. As Kat dropped the weapon, she felt her ankle blow out from under her as the killer kicked. He rolled as Kat slipped, as the drone called for them to stop moving. The killer, with Kat's cable around his thigh, rolled to the roof's alley edge and kept moving, pulling himself over and off.

What? Had the man just killed himself?

Kat felt the cable spooling out from her wrist, did a lightning quick calculation. Not enough slack to get him to the ground, which means he'd pull her over the edge too. She snapped her wrist, disengaged the cable's clamps, and felt the thing go slack a moment later. She went to the edge, looked down towards the alley, expecting to see a broken body.

Instead, she saw a dented dumpster and a limping form vanish around a corner, further into the alleyways.

"Stop now!" the drone called again. "Or I will fire!"

"No need," Kat said, turning back to the drone and showing her hands, the stun gun returned to its holster. "I'm not resisting."

"She's not the target!" Calvin yelled, this time, from the next roof over, climbing up a fire escape ladder. "It's the dude in black, man!"

The drone swiveled between Kat and Calvin, confused.

"The one I was fighting with," Kat said, sitting on the edge. She could have tried chasing the killer, but diving off the roof seemed a bad call. "Go after him. He's the one shooting people."

The drone finally seemed to get it. The machine ordered the two of them to stay, then drifted off in the killer's direction. Maybe it would get lucky, more likely it would catch nothing but air.

"He got away?" Calvin called over from the other roof. "I thought you had him?"

"I did, till that thing showed up." Kat re-spooled her cable. "But it's not all bad. We can find him, now."

She pointed a couple roofs away, to the killer's rifle, still set up and waiting to lead them to its owner.

Generations

Downtown Chicago in February stayed true to its old moniker, and gusts buffeted Zhan-Yo along the sidewalks as he went, hood up, beneath glass and steel towers. No tachi today, and he kept his head down, dodging eyes from walkers going to and from work, play, shopping. Everyone, in fact, seemed to be matching his downward stare, keeping their faces from the wind's chill kiss.

Crossing beneath Lake Shore Drive, its wide avenues once glorious, now shrunk to match a pod's increased efficiency, their asphalt ripped up and given over to more grass, trees, the natural things that had been demolished in humanity's conquest. He had nothing against the greener things in life, but Zhan-Yo felt that familiar pain: another childhood memory made only that.

Lake Michigan's vastness, coated with floating frozen slabs like the scene from a daring arctic rescue, cured any malaise. While the breeze stayed as brisk as ever, it seemed less hostile here, with the wide shore stretching in either direction. Zhan-Yo crossed the path, normally crowded with bikers, walkers, and randoms like himself but now a barren stretch, to the walled edge and leaned on the cold stone, elbows down and face forward.

For a long time, this view had served to center him. Clouds filtered the sun today, but its soft orange still proved inspiring, a chance to connect with more than immediate sensations. A chance to draw deeper into his purpose. Everyone should look at a view like this and feel that they, too, could hope for a brighter future made possible by their own actions, not a Paragon's largesse.

His Tama beeped and vibrated, the telltale double signal calling Zhan-Yo back from reverie to the present's demands. The thick jacket sleeve had a velcro window that Zhan-Yo opened up, letting him see Sylvie's brother on the Tama's screen. The man's voice came through muffled, the wind blocking it out, so Zhan-Yo had to lift his own arm, hold it close to his ears, like a phone from ages ago.

"I made contact with those two Paragons you mentioned," Mathieu said. "I wouldn't trust them with anything important, you want my honest opinion."

"We don't need them for anything other than getting me inside," Zhan-Yo replied. "They can get me past whatever's watching the entrance. From there, we leave them out of it."

"So now you want to get them over there too."

"Wexley will manage that. Tell him how many seats you need," Zhan-Yo said. "Get it done. We're almost there."

"And the other thing, the packages?"

The cryptic dance. Zhan-Yo smiled into the wind. He hadn't mentioned the summit, where his turncoat Paragons would be flying, and now they were discussing that spy movie cliche: packages. Any Paragon actually listening to the conversation would probably be confused, suspicious even, but the evidence wouldn't exist. They couldn't plan against it. Zhan-Yo had always thought this sort of stuff seemed foolish, a waste, but now, actually talking like a spy?

He could get used to it.

"Exactly as ordered," Zhan-Yo said. "We can't mess this up, because there won't be another chance."

That's what Zhan-Yo had thought with Aegis as well, and he'd found his second chance, but getting so lucky multiple times seemed like a poor plan.

"No, there won't."

Between the wind, holding the Tama to his ear, and squinting as he looked over the lake, it took Zhan-Yo a moment to register the voice saying the words wasn't Sylvie's brother, and that they hadn't come from the Tama.

With nerves spasming into an exciting cocktail, Zhan-Yo turned around. Standing across the path from him, clad in similarly bulky winter gear that framed her face in a deep blue jacket's halo, stood a woman Zhan-Yo did not recognize.

"You don't know me, do you?" the woman said. Zhan-Yo glanced at his Tama, Mathieu's questioning face looking back at him, and Zhan-Yo left it alone. He couldn't know what might happen next, and letting a friend listen in might be valuable. "You hurt me, and you don't even know who I am."

Grudges accumulated during a life like his. Running a company like Ziran meant countless decisions that left winners and losers. How was he to know which one had finally decided to take their grievances to a physical end?

"I have many enemies," Zhan-Yo replied. "Which one are you?"

"Your worst."

The woman took three long steps across the walk, like she was going to deliver a hard kick, or maybe a punch. Of all the things Zhan-Yo couldn't have happen, an open brawl on a well-trafficked street numbered up there: the Paragons would come, and then he'd get detained. So instead Zhan-Yo offered up his hands, held them in front of his face and took the pitiful route.

"Stop it," the woman said as she crossed to Zhan-Yo's side, not striking him. "Put your hands down and fight me like you did my father."

And there it was. The hint he needed. No business-man's daughter would come attacking him off the street. But Aegis?

"If I lower my hands, will you let me speak?" Zhan-Yo said. "Or did you come only to kill me?"

"Only to kill you."

To the point, then. Zhan-Yo could admire that. Would admire that, except dying would ruin his plans.

"Then you'll never know why," Zhan-Yo said, still keeping his hands up, now backing until he felt the wall behind him. "I didn't want to kill your father."

"Don't care," the woman said, and Zhan-Yo parted his hands ever-so-slightly to see her walking after him, breath sending clouds as she moved. "What matters is the end result."

"Then you're as short sighted as your father was," Zhan-Yo said, taking a chance.

Aegis's daughter did not take the bait. She quick-stepped up to Zhan-Yo and sent a swift elbow jab into his stomach. Hard-nosed pain radiated, and Zhan-Yo sucked in cold air by the lungful, bending over and coughing it back out. Of course Aegis would have taught his daughter to fight.

Maybe she was an anomaly too, and could break him in a dozen ways.

"Last words?" the woman said.

Zhan-Yo let himself fall forward, into the woman, who sidestepped him with a disgusted noise. As soon as Zhan-Yo's elbows hit the ground, he rolled forward, ignoring his wounded abdomen's protest. Exiting the somersault with a twist, Zhan-Yo stood up into a fighting stance, resting easy on his knees.

The woman laughed at him, even wiped away some tears from her eyes, "How many of you did it take to hurt my father, if this is all you are?"

Around them, nothing seemed to move except occasional pods back on the road and, beyond them, the slow-stepping giant statues in their eternal orbit around the park. Despite the woman's remarks, the space had an epic feel, that buzz when destiny strikes home.

Zhan-Yo couldn't repress a grin. He craved this energy.

"What's your name, little one?" he asked as the woman came towards him again with confident steps. "What did Aegis call you?"

"Celice," the woman answered. "And you don't get to say his name."

Again she burst into a rush, and again Zhan-Yo back-pedaled across the walk and onto the snow dividing the people's trail from the pod's expressway. His feet collapsed the crunchy top, biting into fluff beneath, and Zhan-Yo used it: stopped and kicked the snow up into Celice's charge.

The cold flakes didn't do any damage, but they did cause Celice to close her eyes, to shift a hand to block her face for a second, and in that moment Zhan-Yo stepped forward and to the side, catching Celice as she followed him into the snow and throwing her past him, snaking her ankle with his own. She crashed into the snow, picked herself up almost as quick, standing with flakes coating her hands and spilling hair.

"Aggressive, Celice," Zhan-Yo said, settling in. "Like father, like daughter."

The fight might mean his end for many reasons, but if he couldn't leave it, then Zhan-Yo would, at least, enjoy it.

Celice stared at Zhan-Yo for a long moment, long enough that Zhan-Yo wondered if she was stalling. Maybe give the drones a little more time, but he couldn't see any black orbs rushing their way. Yet.

"My father loved these fights," Celice said, finally taking a slow step towards Zhan-Yo, who stood sturdy on the sidewalk. "He would talk for hours about who threw which punch, snapped which kick. Because in the end, he thought being physically *better* than someone proved you were right."

"A simplistic view," Zhan-Yo replied, back-stepping to keep the distance between them.

Celice put an edge into her voice that made Zhan-Yo ever-so-slightly nervous. A curious calm, coupled with a dead-eyed look, raised the possibility that Celice had cut away her humanity's last bits, leaving cold revenge and its brutality her body's sole command.

"I always saw it different," Celice kept talking, kept walking. "Aegis would beat up his enemies, but they would keep coming back, because you couldn't knock out a movement with a jab. Couldn't destroy an organization with an upper-cut."

"So you did play a part," Zhan-Yo said. "Your father's little helper."

"His protector," Celice replied. "He took care of the surface, I pulled out the roots. Now, I have to do both."

Celice quick-stepped at the last, cutting the distance to Zhan-Yo and driving with a right-handed cut towards Zhan-Yo's stomach. He brought his arms down to block, realized Celice was feinting as she drew her hand up, kicking along with it.

The high strike nailed Zhan-Yo's chin and knocked him back. The sidewalk's soft crunch let him know the follow-up was coming even as Zhan-Yo tried to get his eyes back down, stop the sudden blur in his vision.

Instinct saved him, threw Zhan-Yo forward into Celice's body, barreling into her punch and cutting its effectiveness. He motored his arms, driving quick, close jabs into pressure points while Celice tried to keep herself upright, and failed.

When Zhan-Yo felt her balance falter, he flattened his palms and shoved, sending Celice to the ground, where she slid a meter, glaring up at him with pain etched on her face, blood dribbling from her lip. Zhan-Yo, too, felt the bruising along his jaw where her kick had hit.

With Celice down on the ground, the fight had reached the conclusion. Zhan-Yo, massaging his face, started towards Celice's side. A sharp kick to the head and that'd be the end of it, and Zhan-Yo might even get away.

No drones yet.

She pulled the gun faster than Zhan-Yo thought possible. One second, her hands were on the cold ground, propping her up. The next, they'd slipped inside her coat and emerged with two very illegal handguns aiming right at Zhan-Yo's closing form.

He'd never, ever had a gun pointed at him. Not once in all his years had Zhan-Yo dealt with the immediate life-ending peril put forth by those black barrels.

Zhan-Yo froze. Put up his hands. His mind dashing between what he could say, could do, could believe that would change the outcome.

"Your father never used those," Zhan-Yo said.

"I'm not my father," Celice replied.

"But you're not a killer, either," the voice wasn't his, and Zhan-Yo looked up, along the sidewalk to see Mynx standing there, Paragon uniform bright against the day, black hair riffling in the wind. "Put the guns away, Celice."

"He killed him!" Celice shouted, not turning away from Zhan-Yo. "He killed him and you want me to put these away?"

"He's already taken care of," Mynx said, and Zhan-Yo raised his eyebrows, opened his mouth to ask a question, and felt two sudden slams into his back knock him forward.

Zhan-Yo didn't stay awake to see the ground he hit.

36

Daughter's Rage

The drones shot Zhan-Yo. Hit him with two stunning darts, and then Mynx helped drag the man's limp body into one of their cramped cargo holds. With a short command to take Zhan-Yo to the airport, the drones left Mynx and jetted away.

"I want him all the way out," Mynx said. "Back to our facility."

"Near home?" Reeves, her AI, spoke over the Tama. "Isn't that close to the summit for someone like him?"

"Close enough that I can wring whatever he's got left out and still make it to my event."

"Isn't that a risk, though?" Reeves replied. "I don't want to seem nervous, but putting Zhan-Yo close to the Champions is asking for catastrophe."

"He'll be sealed in and sedated," Mynx said. "As soon as we have our chat, I'll ship him off to the island. See how long he lasts with all those other anomalies. Maybe Thane will bite his head off."

"That's a grim image."

Mynx didn't disagree, but she did look down the sidewalk, where Celice had stopped her stalking and watched from an overlook. Waiting for a conversation that had to happen, one Mynx wasn't looking forward to.

What did you do with your best friend's dangerous, ambitious daughter?

"Where are you taking him?" Celice asked when Mynx closed in. They both turned to watch the lake and the ice floes, what Zhan-Yo had been doing too. "Off to some secret torture chamber, I hope?"

"We'll get what he knows. Apinya's coming to the summit. If Zhan-Yo won't talk to me, then Apinya will take his mind."

"What do you think you'll find? Some grand plan?" Celice laughed. "You think a guy who wanders by the lake, by himself, has some big force waiting for the word go? You should have let me shoot him."

"That would've done you no favors either." Mynx put a hand on Celice's shoulder. "Have you ever taken a life?"

Celice shook her head. "He should have been my first."

"No," Mynx replied. "You should never have a first. Keep your slate clean. Your dreams won't be so terrible."

"That's what dad used to say," Celice brushed her hair from her face, set her hands on what must have been ice cold stone. "Every one sticks with you."

"For him, I'm sure."

"But not you?"

"It's different when you're in a machine, or controlling one," Mynx said. "I don't get too personal."

Aegis had struck a deal with Mynx, when the Champions realized delivering knockout blows wasn't quite enough. When their enemies progressed from anomaly criminals to armies and rogue states. Mynx designed weapons able to level hundreds, thousands.

Making drones to destroy had been easy. Mynx had gone along with the idea, powered by Aegis's rhetoric and Apinya's philosophical necessity: create a new world, powered by those with powers rather than greed and corruption. She'd delivered, and when those first enemies fell, torn apart by missiles and bullets, Mynx hadn't felt the pain. The soul-rifting agony Aegis said came with every fatal blow.

But maybe she had, and didn't know it. Maybe the numb, cold view Mynx had adopted in the years since, where hostile lives were obstacles rather than people, had come with those early days and never left.

"Dad liked to say the Champions didn't practice vengeance," Celice said. "I never thought that was true. He'd hold on to people that crossed him or the Paragons. Talk about them with me. My friends at school would laugh about the movies or some theme park while I'd hear about some brutal monster halfway around the world with dinner."

"You were his outlet. Aegis always tried to keep the organization clean. I didn't care, but he knew people wouldn't follow us if we kept grudges. If the strongest anomalies on the planet couldn't forgive, then how could anyone else? The Paragons have teams that stay away from the spotlight. They catch important criminals, then we haul them to justice."

"Away from the spotlight. That's funny. You run the trackers. Aren't they just like me? Dedicated to hunting down lawbreakers?"

"Reeves runs the trackers more than I do," Mynx shivered, her kinetic suit was about empty. Time to make tracks towards somewhere warm. "I'm not going to preach to you, Celice. Your dad was murdered, how you deal with it is up to you. But Zhan-Yo committed a crime, and he has to pay for that crime publicly. With Paragon justice, and nothing else. So whether you leave him alone to spare your soul, or because your father would have wanted you to, I don't care. Pick one."

Mynx pushed off the wall, turned to head towards a waiting pod.

"I thought you were my friend?" Celice asked Mynx's back. "And that's what you say to me, about the man that killed my father? Pick one?"

"We all had to make hard choices to get here, your father included. You want to stay with us, you have to learn. The Paragons, the Champions are bigger than you and what you want. So yes, pick one, and move on. The world already has."

Harsh, maybe. Then again, Mynx had faced similar choices as she'd grown older, as the Paragons had grown. Too many times to count, they'd had to make the call whether to eliminate enemies, and former friends who no longer agreed with the Paragon's growing power. Losses, too, had to be dispensed with. Give them a cry, a funeral, and move on.

If Celice still wanted it, after Zhan-Yo had his trial, had his guilt and shame displayed for the world to see, so anyone else thinking his thoughts would see how far they could fall, Mynx would let her pull that trigger. Celice could do it in a back room, with nobody watching. Excise her anger, and see if expelling Zhan-Yo from the living would give her any satisfaction.

A body had never offered Mynx any solace. The victory, yes. The solution, yes. The final act? No. Mynx left that to the machines now. They didn't care, and they didn't fail.

Mynx watched Celice as the pod pulled away, Aegis's

daughter had turned back to the lake, staring out over it as though her answer lay among the ice.

Who knew, maybe it did?

37

The Beach

Arthur's plan would kill them all. Thane knew this as well as he knew anything, though Arthur's showy presentation, complete with a sand diagram embedded into a crude table, seemed to sell Cassidy and the other anomalies in the wide room.

That they stood in a room at all testified to Arthur's power on the island. If Cassidy's group had beachside huts and fishing nets, the Duchess improved upon that with an actual town and bigger, if still thatched, homes. Arthur had a brittle village.

The explanation, as they had walked through a fully-functioning wooden gate, settled on several anomalies whose powers could work in unison to mold sand into stable, resilient glass. The binding shaded the sand darker, making the village's walls, homes, the gate, all appear like shiny mud.

An interesting look, and not one Thane would choose given any options, but on an island like this, you worked with what you had, and what Arthur had beat out the rest.

Here, in this room, Thane even had a chair. Cushioned

with a grass and leaf weave, the chairs ringed Arthur's central table in a house lit with torches. That table, uncovered now to reveal a sandbox inside with drawn diagrams, pulled Thane back to Paragon planning meetings long ago. While crude compared to computers, the table's real power came from everyone standing in the same place, sharing opinions and ideas.

"Anywhere else, you'd burn the place down," Arthur said as he demonstrated his own power to light the first torch. Thane couldn't detect the dimmer light around him as Arthur drew the sun's energy for the first flame, but all the other torches dwindled when Arthur siphoned their photons for the next one in line. The anomaly touched each unlit wick, his arm glowing, and fire sparked and spawned. "But our houses are strong, fireproof. Better than home, I think."

Sure, if you didn't mind dirt floors, no indoor plumbing, and lived only in places with ideal climates. Thane, though, kept his mouth shut. Let the man show off his toys.

Thane could take them away later.

In the sand, cradled by hardened versions of itself, Arthur had drawn out his way to escape the island. Thane, Cassidy, and several other anomalies had watched as Arthur illustrated various positions, responsibilities, and timings that would, if carried to an absolute perfect ending, ruin enough drones to let them escape.

"We can't fight them directly," Thane said, not for the first time that evening. "Most of these anomalies don't have combat training, gear, or abilities. They'll be slaughtered."

"They'll be protected." Arthur jabbed a glass poker into the sand's center, where he'd drawn an A to mark his spot. "I'll draw the drones, remember? Anyone not able to contribute to the ambush will be hidden away. They'll jump on the arks and wait."

"Mynx made these drones. They won't fall for your trick."

Arthur pointed at Cassidy, "What about you? Awfully quiet. Going to let this one keep throwing insults at my plan?"

"I'm with Thane," Cassidy said. "We can't win a war. We can, maybe, manage an escape."

"Right," Thane continued, trying to keep his anger in check so that he didn't start slurring words, lose his ideas. "An arrow. From your docks and straight south, to Hawaii. It's the closest inhabited place."

Blocked by Thane and Cassidy, Arthur turned to the other anomalies now, spreading his hands like a salesman disgusted by the foolish words he heard.

"Ah, yes. Go right to where Mynx, this person you claim knows everything, would suspect," Arthur said. "If you don't destroy the drones, then they'll follow you. Break through their line and they'll hunt you down."

Thane couldn't argue with that point. The drones would definitely follow, and would do so with lethal intent. Escaping would mean a fighting retreat until they could lose their pursuit. Which, they could.

"That's where we need help," Thane said. "But with what I'm seeing here, I think we can manage it."

"Manage it?" Cassidy asked. "I didn't think we'd worked that out yet."

Arthur laughed, "See? They don't even know their own plans!"

"No," Thane said. "You're the key." Was Arthur really the key? Thane couldn't know for sure, but it generally helped to butter up someone's ego. "The ones that make your glass? They can dome the arks. Seal them tight, but leave a door. Then, we head off and keep you protected. You draw in the sun's energy, send it into the sea."

"Making steam." Arthur said, his grin settling into a straight look that Thane took as a positive sign. "Blind the drones for a moment, and then submerge. If the timing's right, we might lose them."

"And we won't leave so many anomalies to die," Cassidy said.

Now Arthur nodded along with them, "We'll still need to draw the drones into the center. Without that, they'll just surround us, and submerge or no, we'll be followed."

"Anyone we send to the center won't make it back in time," Thane said. "It would be suicide."

"Not so!" Arthur said. "And here I see a way our plans can come together. We had never intended for the volcano to be our last stand, but rather a gathering point to draw the drones in, where I could use the lava's light and energy to destroy them. Such a thing might rupture the volcano itself, so we have been making gliders."

Cassidy snorted, crossed her arms, "Gliders? You're going to blow up all the machines and just float back home?"

"Of course," Arthur said. "We had been working with the Duchess to stock them, but you must have dealt with her before learning about our deal?"

"We didn't talk much," Thane said.

"Well, thankfully, we did." Arthur jammed his stick in the sand's center, like a flag. "We draw the drones in, destroy what we can, then glide to you and make our escape. Perfect."

"These gliders," Thane said. "How long until they're ready?"

Arthur looked over at another anomaly, a thick-set one

with manic eyes and hands that, Thane noticed, never stayed still.

"We have the design," the anomaly rumbled. "Another month to build the prototypes, another to test and perfect, another just to be sure. Three months?"

"No," Thane replied. "Too long."

"Too long? You've only just arrived. We've been here for years. Why the hurry?"

"Because you've been here for years." Thane jabbed a finger into the sand, circled the ship. "We have enough anomalies. Together, we can break our way to freedom without the gliders. And we can do it tomorrow."

"Tomorrow? That'll never work. No. We need time to prepare."

"You've had it. I've seen your town. You have food to store, most of the island's anomalies that want to leave are here already. Waiting only makes leaving harder."

"Your haste will get us killed."

"Your laziness will keep us here forever."

"But we will be alive," Arthur said, then held up both his hands, one going to his forehead for a soft rub over closed eyes. "I'm sorry, but I'm exhausted, and this argument is doing nothing for my headache. We'll continue this conversation in the morning."

AFTER A SESSION LIKE THAT, Thane didn't feel at all tired. Neither did Cassidy. Arthur, after his declaration, made a second about his imminent bedtime and the other anomalies did the same, letting Thane and Cassidy escape into the night and a village at rest.

They didn't have to talk to know where to go: the beach, where Cassidy's bunch had already settled with their ragged bed rolls. Cook fire remnants spoke of a meager dinner, but thus far there hadn't been a single fight.

"Do you think it can work?" Thane asked Cassidy as they wandered away from the others, waves licking at their feet.

"You're the one who fought so hard for it."

"I know, and I believe in it. But I need you to trust the plan as well. Their courage will falter, and the others will look to you, not me."

"Hah," Cassidy said, then pointed to a spot on the beach a meter ahead. A hole appeared, as though an invisible spoon had scooped out the sand. Seawater rushed in to fill it. "See that? I trust that. Anything else is just a guess."

The display had Thane confused, "I don't understand. If you had so little confidence, then why did you come along? Why help me?"

"It's not you." Cassidy stopped and turned out towards the horizon, hugging her shoulders. "It's all this. Everyone. I know we're killing each other, I know we don't have all the things I used to love. I know my family isn't here. But Thane, like Arthur said, we're alive."

She looked at him, and Thane felt his muscles growing tired, softer as he tried to puzzle her out. Tried to put himself in her mind.

"Stop," Cassidy said. "You're changing. Just, let me talk. Then you can do your mind stuff if you want."

Thane used Cassidy's order as motivation. Held onto the tiniest pricked pride and let that wound build him back up. Cassidy waited, alternating looks towards to the waves and Thane's face.

"You about normal again?" Cassidy asked.

"I have no normal," Thane replied. "But, I can't read your thoughts, if that's what you mean."

"Good enough, I guess. What I'm trying to tell you is

that I'm afraid. I have a lot to lose here, and I've been wondering, for a while now, if that wasn't Mynx's whole plan. If she put us here to see whether we could become better people than we were."

"She's not coming back for you."

"You don't know that. Those drones watch our every move. Maybe all we have to pass is some algorithm and a plane will show up, take us home. We fight against the drones, maybe we lose all that. Maybe we lose everything."

Thane said nothing. It was a choice, as it had been for Cassidy every minute she'd been on this island. Run, or fight. She'd been running so far, and all it had brought her was smoked fish and the constant threat that some anomaly would slaughter her as she slept.

He wanted to say all that, but it seemed cruel. Unnecessary.

"Then you have to choose," Thane said. "Me, or Mynx. You could leave tonight, go back to your huts, and spend your days waiting. Or you could act, with me, and control your own destiny."

"Easy to say when you're so hard to kill, when you're risking so little."

Thane shook his head, "I'm risking you, and that is no small thing."

The words surprised him as much as they must have surprised Cassidy, but they were true nonetheless. Thane had only known the Void for a few days, but they had spent hours and hours together, known danger and hope together, and, logically, Thane supposed it made sense.

It had been so long since he'd cared about anyone beyond himself. So long, he wasn't sure he still knew how.

But when he felt her fingers find his, Thane still knew how to hold her hand.

38

Detective Work

The killer didn't want to be found. Kat gave the rifle another once-over—a somewhat surreal experience sitting on her couch with a weapon that large—and confirmed every single identifier had been scrubbed. If, indeed, the rifle had ever had any to begin with. The barrel and body seemed new, or kept up with fanatic care. While most bullet-firing weapons like this were from pre-Paragon control, Kat would bet this one had been made only months ago.

Paragon law forbade these weapons because the Champions weren't invincible. Most anomalies weren't Aegis, and could be downed from distance with a well-placed shot. If Kat remembered her history right, the first Paragons lost large numbers fighting against things like this, and its faster-firing brethren. Then, they changed tactics.

Her parents had told Kat stories about those days, back when the Paragons were emerging and anomalies were choosing sides. Those with the strongest abilities, the ones able to wipe out dozens or hundreds or thousands with a wave, or able to neutralize armies with a blink, became commodities. Nations played loyalty cards, trying to convince their genetic lottery winners that they should put their country before their powers. Join the rank and file, fight for your leaders.

The Paragons offered change. Equality in an organization that respected and would fight for you. With Aegis standing at the front, surviving one assassination attempt after another as the normals saw their looming end, any anomaly true to their kind knew which way to go.

One night, as the world edged towards global conflict, the Paragons made a clinching move. Kat didn't remember names, but she remembered the images. Held up like treasures from a legendary past, the pictures, videos, and anecdotes gave the night—referred to by the Paragons as 'the Pacifying', by everyone else as 'the last time normals ruled the planet'—its due: Paragon strike teams, using anomalies and their combined powers, destroyed or rendered useless almost every significant military outpost across the world.

Kat's mom seemed to struggle with the implications that represented: if the Paragons were so afraid of these things, yet had the power to obliterate them all in less than twelve hours, weren't the Paragons even more dangerous? Her father, though, exulted in the moment. That was when the Paragons crossed the line from fringe group to a world-wide force, from a blip to an inevitability.

"We knew true heroes changed the world," her father had said, once, before they knew Kat wouldn't have any powers, wouldn't be an anomaly. "That day, we proved we could really do it, and they couldn't stop us."

Talk about a phrase that'd turned as Kat grew up, as she went to her own Gateway test, double-anomaly parents excited to see what their daughter might do with those mighty genes, and nothing. Nothing.

Rifles like this one had been the normal's power for so long. The stun guns Kat used, those pale imitations, they fit the Paragon's legal lines. Kept any normals from getting too strong, from doing exactly what this killer had in mind.

The days after her Gateway had seared into a long stretch in Kat's memory. Her parents tried to spare the pain, embarrassment by telling relatives themselves, but Kat didn't care about aunts and uncles, grandparents, cousins. Not even the other kids at school, most of whom turned out like her. Any granted anomaly gifts by the genetic gods disappeared into the Paragon's programs.

The small changes hurt. How her parents reacted when Kat came down in the morning, how they spoke, more now, of what she might want to do when she graduated. Stressed optimism tinged their voices, and what had been love began to feel less so, a toxin seeping in through touch and tone.

So Kat took to leaving. Spending nights with friends, or at the park, or the library, or anywhere else but in that house where everything reminded Kat that she had failed. Until her sister, through lottery luck infinitely worse than Kat's, solved that problem and created millions more.

The rifle didn't have a number on it, didn't have a name attached, but that didn't mean the weapon couldn't be traced. Someone had made the thing, and it wasn't the first time Kat or the Paragons had come across something like this. The nice thing about ruling the world: you tended to have resources.

WITH THE DRONES running surveillance and handling most policing duties, the old stations around Chicago and, Kat supposed, everywhere else switched to support Paragon needs instead. These went from the usual complaints about a drone knocking over this or that, to pleas for anomaly help in rescuing, say, a lost pet. Kat used the stations to drop any anomalies she'd rounded up, and occasionally, to access some services the Paragons kept to themselves.

Like who might be manufacturing illegal weapons around the area.

"That's a pretty one," said the Paragon, an older woman in that bright blue uniform, hair pulled back in the one concession she made to severity. Everything else, from her slouch to her half-lidded eyes spoke to a crushing boredom not even the rifle could penetrate. "Give it over."

Kat had crossed the station's threshold, from its boring lobby with its carbon-copy Aegis statue—these would be, no doubt, replaced with Atlantis's new Champion eventually—to the warren hallway network lying behind. Anomaly and normal holding cells adjoined equipment lockers, split from offices with thick walls.

Kat had heard the marketing pitch for the gray-scale concrete walls, supposedly 'power-proof'. Normals with pre-rep fortunes burned it all on homes made with this stuff. Ridiculous. Nobody could guarantee an anomaly wouldn't be able to blow something apart. Or turn it into jelly. Or nothing at all.

Now Kat watched as the woman lifted the rifle, balanced it between her hands. Kat could have sworn the woman's uniform suddenly glowed a bit, like a lamp turning on, and the woman nodded.

"We've seen ones like this before," the woman said, setting the rifle on her desk and tapping on her Tama. "They're all coming from the same place. Not too far from here actually."

"What?"

The woman glanced up, as confused as Kat, "Did you not hear me?"

"No," Kat shook her head. "No, I don't get it. You said you have more of these?"

"Oh, yes. Not rifles like this one, but smaller weapons," the woman chuckled, as if lethal tools were just hilarious. "Amazing how many these people lose. We get them turned in all the time."

"These people?"

"It's a group." The woman chuckled again, though more dire this time. "If you want to call it that. They collect these guns from outside the city. We don't know what they're doing with them, but every so often they screw up, get caught or drop one of these things."

"Wait, so this happens often? Like, it's ongoing?"

Kat's tone frosted the woman's attitude, and she leaned back behind her desk, holding her arms straight against the surface, as though pushing Kat away.

"You're sounding judgmental, tracker," the Paragon said. "I'd watch your tone."

"Watch my tone? You're telling me you've been letting a bunch of armed killers run around the city?"

"Killers? Hardly. They don't bother normals. They don't bother us."

Kat wished she was naive enough to take that response and be fine. Wished she couldn't connect the dots, wished she didn't understand how the Elementals and the Paragons, who both wanted to avoid anomalies fighting in the streets, could use other agents to get after each other.

"So because they're targeting Elementals, mostly, you don't care," Kat said.

"That's what Innis said. They stay in their lane, we stay in ours. It's not like the Elementals are helpless: all the weapons we get come from fights they win."

"Yeah, well, not anymore." Kat pointed at the rifle. "These people aren't playing fair. They took a shot at Calvin. A Paragon. And, I don't know, do you not care, at all, about being on the good side here?"

The woman considered Kat for a long moment. Maybe reconciling her current self with the one who, however many years ago, had stepped into that blue uniform with something larger in mind than blithely letting killers go to work in her neighborhood.

"Look," the woman said. "I'm not a fighter, and, really, none of us here are. That's what the drones are for. You want to pursue this, I'll send the address to your Tama. That's where all these weapons get picked up."

"Thanks," Kat said, then took one more look at the long rifle. "How do you know? Can you read it somehow?"

The woman offered a sad smile, "When someone attaches a strong emotion to an object, I can see that moment. Trace it. You want to kill or hurt someone, that's a big deal. All these guns, that beacon comes from the same spot."

A spot Kat would be going, ready to mix it up, and ready to do what the Paragons wouldn't. Because someone had to, damn it.

39

Interrogation

Zhan-Yo crackled like melting ice. His bones ached, his muscles twinged as nerves flailed, and his brain filled with fog. Even so, he could see the walls, gray and smooth, like unpainted, perfect concrete. The floor matched, and when Zhan-Yo realized he laid on that hard surface with nothing in between, the aches made sense.

Especially when his Tama told Zhan-Yo he'd been lying there for hours.

Worse, his Tama told him nothing else. Total disconnection from any network. Only a blinking clock and an error symbol came from the device on his wrist, Zhan-Yo's connection to the world.

A lone door sat on the far side, slotted even with the wall, and a shiny silver. No windows, and the white light came from a glowing ceiling, as if the whole thing constituted one large lamp.

Mynx had taken him, Zhan-Yo recalled that much. Probably saved his life, as it looked like Celice had been about to pull that trigger. If Zhan-Yo had to guess, though,

Mynx would probably finish that job as soon as she extracted whatever information she wanted.

And how would she get that knowledge? Would she torture Zhan-Yo?

The thought came with a strange emotional mix. Apprehension, yes, but with a little excitement. Zhan-Yo had never been captured before. A man could be measured in many ways, and seeing how long Zhan-Yo might stand up to interrogation was one of them.

His rational side dismissed this notion as stupid, foolish. Embracing a toxic perspective. Zhan-Yo should be afraid, should be readying what he could give up to save his own life. The revolution only stood a chance with him at the head, no matter who he had to give up to stay there.

The door cracked open, a pop-hiss that told Zhan-Yo the air in this particular cell could be sealed away. Suffocation, gassing, all possible. All unsettling.

The first thing through trundled in on five narrow legs, each one ending in a flexible metal claw. A gleaming, boxy machine about a meter high, a black nub camera sticking from its top like a boil. Following that came Mynx, and behind her a third, a humanoid drone that Zhan-Yo recognized from security operations around Chicago. The last one held an assault-grade stunning rifle, blue lines running across the weapon's gray metal giving away its purpose.

"We never had a proper introduction," Zhan-Yo managed, sitting up and hiding a pain-induced grimace. "Thank you for saving me."

"I wouldn't be so happy," Mynx replied.

Despite all his stature, his goals, and his experience, Zhan-Yo's heart curdled as Mynx sent her set stare his way. Being in a legend's presence warped reality—Zhan-Yo had watched, and rooted for, Mynx and Aegis and the other Champions for a long time before souring on their efforts

— and the room and its contents fuzzed. Zhan-Yo's ears rang, and his eyes burned as Mynx continued her silent judgment.

It felt like his mother's disappointment. His own shame.

Logic struggled through the emotions. Fought against the tide as Mynx waved the spindly drone forward. Zhan-Yo wasn't a child. He'd considered the consequences, and knew them before he'd acted. The Champions weren't his parents. They had no moral high ground. Mynx, Aegis, weren't the heroes Zhan-Yo had idolized: those were myths, these were people.

Flawed people.

One breath, two. Focus, as Chloe, his martial arts instructor, often said. In conflict, throw out the extras and focus on the here and now. Like how this robot had come very close, and how Zhan-Yo didn't want the thing to touch him.

"Don't fight, or I'll knock you out again," Mynx said as Zhan-Yo edged away from the drone. "And I'd love to do that, but it makes talking difficult."

"What is that thing doing?"

Zhan-Yo rose to his feet, so that the drone only came up to his waist. The change didn't stop the drone, who kept crawling after Zhan-Yo with a patient pace. The machine seemed to know Zhan-Yo had nowhere to escape, which did nothing for Zhan-Yo's tired nerves.

"I believe you're a smart man." Mynx and the other drone hadn't moved from their spots near the door. "And you were a very wealthy one. Someone like you doesn't risk it all without a plan, and I think a plan like yours requires help."

Zhan-Yo backed into a corner, then loosened his knees as the spider drone drew nearer. If he had to fight the thing, he would. As the drone crawled within a meter, Zhan-Yo snapped a kick. It didn't connect. Or rather, his foot hit the drone's leading claw, which had risen up at ludicrous speed to catch Zhan-Yo's attack. The drone jerked Zhan-Yo's kicking foot, and Ziran's former leader, the revolution's spark, found himself landing hard on his back, staring at the white ceiling trying to catch his breath.

"I don't expect you to tell me the truth. Not without some confirmation," Mynx said, and from her voice, she'd moved closer. "You know that we did not design the Tama. The Champions, I mean?"

Zhan-Yo raised his head as he felt, saw, the spider drone's second claw land on his chest and spread. The machine pinned Zhan-Yo, and when he tried to move, the pressure increased to stick him down, force the air from his lungs. When Zhan-Yo laid back down, the force relaxed, letting him breathe.

Those were the rules.

"I know the inventor," Zhan-Yo said. "Ziran invested in his company."

"So did the Paragons, and we were very persuasive," Mynx said. Zhan-Yo looked to the left, and there Mynx stood, only she didn't look at his face, but his left wrist. The Champion nodded once. "Your wrist has everything we need."

"Impossible. Tamas delete everything when they're removed. That's the only way I'd wear one."

"Impossible is relative."

Zhan-Yo felt a prick near his elbow, and within seconds his entire left arm went numb. He raised his head, the machine keeping his chest down, and did all he could to keep his scream in his mind.

When it came to promises in modern times, the Tama maintained an unbreakable one. Your friend, your teacher, your memory from the moment you attached one to the moment you died, your Tama was supposed to be yours, and yours alone. Sure, things you beamed out from it might be intercepted, but the data it gathered about your health, the recordings that it made, the moments it stored away, all driven by algorithms designed to filter out boring and keep meaning, those were yours.

Only yours.

The drone pressed another claw against Zhan-Yo's Tama's screen. The metal ends spread out, covering the face, before tiny flaps all along the claw opened and what looked like a hundred tiny tools sprang out. Little blue-white flashes sparked as the devices spread like a canopy over Zhan-Yo's Tama, and he'd seen enough Ziran manu-facturing to know those lights marked precise measurements.

"How have you kept this secret?" Zhan-Yo whispered as the little tools found their positions. "Nobody would—"

"Walk it through," Mynx said, keeping her eyes on the drone. "You'll figure it out."

The drone, from somewhere deep in its mechanized guts, gave a buzzing whine, and the tools when into motion. Diving into the Tama, digging into micro-sized holes Zhan-Yo didn't know existed, but that must have been there. Must have been put there in the design. Back-doored by the Paragons.

With his left arm numb, Zhan-Yo didn't feel the weight leave his wrist a minute later. Didn't notice that, for the first time in nearly fifteen years, his arms were the same. He could see, though, and the hairless, bleach white spot on his arm looked alien. Tamas used various means to keep their areas sterilized and clean, but they couldn't, didn't ensure the skin they covered matched anywhere else. Why would they? You'd never be alive to see it.

The drone lifted the Tama away, its screen and connecting bracelet hanging loose and limp in the air. For all it contained, the device seemed so small, so insignificant.

"I'm going to go take a look at this," Mynx said. "Unfortunately for both of us, I'm going to be busy, so it might be a while before I come back with questions."

The drone lifted its claw off of Zhan-Yo's chest as it retreated towards the door. The claws release, and the sudden desperation in seeing his Tama flying away from him, sent Zhan-Yo curling up and bursting at Mynx. The only chance to get the Tama back, or to destroy it, lay in taking the Champion hostage.

He never made it.

The stunning shot struck Zhan-Yo before any progress, and his half-rise turned into a spasm as he fell to the side, a far cry from a mighty warrior, from a last stand, from anything. Mynx watched, a frown growing into what looked, almost, like genuine sadness.

"You really do believe in yourself," Mynx said. "If it helps, if it matters, we do, too. And we will do anything to protect the world we've made." Her own Tama beeped, and Mynx looked up, turned to the door. "Get some rest. Try to have some good dreams, one last time."

Zhan-Yo didn't see Mynx leave the room, didn't hear the guarding drone lock him in again, because as Mynx finished speaking, he left consciousness behind.

40

On Site

Despite rending a Tama from the would-be killer of her oldest friend, Mynx felt pretty damn good as she descended into the rooftop landing pad on the stadium roof. Over the last week, drone and human crews had converted the giant venue into a Paragon-blue-clad center ready to host the world's Champions, regional Paragon leads, and countless vendor groups that'd put together hasty agendas. Remarkable, really, how fast companies could move when given the chance to pitch their visions to the world's ruling body.

And it started today. Tonight, in fact.

"Who's arrived?" Mynx asked as the drone touched down, this one large enough for Mynx to sit in an actual chair, compared to her cramped jet or the hands-on, small drone collection she wore for her own exploits. "Tell me it's not everyone."

Yes, eventually Mynx wanted all the Champions to show. Tomorrow would start the real discussions to get to a unified succession message, a template for how the world would go on turning as Champions retired or, as hard as the thought might be, died. She hoped today might serve as a warm-up, a tentative ice-breaking for some who hadn't seen each other in years. Too much personal baggage, too many fragile egos at once and Mynx feared the whole event might collapse before it started.

"Apinya and Burov are on the premises," Reeves replied. "They're talking. Politely."

"Anyone else on the way?"

"The pods show nobody yet, but incoming flight records show all the Champions, including Pixie, have arrived in the LA area."

"So the party could start at any moment."

"I would not call it a party."

Mynx nodded to nothing but air. Reeves would see it, of course, as the AI linked to the cameras crawling the stadium, to her own Tama, to the pods and air traffic control and every other system in Pacifica. Sometimes she mused whether giving Reeves all this power was wise, if Mynx couldn't trust her own code and the limits it placed on Reeves, then she ought to destroy the drones too. And any anomaly with great enough power to cause damage on a similar scale.

In short, potential disasters filled the world, and right now Mynx only had space for one.

Burov held the floor in the stadium's center, standing on a stage and boasting to Apinya about something or other that Mynx had missed, thankfully. She had wandered the maze leading from top to bottom and onto an artificial field, covered with chairs holding signs guiding tomorrow's attendees to their proper rows and groups.

"Thank goodness, our hostess has arrived," Apinya said, looking manicured and bright in a red Paragon uniform, with the logo and seams a pure black. "Mynx, can you rescue me from this torture?" He waved back towards Burov. "I believe if I listen to him anymore I'll lose what sanity I have left."

Burov, who maintained the Paragon blue beneath, in a clever homage to the old countries that had made up his region, a jacket seemingly laced from their flags. Los Angeles kept it warm in February, so Mynx wasn't sure how the Champion avoided the sweat, but Burov seemed as pristine as Apinya.

The Russian didn't share Apinya's mild-mannered greeting. Instead, Burov leapt off the stage, strode past Apinya and wrapped Mynx in a seconds-long hug. His breath smelled like cloves, and Mynx had to keep herself from coughing when Burov pulled away and draped an arm over an eye-rolling Apinya.

"We've come!" Burov announced. "The Champions together in this magnificent place you've built. Look at all this blue. How many cameras will be rolling? Are we on right now?" He cast his wide grin around, then shook his head while Mynx stared, eyebrow arched. "Mynx, I know you've never been one for the show, but this is an opportunity not to be missed!"

"And yet, how I wish I could," Mynx replied, failing to hide a smile. "It's good to see you two, and I'm glad you're here early. If we can establish a position, then I think the three of us can get the others to go along."

Around them, field workers continued setting up, all observed by several hovering security drones. Blue-uniformed Paragons from Pacifica roamed the grounds and used their abilities to add sparkling flare to the decor, to float up to other levels, or to practice placing illusions for the opening ceremony. Activity aplenty, and that brought listening ears, so with Burov complaining about the sudden switch to work, the three of them abandoned the stadium's center for one of the dull, but far more private, boxes.

. . .

THE TRIO MADE it as far as the outer concourse, heading for escalators up. The churning black steps almost covered the approaching feet, but the Champions, with battle-forged habits, couldn't ignore the running footfalls.

Three people, decidedly not in Paragon blue or anything close to it, closed at a sprint. The area around the escalators, a wide open concrete vista with curved floor-to-faraway-ceiling windows on one side and the stacked levels on the other, provided an ideal battleground. Which would fit the people coming towards them perfectly.

"Don't," Apinya muttered as the trio closed. "They're not going to fight."

Strong words. Rosamund led the three, her refined composure rankled by the run. The other two, a youngish man—Mynx had lost the ability to guess an age with any accuracy—and an older woman, seemed to fare better, but their tans told of homes close to here, while Rosamund had come quite a long way from the northeast. Not that the distance had calmed the cold fury on her face.

"No invitation!" Rosamund said by way of a greeting. "None. Yet you call this a meeting to determine the plan-et's future?"

Though Rosamund spoke straight at Mynx, Pacifica's Champion didn't have a chance to breathe before Burov stepped in front, once again with his arms out wide, a showman mocking his audience.

"Ah, if it isn't the Elementals? Feeling left out, were you? Too bad! If you want, I invite you to come to my region when this is done. Plenty of fun there for all of us."

Rosamund threw the Russian a narrowed look, then stepped around him and went right to Mynx. Not a bad play. Burov, unlike the other Champions, had taken a hard line against Elemental operations in his part of the world. Any anomalies unaffiliated with the Paragons were caught, traced, and put back into operation, and that was that. Didn't matter what organization you said you belonged to.

"Are you going to let this beast speak for you?" Rosamund said.

"Burov, please." Mynx sighed. "This is my home, not yours."

That earned her a dismissive shrug from the Champion, but Burov moved aside, which was as much as Mynx could hope for.

"It's our home too, and we want a chance to fight for our place in it," Rosamund said, thankfully backing off a step. "I—"

"How did you get in?" Mynx cut her off. "I need to know if security has holes."

"Your security is fine," Rosamund said, and Mynx caught a slight pupil shift to Rosamund's left, towards the young man. "Nobody else can do what we did, and we're not here for a fight. Obviously."

"Not obvious," Apinya observed. "Everything about your approach says otherwise. I thought the Elementals wanted more than blood in the streets, yet here you are, like any other villain. Refusing to play by the rules."

"The rules are rigged," Rosamund said. "You all know it."

That's because those in power made the rules, but Mynx didn't say that. She let Rosamund and Apinya banter back and forth, their arguments getting increasingly esoteric and abstract. There were solutions here, and they went from hard rejections to giving the Elementals a slot to present their point of view, which, no. Never.

"You can attend," Mynx said. "You, Rosamund, and that's it. And you can listen, but no questions."

Rosamund snorted, "How's that fair?"

"It's not, but that's what I'm willing to give you," Mynx said. "You wanted in, and I'm giving you that chance. If you don't blow it, maybe there'll be more later."

Apinya and Burov caught the cue and headed for the escalator. Mynx, after matching glares with Rosamund for a solid second, followed. The Champion felt a headache coming on, and she still had a whole day ahead. Reeves would have to bring some tea, maybe some pills, if Mynx needed to dance like this for hours yet.

"I'm going to be here!" Rosamund shouted up after them. "We all deserve a voice, Mynx!"

And Rosamund, unfortunately, knew how to use hers.

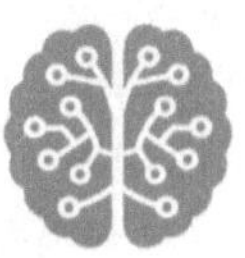

41

The Turn

The surf changed along with Thane. At first, in the early morning dark, every splash came chill and prickly. As Thane willed himself towards determination, towards force and drive, his body joined the dive towards resilience, crashing into the bubbling waves.

Behind and around him on the beach, other anomalies rose to greet the day in their own fashions. Some sparkled to life with their own abilities: one woke and shook off golden flakes, like shedding a skin, while another reached towards the sea and, like a suction, funneled ocean water into his cupped hand and drank it. Rituals cast in iron through days, months, years waking up to the same horizon, the same black line floating out there watching them all.

"You're always up early," Cassidy said, brushing sand from her skin as she came up beside him. "And this water's freezing."

"Is it?" Thane said, looking down at the surf. "I don't feel much like this."

"I noticed." Cassidy squinted as the sun began its entrance.

Watching dawn had become commonplace since Thane had made it to the island. Something about lacking unnatural light had him getting up when the sky turned frozen blue, then purple, then orange. There never seemed to be any clouds right then, and the stars would wink out one by one, the universe saying goodbye as Thane zeroed in to Earth.

Neither one said a word until the sun had its full bulk over the horizon, three black specks marring its perfect surface.

"Are you ready?" Thane asked.

"You're not giving us much time."

"I don't have much time to give," Thane replied. "Every day we spend here is wasted. Those who want to stay will stay, and those who want to leave lose time we will never get back."

"But we could find a better plan," Cassidy said.

To their left, an anomaly approached the ocean, but she kept looking over their way. Thane recognized her, but couldn't place the name until Cassidy said it, aloud and with enough spice to catch Thane's attention.

"She left us," Cassidy said when she noticed his questioning look. "We were friends, I thought. Until she didn't come back."

Sienna, her long hair—most everyone on the island had long hair—spreading out behind her in the breeze, gave Cassidy a small smile, then turned towards the ocean. The anomaly stood still, as if falling into some meditative trance, then Sienna's right arm, hand balled into a fist, punched skyward.

Sienna pulled her arm down, then punched it up again, and again, and again.

"What is she doing?" Thane said. Anomaly powers could be anything, but he hadn't seen one like this. "Hitting the air?"

"Just watch," Cassidy glowered.

The ocean, out some meters, frothed and bubbled. Waves crashed where they hadn't before, pooling around some hidden obstacle. One that showed itself moments later with another Sienna fist pump.

A ship. No, a boat. Too small to be a ship, and too crude. Thane estimated fifteen meters long, maybe half that wide. A boxy thing that nonetheless caught the sun's light on its brown palm bulk and glimmered like a lit-up ornament.

"It's tinted glass," Thane said.

That couldn't be right—glass boats didn't exist—and yet, there it was. Smooth and shimmering. The boat rose up to the surface, and Sienna kept punching her fist, now throwing rocks that had been loaded onto the boat off and into the ocean in cascading, giant splashes.

Thane had figured Arthur's escape craft would come from some anomaly, perhaps molding a giant ship out of sand. But this, this worked too.

"Sienna has quite the power," Thane said. "I can see why you wanted to keep her around."

"She wanted to leave as much as you did," Cassidy replied. "Siblings back home. I think I didn't move fast enough for her."

"You are now."

Cassidy nodded. "We're leaving this afternoon?"

"We are. With as many as want to come."

"As many as we can fit." Cassidy walked by Thane, heading for Sienna, who had ceased her sky attack, her face flushed and arms rubbing each other.

Other anomalies began tending to the boat, shifting on

provisions and cleaning off seaweed and other random ocean junk that'd found its way aboard. Beyond its bulk, the boat had several oar slots and a simple cabin towards the front, enough to provide shelter for a half dozen in a storm. Thane saw an anomaly lift a hatch and toss some coconuts inside, so there was, at least, some cargo room.

If they made it beyond the drones, who knew how long they'd be sailing. While the anomalies he'd spoken to, Arthur included, pegged the island near Hawaii—the constellations in the sky seemed to confirm it—Thane would take every calorie he could.

"Boss. You all right?" Sook asked, coming up, as the man did far too frequently.

"Are you hungover?" Thane judged the man's baggy eyes and sweaty face.

Thane wouldn't say the island made drinking easy, but the anomalies had figured out how to make wine from fermented fruits, and the results had been on display last night. One last party for their island prison.

"Nothing a little sun won't take away," Sook said, then leaned down and splashed salt water on himself.

"At least someone's having a good time." Thane looked back towards Arthur's camp and its growing action. "Looks like Arthur is mobilizing for our escape."

"Are they?" Sook, face dripping, mirrored Thane. "Didn't look that way when I came over here."

"Look at them. Like ants, scurrying."

"Right, but, like, that one? Over there?" Sook pointed to an anomaly walking into the ocean and, with a heave, returning a simple trap to the sea. "Why're they setting up the traps if we're going to leave?"

Sook pointed to another before Thane could come up with a reply. "And those two, they're still working on a new hut. Why bother, you know?"

Cassidy's warning drifted through Thane's mind. Not all anomalies would want to leave the island, not all would want to sacrifice this for an unknown, Paragon-controlled that.

"If some want to stay, that's their choice," Thane said. "Provided we get the necessary ones."

The boat, the drones, required enough anomalies with useful abilities. Without getting their support, the escape would wind up killing them all. Or wouldn't get going in the first place. A pathetic end to a dream Thane wasn't willing to sacrifice.

"Walk with me," Thane said. "Let's look around."

Sook fell in line, and as they went away from the kissing waves, Thane noticed several other anomalies shift to go with them. He recognized these, and realized, with a sparkle, that Sook had taken his job seriously. The body-guard had kept his promise, had recruited watchers.

Sometimes the best people came from the most surprising places.

Arthur's camp proved as busy as it looked, but for every anomaly Thane saw loading provisions into the ship, or pulling together equipment for the journey, he counted another focused on useless tasks. New buildings, planting and tilling gardens, shoring up dune walls that'd been damaged by winds.

A woman who'd been in Arthur's house the prior night, when they spoke about the plans, hunched over a muddy pit, molding what stiffer soil into a pot. The anomaly's hands left faded red trails wherever they touched, trails that smoked and seared the mush, turning it hard.

"You're making pottery." Thane started the conversation, standing over her. "Why?"

"Because we need it," the woman replied without looking up.

"For what?"

"Storage." The woman began tracing, with her right hand, a lazy spiral into the pot's side. "Our harvests are large enough now, we need someplace to put the extras."

"Except we're not going to be here after today, and we won't need any pots on the boat," Thane felt a little stupid, stating what seemed obvious.

"I'm not going," the woman replied.

"Why?"

She looked up at him, her dirty hair clumping around her shoulders, her teeth tarnished and her skin salted and dry, "Because Arthur asked me to stay, so I'm staying."

Thane asked and the woman answered more questions, growing more and more mocking with every response. Thane would get his true believers, the ones who really wanted to leave the island. Anyone else, those on the borderline, who didn't see dying under drone fire as a noble end to their life, would stay. Arthur would welcome them.

Arthur would support them.

Because the damned villain wasn't leaving either.

42

Into Her Own Hands

As last meals went, Kat savored the sandwich and fries. The grease, the mustard and the toasted bread. The place wasn't fancy, but it had proximity: two blocks from the destination. Kat had her suit on, but kept the mask down. People tended to get nervous when she went full battle mode in a crowded space.

Kat paid for the food and swept back out to the cold street, asking herself for the fiftieth time in the last hour why she had decided to do this alone.

The reasoning went like this: Gordon, still recovering, wasn't in a position to fight, even if he wanted to. Calvin, a runaway who'd spent his time hiding from enemies rather than confronting them, might hold his own, but the anomaly hadn't helped with the killer. Better to keep Calvin in reserve, watching Seeker and waiting for a call.

Mostly, though, Kat preferred it this way. No baggage. No concerns about anyone other than her own armored, highly-skilled self.

For a house dealing in deadly weapons, this one didn't look all that dangerous. Faded light blue paint meshed with a white-washed front porch, deeper blue shutters, and a snow-coated lawn to check all the ordinary boxes. Hanging from the second floor windows, as if to confirm the bored vibe, a few Christmas light strands still hung, their owners too lax to clear them away after the holiday.

A question: to mask now, or mask later? Maximum protection dictated going in expecting death and destruction, but fights tended to start when a player walked in ready for one. If Kat came in to talk, the people here might be willing to indulge. She couldn't be sure the killer was here, and scaring away her sole lead wouldn't help anything.

So Kat picked the middle ground. Twitched her wrists to ready the flash bombs, adjusted her collar so that with a quick nod the mask would spring up, but otherwise left her red-nosed, half-frozen face open to the world.

No doorbell, no Tama scanner, so Kat knocked on the tan cedar door. Waited. Puffed a few smoky breaths. Knocked again. Waited again.

As if timing her thoughts and their trend towards smashing in the door, a man swung it open. Stood behind the screen in an outfit Kat described as tactically tasteful: A sweater bearing reindeer fit snug over an obvious bullet-proof vest, while black pants loaded with pockets left just enough space for snowflake-coated socks to poke through.

"Not every day I get a tracker at my front door," the man said, through the screen. "What can I do for you?"

Wait, what?

"How'd you know I was a tracker?" Kat said.

The man tilted his head, then shrugged and opened the screen door, "Not many normals wear gear like that. And before you ask how I knew you were a normal . . ." He stepped aside, pinning the doors open for her. "Why don't you come inside?"

"You're letting a stranger into your house?" Kat tried to buy some time, understand the man's game.

"Better than losing all my heat," the man replied. "Come on in, promise it's nice in here. Coffee and everything."

Kat flashed a brief, cold smile, "Well, if there's coffee . . ."

She went by the man, keeping her muscles tensed and eyes moving the whole time. Immediately inside, the house gave away its basic origins. A central stair leading up to a second floor, rooms to the right and left filled with generic, soft colored furniture that said nothing about the owners, and a hall back towards what Kat would bet was the kitchen.

All the tension meant she jumped a bit when the man shut the door behind her. Kat turned as the man laughed, felt a flush climb her cheeks and hated it.

"What're you so nervous about?" the man said. "You came here, remember? Now, c'mon back. Let's talk."

"Stop," Kat said, keeping her arms down by her sides, where, with another motion trigger, her stun gun holsters could sweep out for a micro-second draw-and-shoot. "Who are you, and what's going on?"

"Rhimes," the man said, reaching out as if to shake Kat's hand. She eyed the offer, eyed his wide toothy smile, and gave him a single shake, saying her name with the gesture. "And Kat, what's going on is you showed up on my front porch looking like you're ready for something rough. I'm ready for a warm drink, so I'm choosing that option, if you're fine with that?"

"I hear what you're asking, but what you're wearing says something else."

Rhimes let his smile break for the first time, "Kat, let's save ourselves some time and stop playing dumb. I'm willing to bet you don't show up everywhere looking like this, which means you know what's going on here, and what we provide. So, let's talk about how I can help you."

Blunt honesty. Kat admired that, really. Made things go a lot faster. When Rhimes finished the admission with a walk towards the kitchen, Kat followed, keeping up the inspection and finding nothing more than generic artwork that matched the lived-in, lifeless house.

A small table served as the tiled kitchen's resting place, and Kat took a seat on a crunchy wooden chair while Rhimes grabbed a couple mugs and a pitcher from the one thing that really stood out in the house: a luxury-grade infuser, made by anomaly hands to syphon the optimal flavor and caffeine from the beans based on how much water you put in. The things were marvelous, and Kat kept debating whether to splurge on one, always falling on the side of more toys for Seeker instead.

"That's really good," Kat said after the first chocolate-nut sip.

"Always is," Rhimes replied, nursing his own mug. "So, I didn't think trackers liked the lethal business? Cuts down on your future earnings?"

"When I saw what happened to Aegis, figured I should get better protection," Kat replied, rolling up a story. "Not everyone plays fair."

"Of course. The Paragons don't have anything for you?"

"They're not paying much attention to me at the moment."

Rhimes laughed, which he seemed to a lot.

"Right. Makes sense. Let me ask a different question. How'd you know to come here? We like to know who gives referrals, so we can credit them, you understand."

"Ran into someone while I was working. He had some

impressive stuff. He didn't want to tell me right away, but managed to pry this place out of him."

"It's a tight group, our crew." Rhimes finished the coffee with a long gulp. "Don't mean to rush you, but we've got more folks coming soon, and I'd rather get you out the door before they come in. Customers don't like seeing each other, you get my drift."

"Sure. What do you have?"

"Follow me," Rhimes said, standing. "And, if you would, leave the coffee. Don't want to risk things getting messy."

Kat would've rather finished, but delicious coffee ranked somewhere below the need to find the killer, to understand how this crew worked. Buying a weapon from Rhimes wouldn't get Kat quite what she wanted, but seeing them might help her figure out where they were getting the guns.

When Rhimes went to a plain door, swung it open and revealed the basement as their weapon's cache, Kat didn't have any surprise to hide.

"A little cliche, isn't it?" Kat said as Rhimes led her down sturdy steps, metal ones that broke from the house's usual wood vibe. "Keeping all the secrets in the basement?"

"I find, when dealing with dangerous people, it helps to be predictable," Rhimes replied. "People keep their fingers off the triggers if they know what's coming."

Sure, whatever man.

Kat didn't need to come up with a response, because getting to the basement proper, where the lights came on automatically—motion detection, probably—served to kill the conversation.

Kat had never seen anything that justified the word 'arsenal' until now. Kat wandered past Rhimes, who stayed at the stairway's end with a knowing grin, and looked at guns, knives, long rifles, and things more suited to straight military action, all mounted on slate-gray walls and organized by lethality.

The basement had a second room too, and Kat glimpsed the opposite end through a doorless entry: armors, vests, boots, and all the gear a discriminating monster could want.

"Impressive."

"Isn't it?" Rhimes said, behind her. "It's what you were looking for, right?"

"More a who, than a what. Do you keep a client list? Names, numbers, things like that?"

"Of course. But we wouldn't show that to anyone. Not even a tracker."

Kat turned back, faced Rhimes dead on, "The Paragons might be a mess, but I bet they'd get a team together if they knew what you had here. This is way more than a few guns."

Again, Rhimes let his grin fall away to a studied frown. The man was a facial expression master, all exaggeration to the point where Kat couldn't tell if Rhimes was being serious or not.

"I thought we were having a nice afternoon," Rhimes replied. "Sorry to see it spoiled." He reached over, pulled his sweater sleeve up over his Tama, tapped away at it for a second. "I have our list right here. A simple Tama transfer work for you?"

"You're just going to give it to me?"

"What are my options?" Rhimes walked over to her, holding his left arm, with the Tama, out in front. "I say no, you have the Paragons wipe us out. I'd rather lose one client than all of them."

A reasonable play, though Kat still felt the negotiation

had gone too fast. Too smooth. All the same, the client list would whittle down the mystery. With the Paragon's own database, she could pin some likely suspects and send drones to spy on them all. Once they found the right one, Kat could have the drones solve the problem too. Easy.

Kat held her own Tama out, just forward on her wrist from her cable-launching gauntlets. Rhimes came in close, held his Tama out to touch Kat's. A chime sounded from both, proving the connection. Now Rhimes needed to send the document over, and . . .

The man held a gun in his right hand.

Kat couldn't see it while the Tamas, together, blocked the view, but she knew a drawing motion when she saw one. A small weapon, going by how easy Rhimes moved, how close he wanted to get to use it.

Kat didn't give him that chance.

Kat snapped her head back, and the mask shot up, coating her and instantly highlighting the drawn gun as a threat. Rhimes pulled the trigger and the bullet glanced off her sudden shield, leaving a solid crack in the mask's glass —damn expensive to repair too—and sending Kat's head for a short spin.

She reacted with instinct more than anything. Rushing forward, using her left arm to push Rhime's gun away while Kat's right hand delivered rapid jabs to pressure points. Rhimes, though, had apparently been in fights before and kept blocking, blunting the attack.

Worse, the mask picked up and highlighted, with little green pulses, noise from upstairs. Footsteps coming quick. The front door slammed shut too, after apparently being opened with quiet intentions. Reinforcements.

Not good.

Kat swapped her strategy. Reached over, grabbed Rhimes's right wrist with her free hand and snapped it, causing the man to drop the gun. Kat kicked it beneath the stairs as Rhimes tried to bulldoze her away. Kat dodged to the side, felt Rhimes tug at her as he passed, and she burst towards the stairs.

She had to get out. Now.

Kat hit the first step, saw the basement door open to show another black-masked man—too chunky to be the killer—standing there. She raised her left wrist, snapping it to the cable, and fired. The man stared at his left thigh, suddenly sporting a shiny steel hook, and Kat pulled. The man's leg came out from under him and he slid, on his back, down the steps.

Detaching the cable with another wrist snap, Kat jumped, legs pumping as she stepped over the sliding man like someone hoofing over an obstacle course. Up the last few steps to the hallway, and—

"Stop, or we shoot!" shouted another voice, a woman's this time.

This one stood guarding the house's front door, what looked like a rather heavy rifle in her hands. A second shout came a breath later, from behind Kat. In the kitchen. Her mask hazed both back and front with red, then threw in another as the steps announced Rhimes's ascent.

"You don't want to die here, Kat!" Rhimes called from the basement steps. "It'd be a waste."

"A waste of what?" Kat said, turning both ways, trying to find an exit. "And didn't you just try to shoot me?"

Her suit could take a couple hits from small guns, but it wasn't designed to handle heavy weapon fire. Trackers weren't supposed to go after gun-toting villains, but rather low-level anomalies jumping ship. The Paragons ought to be handling this, not Kat.

But they weren't here, and she was.

"I gave you the second to save yourself," Rhimes said,

getting closer. "You're a normal, Kat, and a good one. Don't want to see you dead."

"That's comforting." Kat burst as she said the words, dove back towards the kitchen.

The man there was slow on the trigger, and the woman at the front didn't even try to fire. Probably good, as with Kat diving away, the shooter's partner stood square in her sights.

Kat caught her dive as she hit the tile, springing right towards the glass doors and the snow-covered porch beyond. She'd go right through them, head to the side and disappear.

Or she'd feel the gunman tackle her, throw Kat back against, through, the table with the coffee mugs still on it. Kat's leftovers spilled across both of them as she hit the man with a punch to the neck before throwing him off.

There Rhimes stood, sweaty and with a tear across that sweater, holding a stun gun that looked very familiar. Kat felt her right thigh, where Rhimes had run into her down below, and came away empty.

"Like I said." Rhimes raised the gun. "Don't want to see you dead."

The dart hit the mask, right at the crack Rhimes had made earlier. When he'd tried to kill her, no matter what he said. Kat felt the prick in her forehead, the icy numbness that followed.

Kat would get him for that. Get'em all.

Right after she remembered how to walk, talk, think, or stop her eyes from shutting.

43

Another Chance

No windows, no Tama, no time. Zhan-Yo couldn't be sure when he woke up, only that he woke up alone. Still in the sealed room, left there with a headache, a growling stomach, and a dry throat. The ideal state to contemplate failures. Missed opportunities.

If Zhan-Yo had been frustrated when Aegis's death failed to create a vast uprising, he at least had hope that he could try again. Kickstart a revolution some other way. Now, though, his Tama would give Mynx all the information she needed to go after anyone who'd ever helped him. Wexley would go first, and likely Ziran itself would follow. Then Mynx could set about rolling up every corporate head, fiery citizen, and true patriot Zhan-Yo had met with over the years. A total clean sweep, like something from humanity's more brutal eras.

All because he'd taken a walk to the lake.

Zhan-Yo drummed his fingers on the cell floor, watched them move and traced the veins on his hands. They stood out more now, with his thinning skin. A living metaphor as Zhan-Yo lost his life's extra pieces, trimming to the essentials. Sylvie might have appreciated that assessment, but then, she'd always been one hundred percent essential. No distractions, just the job.

He rose, sniffed and coughed at the smell on his clothes — still the same that he'd put on before leaving Wexley's place. Dehydration meant Zhan-Yo had no need to use the bathroom, which he found by accident when he stood on the one floor tile shaded a bright blue. Behind him, a tile had slid away to reveal a hole and, folding out from the side like some clever toy, a tiny rig with sanitizer and toilet paper.

Truly, he lived in marvelous times.

In an idle exploration, Zhan-Yo tried playing with the toilet thing now. Wrapped his hands around the metal rod carrying the roll and the sanitizer dispenser and tugged. It did not come free. Didn't even move. Perhaps some Paragon far away, or maybe a drone, laughed at him.

Or perhaps somewhere closer.

He heard a short staccato, what might have been true guffaws. Mynx might have programmed the drones with the most demeaning laugh out of spite, subjecting Zhan-Yo to ruthless mockery. They came again, louder this time, each one draining into the next, as though the person could not stop laughing.

"Yes, yes!" Zhan-Yo shouted towards the door, stepping off the plate and letting the toilet descend into secrecy. "I'm sure it's all hilarious for you."

He would have continued shouting at his nameless tormentor, but even shouting the one line scratched his throat, the words coming out ragged and harsh. Instead, Zhan-Yo went up to the door and banged on it. Then hit it again, and again.

The laugh met his third knock, loud and hard. Vibrating the door. Deep and sharp. Unlike any laugh

Zhan-Yo had ever heard, and strange enough that he backed up, wondering if Mynx had decided to off him right now. If she felt keeping Zhan-Yo, the joke revolutionary, had grown tiresome.

Another thunk outside and the cell door popped, white smoke wisping around the edges, before swinging open. Xander, one of the traitorous Paragons from Chicago, walked in, looking as confused and frightened as Zhan-Yo. Behind Xander, Zhan-Yo could make out others, hear shouts and more bangs. Not laughter, he realized, but guns. Actual guns in a Paragon facility.

"What're you doing here?" Zhan-Yo said, tilting his head.

"Getting you," Xander replied. "We need to go, now. Before they figure out what's going on."

Zhan-Yo had seen enough movies, read enough stories to know a prison break when he saw one, and while those tales tended to punish someone for running, he didn't exactly have much to lose. When Xander started speaking, Zhan-Yo had already begun moving for the door. By the time Xander finished, Zhan-Yo had gone through it.

Zhan-Yo had expected a hallway, cells lining solid walls with all the grim trappings meant for prisons. Instead, he left his cell and entered a wide space, an entire floor with its middle section coated in glass. Zhan-Yo's cell did, indeed, join others around the floor's outer rim, each one opening to hard slate tiles. No windows, except that central pillar, whose transparent build extended, apparently, from the bottom to the very roof.

The sunlight coming in revealed the work done by Zhan-Yo's would-be rescuers, as drones littered the space, crumpled over and sparking in corner clusters as masked men in black tactical gear dragged and dumped the robots with each other.

"So you are still alive," Mathieu said, walking over and giving Zhan-Yo someone to focus on, to try and overcome his shock. "We couldn't be sure that she didn't kill you."

"How?" Zhan-Yo nodded past Mathieu at the crew, and noticed Stubbles was there too, looking ill as he helped pile a spider drone onto its gladiatorial comrade.

"Your Tama," Mathieu said. "Wexley had it tracked, and so we knew you'd come here. When you disappeared for a bit, while we were still coming, we thought you were dead. Then your Tama came back online."

"Mynx took it."

"Still has it, I think," Mathieu said. "It's in the building, but we don't have time to dig for it. Mynx is probably already on her way."

Zhan-Yo wanted to hear more, but with the last drone clustered, the mercenaries set what looked like plastic explosives—beige cubes with little black detonators—next to each bunch. One signaled to Mathieu, and Zhan-Yo didn't need a translation to know they needed to leave.

Only, how? There didn't seem to be a stairway, or an elevator.

"Come on," Mathieu said, stepping onto the glass. "Gotta admit, I think it's a pretty clever way to get around."

"What is?" Zhan-Yo said, stepping onto the glass.

Marcus, the other Paragon traitor, went over to them, gave Zhan-Yo a cautious look, "Ready?"

"Let's go," Mathieu said.

Marcus tapped away on his Tama, selecting things Zhan-Yo couldn't see, and the entire floor shifted, sinking down towards the ground. The white tile, along with its drone bodies, stayed still.

A floor-wide elevator. Inefficient, unless you wanted to keep your prisoners from breaking out. If Zhan-Yo had managed to get through his cell, he would have found a dozen meter plummet waiting for him.

"Good thing we found these Paragons," Mathieu was saying. "Looks like this is a regional center, a bunch of worthless scrubs kept in here. Marcus, Xander could waltz right in with their credentials."

"They won't have any for long," Zhan-Yo said.

"We were going to lose them anyway," Xander said, though his downcast look hinted that cost wasn't free. "Alone, we'd be dead. With you, maybe we have a chance."

The glass elevator hit the ground floor, slotting into the lobby. Mathieu ordered everyone out the double doors leading towards the afternoon sun, then grabbed Zhan-Yo's arm. Handed him a little black device.

"Want to do the honors?" Mathieu said.

Zhan-Yo did, and they ran out as bangs sounded above, shrapnel raining behind them in beautiful metal clatters.

Three large passenger pods waited, no doubt disconnected from their central network. Mathieu confirmed Zhan-Yo's assumption when, after sending Xander and Marcus to the first car, he slid into the second's left seat, with the emergency steering wheel up and active. Zhan-Yo took the right, and another two mercenaries filled out the vehicle.

"I have contacts with a safe house to the east, near the desert," Mathieu said. "With the summit, I bet we'll have time to figure out where to go next before anyone comes hunting."

Yes. They could crawl back into their holes, they could hide and wait for Mynx to come find Zhan-Yo again, this time with lethal force. With his Tama gone, Zhan-Yo didn't have any bargaining power. She'd just kill him, and everyone else.

"You said Marcus and Xander, their Paragon status is still active?" Zhan-Yo said as the pods started up.

"That's how we got in the building."

Zhan-Yo glanced back towards the prison. Without windows, with all its thick brown stone, their bombs hadn't made a mark. Too much like Zhan-Yo's own efforts.

"We're not going to the safe house," Zhan-Yo said. "Take us downtown, but split us up. Don't make it suspicious. We can still execute the plan."

"When she hears what's happened here, Mynx isn't going to let anybody close," Mathieu said. "The plan's a bust, Z."

"No." Zhan-Yo looked out the pod's windows towards LA's distant downtown. "I've been where Mynx is now. She won't call it off, she won't declare an emergency. Mynx is hosting all of her rivals, and she cannot look weak. We go."

44

In The Box

With the Elementals mollified, Mynx, Burov, and Apinya made it to the upper box for a late lunch. One that Mynx, already feeling her social stamina fraying, hoped would be small, with only one surprise guest.

Pixie, alone in the room, picked at a central buffet stuffed with Pacifica food. Tacos mingled with fresh-caught fish and Hawaiian pineapple. Almonds and cashews lingered in bowls at the room's edges, perfect finger food. Reeves, who Mynx had tasked with catering duties, had done his job.

"You beat us here," Mynx said, leading Apinya and Burov into the room and summoning up the warmest look she could find. "The Elementals arrived and made a scene."

Pixie, with the weathered patience found only in mothers, nodded, "I heard they might be coming."

"And now they are here," Mynx said. "But, they agreed to behave, so let's do what we mean to." An awkward pause—segues were not Mynx's strength. "Pixie, this is Burov, and Apinya. I don't know that you've met?"

"We haven't," Apinya extended a hand which, after transferring her small plate to the table, Pixie shook. "Welcome to our little club."

"Yes!" Burov echoed, taking up Pixie's hand as soon as Apinya let go. "I don't envy following Aegis, but I wish you luck. Such a legacy would have me running out that door and far away."

"Burov," Mynx said. "Please."

Pixie, though, laughed. Deep, yet soft, with genuine warmth.

"Aegis and I were good friends. We fought together for a long time, and with New York so close to Boston, we were more partners than anything. I don't see this as me stepping into his place, but rather standing alongside what he built, and doing what I can to make it better."

Silence. Mynx couldn't help but be impressed. Especially after Innis, the traitorous bum, regional Paragon leaders had fallen in Mynx's estimation. Here, though, came Pixie, ready with grace and humility to walk in a legend's shadow.

Mynx would have hidden herself away. Buried herself in work to distract from the moment until it had passed entirely. A younger version might have felt jealous, envied Pixie and her confidence. Today's Mynx appreciated, respected it.

"Well, I feel we've made the right decision," Mynx said. "Pixie, I'm thrilled to welcome you to our ranks. The other Champions should be filtering in over the next few hours, and I hope you can meet them all before we announce you to the world."

THE LUNCH WENT ON, the foursome pressing through food and free-flowing conversation without, somehow, the drama that tended to percolate when the Champions gathered in a single spot for more than a minute. Even Burov, with his waxy face hiding whatever emotions he'd stolen for the day, seemed less creepy than usual. Mynx may have even laughed.

Twice.

One hour stretched into two, and Mila arrived, followed by Lukas and the others until the whole group milled around, swapping stories. Altogether, Mynx was astounded. Not one outburst, not one threat or old grudge came up.

"Mynx," Pixie said, appearing by Mynx's side as Pacifica's Champion sought a breath while refilling her water glass. "A question."

"Ask it."

"I know some of the other Champions have families," Pixie said. "But, with what happened to Aegis, I'm hoping I can get some of your drones to watch over my children. And my husband."

"Pixie, you command every drone that's in Atlantis," Mynx said, pulling back her full cup, a Paragon-blue plastic that would, after this event find its way to an anomaly-powered recycler. "You can order any of them anywhere."

"No, I mean, I want something better," Pixie said, and Mynx caught the tone. "I'm not Aegis, I'm not the same kind of fighter, and I don't live in Bastion. My kids are vulnerable."

A hard question to answer. Yes, Mynx could design a new drone. Could attach all manner of gadgets and gizmos to make it the best machine ever built. But that wouldn't get to Pixie's core question, her core concern.

"You're a Champion, Pixie," Mynx said. "You will be a target now. Your family too, maybe. But you are not alone.

You have all of us, you have the Paragons. The drones. Anyone that strikes at you will be found, and dealt with. I can promise you that."

"I don't care about revenge."

"Then you do the best you can to protect them," Mynx said. "Move to Bastion. Do what Aegis did. Hire tutors. Keep them with trusted Paragons."

"Doing that would keep them from a normal life. They would lose their friends." Pixie glanced at her Tama, buzzing with a message from, Mynx assumed, one of those same children. "I didn't mind managing my region, but this?"

"This is what you are now. I'm sorry, Pixie, but there's no backing down. We chose you. Atlantis, the world, needs you. Would you abandon us?"

"For my family? Absolutely."

Mynx took a deep breath. This wasn't the conversation she should be having. Apinya would be better at this. Pixie, though, looked like she needed an answer now.

"Pixie, I—"

The room's doors burst open hard enough to bounce on their hinges. Celice, still in the same gear she'd worn in Chicago, ready for a fight, pushed through, firing glares at everyone all at once. After a hot second scanning the room, during which Apinya made the first flowing step her way, Celice narrowed on Mynx and Pixie.

"Here she comes," Mynx said. "You're about to see why we need you."

Pixie didn't say a word. Smart.

"What'd you do with him?" Celice opened the conversation. "Where is he?"

"Safe, secure," Mynx replied.

"Who are we talking about?" Apinya joined the conversation, letting Pixie fade into Mynx's shadow, away from Celice's heat. "Celice, we haven't seen you in so long!"

"Shut it, Apinya. I'm talking about my father's killer. Mynx has him, and I want to know where."

Apinya looked Mynx's way, and she gave him a slight nod, otherwise keeping her mouth shut. Let the diplomat handle this one.

"Because you want vengeance?" Apinya said.

"Damn right I want vengeance," Celice replied, sticking a pointed finger towards Mynx. "I nearly had it in Chicago before she took him away. I hoped, maybe, I'd see something on the way here that you were doing something, Mynx. Anything. But no. Everyone still thinks he's out there, free."

"He's not," Mynx replied. "If we tell the world we have him—"

"Then you show that you pay a price if you attack the Paragons," Celice said. "You show that my father is going to get justice."

"Is that how it works?" Apinya said. "Justice? I seem to recall announcements like this spur more danger than quell it. Drive, perhaps, this man's supporters into the open. Instead, we disappear him for a while, and the fervor dies. Then, when we show a broken, lost man, the cause is forgotten."

Celice closed her eyes. Balled her fists. Mynx knew the signs: Apinya working his ability, massaging her mind. Not something Mynx had ever seen done to another Paragon before, much less someone like Celice, who knew what Apinya could do. Nonetheless, like the tension being loosed from a string, Celice's face settled, her shoulders drooped, and a few stray tears replaced the fury that'd lit Aegis's daughter a moment before.

At a wave from Apinya, Burov strode over and placed a

gentle hand on Celice's shoulder. Beneath that mask, Mynx couldn't see what happened, couldn't see those splotches shifting, but when Celice broke into a full-blown sob, she saw the effects. Apinya had primed the woman, and Burov had pushed her over the edge.

Before Celice opened her eyes, the Russian stepped away, turned back to Mila and Lukas, as if he'd never been near.

"I'm sorry," Celice said. "I just, I just can't keep going like this. He was all I had, really."

"Come on." Apinya put a gentle arm around her. "Let's get you some food, a lot of wine, and you can tell me all your favorite stories about your father."

A line like that wouldn't have worked on a clear-headed Celice—or on Mynx herself—but with Apinya nudging her along, Aegis's daughter took the salve and went over towards the buffet.

"That," Pixie said, "that was amazing."

"Horrifying, really," Mynx replied. "We do have him, though. Zhan-Yo. Soon we'll have everyone he ever worked with. Round them all up. I'll even let her pull the trigger, if she wants."

Her Tama buzzed. Angry, urgent. A vibration reserved for emergencies. Mynx looked at it. Read the message once, twice.

"What's wrong?" Pixie asked.

"Everything."

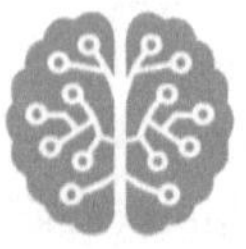

45

The King in His Castle

Arthur's house—impressive for the island, a hovel anywhere else—buzzed as the morning moved into full swing. As Thane approached the building, located on the village's edge, atop a small hill that presented a scene-stealing view, voices carried along the breeze. Laughter too. The conversational cadence that comes when one speaker is presenting to an adoring audience.

That Arthur would be attempting a betrayal, would be trying to keep the most valuable anomalies for himself, didn't surprise Thane all that much. You couldn't forget that everyone on this island had been sent here for some grievous misdeed. Why wouldn't they perform another?

And yet.

Hope hadn't been Thane's key quality. He'd survived on grit, through forced medical treatments, and the gradual realization that nothing in his life would ever be charmed. Work, fight, rend, rip and maybe Thane would get somewhere. For the first time in forty-some years, Thane had the real chance to forge his own direction.

Hope lingered in that possibility, and Arthur wanted to take it away.

Why?

Thane approached the door, a leafy shield that presented little more barrier than air, but gave privacy a slight nod. Inside, on the same dirt floor he'd walked the night before, he saw enough new footprints to confirm the sounds. No small gathering here.

The monster had many friends.

As soon as Thane went through the plant door, the talking stopped. Not in the whittled down way common to conversations weaving towards an end, or in the sudden hushes claimed by gossipers whose subjects have appeared in their midst. No, this silence came with vacuum force, as if Cassidy had sent a void and sucked away the entire audience.

Yet, when Thane rounded the hall and came into the house's central room, with its sandy mapping table and its woven chairs, he saw mouthes moving, a dozen anomalies chattering to one another without a single sound making its way to Thane. Arthur, already standing and heading Thane's way, put on his showman's grin.

As Arthur crossed some invisible line, his footsteps found their sandy swish, like Thane's own. The man's knuckles cracked as he flexed his hands before spreading them wide.

"An unexpected guest," Arthur said. "Whatever brings you here, Thane?"

"I can't hear them?" Thane cut to the question. Arthur no doubt knew why Thane had come, and Thane would rather understand potential threats than bandy pleasantries. "Which anomaly?"

"Only a small bubble," Arthur replied. "Very useful in

a world without walls to have a chat without prying ears. Like yours."

"Like mine." Thane tamped down on his anger. Now wasn't the time to break into a fight. He needed his mind for this, not his muscle. "What wouldn't you want me to hear?"

Arthur moved to put his hand on Thane's shoulder, and Thane took a step back, forcing Arthur into a shrug, then a glower.

"You want to leave the island today, right?" Arthur said. "That's why you have all these anomalies working to get that boat ready?"

"That was the plan."

"Not everyone runs on your time. Some of us, it turns out, have grown fond of this island. We like it here."

"I gathered." Thane pointed behind Arthur, to where the group had stopped their conversation and, still muted, watched the confrontation. "Is this your meeting to carve up the island after we're gone?"

Arthur laughed, "They told me you were smart! You didn't like my plan, I don't like your plan, so some of us are choosing to stay here instead."

"You heard my plan last night." The desire to throttle Arthur began to overpower Thane's reasoning. "We're leaving the island today."

"Ah, but Thane, that's the thing. Plans change. My plans, specifically. Your plans, not so much. Take the boat. It's yours. Go with my blessing."

"I don't want your blessing."

"Then why are you still here?" Arthur managed to look confused. "None of us want to go with you."

"I'm here because this plan requires some anomalies to succeed. The ones we don't need can stay, the ones I decide we need, will go."

"Oh, I don't think so." Arthur shook his head. "No, no, that's not going to work. Every anomaly on this island gets to make their own choice, my friend, and you have to live with who you can persuade to go along on your little doomed boat ride."

Thane counted ten others in this room. Nearly a quarter of the anomalies in the camp. Already a dangerous ability decline, and who knew how many others had seen the ship, taken a look at the drones this morning and found their faith wavering?

Could Thane fight his way to victory here? Beat up and break down Arthur's house and his contingent, then try to force everyone onto a boat, where they'd have to work together to overcome the drones?

An unlikely idea.

"You okay, Thane?" Arthur continued. "Just staring off into space there? Kind of scaring me."

"I'm thinking about whether to kill you."

"Ah. Carry on then. Just know that if you try, I'll fry you, then have you for dinner. Bet you'd be a bit gamey with all that muscle. Not my preference." Arthur laughed again, an obnoxious chortle. "I prefer the fatty stuff. A good fish. Some pork belly. Haven't had that in a long time. Maybe, if you get away, you could send us some? Air drop?"

"Please, please shut up."

"No, don't think I will." Arthur flashed a smile at his audience, one that they returned. "This is my turf, Thane. These are my rules. You're leaving today, and who you're leaving with is entirely up to them."

"Then bring them together. I want everyone on the waterfront. We'll make our pitch, and see who chooses to leave, who chooses to stay."

"A daylight debate? Sounds lovely. I'll be there."

Thane didn't wait for any more words. The noise came back as he left Arthur's house, walked down the hill and went back into the village. Found breakfast, and bit into the smoked fish with ravenous abandon, frustration fueling Thane's mouth. Sook stayed at a safe distance, keeping others away.

Over near the shore, Thane saw Cassidy still talking with Sienna. Other anomalies shifted around, looking towards the boat or lingering by their huts, over their cooking fish or broken coconuts. Caught between a stagnant, stable life and hoping for a better one.

Thane would make his argument, he would spread his vision for a bold new world spearheaded by those who had lost the current one. He would persuade them to climb aboard that boat, to use their powers to shield, destroy, and flee the drones. An anomaly army making its first foray.

Then Arthur would make his own, and when the little man had finished, Thane would see the impact. If Arthur had done well, if he saw souls wavering, too many, then Thane would simply snap Arthur's neck right there. Kill the movement with the man.

Thane would get off this island with the anomalies he needed. Today. No matter the cost.

46

The Man Behind The Mask

Someone held her hand. Not in a loving way, but with a tight grip, keeping it pinned to the soft faux-leather found in high quality pod cars. The ones people paid extra reps to reserve.

Kat wanted to open her eyes, but the lids felt heavy, and seeing what lay beyond them probably wouldn't improve her mood. A headache took turns with her sore body—not aching, more like a medical shock—easing up from the stunning bolt. Thankfully, someone had pulled the dart from her forehead.

The other reason she kept her eyes closed? People were talking.

"But did you expect the dive?" Rhimes said to someone else, his voice near enough to tell Kat he held her wrist. "Think if I tried that, I'd make a fool outta myself."

"You would," a woman's voice—the one with the gun? "I've seen you try to run. Not pretty."

"I may not be smooth in the action, but who talked her down there?"

"And who let her get out?"

"You ever pin a tracker before? I don't think so."

Kat felt the pod car slow down, take a long left turn and barely speed up. A small road, then. She wanted to look at her Tama, figure out where they were taking her, but held back. Instead, she took another bodily inventory, tested out nerves and traced the aches to confirm nothing felt broken, or tied. Aside from Rhimes holding her wrist, they hadn't bound her.

Bold, and stupid.

"Rhimes," the woman's voice changed now, softer, less confident. "You heard about the Paragon building, right?"

"What about it?"

"I don't think we've had a word from Innis since."

"So?"

"I didn't sign up for this to get killed." A sound, someone shifting on the wide pod seat. "We had our deal, but without Innis keeping us safe, how much longer can we do this?"

"As long as we're getting paid to." Rhimes, unshakeable.

"He's got you, doesn't he?" the woman replied. "What does he have?"

"Reps."

"What're those gonna be worth if we're dead, or, hell, if we win?"

"Then maybe it's loyalty. Or the contacts. What're you asking me all these questions for?"

The pod slowed, stopped. Kat tried to keep breathing shallow, even. Tried to parse the words, get to some conclusion, and failed.

"I don't know. Guess pod rides get me reflective. Guess maybe I'm worried." The woman opened her door, a soft thunk.

"Do me a favor," Rhimes said, not moving. "Keep your worries to yourself. They're not helping right now."

If the woman replied, Kat didn't catch it. The woman's door shut, and a few seconds later the door behind Kat popped open, causing her to slide until hands reached out, caught Kat's back.

Cold air slapped Kat's face, sliding in through the mask's crack and getting trapped along her cheeks, her neck. Kat couldn't keep down the shiver, and popped her eyes open, looking right up into the woman's face, which screwed up into a nasty smile that fit right in with her dry, freckled skin holding more wrinkles than the woman's years deserved.

"Look who's awake?" the woman said, and she dragged Kat out.

Kat had enough feeling to get her legs beneath her as she left the pod seat, preventing a stupid and embarrassing collapse to the ground. With the woman lifting and Rhimes letting go, Kat stood, took a look around.

And saw no less than three guns pointed at her.

The man from the house, plus another two, all in that same black gear, stood back from the pod, spaced just enough to keep Kat from hitting them all at once. They each had their weapons pointed her way in a solid form suggesting a career's experience.

A career that had led them all to a park, apparently, and one far enough away that only distant buildings, peeking over leafless treetops, gave hints to Chicago's proximity. Sparrows flew around overhead, tweeting away, while the chill breeze blew exposed prairie grass tops back and forth. A warming house sat at the lot's end, adjacent to a skating rink.

All empty. Strange, for a place so beautiful on a sunny winter day.

"Kat Collins," a new voice announced, coming up with Rhimes and the woman by his side. "Chicago's top-ranked tracker, here in the flesh. Welcome."

This guy, unlike the others, wore a businessman's overcoat, black leather gloves, thin sunglasses and close-cropped blond hair. Such a perfect movie villain look that Kat almost laughed.

Almost, because she noticed how he walked, how the shifting coat revealed a hip holster with a handgun in it, one she recognized.

With a twitch, Kat sent her mask folding back into her suit, the crack splitting and sprinkling some glass in the process. That'd be expensive to fix, but better some more damage than going into a confrontation with blurred, scratched vision.

And she really wanted to see this guy straight on.

"You're the one who shot me," Kat said as the man came up to her, careful to keep himself removed from his allies' firing lines. "On the rooftops."

"In fairness," the man said, clasping his hands. "You weren't my target, until you didn't give me any choice."

"Because I didn't want you shooting my friend."

"Which one was that?" the man asked, then threw a look around to the other mercenaries. "Did any of you shoot her friend?"

"Calvin's his name. One of you tried to kill him."

"Is he an anomaly?"

"He's a Paragon."

The man folded his hands, shook his head. Enough faux regret to win an award.

"Ah, then I'm so sorry," the man said. "We should have killed him in the first go around, spared us this difficult conversation."

Kat counted seven to one against her in the lot. She

had her suit's gadgets, though her thighs felt light enough that Kat suspected her stun guns had gone missing. Even with them, jumping into a fight against people armed like this would, uh, not end well. So she swallowed her spit and vinegar.

"Who are you?" Kat asked. "And why'd you bring me out here?"

"The second one leads to the first. To keep things short, I brought you out here because I know who you are, and what you aren't."

Kat waited. Let the man give himself away.

"The tracker with Paragon parents," the man continued when Kat didn't speak. "Always holding a grudge against the anomalies, even as you profited from them. How many times did you take one out, bring them in and wonder why fate didn't give you what they had?"

"Doesn't matter," Kat said. "Get to the point."

The collective hesitation around her at Kat's reply confirmed the boss-toady relationship between the man and his gun groupies.

"Efficient. I like it." The man did another sweeping glance around the lot, as if to say this, here, was the point. "You're getting crushed beneath the anomaly boot. We're working to destroy it."

"By murdering them?"

"Balancing the power. That's all. Making it fair for those of us fate didn't bless. We have to show them that normals deserve to be treated right, as equals."

"You have a funny way of doing diplomacy."

"Then, I ask you, join us. Help us get better," the man said, and Kat found herself believing the words, even if she'd already labeled him a psychopath. "If you can find a peaceful road to what we deserve, then we'll take it. Until then, our only option is fear."

"I was afraid for a long time," Kat replied. The man's offer made it clear what would be happening here, especially if Kat said no. Which meant every second she bought gave her another chance to solve the puzzle, find a way out. "I avoided every anomaly I saw, ran from Paragons. But after years, I realized that's no way to live. Anomalies don't choose what they are. It's not their fault."

"So you joined them."

"I decided to live my life, rather than let my past control it."

The man sighed, pulled up his left sleeve and glanced at his Tama.

"I had hoped, by coming here in person, that I could convince you," the man said. "But I get the feeling you're saying no."

Kat, in fact, said nothing.

"Unfortunate, but if I cannot turn a problem into an advantage, then I will remove it."

The man held up a hand.

"Wait," Kat said, sharp and sudden. "You never told me who you were."

"The dead don't need to know," the man replied, flicking a single finger towards Kat as four rifles raised, fingers pressing on the triggers.

47

Infiltration

So far as Zhan-Yo knew, no guide existed for infiltrating Paragon gatherings. And even if there was one, without his Tama, Zhan-Yo wouldn't have been able to find it. This, though, did not stop him splitting away from Mathieu and the other mercenaries and heading, with Marcus and Xander, to the summit.

Mathieu had protested the arrangement until, with some convincing, the whole group agreed on a plan that would put Zhan-Yo center stage. He would get the spotlight, and then the whole world would witness what his revolution stood for.

With the stadium standing large outside the pod—this a smaller, normal pod notable only for its dirty green blandness—Zhan-Yo and his Paragon partners exited into the late afternoon sun. While LA wasn't warm by summer standards, compared to a Chicago February, Zhan-Yo felt like he ought to be in shorts. A t-shirt. On the beach.

Zero for three on that front.

Though they had found time to stop by a reasonable store on the way for Zhan-Yo to throw on a reasonable suit—he'd endured strange looks from the store's owners at his Tama-less arms, but they'd let Mathieu buy the clothes without comment. Now the revolution's leader looked more like a mid-level executive than a change warrior, but given that Zhan-Yo was supposed to be rotting in a cell, complaining about fashion seemed a little much.

Marcus and Xander had brought their Paragon blues, so they looked the part as the trio approached the summit's main entrance, a glitzed thing hanging over with blue and gold glitter, streamers, and painted four-meter gladiator drones looming. Behind the colors, Zhan-Yo caught slap-dash evidence: the summit had been thrown together in a few days, and behind the hurried decor, the stadium's raw gray concrete and metal gave the whole thing an incomplete feel.

"Ziran threw better-looking events than this," Zhan-Yo said to Marcus as they approached the drones.

"Ziran's trying to sell Tamas," Marcus replied. "Paragon's aren't selling anything."

"Only their entire government."

"Mmmhmm," Xander muttered while Marcus shrugged, looking at his Tama and tapping to his Paragon profile, uninterested in whatever Zhan-Yo was trying to say.

Because of course. Why would Xander and Marcus care about the world, about those who ran it? The kids were looking out for themselves. Short-sighted, but Zhan-Yo could accept that.

These two were just means to an end.

The two drones stepped in unison as the trio approached, closing ranks across the entrance and flaring their helmet lights—eye facsimiles that glowed bright white. Marcus and Xander held up their Tamas and both drones, each tilting to look at a Paragon, flashed their eye lights green. Both, then, turned to Zhan-Yo.

A face that should have been registered on every watchlist the Paragons had, that should have prompted an instant capture, instead earned hesitation. Zhan-Yo didn't need to look to his left to see Xander performing his magic, manipulating the light waves between the drones and Zhan-Yo. The kid had promised Zhan-Yo wouldn't be recognized, and the fact that he hadn't been blown to pieces yet seemed to verify that promise.

"We're escorting this normal," Marcus said. "He's got a meeting with the Champions before the summit starts."

Whether the gladiators would process Marcus's words or not became a moot question when the two machines pulled back, stepping aside to show another Paragon. Not one Zhan-Yo recognized, but apparently his collaborators did, because both stiffened at the sight.

A shorter, stout woman with a frown, and dressed in an airy outfit—still blue, still with the Paragon *P* on the chest—came between the drones and gave Zhan-Yo a good look.

"What's the name?" she asked, a bullhorn voice startling Zhan-Yo into responding.

"Wexley," Zhan-Yo said. "Just here about sponsoring."

If he'd convinced the Paragon, Zhan-Yo couldn't tell by her face. He still couldn't tell when the woman faded, became translucent and then burst into a billion tiny particles. The dust blew through Zhan-Yo's suit and out the other side, where, when Zhan-Yo turned around, he found her watching again, frown even deeper.

"No Tama, no identifiers," the woman said. "This summit wasn't exactly well-planned, so we don't have a list, which means you aren't on it. Can't let you in unless you have a Champion vouching for you."

"C'mon Settra," Marcus said. "He's local. Said he has a sandwich chain in the area and wants to offer coupons."

Sandwich chain? Coupons?

Zhan-Yo tried so, so very hard to keep an innocent smile on his face. He'd pushed for this, tried to seize the moment, and when you went fast, sometimes you dealt with amateurs. He had to remember there was a reason Marcus and Xander were pulling crap Paragon duties back in Chicago.

"Coupons," Settra replied, as incredulous as Zhan-Yo at the idea. "And how would two Paragons from Chicago know a local sandwich shop owner?"

"I know his father," Zhan-Yo interrupted. "Way back, from college. I reached out when I heard the summit was happening, since I knew they were Paragons. I wanted to see if they could get me a meeting? For my stores?"

"Right, yeah," Xander added. "Just, uh, helping out."

Settra had a look that said more questions would be coming, until the drone on their right, standing watch, shot sparks from its back leg. The thing knelt down, its white eyes flashing yellow. Settra glared at it, cursed.

"You two," Settra said. "You've got the summit map on your Tamas?" Marcus and Xander nodded. "Then take this guy to the main entrance. That's where the media's going. Someone will help him there."

"Got it," Marcus said, and the three turned to head inside.

"And don't lose him," Settra said to their backs. "Anything stupid happens, I'm holding both of you responsible."

Neither Paragon replied, but Zhan-Yo caught the fear in their walks, their eyes. These two were kids playing a dangerous game, and now they'd made a move they couldn't take back.

"Good call," Xander managed once they'd crossed the stadium's threshold, the concrete floors banding above them. "She wasn't going to let us go."

"Not the first time I've had to take out a drone," Marcus said, with that false bravado Zhan-Yo had seen so many times from people trying to prove themselves to their peers. "A little juice right on the joints, and they pop."

Zhan-Yo had them pull up the summit map as they meandered towards the main entrance. Once they were beyond Settra's sight and well within the roving Paragon crowds, which were starting to build up for the summit's opening, Zhan-Yo pulled them off to the side.

"You know your roles," Zhan-Yo said, and the two Paragons nodded. "Then get to it."

They didn't ask any questions, and despite how annoyed he'd been at them earlier, Zhan-Yo lingered a look on the two Paragons as they mixed with the crowd and left him. The two boys had done their job, had put themselves to the test, and succeeded.

The revolution hadn't been about destroying the Paragons. Not about ending anomalies or casting them out. Zhan-Yo wanted to raise up normals. Bring about parity. There were good people in both camps, and, working together, they should be able to create a better world.

The Champions, though, would never see it that way.

Zhan-Yo confirmed that view as he joined the crowds, slowly making his way towards the stadium center. As he mingled, keeping his mouth shut and his ears open, Zhan-Yo heard blips wondering about why the summit was even happening, standard celebrity comments about the Champions that'd been sighted, and, more important, tense whispers about Aegis and what would be coming in his aftermath.

Coupled with that last came the slurs Zhan-Yo expected, but still saddened him to hear. The Paragons had always looked down on normals, but, in public, tended to paper over those feelings with uplifting platitudes and plastic paeans to some unified Eden. Here, instead, came vengeful promises, angry aspersions, and lies all meant to turn the average citizen into a suspicious monster waiting for a chance to stab any anomaly in the back.

Aegis had often spoke in his speeches about cleansing society's disease, removing hate and anger and replacing them with cooperation and love. If Zhan-Yo respected one thing about the man, it had been the legend's ability to hold true to those principles even if the organization he led disregarded them. Sure, Aegis would throw punches, but he did it with a genuine hope that every fist fight would make the world a better place.

Zhan-Yo would, did do the same. Unlike Aegis, he would succeed.

At the next cut in, Zhan-Yo turned right, slipping past blue uniforms and the occasional buzzing drone to duck into a tunnel heading towards the green grass at the stadium's center.

Sun slanted onto chairs laid out in row upon row, looking in, like the raised seats, on a central circle stage. Zhan-Yo walked an aisle—here, there were fewer Paragons, some still assisting with setup, others taking pictures on their Tamas. Nobody paid any attention as Zhan-Yo brushed his fingers over the warm metal chairs, stepped on the faded white lines meant for games not being played today.

Blue cloth draped the stage itself, featureless otherwise. No doubt any speakers would be mic'ed, or amplified by anomaly power. Zhan-Yo touched the lip, felt the fabric.

He'd promised his backers a sign. He owed the world the same.

Putting both palms down on the stage, Zhan-Yo heaved. Pulled himself up into plain sight. Hundreds, maybe thousands who wanted him dead now had a clear shot, and nobody would protest if they took it.

But when Zhan-Yo stood, he stood tall. This was his time, and no Paragon could take it from him.

48

Watching

Given a choice, Mynx would always choose her Factory. The bustling, machine-filled construct accommodated her dreams without the drama, let Mynx play with her ideas without idiots running amok, ruining everything.

Unfortunately, Mynx did not have a choice. She watched Zhan-Yo mount the stage from the Champion box far above and slowly, ever so slowly, bit through the carrot she'd dipped before Reeves alerted her to the unwelcome intruder.

The AI had mentioned the prison breakout as it happened, had scrambled drones to prevent it, but Zhan-Yo, the slippery bastard, had escaped. Mynx had figured the revolutionary would run to some hidey-hole, escaping to deep down dirt to molder away with his schemes. Instead, and Mynx had to give Zhan-Yo some angry credit for this, the man went for impact.

Not that Zhan-Yo would get much to the wider world from right there. The summit hadn't officially opened, and media had been corralled into an entrance area to take splashy photos as Champions arrived. Whatever Zhan-Yo said in there, whatever protest he made in the moments before Mynx had his existence erased, would be heard only by those Paragons wandering by.

Hopefully, the man's words would fall on deaf ears, and Mynx wouldn't need to add more clean-up to her full list.

"Apinya is going to handle the man," Burov said, joining her. The Russian's bombastic attitude had mellowed since Celice had appeared, as he continually snuck by Aegis's daughter to steal away her anger and hysteria. "We need to keep her away."

Mila and Pixie, right now, were on Celice duty, keeping her from the windows and by the snacks. If Mynx could hear correctly, Pixie plied Celice to take a higher position in Atlantis. The Paragons might not make her a Champion, but keeping the legend's daughter, skilled enough in her own right, on the team would make a good media move.

"I hate this," Mynx said.

"Which part?"

"Every one."

"I could take care of that for you," Burov said, and Mynx rolled her eyes before she caught his straight face.

The man thought he could suck away her dislikes? Morph her personality into a socialite, spotlight-loving Champion?

"Keep your powers to yourself," Mynx said, then poked towards the window. "I'm going down to give Apinya some back-up. If we need Zhan-Yo annihilated, better to have someone ready to do it."

"Kicking off the summit with a murder," Burov mused. "A bold move for you, Mynx."

"Might be my only one."

Mynx dumped her plate and, with a final nod towards Pixie, in which their looks exchanged their respective missions for Zhan-Yo and Celice, Mynx headed back into the concourse.

The opening ceremonies were a couple hours off, but Paragons from across Pacifica and those who'd made journeys from around the world were already clogging the walkways. As much as Mynx had made the summit so the Champions could talk, various Paragon groups had pooled their hasty resources and formed sessions, classes, and more.

The sheer production had so far eclipsed Mynx's own plans for the event that she couldn't help but be impressed as she saw signs coating every intersection, detailing which rooms and which stages would hold what conversations. Sometimes she forgot that the Paragons were far more than a few Champions; they ran the world, and took it seriously.

Not far beyond the box, at a buzz from her Tama, Mynx took a left turn and went to the concourse edge. She could look out through the tall windows into the LA afternoon here, the height showing pod stations and neighborhood shops and restaurants. Mynx also found space, and a drone found her.

Tiny machines, each one a candy bar size or smaller, floated up and around her, lodging onto her uniform like so many decorations. By the end, it looked like Mynx had festooned her Paragon suit with jewels. Armlets and anklets wrapped her limbs. A little ridiculous, but given what some anomalies wore here, nothing that would merit much notice.

"Took you long enough," Reeves admonished, the AI's voice now coming right into her ear, courtesy of her new, mechanized earring. "Statistics hold that an attack was likely as of an hour ago."

"Couldn't get away," Mynx replied, still staying in her

space, watching out the windows. "Give me the rundown."

She could have read the information on her Tama, but Mynx found it easier to play with ideas while listening to a verbal narrative. Let Reeves describe the problems while she solved them.

"It's looking like a rough day," Reeves said. "First, you have the prison breakout. Early reports say the guard drones were disabled by conventional arms, then blown by set explosives. Other prisoners were unaffected."

"Well that's something. Any idea who broke him out?"

"A normal group. Ex-military, going by the videos."

"Of course. Activate warrants. Kill on sight." Mynx drummed her finger on the rail.

"No capture?"

"No capture. We have Zhan-Yo's Tama. No hired gun will have better information. And Zhan-Yo already made his position clear. Anyone helping him is complicit."

"Done," Reeves paused. "This next piece is unusual."

"Wait."

Mynx looked back towards the concourse, towards video monitors that had come on and were focused on the center stage, where Zhan-Yo stood tall and looked to be yelling things. Without a mic, thank goodness, she couldn't understand what he said, but, given how many Paragons had turned towards the field, that barrier wouldn't be one for much longer.

"Keep talking," Mynx said as she left her oasis behind and began pushing through the crowd, making her way to the middle. "Things are getting worse here."

"And everywhere," Reeves replied. "Our little anomaly island is having problems. It seems they have built a boat."

"They know the rules. Have the drones destroy it."

"Will do. However, this event also signals cooperation on a level we did not anticipate. If the anomalies combine their abilities, I calculate the drones may have difficulty succeeding."

"Reeves. You have lethal drones by the dozen out there. I don't care what you need to do, but take care of it. I can't focus on a few distant anomalies right now."

"Of course."

Mynx made it to the ground level, intentionally keeping away from the main entrance and what would certainly be questioning cameras. Reporters. She saw Rosamund and the Elemental crew making their way ahead, splitting Paragons as they marched onto the field. Figured they would be right up front, wanting to hear from anyone castigating the world order.

"There's something else," Reeves said. "About Zhan-Yo."

"Say it."

"It looks like he may have entered with two other Paragons. We're searching for them now."

"So more traitors." Apparently the Paragons needed another formal cleansing. Apinya and Burov might have to go person-to-person again, no matter how much time it took. "Why is that news?"

"Because I'm having trouble figuring why Zhan-Yo would come here so fast after his breakout," Reeves replied. "There's no good reason for it. Coming here guarantees his capture, or his death, or both, and we can control the narrative."

"Unless?"

"Unless he is planning something bigger."

Mynx left the tunnel, stepped onto the bright grass. The sun had fallen, partly, behind the stadium's outer wall, and its fractured light blanketed the field in blazing orange. Zhan-Yo's voice came out clear, now. Some haranguing speech about how the Paragons were no different than past dictators, that the world deserved equality and other point-less platitudes.

"Mynx, are you listening?" Reeves asked.

"I heard you." Mynx stopped, saw Apinya had closed with the platform. She looked around the stadium, spotted the Champion box, with Mila in the windows, shrugging her way. "What's bigger than killing Aegis?"

"Getting the rest of you?"

Mynx didn't feel ice in her veins very much any more. She'd seen most one could see in life, in danger, and had survived. But, she'd also built a whole world from the ground up. Its architects were now in this very space with her, and that made them vulnerable, no matter how powerful they were.

Reeves had so much security around the stadium, though. So many drones and so many anomalies pressed into protective detail. How could Zhan-Yo, so recently taken captive, orchestrate anything complex enough to get by their measures?

Mynx looked back towards the stage, towards the speechifying monster on it. Aegis had underestimated the man, assumed his own invulnerability right up until the end. Mynx wouldn't, couldn't make the same mistake.

"Reeves," Mynx said. "Order—"

She felt a hand on her shoulder, one that pulled her around, and Mynx turned to see Celice's wild, angry face.

"You said you had him," Celice snarled. "You lied."

Mynx didn't see the fist coming, didn't ever think her best friend's daughter, a girl she'd known and loved for so long, would strike, but Celice hit her hard, right across the jaw, and Mynx was out before she hit the grass.

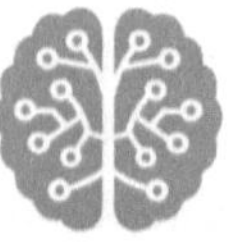

49

To Sea

Thane didn't play the political game. He didn't canvas for support, pitch his position, or give grand speeches extolling people to follow him. Threats, reps, and the lust for power tended to be Thane's preferred mechanisms. When you were right, when everyone saw how much they had to gain by following you, how much they might suffer if they didn't, why did you need democracy?

This strategy fell hard on the run up to lunch. Thane had Sook and his other bodyguards quiz every anomaly they could find on where they stood: leave or stay, and, if the latter, what ability did they have?

Thane told them to be nice, knowing he didn't have that ability himself. Instead, he chose to serve his own effort doing something he understood. Thane made his way back down to the waterfront—Sienna and Cassidy had left the boat, vanished off somewhere—and climbed aboard the ship. Walked its deck aft to bow and inspected its shimmering surface.

Sunlight glared off the boards, crudely fashioned pieces molded into place by anomaly powers rather than craftsmanship. Many still glistened with ocean water, salt crystals visible where the heat had done its work. The protective glaze didn't provide invincibility, though; Thane noted spots where the wood had rotted, where sea creatures had made holes and homes, and boards that felt spongey. This boat might float for a while, but it would not survive an extended sea voyage.

As Thane made his way, he nursed that tiny, angry flame. Fed its hunger so that he grew taller, stronger. A giant amid the working anomalies. The puny others would see their leader, great and terrible.

The meek ones shied away from him, even as they loaded more food. Brought spare wood aboard. Slotted poles and slapdash oars into equally crummy slots. Tools for lesser bodies. Thane could swim the whole way. Eat a fish with one hand, kick with his legs.

The greatest, the strongest.

The littlest man announced his way to the beach later, interrupting Thane watching fish in the waters, wondering how they might taste if he grabbed and ate them right this minute.

Arthur.

The man's name took a fuzzy spot on Thane's tongue. One to destroy if things turned sour. If Thane's stomach rumbled too much.

Anomalies trailed Arthur, including ones Thane recognized, even if their labels didn't come to mind. Not food, those, but friends. Ones to protect. Who would help him later. One, a brown-haired woman, waved Thane away from the boat. He should leave it, get close to the little man. To the snack.

Fine.

Leaving a big splash behind him, Thane stomped next to Arthur, his huge feet sinking into the wet sand. Arthur didn't seem to notice. The man spoke to the crowd, saying things Thane didn't care to listen to. They were boring words, given by a weak man.

But the weak man had the attention. Eyes focused on Arthur, and Thane saw nods. A few smiles. Even a laugh. Thane grunted. That was not the plan. They were supposed to like Thane, what he offered. To follow him onto the boat and beyond.

Thane reached down, put a big hand, its skin stretched taut over long bones, on Arthur's shoulder. Thane didn't mean to push, not really, but he shoved Arthur into the sand. Arthur stopped speaking, and Thane saw those smiles vanish. The eyes turn to him.

"Weak," Thane said, pushing Arthur further into the sand. The man tried to move Thane's hand away, like a gnat trying to lift a boulder. "Strong."

Thane raised his other hand, fingers curled into a giant fist. He stepped to the side, keeping his right hand on Arthur's shoulder, and pointed towards the boat.

"Free," Thane shouted. "Us!"

Rather than applause or a rampaging stampede towards the boat, carrying Thane along with it, the anomaly felt a sting. Smelled the acrid whiff as flesh burned.

His flesh. His arm.

Arthur, a dark shadow surrounding him as the man pulled in ambient light and twisted it to a burning coat around his hand, looked little like the hapless prey he'd been a moment before. Instead, his every part lacked light: his eyes were slate gray, the tan skin gone ash, and even his teeth appeared like hollow dust.

So Thane threw him. Jerked his right arm, pulling Arthur and sand up and away. Arthur flew and splashed into an oncoming wave, roiling black and bright as nature threw its anathema back onto the beach, where some other anomalies went to help him stand, coughing, as normal color came back to Arthur's body.

Thane's arm stayed hot red and white where Arthur's grip had seared him. The pain should have made Thane angry, should have pushed him into a rage, but no. Instead, Thane rubbed at his arm, wrinkled up his face, and tried to understand.

This part, this form, it didn't feel pain. It didn't get hurt. Thane could get knocked around, could get trapped or stunned, but pain? Damage to his body? Never. Not like this.

"Thane, calm down." A woman spoke, coming up to him. "If you lose it, we'll lose all of them."

The woman. Thane knew her, and she didn't look afraid like most of the ones watching him. He could fight them, eat them, destroy them. But he looked towards Arthur, now calling something else to the assembly, something angry.

That one could hurt him. Thane rubbed his arm again. Could maybe kill him.

And for the first time, Thane felt fear.

Except, what did he have to be afraid of? Thane shook his head as his body shrank, as his muscles atrophied away until a normal, older man stood along the beach. Sook and his bodyguards took the cue to form a soft line between Thane and the other anomalies.

If Arthur tried to make any move, Sook would defend him. Cassidy would open a void in the man's mind. Thane had allies here, and if things turned truly terrible, well, Thane would still bet his crushing anger against Arthur's light show. Until that moment, however, another method would be better. He'd tried strength, now Thane had to use the silver tongue.

"That's your choice!" Arthur started yelling again. "That maniac, or me! The one who's led you this far!"

"The one who will lead you no farther," Thane announced, then tapped Sook aside so his audience could see him directly. "You should thank Arthur for his service, but he has completed his journey. I ask you, have you finished yours?

"The Paragons that put you here have not been punished. Your families live without you, wondering where you have gone. Whatever ambitions you may have held, how can they be met here, wasting away in this prison, allowed only what the Paragons give you?"

Faces turned back and forth, to Arthur standing at the beach head, his village behind him, and Thane, framed by the boat.

"The Paragons gave us our lives," Arthur countered. "I have no love for them, but I have no desire to die either. Thane would lead you to nowhere except the bottom of the sea."

"I choose not to live in fear of those drones," Thane said. "I choose not to live in fear of those who preach it. It's time to show the world we are not done with it. Come with us now, or you will never see another chance to leave this island."

If Thane could declare a single argument more effective than any other, this last seemed to hold the most attention. Every anomaly Thane could see fell into themselves, looked towards the sea or the island's volcano and, no doubt, played out their lives towards their inevitable end: days spent grabbing fish, weaving new clothes, and watching the clouds soar by until some storm or simple disease claimed them decades before their due.

Thane gave them three long breaths, then turned and waded into the water, heading towards the boat. Cassidy,

Sook, they understood and followed. A little earlier than planned, but now was the moment.

The brain prevailed where the beast failed, but Thane would have his escape. The splashing, smashing sound of feet stepping into the waves proved it.

50

Botched Execution

The man ordering her death returned to his pod, leaving five-to-one odds against Kat in the snowy parking lot. Rhimes, flanked on either side by assault weapon-wielding mercenaries, kept his hand up and the fire order stalled while their leader's pod geared up and crunched away. Had to get the king away from any possible misfires.

"Satisfy a dead girl's curiosity," Kat said. "How much does he pay you?"

As Kat asked the question, she twitched her left wrist ever so slightly, sending the suit rotating her gadgets.

"Pay us?" Rhimes said. "Doesn't matter. Once we're all done, reps won't be worth a dime."

"So you're doing all this outta what, love?"

"Ever hear of loyalty, tracker?" Rhimes glanced away, towards the pod as it rolled into the street and picked up speed. "Or are you too alone for that?"

Kat clenched her left hand. Two small, silver orbs shot from her gauntlet, slamming hard into the snow-coated asphalt and bouncing back up. Everyone's eyes looked to the objects as Rhimes lowered his hand.

"Oops," Kat said, and *moved*.

Twitching her neck to the right, Kat popped the damaged mask back up as she shut her eyes, pushed towards the nearest gun-thug. The silver orbs burst, a flash bright in the dwindling twilight. The mask blocked enough that Kat only had a brush come through her eyelids, a purple-blue splash against the black.

Kat opened them again as she reached out and caught the first thug with her right arm, kicking with her right leg into the man's knee and breaking it as his hands went to his seared eyes. The man's rifle, hanging by a strap, swung in the air as he fell, and Kat caught it, crouching with the move and scooping up the weapon.

Kat's experience firing projectile weapons, rather than the no kickback stun darts, lay entirely at Paragon-approved ranges. The recoil made her aim jump, but at this range that hardly mattered. Bullets sprayed as the other four stumbled around, Kat aiming first at the nearest thug, then swinging the muzzle around to the farther two, catching all three with her fire.

Rhimes, that bastard, managed to keep enough composure to fall and crawl to a pod's far side, dodging Kat's initial onslaught by hugging the ground, and her second sweep thanks to the premium pod's thick construction. The vehicle's glass shattered, sure, but its frame held strong.

Kat let off the trigger, her shoulder sore as the weapon had shoved itself against her a thousand times in those few seconds. Beyond Rhimes, she didn't see a single other enemy moving around. No twitches either.

Had she just killed four normals?

A sudden urge to vomit surged in her stomach, quenched only by Rhimes calling from his hiding place.

"Not a bad trick for a tracker!" Rhimes said. "Guess we shouldn't have underestimated you."

Rhimes kept talking, but Kat stopped paying attention. She had to focus. Stay in the moment. Moral arguments could wait, self-pity had to. Survival mattered most. Rhimes first, Kat later.

"Stop!" Kat yelled back. "Just, just stop."

Rhimes, thankfully, did.

"You're done, all right?" Kat said, sitting now next to the guy who's leg she'd smashed. That one, at least, lived, moaning next to her and gripping his knee with both hands. "It's over."

Or close to it. The gunshots had already triggered her Tama's alert, which meant drones would be coming, even this far away. Any nearby Paragons would also be notified. If Rhimes and his crew had fired and left, they would probably get away. Now? A Paragon prison was their best hope. Death, their worst.

"Over?" Rhimes said. "Kat, this is just the start."

Where did this guy get his bravado? Kat leaned over, unclipped the rifle from the groaning guard, stood up, and saw Rhimes dash around the corner towards her, hands pumping. Kat raised the rifle, hand pressing on the trigger, but Rhimes slapped the barrel aside and slammed his shoulder into her.

On the slick asphalt, Kat's feet went out and she fell back, cracking her head on the hard ground. Her hood and mask blunted the worst, but the rattle had her sucking in her breath, even as she reached up, caught Rhimes's foot as he tried to step on her, and yanked it out from under him.

Rhimes fell back and Kat heard the knee-guard shout as his boss landed on him. She didn't wait for Rhimes to get back up; curling forward, Kat pulled to her feet, twitched her wrist to the steel cable, and raised it.

Fired.

Rhimes twisted, burying the cable in his gear-coated chest rather than the arm Kat had aimed for. The man winced, then grabbed the cable, and yanked, pulling Kat towards him, giving Rhimes the leverage to get to his own feet.

Being tied to a man like Rhimes was not good. Kat tried to disconnect the cable, but the thing only strained against Rhimes's clothes, failing to break through. Her attempts helped Rhimes close the gap, and the man again barreled towards her, brushing through Kat's attempted kick.

Getting crushed beneath Rhimes was not an option.

Kat kept her feet dancing behind her, retreating against Rhimes's push, even as they stepped beyond the lot's boundaries and into thicker snow. She threw jabs with her left hand even as Rhimes caught her right with his own. Giving up the tackle, but still tied in close with that damned cable, Rhimes swung for Kat's head, and missed.

A stupid dance. A deadly one. Two desperate fighters stuck together and in between the dodges and the adrenaline and the punching all Kat could think is that she might die out here, next to a frozen pond, and how she'd never expected she'd go this way.

No gunshots, no brawls. Kat wanted an old woman's way out; asleep and safe.

"I picked the wrong job," Kat said, ducking another wild swing.

"Me too," Rhimes replied, pushing Kat further back through the snow, down the slope.

Kat's left foot landed on something that wasn't snow. That was, in fact, ice. She slipped, spun, and pulled

Rhimes around, the sheer force giving the cable enough momentum to tear through Rhimes's vest, leaving a rent through the middle but, at least, freeing them.

For a hot moment, the two stood, facing each other shrouded in their own breath. Reality had its moment to sink in.

"You killed my soldiers," Rhimes said, no jolly smile here.

"They were going to kill me."

There were strategies. Ways to win on a surface like this. Kat just needed to bait Rhimes into another charge and he'd likely fall. Then, a swift strike to the head and Rhimes would be out, and she'd have a prisoner. Someone to deliver to the Paragons, or the Elementals, or whomever wanted to face the rest of these gun-toting maniacs.

While Kat would go and get some therapy. And a long nap.

"You had a choice!" Rhimes said. "He made the offer."

"And what an offer it was." Kat glanced to the right, towards the sky. Searched for drones, saw none. How far out had they gone? "I say yes, I get to join your killing crew. I say no, I die."

"No, that wasn't the choice at all. He offered you a chance to escape. You're living in a prison that you can't see, eating from the spoon the Paragons feed you. With us, you could have had freedom. Could have helped the world see what's been blinding them for so long."

Great. What's worse than killers for hire? Zealots. First the Elementals, now these guys. Why'd they always come for her? What about Kat made her so attractive to these people?

"Maybe I like my prison," Kat said. "It's got a nice dog. Good whiskey. A warm bed. Now, if you could please let me go, I'd like to get back to it."

Rhimes shook his head, "Nah, can't be doing that. Join or die, Kat. That's the game."

"What a crappy game." Kat held up her left wrist, ready to fire the cable.

Rhimes saw the move and charged, feet slipping on the ice. Kat held her fire. Let Rhimes's panicked burst get him out of control. The man came stumbling towards her, hands reaching for Kat, and she sidestepped him, planting her own feet flat so they stuck. As Rhimes went by, she delivered a kidney strike with her right, punching him off course and sending Rhimes crashing to the ice.

She kept on the opportunity, quick-stepping over to Rhimes, sliding a bit, but managing to keep her footing. Rhimes, his face scratched up and bloody from the fall, tried to pick himself up, slipped and hit the ice again.

"Guess you lose this round," Kat said, aimed her foot, and fell as bullets came from nowhere, blasting around her.

Rolling as Kat hit the ice, she looked back towards the attack, saw the guard—must've been the knee one, giving how he leaned on the pod—holding his rifle, aiming it her way. Pausing his fire.

"Let me get free," Rhimes said, his feet scraping along the ice away from Kat. "Then kill her!"

Hands on the ice, boots slipping as Kat tried to get a grip, she looked through the mask at the rifle, at the thug's hand as it slipped down to the trigger.

It really was a crappy game.

Soul of the Enemy

Admittedly, Zhan-Yo hadn't expected to begin his inspiring, revolutionary speech by yelling at roaming Paragons to pay attention. Somehow, he'd thought that taking the stage in the giant stadium's center would be enough. Cameras would appear and Zhan-Yo would be projected across the world. That's usually how it went at Ziran conferences, when he'd taken the stage to pulse-pounding music, applause, and a thousand adoring stares waiting to know what new Tamas would be released that year.

Zhan-Yo counted maybe a dozen blue suits among the seats watching him. One looked with enough intensity to suggest she knew who Zhan-Yo was. As her face turned to a frown that grew ever deeper, Zhan-Yo wondered if she might just obliterate him on the spot. Summon some laser from the sky, or perhaps turn his insides to jelly.

"Paragons!" Zhan-Yo shouted, again. He threw his hands up, as though trying to catch the sinking sun. "Listen to me!"

They did not. The opening ceremonies, as Zhan-Yo

understood from the signs posted all around the stadium, were several hours distant and the Paragons seemed more interested in meeting friends than listening to the strange human on the stage.

Except one.

Walking down the middle aisle directly towards Zhan-Yo, with a serene beam on his face, came a Champion Zhan-Yo had never seen in person, but knew well enough. Wrinkled, longer hair tied back, Apinya wore a red and black Paragon uniform, and while he didn't walk with a staff, Zhan-Yo couldn't help but picture one in the Champion's hands. An old wizard coming to cast a spell on the upstart.

If the Paragons didn't pay attention to Zhan-Yo, they certainly gave Apinya all the love. Blue suits followed the Champion into the center, flowing out behind him and standing amid the seats, watching to see what might happen, whether the legendary mind master might dispense with some wisdom or another.

"Here you are," Apinya said as he approached the stage, and not with the booming voice Zhan-Yo expected, but a mild tone. A conversation between two people, not a public haranguing. "In the middle of things."

"At the start of them," Zhan-Yo replied, and he abandoned center stage to head towards the edge, standing before and above Apinya. "Today we begin something new."

"Do we?" Apinya tilted his head ever-so-slightly, showing no annoyance that Zhan-Yo had claimed the high ground and, apparently, meant to keep it. "And what is this something?"

"A new beginning for us!" Zhan-Yo looked up as he said this, dashed Apinya's conversational volume. His audience here wasn't the Champion. Wasn't, really, the

Paragons in the stadium. They were bystanders to the true targets: the public. No doubt someone was recording this, possibly sending it live to the world. "The Paragons and the Normals. Today we start again. Together, as equals."

"A bold claim," Apinya replied. "One, I think, that lives more in words than deed."

While Aegis spent his glory days plastered on magazines and mugging for the cameras at every opportunity, embracing the legendary role and reveling in it, Apinya snuck into second paragraphs, background photos. He played the mediator, the problem-solver, the subtle dealer. The Champion would try to play with Zhan-Yo's words, break his argument down in public and turn the revolution into the ridiculous.

Zhan-Yo wouldn't, couldn't let him.

"I know you think what you're doing is right," Zhan-Yo declared, again ignoring Apinya for his worldwide—maybe—audience. "That you're preserving a peaceful system. But I tell you to look around, to see all those that you, the Paragons, are crushing each and every day beneath your boots. You hold yourselves honorable, defenders of justice, and yet, you refuse to let those you defend pick up their own shields, take up their own causes. Through chance, humanity's billions are rendered into their stations, like the old divine kings."

He had to take a breath. The air went into his lungs, refreshing his words for new lines. By the time he started speaking them, he no longer stood on the stage. No longer preached to a rapt world.

Instead, Zhan-Yo sat on a stone stool on a mountaintop. A granite chessboard, game all set to start, sat before him, and on its other side, on a similar squat stool, sat Apinya. The Champion had that same smile, the grin one might give to a child who persists in their strange, harmless behavior.

Zhan-Yo couldn't feel any wind, and while he could see snow at his feet and clouds moving beneath him, no chill touched his skin. No altitude thinned his breath, not that he even breathed.

"Everyone's mind is different," Apinya said, then reached out and shifted a central white pawn one space forward. "I used to greet people on their own terms, try to make a home that fit their experience. I came to realize that did not help my efforts. So now I bring them here."

Apinya nodded Zhan-Yo's way.

Ziran's former leader knew how to play chess, but knowing the rules and being any good at the game were two different things. So he copied Apinya's move, and tried to think up a response.

"I know you might be confused, even frightened," Apinya said, shuttling his queen forward into the pawn's vacated space. "But no harm will come to you here. And little time will pass out there. Our words are light, our bodies beyond physical bounds. Here, we can reason without emotion, resolve without rage."

Again, Zhan-Yo copied his opponent.

"I don't have anything to argue," Zhan-Yo said. "You know what I am fighting for, what I want."

"Normals on an even plane with Paragons." Apinya shifted another pawn. Zhan-Yo stopped caring about the game—he would copy Apinya's every move until the Champion won or it became a mess. "A noble goal, if a misguided one."

"The people in power often want to keep it."

"You are not young." Apinya added a lecturer's touch to his tone. "You witnessed our rise, and you know the world that came before. The chaos that ruled as leaders pursued their greed, their vendettas and their selfish ideas. You flourished in what came after, and yet you would do away with it?"

"Not do away. Share it. Keep your Champions, keep your Paragons, but let us inside the doors. Give normals the chance to decide our own fates. Bring government back to all the people, rather than a few."

Apinya and Zhan-Yo played through several moves in silence before the Champion spoke again.

"You claim that such a move would benefit the many, but where is your evidence? Democratic societies existed before the Paragons, yet were unable to prevent our rise. They faltered beneath flawed leaders."

"And so will you. You're already seeing it, after Aegis. Not every Paragon is honorable. Not every Champion is you. What happens when one goes off on their own? What happens when millions die because a Champion doesn't care anymore?"

"Then they will be dealt with."

Zhan-Yo wanted to laugh, wanted to cry. "See? This is what I mean. There are no controls, no levers for the common people to pull to keep you in check. The police police the police, and the normals suffer for it."

Apinya took Zhan-Yo's queen. A stumbling setup that would have been obvious if Zhan-Yo had been paying attention. While he couldn't copy Apinya's moves anymore, Zhan-Yo resolved to play with erratic abandon, swapping one piece for another to bring the game to a rapid end.

"You killed Aegis," Apinya said. "No matter what you say, we cannot listen. By plunging that sword into his back, you destroyed your own position."

"That was a mistake," Zhan-Yo replied. "I didn't want to kill him. I just wanted him to see my side of things."

"And he did not see?" Apinya took another piece, a knight this time.

Zhan-Yo took his revenge, even if taking Apinya's knight put his own bishop in jeopardy.

"I . . . he did not believe me. He thought I was arrogant. That I was making a mistake."

Apinya nodded slowly as he took Zhan-Yo's bishop and left himself protected from any real counter.

"Do you think, if a legend suggests you might be making a mistake, perhaps approaching your problem from the wrong angle, he might be right?"

Zhan-Yo tried to consider Apinya's words, but they seemed less like an argument and more like a feeling welling up inside, the cold doom that comes when the wrong path is chosen, is walked.

"I'm doing what I think is right," Zhan-Yo said. "But I might be doing it wrong."

He moved a piece aimlessly. A pawn scratching forward. Apinya took Zhan-Yo's last knight. Let Zhan-Yo move again in silence, and Apinya snagged another piece. The game had become a full-on rout.

"Remember, we are all invested in humanity," Apinya said. "Together, normals and Paragons advance society. You, yourself, have transformed the world with Ziran's efforts more than almost any of us."

"True."

Another move. Zhan-Yo only had a couple pieces left, surrounded by Apinya's hordes.

"Then don't you agree that we have our roles to play, the normals and the Paragons? That this revolution of yours is spending lives and energy that could otherwise be used to help those in need?"

Zhan-Yo couldn't put together a coherent thought. Words slipped away as he tried to say them. Instead, like a powerful drug's onset, Zhan-Yo felt only that Apinya's argument held immeasurable truth. This revolution, this cause, was a waste. A misdirection that would lead to sorrow and little else.

"I understand," Zhan-Yo whispered.

Apinya moved his queen, combining with a rook to send Zhan-Yo's king into a checkmate prison.

"Then agree with me," Apinya said, that grin never leaving his face. "Invite me up on your stage and tell the world that you see a better path. Together, we can unite our people and forge a way forward to a better world."

Zhan-Yo reached out, pushed over his king, nodding the whole while. Apinya had it right. There were too many important things to be done for a silly fight between Paragons and normals. Better for each side to stick to their roles, helping advance society as best as their abilities allowed.

The board, the pieces and the mountaintop faded out and, for a moment, Zhan-Yo felt like he fell through those clouds, until he crashed back into his own body, on that stage, with Paragons looking at him, drones floating above him, and death seconds away.

"We have made a deal," Apinya announced. The man wasn't boisterous, but the drones picked up his words and amplified them. "Together, we will bring about cooperation. A partnership between Paragon and normal."

Zhan-Yo nodded from the stage, beckoned for Apinya to join him on it. The older Champion began heading to the side, where a small stair had been placed for anyone not of scrambling mind to climb. As the Champion walked, Zhan-Yo turned back to the expectant Paragon crowd, to the drones crowding around.

Towards the back, pushing her way forward, he recognized a face. The woman that had tried to kill him in

Chicago. Zhan-Yo had to tell her that he had made a mistake. That he had it wrong. They should not be at war, but should be allies fighting to preserve this perfect world.

Zhan-Yo raised his right hand high, waved it towards her, saw Celice look his way, the hatred on that face. So strong, so angry. Zhan-Yo went back a step, two, and dropped his hand, unsure and unsettled.

How to build a bridge to that one? Zhan-Yo didn't know, and so he turned to Apinya, just now getting on the stair, and looked for answers.

But the Champion's smile vanished with ripping, roaring earth. Rattling explosions, spitting fire, and a sudden dark sucking Zhan-Yo down, down, down.

Assessing the Damage

Mynx.

MYNX.

The noise jolting her eyes open wasn't a word, but a seamless sound sent straight to Mynx's mind, designed and tested to ensure a visceral response every time. The ping bounced, blared, and broke the blinders holding Mynx unconscious, and revealed the stadium beneath her.

Beneath?

Wait.

As Mynx blinked into reality, small squares appeared across her vision in blues, greens, and reds. They shifted and centered on various spots around . . . disaster. Smoke rose, with flickering fires beneath, as bodies moved or lay still. Shouts for help and screams for those lacking it echoed as emergency sirens drew near. Amid hollowed out bleachers and torched, pitted turf, the stadium's concrete shell still stood, like a fractured, empty skeleton. One she had left behind, that she floated above.

A suit. That's where she was. Mynx mushed her way through the mental backlog as more and more squares popped up on her visor, slamming over and onto one another. So many, and so few moving.

"I evacuated you before the explosives went off," Reeves said, the AI coating his words with the appropriate sadness. "After Celice struck you, I had the emergency suit going anyway."

"How did you know?"

"Know what?"

"I'm assuming there were bombs?" Mynx said. "That's why the stadium looks like this? Or did an anomaly lose their mind?"

"Analysis pegs Zhan-Yo as the likely source. When he took the stage, I began an immediate security analysis given that—"

"He doesn't have suicidal tendencies," Mynx interrupted, letting cold logic numb the sick desperation growing in her gut. "Skip the details, give me the cause."

"There doesn't appear to be a single fault. Different explosives went off throughout the stadium."

Mynx took the suit's controls, began a controlled descent back towards the stadium. The emergency suit, more a big, safe box than a means for combat or service, had two flexible arms that Mynx could use to lift some bodies out. Now that the situation called for a hero, Mynx might as well be one.

"Small bombs didn't do this," Mynx said. "We planned for things like that. Any riots. Small arms attacks by Zhan-Yo's people."

"They didn't have to," Reeves said. "Whomever planned this knew what they were doing, Mynx. The attacks didn't come from outside. They were already hidden in the stadium."

"Hidden where?"

"Everywhere," Reeves replied. "The merchandise, the

food, the chairs and the stage. Within stadium vents. I think the only reason the stadium's still standing is enough anomalies reacted, suppressed the damage with their powers. All of you should be dead."

Reeves was saying their entire summit, every piece of it had been compromised. Mynx had established security, yes. Had placed drones around the entrance and had vetted the companies providing every item. All had checked out. All had been doing business with the Paragons for years and years.

So either someone had managed to sneak in explosives, or the Paragons had been compromised at the very start. Supplies had started arriving two days ago, bulk shipments matching the summit's haste. Mynx thought they had done their best, but perhaps mistakes had been made. Assumptions assumed.

Who would dare strike against the Champions, after all?

As she dropped, Mynx saw Paragon flags blowing their tattered selves in the dusty wind. More shouts filtered through the suit's speakers, and when Mynx touched down in the stadium's broken center, with torn up turf, chair pieces, and shattered glass everywhere, she fought to suppress a sob.

The Paragons were doing what they ought to: Those heroes not destroyed by the explosion bounded around, shifting debris and making way for medical drones and, by now, normals to lift the wounded out and away. Nobody paid attention to the woman in her suit in the center, watching her disaster unfold.

Mynx ran through more checks with Reeves, numbly confirming emergency response, ensuring all the LA drones were either assisting with the disaster or scanning for those responsible. When she reached the end, with

Reeves continually telling her that he'd already done all this and more, Mynx took a long, shuddering breath.

"Let me out," Mynx said, and, despite Reeves's protest, the suit obeyed.

Its glass shield opened, and Mynx stepped out onto the ruined surface. She wobbled a bit, her head hurting, but managed to steady herself with an outstretched arm. Without the suit's filters, Mynx breathed in who knew how much dust, how many chemicals. She felt heat from residual fires, their sparking flames glowing around her as the sun dropped away. And she heard, oh she heard.

Champions had seen it all before. That's what Mynx had thought, that's what she'd told herself before innumerable missions. Nothing could surprise her, and no horror could be too much for her icy veins. Mynx could stand it all, shut it away and go back to her machines. Make them more ruthless, more effective, so the Paragons who couldn't handle humanity at its worst wouldn't have to.

And yet, here was something she hadn't seen. Her friends, some among her closest confidants, might be buried around her right now. Others might be dead and gone. Vaporized or spirited away in ambulances, only to be seen again at a funeral or a morgue.

Mynx considered herself a logical creature. Built on numbers and proofs, facts and figures. Apinya, Burov, they handled the emotions. They were prepared to deal with this on the level it required. Mynx could only cope by turning emotions into numbers.

If even half of the Champions had been killed today, the world would be thrown into chaos. Power struggles like the one in Atlantis would erupt, and factions like the Elementals—did Rosamund survive?—might take advantage, form their own little territories. The Paragons might be able to claw things back, but it would require massive efforts.

Mynx would need drones by the thousands, by the millions. But who would trust her, now? She would be alone, having drawn the Champions and so many Paragons into an obvious trap. Mynx wouldn't get any respect, and she wouldn't deserve any.

She walked, because what else could she do?

Not too far from her, a Paragon in a shredded blue touched a concrete chunk and it fizzled, dissolved to dust, revealing a crumpled form beneath it. Two smaller drones zipped in, latched onto the body and lifted it away while the Paragon moved on to the next.

Mynx went around her landed suit slow, as if in a nightmare, keeping a hand on the machine and herself stable. Physically, mentally, she frayed.

The stage had splintered into pieces. A bomb must have been beneath it. No bodies there, no pieces around. No Zhan-Yo in sight, no Apinya either, though the two had been right here. In the center.

Apinya should have stopped Zhan-Yo. The Champion could turn anyone against anything, or into nothing at all. Now he'd vanished himself. Perhaps blown away. Mynx could only hope Zhan-Yo had suffered the same fate.

"Mynx," Reeves said, speaking through her Tama now. "Please. I'm getting too many requests to handle. The Paragons need direction, and they need it from you."

"After what I did? What I've done?" Mynx reached out, touched the stage's torn, flopping fabric. "What do they want with me?"

"Remember when you told me, before all this, that you were going to be a Champion again?"

Mynx said nothing. Blinked dust from her eyes. Watched the drones, Paragons fly around.

"You said you would. You said you would be what the world needed now that Aegis couldn't."

"That went well."

"It's still going. We should have a casualty list soon. Mynx, I can't be the one to tell the world what's happened. A computer shouldn't deliver news like this."

"Oh, lucky me." Mynx sat on the stage. Took a big breath, coughed up the dust.

Being a Champion meant living a thousand lives. Mynx had filled dreams beyond counting in her Factory, adventuring with Aegis and the others, and now the time had come for the tragic side. She wore the uniform—Mynx looked down at herself—and wore it still. Even if she was the only one.

"Tell me, Reeves. Who did we lose?"

53

The Black Horizon

In the dripping wet moments after the stampede through the waves to the boat, Thane and the other anomalies had to stop their rush to escape and confront reality. Namely, they had a boat with no motor, some supplies, and a couple dozen powered people with no idea how to work together. With the day dipping into afternoon and nobody wanting to be battling drones in the dark, Thane shriveled himself up to get things sorted quick.

As Cassidy shouted out an anomaly roll-call, Thane leaned on her and placed every answer into its optimal position on the boat. Sook, with his air-gusting abilities, made a natural engine. He'd be at the back, rotating out with Sienna, who could redirect her kinetic energy to give the boat a boost.

Another anomaly, Avery, claimed to be the one who'd sealed the boat in the first place. Able to turn surfaces into smooth glass, his power at first seemed pointless, but Thane had to think about more than the calm waters in Arthur's bay; out beyond where waves might rise up tall and the little boat could be rocked by surf, sealing the surface into a straight, smooth line might be essential.

Other anomalies could twist energy, mold their own skin, or weave hard nets between molecules at a distance. Thane gathered these around the boat's midpoint, where they could shift to counter wherever the potential drone attack would come from. Ideally, the escaping anomalies would get time before the drones reacted, would pick up enough speed to break away from the pursuit.

The drones might be able to follow the boat all the way to Hawaii, but Thane held to the hope that, with enough momentum and a little bit of offense, they could punch through the line and outrace the more distant machines, getting to civilization in time to ditch the boat and disappear.

"That's all of them," Cassidy said, and Thane gave a weak look around at the clusters he'd arranged. "Do you think it's enough?"

"We can always use more," Thane said, looking back towards the beach, where Arthur and his cadre stood, watching. "Give them another call. See if any have changed their minds."

"Not sure that's a good idea. I don't think you made many friends with your push back there."

"I'm not trying to make friends."

Cassidy shook her head, sighed, "Thane, you want to be a real leader, you're going to have to learn to act like you care."

"It's not that I don't care. It's that I care about more important things than people's feelings. Ask. If Arthur tries to fight, I'll jump off this ship and tear him apart."

Thane hoped he didn't show the slight fear that trickled in at that idea. His arm still hurt where Arthur had torched Thane on the beach, a singularly strange sensation after decades dealing with pain as a novelty. Still, now was not the time to lose confidence in his abilities. Thane had to be the invincible beacon.

"You get us killed, I'm going to be very upset," Cassidy said, then handed Thane over to Sook to support and made her way off the ship, back into the water.

"Bring me to the back. I want to see what happens."

"Sure thing, boss," Sook said. "By the way, pretty impressive. You know, didn't think this was actually gonna happen when I found you in that cave. Thought we'd be dead by now, really."

Sook, the bedraggled, lanky bodyguard had thought Thane would lead him to his death, and came anyway?

"Thank you, I suppose," Thane said. "I do owe you for getting me out of that cave. When we get to a real city, I'll see your debt repaid."

"Don't worry about that. This has already been more than enough. More than I thought I'd get, anyways."

With Sienna on one side and Sook on the other, Thane watched Cassidy approach the beach. Arthur came up to talk to her, and while Thane couldn't quite hear what Cassidy said over the ocean's noise, he could see that she spoke around him, to the anomaly cluster on the beach.

Arthur shook his head even as Cassidy started, then gestured for her to stop, his face getting more and more red with every word. The anomalies behind him didn't seem to care about Cassidy either, standing stone-faced as the Void made her plea.

Or tried.

With a sudden darkening, Arthur thrust his hand into the air and drew the light around him, around the beach, such that everyone's shadows pulled towards the anomaly. Cassidy backed away a step, but Arthur didn't seem to be looking at her anymore. Instead, he stared past her, past the boat, and kept sucking in the light.

"Is he about to blow himself up?" Sook said.

"One can only hope," Thane muttered.

Arthur did not, though, go nova. Cassidy broke and ran back towards the boat as Arthur kept drawing in the light, splashing through as she went, as a bright afternoon turned into grim sundown, then to a lightless night.

The anomaly blazed like a beacon, with yellow-white light swirling around him, as if Arthur had become his very own star. Thane thought he could hear Arthur yelling, now, a wordless scream.

Maybe Sook was right. Maybe Arthur would protest this whole adventure by exploding himself, casting everyone to oblivion. Thane couldn't even be angry at the thought—there wasn't time, and, in a way, this sort of grand end would be too impressive to fight against. There was nothing to do but watch and see whether Arthur would blow them all to ash.

Then, as if pitching a fastball, Arthur bunched himself up and launched an arm forward. All that light within him, all the light that Arthur had sucked from the day, siphoned into that arm and out its end, rocketed off and over the boat towards the far horizon.

In the instant the light left Arthur, like a cloud moving away or an eclipse meeting its end, daylight returned in a wave as everyone wheeled around to see whether Arthur had been making a pretty show, or if he had a purpose.

Arthur's bolt moved fast enough that by the time Thane turned around, he only saw the aftermath. A rippling, spastic explosion out at the dark drone line, one that burst and expanded, climbing between the drones like a virus and exploding one after another until five or six directly in the boat's intended path had vanished in the nova.

"He's helping us?" Sienna said. "What?"

Thane didn't understand either. Why would Arthur care about their escape, why would he go through all that trouble to blow up the drones in their path? Kindness after Thane embarrassed him on the beach didn't seem like Arthur's trait.

"Thane!" Arthur's voice carried over the waves, barely. "I hope you liked my show! It'll be the last one you ever see!"

A stupid threat. Thane wanted to look back at Arthur, reply in kind, but points and shouts across the boat kept his attention on the horizon, on all those other black dots.

Drones ringed the island, and now they were moving, responding to Arthur's attack, a bolt that would lead them right here. Right to Thane and their escape.

And the anomalies weren't moving at all.

"Go," Thane said. "Get the boat moving. We have to leave now!"

Cassidy came up, grabbed Thane as Sook and Sienna turned to get the boat going. Thane kept shouting for anomalies to get to their positions, to get ready for the attack, for the drone swarm to arrive.

As Cassidy pulled Thane to the boat's cabin, he shifted, took one last look towards the beach where Arthur had been. Where the drones would, should find him. He might attract attention to the boat, but Arthur would draw Mynx's robotic wrath on himself as well.

Except when Thane turned around, Arthur and his remaining band had vanished, as if they had never been there at all.

"Can't worry about him anymore," Cassidy said. "It's all on us, now, and we're following you, so lead."

Thane could have said that leading the Elemental's hired guns in a futile stand against Paragons was very different than . . . well, maybe this wasn't so far off. The goal back in the northeast had been to last long enough to get the Paragons to make a deal. Here, they needed to last long enough to live.

He could work with that.

"Positions by your powers!" Thane called, stepping away from Cassidy into the boat's center, turning as he did to catch everyone's eyes. "Protectors in front, fighters in the middle. This won't be quick, so talk. Find your friends and work together."

Whether the moment's desperation crystallized the response or some anomaly power spurred everyone to coordinated action, the boat rocked as anomalies found their positions. Seeing the response, Thane felt a bitter pride: all these villains and misfits throwing aside their charred pasts to come together in what would probably be a doomed effort.

If it was, then Thane would be happy to stand beside them. His very first, true team.

The drones didn't care one bit about Thane's team, true or otherwise. The little black dots grew to car-sized monsters as the boat picked up speed heading away from the island. The flying machines streaked in, one after another.

"As soon as they're within your range, fire what you have!" Thane shouted. "If you have a shield, work with your partners and raise them in turn!"

Not the most unified defense—with more time, Thane could have worked out firing sequences so anomalies didn't waste their energies attacking or defending from the same targets. Thane didn't have that luxury—they would have to learn on the fly.

As soon as he finished speaking, Thane saw two anomalies in the boat's center point towards the oncoming drone. A small board shot from the boat's surface, grew long and sharp before slicking over—the second anomaly's work, Thane imagined—into a shimmering spear that drove into the oncoming drone's shell, splitting the machine into sparking, fiery halves that disappeared into the water.

A cheer went up, one that died quick as several more drones approached, and dozens more buzzed behind those.

How many more could this ragged band destroy?

54

Connection

Know the best way to dodge a bullet? Get a dog to bite the shooter first.

Kat figured she was about to take another trip to gunshot hell, but Seeker's black-white blur tackled the kneeling gunman before he could crack his shot. The husky bore the attacker to the ground, snarling and snapping at his wrist.

Kat didn't blow the opportunity, pushing herself to her unsteady feet and making a slow dash towards the pond's edge. Rhimes went that way too, getting there first and making a shouting way towards the top, yelling curses at Kat's dog. At least until Calvin came running up behind the puppy.

And definitely when Calvin stuck one hand in the snow and another on the downed man's body. A human icicle tends to make you reconsider your actions, and Rhimes turned his from a rescue charge into a straight line flight through the snow, cutting between Kat and Calvin, heading for the pods.

"Don't let him get away!" Kat shouted. She tried to

aim the grapple, planted a foot wrong and face-planted into the pond's snowy shore.

She stuck her head up out of the snow to see Seeker still hadn't dropped his victim's hand. Calvin had broken into a run after Rhimes, but, despite some icy blasts that broke against Rhimes's back, failed to catch him.

"After this," Kat snarled to herself, spitting out snow as she did so and breaking to her feet, "I'm moving south."

Rather than trace Rhimes's path along the snowy bank, Kat went right for the parking lot. She broke onto the asphalt, winced at the bodies still covering it, and saw Rhimes diving towards the pod they'd brought here, back when Kat had been sedated.

That felt forever ago. Time really moved fast when you were getting shot at, punched, kicked, and tossed around on the ice.

Calvin sent another frozen crystal barrage towards the pod, leaning over as he ran to drag his hand in the snow. The ice cracked and shattered against Rhimes's vehicle, doing precisely nothing as the pod reversed and turned towards the park's exit.

Kat aimed, thought about firing the grapple, then let her arm fall as Rhimes rolled away, abandoning his soldiers. Even if the grapple had been able to get a grip, and Kat doubted the thing would have stuck the pod, all that would've done was drag Kat on a really cold, uncomfortable ride.

"You alive?" Calvin said, clomping over and sparing a long look for the bodies. "I didn't think we'd timed it right when I saw the carnage."

"Timed it right?" Kat said, coming to terms with the fact that she was, in fact, still alive. "You were way too late. I should've died about a dozen times."

"Too late?" Calvin said as they both turned towards

Seeker, still holding firm on his human snack. "I thought you didn't want us to be early? When you sent the signal, I waited as long as you said."

"I didn't think I'd get knocked out," Kat said.

Using Tamas for pre-programmed notifications wasn't exactly a secret. Whether you wanted to send someone a note when you walked into work, or when you spoke their name followed by a task, building a subtle beam to a friend didn't hit super spy levels. Kat had gone to Rhimes's house, tracking the weapons, with Calvin keeping tabs on her progress the whole time.

The idea being, of course, that Calvin could call in the drone cavalry when things went sideways. Instead, when Kat had sent the signal during the struggle in the house—two quick Tama taps as she'd run up those stairs did the trick—nothing happened. The house, according to Calvin, had been a dead zone. Kat had blipped off when she'd gone inside, and appeared later, heading north and west towards the pond.

"Why?" Kat asked, going around to each downed enemy and confirming they wouldn't be getting up again, ever. "Why are you and my dog here, and not the drones?"

"I don't know!" Calvin said, and given the hand-flying exasperation in his voice, Kat was inclined to believe the man. "I tried! Literally, I called the Paragon number we all get and said hey, my friend, a tracker, is in trouble and she needs help, and guess what they said?"

"What?"

"We're too damned busy. Guess it's something with that summit. Said they'd call me back."

"What summit?" Kat said, distracted as she felt the fourth one and realized her one hundred percent fatality rate.

She'd doubled her kill count in a single afternoon. And

unlike some trackers, who seemed to take every anomaly bounty and attach 'Dead or Alive' to the conditions, Kat wanted to throw up. Wanted to be alone. Wanted to be with friends. Wanted to forget this ever happened.

"That big one, out in LA?" Calvin said. "Don't know why it's screwing things up for us, but once they said they weren't gonna help, I figured Seeker and I better get going."

"Mmhmm."

Kat closed her eyes for a moment. Four people. Maybe with families. Lives.

"But Kat, you know, Paragons? We get the override codes for the pods? They go super fast! I thought we were gonna crash, but that thing moved. We woulda been way too late without it."

"Calvin, please, quiet."

"Sorry, I'm just worked up."

"Yeah," Kat said. "Me too."

Seeker barked. Drew their attention back to the husky, and to his victim. Kat didn't move fast; the downed man wasn't moving.

Seeker's catch, turned out, had joined the rest of Rhimes's security force in the afterlife. Kat knelt by the soldier, told Seeker to leave the man alone, and took a quick pulse measure. Nothing, which made sense, as ice filled every cavity Kat could see. Ears, eyes, mouth.

"Geez, Calvin," Kat said slow, standing up and shaking her head. "You didn't have to do that."

Calvin didn't look all that apologetic, "Man was trying to shoot you, Kat. I didn't think about being nice to him."

"Feel like there's a middle ground between nice and turning your insides to an ice sculpture." Kat seemed to exhaust the rest of her adrenaline with that line, though. Like she'd slipped on the ice again, Kat felt heavy, tired, and a pounding headache confirmed she'd pushed past her endurance.

"You know, for a rescue, you're really giving me a lot of crap," Calvin said. "Think I, and Seeker, deserve a thank you."

"I know you do. Thanks. But can we get out of here? Someone's going to come looking for these people eventually."

Kat didn't say that no matter who that someone was, whether it was Paragons following up on Calvin's call or the killer's second wrecking crew, she did not want to deal with them. Couldn't.

She already had enough nightmares.

Kat spent the ride back downtown to Gordon's hotel—her apartment, now that Rhimes and his boss had a bead on her, was hilariously out of bounds—stroking Seeker's fur and staring out at nothing. Calvin tried to talk a couple times, but, sensing her mood, turned to his Tama instead.

Beyond sending a message to Gordon, letting him know they were coming, Kat avoided the world. Calvin's expressions, his whistles and muttered curses made it clear something bad was happening, but for the hour they spent in the pod, Kat only thought about the bodies.

She'd asked her parents once, when Kat had been thirteen or so, whether they killed anyone. Whether they had to hurt people like Aegis did every now and then. At first, they'd said no. They'd both said their roles were peaceful. Friendly. Kat had lived with that for another year, until her mother had come home late with a long scratch on her face and her wrist at the wrong angle.

Kat's father had disappeared with her to the hospital, and with Paragon care, they were back in an hour, Kat's mother looking perfect. The evidence, though, had been enough for a follow-up, a pressing question.

Why had they told her the truth? Was it because, by then, they all knew Kat wasn't going to be an anomaly? Were they trying to make Kat feel better when they told her, with a mug of hot chocolate in her hands, that Paragon work was messy? That you had to learn to live with terrible things?

How to do that, how to live with those things, had been a topic left for another day. One that never came.

Gordon met them in the hotel lobby, looking far too grim for someone who finally seemed able to move like a normal person. At first, Kat thought the man's ashen expression came from seeing Calvin again, but when Gordon nodded towards the bar and Calvin agreed, Kat threw out that logic.

And when she saw the news playing across the screens, when she confirmed it on her Tama, Kat joined the crowded bar in its shocked silence, broken only by bottles splashing booze into glasses.

What else could you do at the end of the world?

55

Blast Zone

Collateral damage. That'd been the risk, and Zhan-Yo had accepted it. Ordered Mathieu to tell him as little as possible about the setup, the rapid response Zhan-Yo himself had ordered days earlier when they'd discovered the summit's location. Apinya, other Paragons, might be able to strip the plans from Zhan-Yo's mind. The only clue Mathieu offered, the only escape given Zhan-Yo, had been the words whispered before they split after the rescue: *center stage*.

When the bombs went off, Zhan-Yo expected to die. To vanish in a flaming geyser or be blown high enough to crumple into bits upon hitting the ground. Instead, he fell. Just . . . dropped as the stage cracked up around him, dipping in the middle and letting Zhan-Yo fall down into the stadium's lower labyrinths.

He landed on a fake dirt pile as plastic turf sprinkled around him. Zhan-Yo's ears rang, and Apinya's mental scrubbing had his head feeling numb. Painful pinpricks bloomed.

A blue-white light once embedded against the chamber's ceiling, now hanging by a cord, flickered as debris continued to fall. From the shouts above, Zhan-Yo realized he'd either blacked out, or had been lying on that pile for minutes already. He wanted to lay for minutes more, let the shock wear off.

Except that wasn't going to work.

Zhan-Yo had committed his ultimate act. Destabilized the world. Dying now would definitely not be in his best interest. Would waste this wonderful opportunity.

He moved, gripped and pulled himself forward across the dirt, down the pile and towards the stone ground. Every motion hurt, and Zhan-Yo felt blood's telltale warmth, wet on his legs, arms, down his face. Shrapnel, maybe, or the explosion's concussive force. Who knew.

But he lived, and Zhan-Yo hadn't expected that much.

The cement floor provided cold comfort. Zhan-Yo coughed at the dirty air. His eyes bleared in the dust, burned as who knew how many dangerous substances now floated around. A deep vibration came as something heavy landed above, rattling more dirt and sparking wires free from their damaged containers.

Standing with shaky effort, Zhan-Yo took his first look across the wide room and realized the space covered the stadium's length. The entire field, with doors at either end. Maintenance for the turf, maybe.

What would he do now?

The thought tantalized Zhan-Yo. Future planning had been a risky endeavor, one only approached with broad words and maxims, a vague inspirational tone that left the door open for success's slim possibility. He had focused on the now, but as Zhan-Yo limped along the cement, wandering around the collapsed sections, he played with a new world.

While he wouldn't know how many Paragons, how

many Champions had fallen in the bombing, Zhan-Yo figured the chaos would be absolute. And normal involvement would be too hard to hide here. The world would know that people had decided to fight back against their masters, and those people would need a leader. Would hold Zhan-Yo up as such.

In their rattled fear, the Paragons, any remaining Champions, would have to negotiate. With normals, billions and billions, standing behind him, Zhan-Yo would have the leverage. The Paragons could call him whatever names they wanted, could declare him a monster and a terrorist, and Zhan-Yo would cling to that cleaner alternative: freedom fighter.

At the table, faced with worldwide turmoil, the Paragons would have to grant concessions. Would have to accept equal placement, treatment. A return to democratic government. The people, not divided between normals and anomalies, would have their day again.

And if, after all that, the Paragons insisted that Zhan-Yo still be put to the sword? Well, he could accept that. His life wasn't the objective. History would remember him.

On his left, a creaking-groaning-breaking noise coupled with dirt falling in dark waves had Zhan-Yo stumble to the right. He'd neared an end—in the dark, underground, Zhan-Yo had no idea which end, he just went towards a door—and now it seemed he'd chosen the wrong one. Zhan-Yo kept moving, watching as the ceiling bent and buckled and broke, debris from above crashing down to the floor and sending up dust clouds, springing rocks free, and causing Zhan-Yo to shield his eyes, close his mouth, and hope nothing fatal would find him.

Nothing did, but the same could not be said of the body lying intertwined with the rocks and the Paragon blue turf holding one of the end zones. An arm, a leg, and, nearly swallowed by dirt, a close-cropped head stuck out, scratched and bloody.

Zhan-Yo winced, then kept on. Had to get going, had to get out.

"Help."

Zhan-Yo couldn't be sure she even spoke the words, or if she just groaned and his mind did the rest. Still, he turned back, frowning.

"Help."

Her lips moved this time, and look, she had one eye open. The other looked puffy, not in a good state. The way her limbs splayed suggested broken bones, and you weren't supposed to shift someone like that. Could bring about permanent damage.

He should walk away.

Except the ceiling groaned again. Farther back, towards where Zhan-Yo had first fallen, another hole broke in. The field itself seemed to be falling apart. No matter what damage the Paragon might suffer if Zhan-Yo helped her, it had to be better than dying, right?

"Please."

But this, this was the enemy. Help the Paragon, and he'd be lending aid to the very people he was trying to stop. Well, no. He didn't want to stop the Paragons, really. Zhan-Yo wanted equality. That meant working together.

Yes, he'd caused this disaster to make his point. But this Paragon, this single victim, she wasn't his main target. She might not have any power, but she might remember, later, the person that pulled her out.

Zhan-Yo would remember too, and in the long days and nights that were to come, it might be good to have something with which to salve his conscience. A good deed to sprinkle on his terrible ones.

"Boss, we gotta go," the words came from behind him,

and Zhan-Yo turned to see the open door, Marcus standing there, dusty but otherwise unharmed in his Paragon blues. "They're still confused, but they're getting it together quick."

"Right." Zhan-Yo looked back to the broken Paragon, both eyes closed now. "Come over here, help me with her."

Marcus ran to join Zhan-Yo near the Paragon, but his widening eyes and questioning face matched his frozen hands when he arrived. Zhan-Yo had already started pulling some dirt away, lifting a rock and tossing it aside.

"What're you doing?" Marcus said. "Are you crazy? Concussed? She's not on our side."

"Not yet. We're not monsters, Marcus. Help me get her out."

Shaking his head, Marcus started pulling at the rocks, "Man, you just dropped a stadium on a bunch of hero heads. If you're not a monster, I don't know who is."

"And yet, you're helping me."

"Look, I'm helping you because I made my choice," Marcus replied, hefting off, with Zhan-Yo, a concrete chunk and rolling it away, clearing the Paragon's torso. "Doesn't mean I'm lying to myself about it."

Was Zhan-Yo lying to himself? Had he crossed that line from visionary to terror, like so many self-righteous kings and dictators cast to history's ashes?

With Zhan-Yo guiding the Paragon's shoulders, Marcus dislodged her legs and the hero slid down the rubble pile to the ground. Zhan-Yo did his best to keep her neck straight and level, and when she rested on the concrete, he was surprised at his own relief to see her breathing.

"Let's drag her near the door, it'll be sturdier," Zhan-Yo said. "Then we can leave her."

"The sinner and the saint," Marcus muttered, but he complied. "You're a strange guy, Z."

Z. Wexley and Sylvie called him that. Nobody else, really. It'd been a while. Maybe he ought to bring that up more. Didn't all those historical monsters have big names? Sinister ones? Zhan-Yo could just be Z, simple and light. Someone to work with, someone to work for, someone who could save the world.

They dropped the Paragon at the doorway, and, with Marcus leading, they disappeared into the stadium and the chaotic crush as people and drones worked to save the saviors.

56

Death Count

Mynx could see the ruined stadium's lights from LA's Paragon tower. It lingered outside the big windows, hazy smoke still hovering around it even as drone and human crews ran straight from rescue into repairs. The surrounding blocks, too, needed help; blown out windows, trapped people, pods that'd taken their disaster avoidance programming and scurried into each other.

"You didn't find him, did you?" Celice said.

Somehow, in that catastrophe, Aegis's daughter had survived. A placement miracle, caught up in a Paragon's protective bubble that the nameless rank-and-file hero had popped up when the first explosions came. While Mynx had been hovering above, Celice had watched as the stadium collapsed around her, its great chunks slamming against the shield and sliding away, a half-dozen Paragons crowding inside with her.

"Reeves hasn't noted his capture, or his body," Mynx said. "There's a chance, however small, that Zhan-Yo did not immolate himself in the stadium."

A bigger chance than small. Mynx had found the hole

in center stage. Had sent a drone down through it and had seen the dirty footprints leading away. Then the whole damn field had fallen, burying any evidence—and her drone—with tons of turf and dirt. Whether Zhan-Yo had been caught in that collapse wouldn't be learned for days, possibly weeks.

"Knowing our luck, he probably got away fine and healthy," Celice said. She sat at the table, while Mynx stood, though both drank tea, both looked mostly out the windows into LA's night sky. "Recording some big announcement. Declaring that everything needs to be turned, now. You should have let me shoot him."

"I should have."

Celice, though, didn't sound heated. Didn't sound angry. She sounded lost, defeated. Like Mynx.

"Sorry for hitting you," Celice said, for the third time now since they'd taken refuge in the room. "I just saw him and lost it."

"I understand." Mynx looked down at her Tama, tapped out some quick orders to Reeves, to other Paragons. "I can't say that I would have done the same thing, but I understand."

"I was going to go right up to him. Take him out right there, in front of everyone. That was my plan. All of it." Celice sighed. "It's like my life had a black box around him. I couldn't see past him. Past what he did."

Oh, Mynx knew that black box. She could see it, or so she imagined, off to the north. Her Factory, waiting to draw her back into its whirring, mechanized confines. Projects to play with, ones on hold for too long now. That would have to hold a little bit longer.

"You can't afford that anymore," Mynx said. "We can't afford that anymore."

"Yeah, I think I get that."

"The Paragons are going to need you. I don't know for sure how many Champions are going to make it out of this, but we'll need leaders."

"You don't want me leading anything right now."

"Not want, *need* you leading. Whether you believe it or not, the Paragons look to you as Aegis's daughter. We need your support." Mynx pulled herself away from the windows, sat opposite Celice and took a strong drink from her hot mug. "Reeves kept going at Zhan-Yo's Tama."

"While the stadium blew up?"

"He's a computer. He can multi-task."

Celice nodded slow. Mynx wondered if she looked as tired, wrecked as Celice did. Probably. Maybe worse, as Celice was easily thirty years younger.

"Zhan-Yo's whole plan revolves around getting the normals to push back against us," Mynx said.

"That's stupid. Everyone loves the Paragons. The world's doing the best it's ever done."

"You need to get out more, if that's what you believe."

"Says the Champion that never leaves her Factory."

Mynx acknowledged that truth by raising her mug. Let the argument stall out.

"My point," Mynx continued, "is that he's going to try and turn the public against us. We'll need to counter that. Ordinarily, I'd say the Champions could just laugh in his face."

"But you're weak."

"*We're* weak, Celice. After this, we're very weak. We need to show we're not broken, and that we're willing to change."

Celice sat back, her eyes narrowing to slits, her grip on that mug getting tight, "You want a prop. That's what you want me for. A famous normal, given a spot near the top."

"Not a prop," Mynx countered. Surprised, too, that she

meant it. "It's not easy for me to say, Celice, but I might've been wrong. Maybe we do need normals in the Paragons, maybe we even need a normal Champion."

"And you're saying that's me. How convenient."

Mynx pursed her lips, then straightened them, tried to find the diplomatic line and nah, she just couldn't do it. Not on a day like today. Not now, with her Tama buzzing every second with another casualty report. Another headline declaring the Champions dead and the world in turmoil.

She slapped the table. Hard. Stood and glared down at the little girl who had turned into nonstop trouble since her father had gone.

"You will stop this, and you will stop it now. This is bigger than you, bigger than your pride. We cannot afford to play these stupid games right now. Get on board, or get out."

For a second, an all-too-brief second, it seemed like Celice might actually listen. Like Aegis's daughter might fold to that argument and take the offer.

Celice pushed herself back from the table, stood even to Mynx.

"I asked you once to let me in, and you said no," Celice replied. "You told me the Paragons were only for anomalies. That I didn't belong. You don't get to change that when it's convenient. Life doesn't work that way. I'm not your ticket out, and I don't want to play your game." Leaving her mug on the table, Celice went to the door. "I'm going after Zhan-Yo. I'm going to finish what I started. And when I'm done, we'll see, Mynx. We'll see what kind of world we have left."

"I'll be waiting," Mynx said the words, but by the time they came from her lips, Celice had already slammed the door.

Gone again.

"Mynx," Reeves interrupted the silence. "I've been trying to buzz you."

"Noticed."

"We found Apinya. He's alive."

57

The Way Out

Completing an anomaly inventory while in active combat was not, in fact, easy. Thane, trying to keep his anger and desperation in check and not go off like a raving mad beast, ran around the swaying ship, asking huddled anomalies who could do what and directing them to where they could be used.

Those without offensive or defensive powers went to the poles, helping guide the boat through the reefs and sandbars along the island's outskirts. Others vanished below deck, to the shallow hold stocked with coconuts and dried fish, where they wouldn't get in the way.

More than two dozen anomalies on the boat, though, found places for their powers. Given that Mynx had used the island for dangerous anomalies, Thane didn't find it too surprising that the air around the boat soon filled with streaking lightning, water spouts launched from the sea, Cassidy's gravity-bending voids, and other physics-defying manifestations.

At first the drones took the hits without thought,

sweeping through on their lethal runs, spraying fire that Cassidy swept up in her void. Or, if Cassidy had to take a breather, another anomaly combo package supplied the shield instead: the two anomalies, who'd been with Arthur, worked in tandem. One launched a giant water spout from the ocean, her arms swinging up as she did so, like a showman, and the other would turn the spray into pure salt, creating a thick, white column that puffed as drone fire pelted it.

More offensive anomalies took their shots, bringing down or damaging drones with acid, flames, or straight up concentration that bent and broke the machine's metal frames.

The boat kept moving forward, with Sook and Sienna alternating their gusts and kinetic lunges, and they were picking up speed. They cleared the reef, and larger waves buffeted the boat, sending it flying every few seconds as it crested one after another. The anomaly seal keeping the boat together held, and the craft skidded along the water's surface like it belonged there.

Thane let himself hope, just a little.

But anomalies weren't tireless, and as the day deepened, the drones numbers and endless waves began to wear. Anomalies took hits. Laser burns or bullets knocking them to the deck or over the side. Not that anyone had time to mourn, or do anything other than take the fallen's place.

This escape wouldn't be a quick win, it would be an endurance contest. A challenge to last until they reached inhabited places, and there, maybe they could vanish into the crowd.

Or, a truly grim thought, these drones might never stop. The pursuit might follow them to whatever end, until every anomaly lay dead, whether at the sea floor or crowded street.

"Cassidy!" Thane called as another drone pass left the anomalies gasping. Those on the line switched out, retreated to the boat's center while replacements went to their positions, watching and prepping for the next swing. "We need to change our plan!"

The Void, looking both spent and frustrated at the same time, leaned on Thane as she came away from her position.

"Agreed. I don't think we can keep this up for much longer," Cassidy said, and Thane, feeling the heat coming off her, couldn't argue. "What's your plan? Does it get us out of here?"

"We're playing defense, and that has to change," Thane said. "I'm thinking we'll never outrun them."

"Attack them how?" Cassidy replied. "We're barely staying alive, in case you hadn't noticed."

"You, Cassidy. You're the key."

"That's not what I want to hear."

Thane pulled Cassidy down as salt pillars shot up and the next drone wave shot past. An anomaly standing on the boat's highest point, seemed to take several energy hits from the drones and, turning as they went by, released the strikes back at their makers, sending two machines tumbling to the sea. A ragged cheer went up, even as the anomaly sank to his knees, blood pouring from his nose.

"How big can you make one?" Thane asked. "Could you capture a whole wave?"

Cassidy shook her head against his shoulder. "I don't know, Thane. I'm so tired already. Even if I did, I might burn up. Start the ship on fire."

"I don't want to ask you, but I don't see another way."

The next drone wave wheeled about, two dozen sweeping in for a pass from the boat's aft. "We're going to break, and soon."

"I thought you said, back on the island, that we could do this, together," Cassidy murmured. "I believed you."

"And I won't let you down." Thane pulled Cassidy to her feet, wincing as her skin singed his hands. "We just need this. Now."

The commands came quick once he had Cassidy moving to the boat's back. The Void looked towards the oncoming drones and focused, her skin heating red-hot. Sienna pulled water when Thane asked, spraying Cassidy with ice cold ocean, a continual shower that had Cassidy yelping, had her vanishing in fog as the liquid hit her and vaporized.

Vaporized. Thane glanced at his own hands, shoulders. They were red, yes, but not black or peeling away as if he'd been boiled. He could withstand this much.

Shouts, though, drew Thane's attention skyward, and then he saw why.

The oncoming drones seemed to shimmer and stretch, some fading altogether as a black oval appeared and grew, its edges not a thick line but a blurry haze. Light failing to escape. If Cassidy had created small negative space before, here was an actual void, sucking in everything nearby.

And the drones ran right into it.

What could have been, should have been spectacular was instead a quiet triumph. Without light, Cassidy's effectiveness came from the drones on the formation's edges, the ones streaking just outside the void's strongest pull. Even there, Cassidy's work twisted their flight, yanked the machines around harder than they could compensate for, pulled them in and crashed them into each other, their fiery wrecks sucking back into Cassidy's void as if being vacuumed, stretching away until they vanished.

Not a single drone came through, though Thane could barely tell, as the fog had enveloped the entire boat.

"Stop!" Thane shouted. "Cassidy, it's over!"

Not totally true. There were more drones coming, more waves, but for a few minutes, at least, they had time. Thane ordered Sienna to keep spraying, until, at last, the fog stopped renewing itself and the speeding boat outran its leftovers. Thane laid Cassidy on the deck, her eyes closed, to grab what few seconds of rest she could before the next wave struck.

The plan had worked. A whole drone flight had been eliminated. Do that a few more times, and they could clear the skies. Buy themselves the freedom they needed, and space for Thane to pull together a new idea.

"DID WE WIN?" Cassidy asked when Thane had coaxed her awake with some more splashing, cold water minutes later, as the next drone wave coalesced for its attack. "I guess I'm alive?"

"You were brilliant," Thane replied, still holding her. "You were everything we needed. You got them all. Every single one."

Cassidy huffed a dry laugh, slid her eyes down the boat, "Of that group. I'll have to do it again, won't I?"

Thane couldn't lie to her anymore. Not now, not ever, "Can you?"

"We die if I don't, right?"

Thane had no answer. Only a sad nod.

"You'll have to hold me again," Cassidy said. "Tighter this time. I almost slipped, and it's only going to get worse."

Stand next to a blazing inferno as she saved their lives? Thane could do that. Could reach into the deep unfairness, the sinister world that had brought them to this moment and keep Cassidy standing, keep himself alive.

"I'll be there," Thane said, pulling her to her feet. "Standing with you till the end."

58

The Morning After

Kat couldn't find the fun with the world's end. She didn't want to join some revelry, throw out all the cares and accept annihilation in some giant bender winding out the clock until the inevitable turned them to ash. No. Instead, what Kat, Calvin, and Gordon did, after that first drink, was stare around at each other and the others in the bar, all doing the same thing, and then make their way up to Gordon's room.

They didn't really talk, didn't swap stories or even describe how Kat had barely survived the run-in with Wexley, Rhimes, and his thugs. That whole thing didn't seem to matter in the larger context; when the world order vanished in a hot explosion, Kat's own issues seemed pathetic.

Only Seeker, huffing around and licking Kat's white boots, seemed unperturbed.

Calvin didn't follow them all the way. His Tama had lit up with Paragon requirements, requests, and then orders to report to the headquarters for assignments, for information. Kat tried to quiz him before the anomaly left, get some details, but Calvin had nothing to say except he'd be in touch. The man vanished into a silent, panicked night.

Retreating to Gordon's hotel room felt wrong, or too confined, or too little in the face of . . . existence? What did you do with disaster like this? The Champions weren't friends, weren't relatives, didn't come to Kat's birthday parties—as if she had birthday parties—but the dire reports coming from LA felt like gut stabs anyway.

"I'm taking Seeker for a walk," Kat had said after they'd punched the elevator button but before the doors had opened.

"Good idea," Gordon had replied, neither considering how absurd a midnight walk would be in a city roiling after repeated Paragon calamities.

Neither one spoke as they lapped blocks with Seeker. Pods rolled by, though Kat would've said the streets were emptier than expected—everyone inside mulling their fates. They passed bars still crowded, patrons staring at TVs or Tamas more than drinking. All those neon lights calling out dwindled in worry's thick shadow.

Kat didn't know when sleep came. They collapsed on the mattress, Seeker between them, and woke up much the same, in a surreal state that pushed only one agenda: find out what had happened to their reality?

"There are people trying to kill you," Gordon said as they brushed teeth, washed faces, put on some normalcy. "I know, I know there's the whole Paragon thing. But that'll play out. You can't get distracted. Not now."

"Uh huh."

"I mean, we're trackers. We have skills. If the Paragons don't work, then something will come after them that'll need us. We'll be fine."

"Sure will." Kat stared at herself in the mirror. Not all that bad. A little scratch on her arm from the dive in the gun house, a red scab on her forehead from the dart, but otherwise her coat and jeans hid the bruises from the murderous ice dancing. "Everything will be just as it was, Gordon."

With her uniform packed in the simple overnight bag, stuffing it full, Kat had to decide where to go. She wasn't any closer to finding the killer, and other than returning to the house and seeing if Rhimes wanted round two, there weren't any clear options.

Not to mention Kat had taken out a bunch of lackeys. If the man wanted her dead before, he probably wouldn't like her any more today. She'd be outnumbered, outgunned. Unless…

Kat looked at her Tama on her left wrist. As Tamas did, and as Kat made sure hers did very well, it had recorded every conversation she had yesterday. With the Paragons on her side, Kat could give Calvin the recordings and watch, popcorn in hand, as anomalies and drones did Kat's revenge for her. Went to the house and torched Rhimes. Maybe identified the lead man by his voice and took care of everything at once.

Sure, the Paragons likely had problems, but a murder ring in Chicago had to merit some action. The city couldn't be left to anarchy because of a disaster in LA

"Can I go with you?" Gordon asked as they left the room. "The tracker boards don't have any information. Mynx, if she's still alive, isn't saying anything."

"Sure," Kat replied. "Just remember that I'm apparently a target. You walk with me, you might get shot."

"I'm used to it."

"Are you?"

Gordon shrugged and Kat didn't have enough energy to push the fight. She needed coffee, and food. And, preferably, a return to her apartment without the fear of getting blown to pieces.

Chicago, apparently, felt the same. After a long night contemplating disaster, lines spilled out for downtown coffee shops as people realized normal work would continue even if its normalcy seemed ridiculous now. Kat stood in line, though. Placed the order on her Tama and picked it up when the steaming cup plopped down on the counter.

The reps worked. Paid for the purchase. The whole exchange was enough to get a girl feeling like things might not be too bad after all.

That feeling lasted thirty minutes, until Kat, Gordon, and Seeker reached the Paragon tower. She'd tried tossing a message to Calvin, but he hadn't replied. Morning news just kept on going about LA Apparently some Champions had made it through, Mynx included, though nothing more than some cursory statement about perseverance, finding the culprits, and blah blah boilerplate had gone out.

Aegis would've been in front of all this. He'd have been standing in those ruins preaching fire and brimstone, courage and conviction. Inspiration and determination in tragedy's wake.

Instead, Kat and Gordon found a throng in front of the Paragon tower, crushing out from the building's doors and into the wide streets. Drones and a few Paragon police had set up barriers in the chill morning, routing pods around, but they looked frazzled and just waved Kat by.

"You want to walk into that?" Gordon asked as they stood on the outskirts.

The crowd moved between worried shouts to angrier demonstration, strange words and chants calling for more freedom, more choice, and justice for normals. Signs, some looking way too professional to have come in the half day between LA's crisis and this morning, called for the same.

"What's going on?" Kat asked the air and received no answer. Even Seeker clung to her legs, not wanting to get near the negative energy. "Justice for normals?"

"Sounds like the guy that killed Aegis," Gordon said, shrinking through the crowd with her. "Isn't that what he was all about?"

"Haven't exactly had time to read news lately," Kat replied, but Gordon's comment did sound familiar.

Regardless, it looked like the Paragons would have their hands full. Kat couldn't imagine anyone listening to her request, even if she made it inside. A supposed killer didn't measure up to the government's downfall.

"So where do we go now?" Gordon said as they resumed an aimless trek along the city streets. "Back to the hotel? Wait and see what happens?"

"I want my apartment," Kat said. "And I don't want to be looking over my shoulder anymore."

"I want things too, Kat."

"Difference is, I know how to get mine." Ideas came from the strangest places sometimes, and Gordon's simple reply turned Kat's memory. "Gordon, I need you to make a choice right now."

"Uh oh."

"Damn right, uh oh. I don't know what's going to happen next, but I don't think I can take on these guys by myself. The Paragons aren't going to help, not soon, maybe not ever," Kat said, taking a turn towards the train station. Gordon followed. "I need allies, ones that'll act."

"I'm not enough?"

"You help." Kat flashed a smile. "But you and I aren't a match for this guy."

"Then who is?"

"The killer's made some enemies. Now that I have some idea of how to find him, they might help us take him down. But Gordon, they're not the good guys. We go to them, we enter into a pact with people the Paragons don't like. It might not go well for us."

"But if we don't do this, this guy's going to kill you."

"Probably."

"Then that's all I need to know."

59

Start the War

What do you do when everything's gone right and you still find yourself sitting in a dim trailer watching news reporting on other people, other places, other projects?

Zhan-Yo didn't have a Tama, but Mathieu's hideout had a computer and he'd connected it to his old accounts through a signal-obfuscating web to make tracebacks nigh impossible. He'd been expecting a flood, countless questions and interview requests from news organizations around the globe.

How did he pull this off?

Why did he do it?

What did it all mean?

Zero. And it wasn't like this information was secret. Zhan-Yo's personal contact information had been outed before, including by himself. A cursory peek around the Internet would get you the goods. Yet, nothing.

The Paragons, understandably, took questions by the thousands. Every news network, hell, every private citizen pitched their representatives panicked propositions that portended doom. As if this explosion, a single one in a single, mostly empty stadium meant the end.

Then again, listening to the Paragons, you might think it did.

"How can they say this?" Zhan-Yo gestured at the screen, where LA's regional Paragon lead had just finished warning everyone to be careful, to avoid public spaces until the Paragons brought the criminals to justice. "This wasn't some random attack."

"Better make it seem that way," Xander said, then the young man returned to his dinner, munching into some fish farmed nearby. "Paragons don't want to—"

"Divide the people, yes, I get that." Zhan-Yo hunched forward. His left wrist itched where his Tama used to be. "All this unity nonsense. Where was this yesterday?"

"Didn't need it yesterday."

Zhan-Yo threw an irritated look back towards Xander, but the kid wasn't watching. Was looking at the screen. At least the TV had size going for it; Zhan-Yo might not have a Tama's instant information at his fingertips, but being able to see Mynx's big face as it shimmered onto the screen wasn't nothing.

Worry lit up the Champion's wrinkles. Gray hair seemed more pronounced now, and her eyes looked awfully red. Not enough sleep, and was she still wearing her Paragon uniform from the stadium?

Now that felt like a compliment. Giving a Champion so much nerve-wracking distraction and disaster that they couldn't even get a clean outfit on?

If he couldn't have his revolution, then Zhan-Yo would settle for this.

He ran a hand through his hair, winced as it brushed a cut. Zhan-Yo had plenty of those. Bruises too. And his right ear seemed to miss about half the things coming into it. Mathieu didn't have a doctor handy, but one of the mercenaries had been a field medic, and his once-over review had pronounced Zhan-Yo battered but alive.

"Hey captain," Xander said, and Zhan-Yo looked over to see Mathieu come into the room, bearing two plates and two more sandwiches. The man still wore his tactical gear, as if he had to be ready for an attack at all times.

"How is it playing?" Mathieu said, handing Zhan-Yo a plate. "Getting the coverage we wanted?"

"Coverage yes," Zhan-Yo said. "But it's all on the Paragons. All on how they will cope with the bombing. They're getting to make all of these tearful speeches about a better tomorrow."

"And you don't like that?"

"Not when it doesn't include us," Zhan-Yo replied. "Wexley said that he did his part. The protestors are out all over the place, at every major Paragon tower in every major city. Only they're never on the screen. We're being muzzled."

"Are you surprised?"

"It sounds like you aren't."

Mathieu took a big bite, wiped some lingering mustard off with his hand while the TV rambled on about curfews and heightened drone presence. Sylvie's brother chewed on the sandwich and, much like he did with Mathieu's sister, Zhan-Yo wished he could read the man's mind.

"There are two ways this can go for you," Mathieu replied. "Either you accept this as your best move, you let the results play out and hope that something happens. You walk away from this, change your name and we ship you off somewhere to enjoy your life in peace."

He hesitated. Watched Zhan-Yo's face and no doubt saw his deepening frown.

"I'm not doing this for peace," Zhan-Yo replied. "I'm

doing this precisely because peace has robbed us of our place in our own world."

"Then we look at the second way. Which means we continue walking this road, taking it wherever it leads, no matter the cost."

Zhan-Yo rolled his eyes. Not a habit he liked, nor one he employed, but the moment's frustration eclipsed his restraint.

"Mathieu, what about what we just did screams *civilized* to you? We planted bombs in a stadium. We hurt or killed Paragons, innocent ones, and injured normals outside and around the space. If there's a dark road to walk, I'm already on it.

"However, I refuse to walk this road blindly. I will not consent to murder without a purpose. It's still early. If this fails to get our revolution on track, then perhaps we move away from violence. Perhaps we stop destroying, and start building."

"Not a bad call," Xander said. Zhan-Yo had forgotten the Paragon traitor was still there. "Back when they trained us, the thing was to always find that common ground. Not everyone, even other Paragons, was going to be like you. Had to get them on your team, especially when they're afraid or angry."

Xander fell quiet, watched the two older men. Zhan-Yo thought the Paragon looked so young right there, venturing an opinion to people far above his station and waiting, hoping that it'd be received well.

Zhan-Yo bought himself a moment with a bite. Mathieu did the same, turning back to the TV. Xander did have a point. Zhan-Yo had created the fear, but maybe that fear wasn't quite enough. He had to show what people *could* have if they embraced their chance, shoved the Paragons aside and took their own destinies back.

"Some Champions died," Zhan-Yo said. "Where?"

"Russia, Europe." Mathieu thought for a long second. "I think those are the confirmed ones. Others might be injured, but we don't know."

"I have friends in Europe," Zhan-Yo said. "Openings there. Xander, I like your idea. Here, the leadership is still intact. The Paragons too strong. Across the ocean, however, there might be opportunity."

Zhan-Yo stood, winced at his crackling knees, "I'll tell Wexley that I'm heading abroad. He'll set up the meetings. Mathieu, get your crew ready. We need to move fast."

"Move fast?" Mathieu said, then finished his sandwich in a mammoth bite. "What're we going to do?"

"Deliver order to chaos."

And if more chaos was necessary, Zhan-Yo could supply that too.

60

Recovery Room

Hospital rooms didn't often inspire euphoria, but this one did, because Apinya was in it, and he was alive. The Champion, looking strange in his blue-and-white hospital gown, held a nurse rapt as Mynx entered. From what Mynx could tell, Apinya was giving the nurse advice about her marriage, and given the notes she tapped into her Tama as Apinya spoke, it wasn't all bad.

"You never stop, do you?" Mynx said after the nurse had scurried out of the room.

"Why?" Apinya graced the words with a soft smile. "I enjoy my gift, and so I give it."

"I'm glad you're still able to."

"Yes, well," Apinya lifted his arms, showing off their lack of tubes and ties. "It doesn't seem like I'm in very bad shape. In fact, the machines told me I could leave this afternoon."

"Less than a day." Mynx shook her head. "We really are getting good at this."

"No," said another voice, squeezing by Mynx with two energy drinks in her hand. "I just happen to be here."

Mila, up from South America, may have expected thanks, but Mynx doubted she expected the hug. Deep, long, and not at all stiff, an unnatural mix for Mynx that nonetheless felt necessary here and now.

"How many did you save?" Apinya asked Mila.

"I've already told you."

"Say it again." Apinya nodded towards Mynx. "So she knows."

"Thirty seven," Mila replied, folding her arms and looking at the tile. "Should have been more, but it took too long to get out of the stadium box. The stairs collapsed so I had to go around before I could get to the bodies."

"Nonetheless, a Champion's work." Apinya clasped his hands, leaned back on the bed. "And then you found me here, and turned me from a wrinkled wreck to a healthy man."

"Still wrinkled, though." Mynx shut the room's door. She wouldn't give this place confidential status, but keeping casual eavesdropping at bay would be nice. "We lost Lukas and Burov. Most of the others have already left. Flown back for treatment in their own regions."

The summit had been a horrendous failure, and it continued to compound. Mynx had forced herself, with Reeves's constant pleading, to do a few interviews and put out more unifying statements. It all sounded somewhat hollow, but apparently they were playing well.

Some protests had sprung up, but they were controlled, and regional Paragons had, so far, kept their heads. What would happen when it came time to sort the casualties and fill the holes, Mynx couldn't say.

"I'll be joining them," Apinya said. "This evening, I think. Barring any setbacks. Your little magic doesn't cause any of those, does it?"

"Only if you make me mad," Mila replied.

"Ah, then I definitely must leave as soon as possible."

"Apinya," Mynx said. "I was hoping you could stay another day or two. Just, show some unity for a little while. Keep the impression that things aren't all bad."

"But they are all bad," Mila muttered.

"I would, Mynx. We haven't even had time to catch up." Apinya put a hand towards Mila, who took it and kept quiet. "Unfortunately, like the others, I now have an urgent and demanding public that will not rest while I am away. They'll want answers, and I'll need to give them. In person and with confidence."

Apinya didn't close with an apology. Mynx shouldn't have expected one. This was the way things were. No more, no less.

"Then do you have any advice?" Mynx asked. "With Pixie being so new to this, I'll have to take the front. Be the picture of Paragon pride and all that."

"My advice? I would find the ones who did this, and find them soon. Ruin them for the world to see, and then ditch them where none can find their bodies."

"Celice is already on that mission."

"Is she on it alone?"

Mynx glanced at Mila, who gave her the slightest shrug. Vengeance and anger weren't really Apinya's game, but here came the most fervent words Mynx had heard from him in decades.

"I don't know?" Mynx answered. "She left in a hurry."

"Then go after her. The Champions have been attacked, Mynx. The Paragons have been assaulted. Reason and discourse are useless when the enemy refuses to listen. A threat like this must be eliminated, not accommodated."

Now Mynx folded her arms, faced Apinya head on,

"You spoke to Zhan-Yo. When he was on that stage. Did you learn something that has you talking like this?"

"I learned that he believes in his cause with all his heart," Apinya said. "He will not stop, Mynx. He will not stop until he gets what he wants."

"Well, neither will I."

Mynx left the room a little later, after convincing Mila to stay and fill Apinya's unity roll for the cameras. As Mynx left the hospital, caught the pod that would take her to her Factory, she sent out orders.

All drones, worldwide, would keep looking for Zhan-Yo. If they found him, there would be no capture. No stunning and interrogation.

And if Zhan-Yo played it quiet? Kept himself hidden?

Mynx had infiltrated the most secure places on the planet before the Champions' reign. Had assassinated villains from afar with a tiny, well-placed shot. The drones that had delivered quiet, bloody results for the Paragon revolution had sat dormant for years and years.

Time to wake them up.

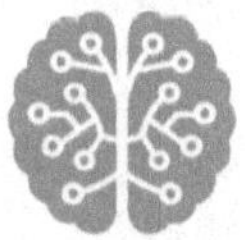

61

The Dive

How many prison breaks involved a couple dozen anomalies blasting across the ocean in a makeshift boat held together by spit and super-powers? Thane bet pretty hard on zero, but he was starting to think this might be a success on the first try. With Cassidy coming in and out, given rest by the other anomalies using their abilities to create cover, the drones had suffered severe losses. The waves behind the boat glittered with black specks, some still smoking, as Cassidy's work left its evidence.

Not that Cassidy herself wasn't exhausted. Thane had to hold her up every time, feeding into his own fear and desperation to keep himself safe from Cassidy's intense heat, even as icy sea water splashed over them. The Void did her work, though, and sucked one drone after another into that dimensional hole, rending them apart and keeping the escapees alive.

The island dwindled on the horizon, its volcano a dark spear splitting the far sky. Arthur and his traitorous band were still back there, safe on land that would be, mostly, uncontested. They could have their trapped paradise. Live out their quiet lives with nothing to show for the great gifts nature had given them.

"What're they doing?" Cassidy murmured, leaning back in Thane's arms as he, in turn, leaned against the boat's port side.

"Who?" Thane looked across the boat, at the anomalies in their requisite positions.

Amazing, really, how fast they'd all fallen in line. Thane only had to bark a few commands and these hardy villains had leapt right to what needed to be done. That failure meant death might have had something to do with it, but Thane had encountered foolhardy anomalies before, ones that used their own egos to shield themselves from reason. Here, though, they had a crew.

Aft, Sook pulsed the boat forward while, at the bow, another, Avery, who had sealed the boat in the first place, used his ability to glaze a path through the waves, creating a shimmering surface like plastic ice that the boat rocketed over. Other anomalies created drone distractions, kept water off the decks, or helped navigate by means Thane couldn't grasp.

"The drones," Cassidy said. "They're not coming in for another pass."

True enough. Rather than clustering for another bolt-spraying blitz—enough anomalies held wrapped arms, legs, or lay prone on the deck getting tended to show the drone's assaults had worked—the drones seemed to be flowing out and around the boat, stringing their numbers into a wide circle. Up close, Thane might consider the maneuver a surrounding threat. The drones, though, hovered beyond anomaly range and, too, their own.

"It's like they're watching us," Thane said. "Which is a problem."

Eventually, the boat would near civilization. The plan

had been to escape pursuit, to vanish on the open sea and make landfall without eyes. If the drones kept on them the whole way, Paragon forces could surround and re-capture, or kill, Thane's small group.

"I can't get them that far out," Cassidy said.

"I know."

Thane moved Cassidy aside, helped her lean against the railing.

At the boat's center, no obvious strategy presented itself. Thane inventoried his remaining anomalies and their abilities, looking for a key to unlock their escape and finding none. Open water didn't offer many options, even to the super-powered. They could keep on coasting forward, and hope the drones spent their energy before the anomalies reached civilization.

Or.

"We dive," Thane said to Cassidy. "You create an opening, a void ahead of us and push it forward, clearing the water. Avery seals the water back as we pass through, and the others keep propelling us forward."

"They'll still be able to track us."

"Not if we go deep enough. Why would Mynx equip aerial drones for that? We get far enough down and we can outrun them."

"You believe."

"I hope, because otherwise the only way this ends is with our death."

Cassidy didn't have a reply to that. Instead, with a shaky sigh, and a grip on Thane's arm, she pulled herself to her feet. Thane shared the plans, and though he didn't find much excitement among the anomalies, resignation worked just as well.

Thane, Cassidy, Avery, and Sienna made their way to the bow. In back, the other anomalies kept watch on the drones, kept the boat moving by pushing air behind them.

"Ready?" Thane asked, and he watched Cassidy take one more look at the noonday, paradise-like sunny sky.

Take in one last beautiful view.

"Ready," Cassidy said. "Once we start, we have to keep going until we can't anymore. Surface too early, and it's pointless."

As Cassidy wrapped her words, shouts rose up across the boat. The drones, apparently seeing something they didn't like, had broken their formation. The flying machines dove towards the boat from all sides, a scattered attack that, with the anomalies out of position, could be disastrous.

"Go!" Thane shouted.

Ahead, the next wave didn't collapse, didn't part, it simply disappeared. The boat dipped forward towards a sudden black emptiness and Thane realized the wave itself hadn't vanished, but the light coming towards them had been sucked away. Cassidy's void grew and pushed, angling the boat down.

Avery pushed his ability around them as water curled around Cassidy's void, the boat shooting behind the minia-ture black hole. Water that should have swept over them from behind and above froze to glass, shattering back to droplets moments later as the boat passed by. Avery himself, a bronzed man who looked between twenty-five and fifty, broke out sweating.

Sienna didn't flake, though. She pulled water from beneath the boat's bow, hastening their descent, and shot it over the group, its ice turning to steam on Cassidy's skin, softening Avery's own, and making Thane shiver so much that he delved into his lingering fear, hope, desperation to fortify himself.

But they dove. Dropped beneath the surface and further down, until everywhere Thane looked, blue, first light and then darker cloaked the boat.

The water would block any drone shots. Would buy them some time. No bolt could get through that much water, no bullet either, and these drones wouldn't have torpedoes on them. At least, Thane hoped Mynx hadn't been that prescient, that paranoid.

"One's still behind!" A cry from behind, and Thane parsed the words enough to look back, into that long and collapsing tunnel.

A single drone, ominous black, had swept inside the boat's tail tunnel. Freed from its formation, the drone darted within the collapsing glass-water, dodging bolts and blasts sent its way from the anomalies with too much ease. As if it could see where each attack would come from, before the anomaly sent it.

Impossible, unless the drone's programming read anomaly body language. Read heat, eyes, breath, and every other hint a living create gave off before it moved. The robot danced as reality exploded around it, and the drone replied in kind.

The drone's own bolts and bullets struck the boat, and without Cassidy's voids or Sienna and Avery's glass-water barriers to block the attacks, anomalies began to fall. The drone shot with precision, each hit marking a fatal end. Sook collapsed when a bolt struck his chest, the boat shuddering as its acceleration faltered.

Another minute, and the boat would be a tomb.

"Cassidy!" Thane shouted. "We need another void! Behind us!"

In front, they needed a multi-meter black hole sucking a path through the depths. Cassidy, already shrouded in smoke from the effort, Thane holding her upright, her skin searing hot against his own, shook at his words. He saw her head turn, those tear-streaked eyes barely open against the pain.

"Please," Thane said. "I believe in you."

A quick roar, followed by metal's twisting shriek, came from behind them. Thane turned, saw the drone breaking apart, its engines still firing, barreling the wreckage towards them. Thane felt shards bounce off his own back, saw them pierce Sienna, Avery. The others.

Saw Sienna stumble and fall off the side.

Felt Avery's concentration snap as his hands went to his shoulder, where a thin metal spike had lodged itself. The glass tunnel fractured, stopped, and the sea began to fold in around them.

Thane gave into his fear, his desperation, his doom. With his arms tight around Cassidy, a nova still, the ocean rushed to claim them.

CONTINUE *the adventure with* REVOLUTION'S RISE, *the Hero's Code Book Three, available at your favorite retailer:*

An Excerpt From
REVOLUTION'S RISE
THE HERO'S CODE BOOK THREE

Shorts, a doubled-up t-shirt to fight the London chill, and new sneakers etching a blister into her heels as she pounded pavement through Hyde Park's stately greens. Celice caught idle glances as she ran, late afternoon urbanites heading for a pub, a restaurant, or just home. Water splashed with every contact, doing Celice a favor by making people clear from her path.

And letting the man, also jogging, as he did every day around this time, stay in sight.

Celice had left Mynx's meeting room in LA, ditched the sob-fest and went to work. If the Champions wanted to play the PR game while the man responsible for detonating a stadium went free, that was their choice. She made a different one.

Her Paragon access let Celice yank the footage from the prison break, where a goon squad busted Zhan-Yo from Mynx's supposedly secure facility. That fancy floor-wide elevator and Mynx's drones hadn't done crap, but at least the Champion had top notch surveillance. Celice absorbed the recording on the flight from LA to New York, then, back at Bastion, she pulled the data on every face she could find on Mynx's cameras.

Zhan-Yo's adopted crew didn't comprise criminals, up until the break-in anyway, but instead people with large holes in their past. Paragon records, compiled with ruthless thoroughness, broke down their lives into nuggets Celice devoured while surfing the sky from New York to London.

She'd picked the European city because damn near every one of Zhan-Yo's group had bought tickets and departed that way in the weeks since the explosion. The flights had come at different times, from different starting points—these people weren't total novices to spycraft—but the same destination made it easy to trace.

Easy, at least, for a super-powered group covering the planet with its all-seeing enterprise.

The man took his usual left, heading towards the park's east exit. Celice followed, maintaining distance and taking the occasional cross-cut along a muddy detour to throw off any ideas. Her zigs and zags moved her parallel to the man, kept him within eyeshot. He hadn't deviated yet, and Celice had no reason to think he would.

Another workday, another routine.

Reaching the park's end, the man did a double-check for traffic. London played the same game as other Paragon-controlled cities—meaning, every city—and held back cars for broader transit, giving way to mag-lev rail, buses, and vans. Nonetheless, this deep in London's heart, randomness abounded, with wealthier citizens taking their cleared vehicles for jaunts or specialty transports delivering their desires. Enough, anyway, that the man had to wait several long heartbeats for a truck to roll on by, batteries whirring and misty water spraying.

Celice caught up, hung a few meters back. She paced, feet pounding the walk without moving, trying to seem every bit the impatient runner not wanting to stop. Her Tama, tied to her left wrist, vibrated. Another call, another message, another request from Mynx's Paragon peddlers trying to find where Celice had gone, what she was doing.

As if the Champion didn't have better things to do with her time.

An older gentleman standing to her left shifted his umbrella to block the now-drizzle from landing on Celice's already sweaty, short hair. Beneath his cloth cap, the man gave her the slightest nod. Celice returned a tight smile, kept her feet going. The truck motored on by and the group shuffled forward.

If any one place had surveillance capacity matching the Paragons, London was it. Cameras littered street corners, giving a person with the right permissions access to scan the city from a desk. Celice, holed up in a rented apartment, called in favors and digitally scoured London's streets for a match.

And now that match ran along ahead, passed stores shutting for the evening and others opening. Shifts changed, laughter mingled with shouted conversations, and Hyde Park's nature lost its scents to kitchens warming up for dinner. The park's simple clarity likewise fell to ad banners and brighter city lights, a sensory shift Celice tried to ignore as she treaded after her target.

Too close.

Her father's words whispered in Celice's mind. Aegis had it right. Those meters splitting Celice from her objective weren't enough. If the man bothered to look behind, if he felt Celice's eyes crawling his back, searching out any possible weapons hidden in his baggy track pants and loose jacket, he'd catch her out against the shambling, coat-covered crowds.

But her father didn't know everything. He'd preach one

stealth lesson after another only to fall back on his fists the minute something didn't work quite right. An easy instinct when Aegis could take a thousand hits and not feel a one.

Celice, though, couldn't fall back. Not here, when intersections and alleyways split off every other second. If the man's route through Hyde Park remained static, he took different options off this street every day. Celice suspected he always circled back to the same destination, but she never found the evidence, not for so many long hours watching fuzzy footage.

Celice bit back a laugh as she worked around a soggy tour group: Aegis wouldn't have spent a minute on the recordings. He would've hit the streets, pulling rank to get what he wanted or smashing through enough walls until he found it.

The man broke right, a casual turn onto a thin alley marked by dumpsters and dripping fire escapes. Celice approached, slowing into a walk, hands on her hips as if her jog had caught up with her little lady lungs.

You're unarmed.

The shorts, the t-shirts, the shoes left little space to hide a weapon. Celice had left the apartment without planning to get in a fight. Look like a runner, figure out where the man went whenever he ditched the streets for London's alleys and then retreat back home to prep the next stage. Now that she'd come this far, however . . .

Turning the corner, Celice spotted the man halfway down the alley. He leaned on a drain pipe, one leg lifted up into a stretch. People shifted along behind her, one bumping Celice forward into the alley's mouth. The man didn't turn around at the scuffle, hadn't seen Celice at all, but she had nowhere to hide if he did.

No way to act casual.

Aegis would like this part. Celice could retreat, could

dip back into the crowded press and make her way home, regroup and try again. If she'd been running this like all the Paragon ops she'd supervised over the years, Celice would've pulled the plug. She had time then, she had time and super-powered fighters on her side.

Another night spent without progress in that apartment, with its bare walls and sparse furniture and gin bottles washed down with lime and little else . . .

Celice picked up the jog, heading down the alley with a smile spreading, a harmless someone who knew they'd be seen.

"Sorry," Celice said when the man heard her footsteps and turned her way. "The streets are so crowded, saw you came this way and thought maybe it's a good route."

"It serves," the man said, holding his stretch and waiting for Celice to go on by.

Make the first move.

Waiting let the enemy take control. Celice ground her left heel, turning in the alleyway and delivering a sharp kick to the man's stomach. The sneaker connected, air blowing out as the man's eyes bugged and his lungs evacuated their contents. The stretch and his single-legged stand meant the man should've fallen to the ground, should've given Celice an easy avenue to a pin and interrogation.

Instead, the man kept his hand on the pipe. The hold let him drop the stretching leg, his feet getting their grip as Celice stepped into a follow-up jab right where she'd kicked. Another wave at the man's stomach and she might get him nauseous, might bruise a kidney and take him out quick.

But Zhan-Yo didn't hire scrubs.

The man knocked away the attack, coughing as he did so, trying to suck in air. He back-pedaled, looking to buy space, give his longer reach a chance. Celice couldn't let him, so she pressed ahead, using the man's bulk as a big target. This time, she varied her strikes, blinking hands and elbows high and low, looking for a vulnerability.

Her opponent took the hits when they came, blocked the ones he could, still recovering from the kick. His stance, growing straighter and more settled by the second, showed Celice's hits to his shoulders, to his knees, and one good nail gouge to the cheek, weren't doing enough.

The swing came off a block, the man slamming down his left elbow to deflect a jab then thrusting the fist right at Celice's eyes. She jerked aside, but not far enough, the blow catching her right temple and sending her back two steps. A bruise there, for sure.

And more to come, going by the man's brawler posture. He had his hands up, feet on their toes and bouncing. Worse, a gleam played on a face ready and eager for the fight.

"Don't know who you are, where you came from, but you picked the wrong alley today," the man said, accent placing him as a Canadian Northwoods product.

Keep him off balance.

"Nope, you're the man I'm looking for," Celice sprang the words with a spirited smile, an earnest look that threw the man for a fractional second.

Long enough.

Kicking through a puddle, Celice sent dirty drops raining at the man, following behind them with a sidestep to the right. Her rival pushed through the trick, trying for a long-reach hit that depended on Celice sticking to the ground, like a normal fighter might.

But Celice, daughter of the world's foremost Paragon, wasn't a normal fighter.

She planted her left foot and jumped, heading at a hard angle towards the alley wall. The leap brought her so far right that the man's swing fell short, his follow-through bringing him right into Celice's rebound. Her right foot touched the wall a half-meter up and Celice kicked off, reversing direction and punching forward with the added momentum.

The man couldn't get his own swing back in time to block, taking Celice's shot right on the chin. Now his turn to stumble, Celice kept on forward, staying on her own feet after the wall jump and using the chaos to grab the man's left leg, twisting it as he recoiled. An undignified plop followed, the tracksuit hitting sopping ground. The man's head came next, cracking on the cobblestones.

Celice leaned over, ready to lay an elbow on the man's neck if he tried to rise. His eyes, though, were clouded and closed, and no longer read reality. Instead, Celice planted two fingers on the man's neck and watched his chest. A pulse beat, the lungs worked their magic. Not dead, unconscious for who knew how long.

"Hey!" A woman shouted at the alley's head, and Celice looked back to see an older couple standing there, watching the evening's improvised entertainment. "What's going on here then?"

Who knew how much they'd seen, how much they'd believe, but a simple excuse would work for most people: The average person wouldn't want their daily comforts disrupted by Paragon business or bloody street fights.

"He slipped while we were practicing," Celice called back. "Get an ambulance!"

She turned back to the man, running her hands through his jacket, looking for something, anything. Getting a Tama off a wrist would take time and tools she didn't have here, and the sheer stillness on his face seemed to mean consciousness wasn't coming back soon.

In the man's left pocket, she found a crumpled receipt.

Coffee, pastry. In the right pocket, a keychain. Only someone paranoid would resort to locks that couldn't be hacked. Celice, keeping low, fingered the two copper-colored keys. She could take them, but then the man would know, Zhan-Yo would know they'd been stolen.

"How's he doing?" came the woman's voice, closer now, excited at being involved. A look confirmed the two were heading down the alley towards Celice. Interlopers being interlopers. "We called, help's on the way!"

Angling her own Tama, Celice captured the keys in three pictures. As the couple came close, Celice stuffed the keys back into the man's pocket and stood up, painting a worried picture across her body.

"Thank you," Celice said as they came close. "I'm thinking he knocked himself a bit hard. I'll go meet the ambulance, if you can watch him?"

The couple, doing their saintly duty, agreed without a second's suspicion. Celice broke off towards the alley's entrance, slipped into the passing crowd, and vanished as a siren's wail broke London's evening peace. Overhead, a drone's dark cloud drifted by, preceding the ambulance call with its own inscrutable eye.

Once, those machines would've filled Celice with hope, with the flush that came with real power in a world that valued little else.

Now, she kept her head down and felt the drizzle turn to rain, the chill fighting off the first pangs from her battered temple.

Continue the adventure with **REVOLUTION'S RISE**, *available at your favorite retailer:*

Acknowledgments and Author's Note

Champion's Call is, despite the by-line, a work that came about thanks to many people. Nicole, my wife, has been a tireless supporter of my writing, giving me many mornings, afternoons, and evenings to spin the tales you read on these pages. My parents too, by reading all of my works and giving me their encouragement.

Readers like you play a huge part, because I'm writing these stories to be read, to be enjoyed and, perhaps, spark a fun question or two.

The Hero's Code is a series that, for me, is about confronting power and its myriad forms, and how many of those forms are both good and bad. The conflict between that power and the ideals of those who live with it forms the crux of this series, and I'm excited to show you where it leads.

Also, superheroes are just fun to hang around, and really, when you're writing these novels, you're getting a chance to spend time with people and places you'll never see otherwise. Aegis, Mynx, Kat—I get to spend time with these marvelous people, and I'm so lucky I get to do so.

Thanks for reading, and look out for the next book, because it'll be here before you know it!

About the Author

A.R. Knight spins stories in a frosty house in Madison, WI, primarily owned by a pair of cats. After getting sucked into the working grind in the economic crash of the 2008, he found himself spending boring meetings soaring through space and going on grand adventures.

Eventually, spending time with podcasting, screenplays, short stories and other novels, he found a story he could fall into and a cast of characters both entertaining and full of heart.

A.R. Knight plans on jumping through to other worlds and finding new stories to tell in the limitless borders of our imagination.

Thanks, as always, for reading!

For more information:
www.adamrknight.com

To Ashe

www.ingramcontent.com/pod-product-compliance
Lightning Source LLC
Chambersburg PA
CBHW031608180726
48284CB00005B/1456